I0659004

Vampires vs Zombies

The Apocalypse

Melissa Hosack

Whimsical Publications, LLC

Florida

Vampires vs Zombies - The Apocalypse is a work of fiction. Names, characters, and incidents are the products of the author's imagination and are either fictitious or are used fictitiously. Any resemblance to actual events or persons, living or dead, is entirely coincidental.

To purchase the authorized electronic edition of *Vampires vs Zombies - The Apocalypse*, visit
www.whimsicalpublications.com

Cover art by Traci Markou
Editing by Brieanna Robertson

ISBN-13: 978-1-940707-34-1

Published in the United States by
Whimsical Publications, LLC
Florida

"Oh shit," he said under his breath. "Aurora?"

"Yeah?" My voice trembled as I slowly backed away.

"Run." With that, he dropped the chair, pushed me in front of him, and did as he instructed me to do. He ran.

I went as fast as I could, but with his six-foot-two frame, it didn't take him long to catch up to me. We both turned simultaneously down the hallway, sprinting for our lives.

"Is there a window in the women's bathroom?" he hollered.

"What?" I yelled back breathlessly, having a hard time hearing over the pounding of my heart and the pursuing monsters.

"Fast! Is there a window in the women's bathroom?"

I scanned my mind, trying to remember the layout of the restrooms, a hard thing to do when being chased by a psychotic monster that wants to eat you alive. "Yes," I said uncertainly, my answer sounding more like a question.

"You better be damn sure, or we're both dead," Damian came back gruffly.

At his somber statement, I really concentrated, picturing the arrangement of the bathroom interior. "Yes! Yes, there's a window."

"Good."

Before I had a chance to take another step, I was thrown to the side. I went barreling into the women's room, forcing the door open with my body as I went.

Damian was a step behind me. He lurched into the room, his tall frame slamming into mine and knocking me off balance.

As the door swung shut behind him of its own momentum, we both collapsed to the floor in a pile of tangled arms and legs. The air rushed out of my lungs as his full weight was thrown on top of me. One of my knees slid dangerously between his, and I accidentally caught him in the ribs with an elbow. "Damian," I groaned, pushing against his chest with my free hand. "You're squishing me."

With a grunt of discomfort, he rolled to sit next to me, breathing hard. His hands ran through his dark hair, and his fingers trembled with shock and adrenaline. While I struggled to a sitting position, he touched a hand to his jaw and winced in pain.

With his weight no longer on me, I was able to convince my lungs to start working again. I sucked in deep gulps of air, my throat feeling raw.

As we both tried to collect ourselves, the door flew open, and three mutilated faces stared in at us.

I stopped complaining. Scrambling to my feet, I threw myself against the door. It closed for a moment before being smashed into from the other side, forcing me backwards.

It opened enough for one of the men to get his arm into the room. I spun around, pressing my back against the door, trying to dig my feet into the floor to give me extra leverage.

Damian was on his feet in an instant. He hit the door hard, his hands on either side of my head, the front of his body slamming into the front of mine. He was jammed up tightly against me with my nose practically in his chest. His head was lowered toward me, and I could see his jaw clench with effort.

The door slammed shut on the thing's arm, and it gave an inhuman screech.

I glanced to the side to see the arm dangling limply next to my head. Blood poured down torn skin and dripped to the floor.

I opened my mouth to scream when Damian pulled back and slammed into the door again, knocking the air, and the scream, out of me. There was a sickening wet noise as the arm detached, landing with a thud at my feet. Without the arm blocking the door, it closed.

Damian reached above my head and clicked the lock into place. With a shaky sigh, he leaned his head against the door just above my shoulder, his body still pressed flat to mine. His breath was hot against the side of my neck, and his body covered me completely. I could feel him all the way down to my toes. He was just a little too close for a casual acquaintance, especially for one I didn't like all that much.

I brought my hands up and pushed on his shoulders. "You can get off me now."

He pulled his head back and looked down at me through his hair, his eyes glinting with amusement. "If I must." He lingered a second too long for my taste before moving away from me.

Acknowledgements

I would like to thank all of my readers! The constant support has been amazing. You guys are awesome! Of course, I also have to thank my family. They put up with my obsessive hours in front of the computer and the fact that my mind is often in la-la land where vampires and werewolves are a normal occurrence. And I cannot forget the astounding people at Whimsical. Thank you for saying 'yes' to my stories and helping me bring them to life.

Prologue

The Zombie Apocalypse

I raced down the hallway of Sandy's Shack, the local burger joint, with my heart hammering against my ribcage and my stomach curling into a knot of terror. A pack of zombies were hot on my heels as I stumbled with shock past the employee kitchen, where screams wafted out into the hall. Before I had a chance to take another step, I was thrown roughly to the side. I went barreling into the women's room, the door forced open by my body.

Damian was a step behind me. He lurched into the room, his tall frame slamming into mine and knocking me off balance.

As the door swung shut behind him of its own momentum, we both collapsed to the floor in a pile of tangled arms and legs. The air rushed out of my lungs as his full weight was thrown on top of me. One of my knees slid dangerously between his, and I accidentally caught him in the ribs with an elbow. "Damian," I groaned, pushing against his chest with my free hand. "You're squishing me."

With a grunt of discomfort, he rolled to sit next to me, breathing hard. His hands ran through his dark hair, and his fingers trembled with shock and adrenaline. While I struggled to a sitting position, he touched a hand to his jaw and winced in pain.

With his weight no longer on me, I was able to convince my lungs to start working again. I sucked in deep gulps of air, my throat feeling raw.

As we both tried to collect ourselves, the door flew open, and three mutilated faces stared in at us.

I stopped complaining. Scrambling to my feet, I threw myself against the door. It closed for a moment before being smashed into from the other side, forcing me backwards.

The door opened enough for one of the zombies to get its arm into the room. I spun around, pressing my back against the door, trying to dig my feet into the floor to give me some extra leverage.

Damian was on his feet in an instant. He hit the door hard, his hands on either side of my head, the front of his body slamming into mine. He was jammed up tightly against me with my nose practically in his chest. His head was lowered toward me, and his jaw was clenched with effort.

The door slammed shut on the thing's arm and it gave an inhuman screech.

I glanced to the side to see the arm dangling limply next to my head. Blood oozed down torn skin and dripped to the floor. The blood would have been frightening in itself, but the coloration was what terrified me the most. There was a gray tinge to it, and it was coagulated so that it fell in thick blobs. No living human should bleed that way.

I opened my mouth to scream when Damian pulled back and slammed into the door again, knocking the air, and the scream, out of me. There was a sickening wet noise as the arm detached, landing with a thud at my feet. Without the arm blocking the door, it closed.

Damian reached above my head and clicked the lock into place. With a shaky sigh, he leaned his head against the door just above my shoulder, his body still pressed flatly to mine. His breath was hot against the side of my neck, and his body covered me completely. I could feel him all the way down to my toes. He was just a little too close for a casual acquaintance, especially for one I didn't like all that much.

I brought my hands up and pushed on his shoulders. "You can get off me now."

Chapter 1

24 Hours Earlier
Thursday, 6:00 pm

I stared at the woman in front of me and wondered what she'd been smoking before coming to class. Her name was Geneva Scott, and she was the instructor of the self-defense class I'd been unlucky enough to be forced into taking by my father. He felt that if I was going to go to college in a big city in the fall, I should know how to defend myself.

Good reason or not, here I was trapped in Geneva's stupid class during a summer vacation where I should be off having one last fun adventure with my high school friends. Instead of lounging on a beach in Cancun, I was here listening to Geneva explain proper breathing techniques to keep calm when being cornered by an attacker. Yeah. When a big man in a ski mask was assaulting me, I was going to calmly remember my breathing techniques. Almost.

All I could think about was what a giant waste of money this all was. I could have fed a homeless man for a week with what it cost to listen to Geneva's little speech. Not that I would. Okay, I could buy a really nice pair of Manolo Blahniks, and I'd get more use out of them than I would this class.

The place was dingy with faded wallpaper and chipped linoleum floors. The lighting was terrible, causing a grim shadow to slash across the floor. It was as if Geneva was trying to recreate the dismal environment our imaginary attacker would be coming from.

The whole thing was rather depressing, in my opinion. I directed a dirty look at my instructor, though I knew it would have little effect. She was too busy harnessing her inner chi to pay me any mind.

As if on cue, Geneva took a deep breath and let it out

slowly, eyes closed to block out any outside distractions. Her long brown hair was tossed over her shoulders and her expression was one of serenity. She had her palms pressed together, her legs crossed Indian style as she sat on a small padded mat on the floor.

I wanted to throw my gum at her. I was curious as to how stress-free she would remain when actually faced with a little bit of conflict. I contemplated calling bullshit on the whole "keeping calm can save lives in the face of danger" thing, but it would probably get me booted from the class. I did not want to face the lecture my father would give me if that happened.

"I want you to practice this technique until our next session. Think about all that we have discussed," Geneva said in her fake, calming voice as she opened a pair of hazel eyes to stare at the small assembled group.

That statement excited me. Not because I was even going to consider thinking about the assignment, but because it meant I could get the hell out of here. As everyone else politely tried Geneva's breathing technique one last time, I grabbed my bag and tossed it over my shoulder, intending to leave as quickly as possible.

"Aurora!"

I paused in rolling up my yoga mat and gave a little groan of disappointment at how close I'd been to escaping. The voice that called my name made me cringe, but despite my better judgment, I stopped and turned around. "Yes?" I stared up at my fellow classmate, Damian Deshea, with a slightly impatient glare.

Damian had been working up the nerve to ask me out over the past couple weeks. I'd been dreading the day he finally got the balls to do it.

There wasn't anything terribly wrong with him. He just wasn't my type. Sure, that's what they all say, but he really wasn't. My type was clean cut, educated, and honest. Basically, everything he wasn't.

Despite the fact that most girls found him to be droolworthy, even Damian's appearance irritated me. He had thick, dark brown hair. Something about that hair incensed me. It was always messy and untamed, curling around his ears and falling over his forehead. It was like the boy had never heard of a haircut. Damian also had a tattoo, another sign of his juvenile delinquency. It was an intricately designed barbed-wire pattern that wrapped around his left bicep.

He'd never once mentioned having a job. This meant he was either living in his parents' basement because he was unemployed, or worked somewhere like a gas station and was too embarrassed to bring it up, as he should be.

He hadn't exactly lied to me, but he'd never told me the truth either. Any time he was asked a personal question, he changed the subject. After the first two times I'd spoken to him, I'd learned I wasn't going to get anywhere in the conversation department. If things got any more personal than shameless flirting, he retreated back into his mysterious shell. Anyone unwilling to reveal even a single personal thing about themselves obviously had something to hide.

I had to admit he was nice to look at, but he was the kind of guy you knew meant trouble, the kind of guy your mother always warned about. He was the bad boy that left girls heartbroken and probably got into fistfights on a weekly basis. He was the type of guy girls couldn't stay away from but were always better off without.

"Aurora," he repeated, flashing me a bright smile.

My eyebrows rose slightly, and with my voice sounding even more impatient, I asked again, "Yes?"

He leaned casually against the wall, one foot hooked over the other. He crossed his arms over his broad chest and upped the wattage of his smile. He'd done this before. "You must be hungry. This class is at such a bad time. I know *I'm* starving after every one."

Because you can only eat between the hours of four and six, I thought sarcastically as I tucked my mat under my arm. I stayed silent, waiting for him to get to the point of his little speech.

"I'm heading out to grab a burger," he said with an air of coolness. "I was wondering if you wanted to grab a bite to eat with me."

I fought not to roll my eyes. I loved how people thought that if you were in a group together, you must have all the same interests. The big flaw with that theory was that I didn't even like this group that much. "Gee, a burger? I don't know. I wouldn't want to dip into your extensive cash flow."

Okay, I knew it sounded bitchy the second it came out of my mouth, but I had to get my point across clearly the first time. I was weak. I might have said yes if he asked again. It might have been the big, brown puppy dog eyes. I had a weakness for those. It didn't matter I knew he was trouble or that he tended to irritate me. I was still a girl, and thus susceptible to his charm.

Damian's eyes narrowed at the sarcastic tone of my voice. "Fine, princess," he said, his words sounding hostile in response to my rejection. "It's your loss."

"I highly doubt it." Internally, I cringed. If I could just learn to control my mouth and temper, I would actually be pretty nice. If only, right? I knew he was only being mean due to the harsh way I'd turned him down. Why couldn't I be even moderately pleasant toward him? It was a mystery, really. Something about him always set me on edge.

As I watched him turn and walk away, I suddenly felt guilty. It wasn't like he'd done anything wrong. I just knew better than to get involved with a bad boy. I'd seen too many of my friends suffer from broken hearts after getting mixed up with guys like Damian.

I wanted to say something to smooth the air between us, yet I couldn't think of anything that wouldn't seem like I was leading him on. I was considering going over to apologize when his arm slid over the shoulder of Brooke, the class bimbo. He started whispering in her ear, his eyes catching and holding mine as he did.

If he was trying to make me jealous, his plan had just backfired. All he'd managed to do was annoy me further. I sighed and rolled my eyes at his childish tactics. "Forget it." He wasn't worth the effort. Sending him a sneer, I marched out of the building. I didn't need to deal with his macho bullshit. If he wanted to hit on Brooke, more power to him. She was more on his intelligence level anyway.

Trying to squelch my irritation, I hustled through the parking lot until I reached my car. Opening a fire engine red door, I slid into the flashy convertible that had been a graduation present from my dad. Leaning back into the hot leather seat, I soaked in the sun, letting it warm my skin and wash away my annoyance. The top was down, so a breeze rustled my hair against my face, instilling me with a sense of calm I never even came close to getting out of Geneva's class.

Feeling much better, I opened my eyes to see Damian walking out of the building. I let my gaze follow his muscled form as he made his way to a beat up truck. He may be nice to look at, but his choice of vehicle was most decidedly not. Shaking my head in disapproval, I turned over the engine of my car and listened to the soft purr it emanated.

Perhaps it was fate, or maybe dumb luck, but Damian glanced in my direction.

With a boastful smirk, I revved the engine. Sure, it was childish, but he had the annoying habit of bringing out the snob in me. Much to my chagrin, he didn't seem offended by my obvious showboating.

Damian merely nodded his head in parting, seemingly not at all perturbed by our earlier argument.

With an aggravated huff at his calm demeanor, I cranked the radio on.

Instead of music, the DJ's solemn voice came through the speakers. "The victim was identified as nineteen-year-old Kelly Sanford. Police are refusing any further comments at the moment, but they assure an investigation is pending."

Those words erased every other thought and left me stunned. I'd gone to high school with a Kelly Sanford. Surely it couldn't be the same Kelly. A chill swept through my body that the afternoon sun would have no effect on. I waited with my heart in my throat for any more information, but the station switched to a song, its sound far too upbeat after their grim announcement.

I sat in dumbfounded silence while the music blared, unable to process what I'd just heard. I was staring out the windshield, trying to collect my thoughts, when my eyes caught Damian's again.

He was staring at me in confusion. The way I'd suddenly dropped the haughty attitude must have clued him in that something was wrong. I'd gone from boasting about my sports car to melancholy stillness.

I quickly looked away from his puzzled, concerned expression. I couldn't handle his pity at the moment, and he surely wasn't who I wanted to be comforted by.

With my eyes trained firmly on the road, I pulled out of the parking lot and started in the direction of my home, hoping against hope the person mentioned on the radio wasn't the girl I knew.

***

Thursday, 7:00 P.M.

An hour after I'd heard the news report involving Kelly Sanford, I was still trying to shake my unease. A quick phone call to my best friend, Amber, had confirmed that the victim was in fact the Kelly we'd gone to school with. The current rumor was she'd been torn apart by a pack of wolves.

Shivering at the mental image that brought up, I made my way out the back door of my parents' house, heading toward our swimming pool. As bummed as I was about Kelly, I was trying to push it to the back of my mind. I was hoping a few fast-paced laps would help clear my morbid thoughts. Running mental images of the horrible incident through my brain was only going to scare me. There were enough things out there to be afraid of without adding freak animal attacks to the list.

As I neared the pool, I spotted my brother lolling at the edge with his legs dangling into the water. A dark pair of sunglasses hid his eyes, but I didn't need to see them to know they were closed.

Older than me by two years, Andrew was the more serious of the two of us. I was no slouch in school, but I would guiltily admit his grades made mine look shameful. With classic surfer-boy good looks, my brother could be gracing the cover of fashion magazines. Instead, he spent most of his time not at the beach, but in his room studying. It was hard to fathom why he would want to pack that much stuffiness into such a pretty package. Yet, despite our differences, I adored my brother.

My lips twisted into a grin as I tiptoed toward him, a wicked idea forming in my mind. When I was inches away, I crouched down next to the top of his blond head and leaned my face over his. "Wake up!" When he jerked upright, I shoved him into the pool.

Andrew gave a surprised yelp an instant before he was submerged. He kicked around sporadically under the water for a moment before surfacing with a scowl on his face.

I couldn't hold in my gleeful laugh, and I gave him a cute grin in response to his annoyed frown. "That's what you get for falling asleep poolside," I said accusingly. "Smarter people have drowned that way."

Grabbing the edge of the pool, Andrew hoisted himself out of the water with ease and stalked toward me. "You're going to be so sorry, little girl."

With a squeal, I attempted to run from him. Unfortunately for me, he was a wide receiver on his college football team, and that meant he was fast, a whole lot faster than me.

Amidst my giggling objections, he picked me up and threw me over his shoulder as if I didn't weigh an ounce.

"Drew, no!" I shrieked, knowing what was coming. I pounded my fists uselessly against his back, but he didn't even flinch. "Drew!" I didn't get to say anything else before I was tossed into the swimming pool. I was airborne for a moment, then the water rushed over my head, and I nearly choked on it through my protesting shouts.

I surfaced with a sputtering cough. Glaring up through my tangled blonde hair, I found him laughing at the edge of the pool as he looked down at me.

His eyebrows lifted in amusement. "Serves you right."

"You're evil," I said as I used the lip of the pool to haul myself out. Shoving my hair out of my eyes, I added, "I spent over an hour working on my hair this morning. I bet you didn't even brush yours."

Andrew's hand swept through his short, usually spiked hair as he seemed to ponder that statement. The look on his face let me know he wasn't sure if he'd actually brushed it this morning or not. With a careless shrug and a laugh, he collapsed into one of the lounge chairs next to the pool. He sat watching the angry scowl on my face for a moment before finally saying, "Would some juicy gossip make amends between us?"

"How juicy?" I asked suspiciously. I didn't want him to tell me that some football player was about to be drafted to the NFL or that one of his friends slept with one of my friends. Okay. Maybe the second example would interest me, but only a little. I sat in the chair next to his, failing at my attempt to appear disinterested. "Come on, Drew! How juicy?"

He leaned forward, lowering his voice, though no one was

around to hear. "Christine told me something hush-hush from the hospital."

Christine was Andrew's longtime girlfriend. They'd started dating in the dark ages, aka middle school, and continued to date through college. Christine had stayed near home, becoming a nurse. Andrew went off to school. They saw each other during holidays, breaks, weekends, and summer vacation. They would probably get married the instant Andrew graduated. Gag me, right?

Pushing aside my disgust at my brother's mushy relationship, I sat forward in my chair, eagerly awaiting the next bit of information. "What did she say?" I asked impatiently.

"You know how old Mr. Smith next door just kicked the bucket?"

"He wasn't old," I said, interrupting him just as he was about to continue. "He was like forty-five. Tops."

Andrew rolled his eyes. "Whatever. It doesn't matter how old he was. The point is that the papers and Mrs. Smith said he died in a car accident."

I glanced toward the neighbor's house. "Yeah. So?"

"Smith didn't die in a car accident."

"Yes, he did. I saw the car. It was crushed. He slammed head-on into that giant oak tree near the park."

"He was in a car accident, but that's not what killed him."

My eyes narrowed with interest. "What killed him then?" If he said something lame like a heart attack, I was going to smack him in the back of the head. *That* was not juicy gossip.

"Christine said, when the body came in, there were weird markings on it. Smith had what she thought looked like bite marks along his right shoulder and down along his arm. There were actually chunks of meat ripped completely off the bone. She called animal control thinking it was some type of wild animal attack." He paused dramatically, shaking his head. "Upon further examination, they realized the bites were human. Someone played Hannibal Lecter on our neighbor."

I gave a startled gasp. "You're lying."

"I almost wish I were. Mr. Smith was murdered. He died before that car wrecked. It wrecked because he was under attack and no longer had control of the wheel. Someone was in that car with him, and whoever it was killed him."

I sat in shocked silence for a minute. "Who would do

something like that? Who would want to hurt Mr. Smith?"

"Obviously someone did, and pretty badly, too. Christine said the body was a mess." Andrew shrugged. "Anyway, Mom's headed over there after dinner to see how Mrs. Smith is doing...and to see if she can coax any information out of her about the murder. Mom said she saw her last night, and Mrs. Smith was pacing around, moping like she didn't know what to do with herself."

"I'm sure she doesn't. Her husband was just murdered."

Andrew shrugged again. "All I know is that something fishy is going on." He glanced at the neighbor's house, his expression thoughtful. "Something's definitely not right with her story."

***

Thursday, 8:40 P.M.

After dinner, I sat curled up on the couch, silently pondering what Andrew had told me about Mr. Smith. The more I thought on what had befallen our neighbor, the more my mind kept returning to Kelly. It seemed like too big of a coincidence to ignore. Two people I'd known had died within a couple days of each other, and both had been eaten alive. I shivered at the thought, my mind filling with images I'd tried to suppress for the better part of the evening. Being eaten while you were conscious enough to feel the agonizing pain was a terrible way to go.

I turned and looked out the window at the neighbor's house. My mother had only been over there five minutes, but already I was dying to know what she'd discovered. Unfortunately, I doubted Mrs. Smith would share much. From what Andrew claimed, she was denying her husband's death was anything other than a car crash. I sighed and slouched down further in my seat. "Do you think she'll tell Mom anything?"

Andrew looked up from the textbook he was reading and raised an eyebrow. "Mrs. Smith never really was the chatty type, and I don't think she cares for us 'rowdy kids' very much either. My bet is she doesn't tell Mom squat."

I stuck my tongue out at him. "Well, you're no fun."

"I'm plenty fun," Andrew said in response, his voice

sounding bored as he flipped a page in his book. "You just don't like the fact that I'm practical."

I opened my mouth to tell him exactly what I thought about him when the front door flew open and banged loudly against the wall. I had my back to the door, but I could tell instantly by the look on my brother's face that something was wrong. I whipped around to find my mother standing in the doorway.

She was holding her arm to her chest as blood dripped down her forearm to the cream-colored carpet at her feet. Her entire body quivered as she stared at us with wide-eyed disbelief.

"Mom! What happened?" I sprung to my feet and rushed to her side. Gently, I peeled her fingers away from her arm in an attempt to see how badly she was hurt. "What did you do?"

My mother pulled her arm out of my grasp to examine the wound herself. "Mrs. Smith did this. She...she *bit* me."

I stared at her in astonishment. "Mrs. Smith did that?" At first, I couldn't fully comprehend what she was saying. For her arm to be bleeding the way it was, our neighbor had to have been gnawing on it.

Andrew had left the room the instant he saw my mother's arm. He returned as suddenly as he had disappeared with a towel in his hand. "You might need stitches. That looks pretty deep."

"It'll be fine," she said in an assuring tone as Andrew pressed the towel over her arm to staunch the flow of blood. "What I need to do is call the cops on that crazy woman." Nudging Andrew back, she marched over to the phone to do just that, leaving the towel draped over her arm.

"What did you say to make her freak out like that?" I asked.

"Nothing! I brought her over some dinner and was giving my condolences over Peter when she just lunged at me. Something's not right in that woman's head."

I sagged down to the couch and watched as she angrily jabbed the buttons on the phone.

A moment later, my mother began speaking into the receiver with a harsh tone, her words clipped and agitated. She quickly repeated what had happened, demanding something be done about it.

I watched as my normally rational mother took her frustration out on the nice receptionist at the police station before she was connected to an officer. As I listened to her rant, I felt a ball of anxiety settling in the pit of my stomach. Today had been frightening all around, but this incident hit home.

After a few minutes of retelling her story to the officer, my mother hung up and turned to me, triumph on her face. "They're sending a car over there now. I hope she tries to bite one of them. They'll put her in her place." Almost as an afterthought, she added, "She looked terrible, too. If Peter were still alive, I'd have thought he beat the hell out of her." She glared toward the direction of our neighbor's house. "She was acting like a maniac."

"You can't just go around biting people," I said with firm agreement. "I don't care if your husband did just die."

"And to think I took her over dinner," my mother said huffily.

"Maybe there's something really wrong with her," Andrew suggested, ever the voice of reason. "You said yourself she looked really bad. You know Grace. When has she ever looked less than perfect? Her husband just died. Maybe she's losing her grip on reality. It's not uncommon."

I rolled my eyes with a sigh. This was just like my brother. He was going for his master's degree in psychology, and that made him feel like he had to analyze everybody. All the time. "If you're so certain she's just going through the grieving process, why don't you go over there and help her through it?"

"Hell no," Andrew said. "She's a biter. Plus, I'm not being paid to evaluate yet. Until she pulls out her checkbook, she's on her own."

"Watch your language, Drew," Mother warned.

"Sorry, but you know what I mean. When she starts paying me, I'll risk getting bitten." His eyes slid to our mother's arm in concern. Blood was already darkening the thick towel. "I think you're going to need something better than that. If you won't go to the hospital, at least let Rory and I run to the store and pick up some bandages."

Normally, I would have been annoyed at him for offering my assistance without consulting me first, but I was spooked enough not to care. I quickly nodded my agreement. "He's right. You're going to need something more heavy duty than a few Band-Aids."

"I can—"

Andrew cut her off before she could protest any further. "You can go yourself, but you won't. Just relax. We'll take care of it." He gave her a playful wink and pushed her to sit in a nearby chair. "You cook dinner for us every night. The least we can do in return is make sure you don't bleed to death."

My mother reluctantly gave in and settled back in the chair. "All right, but be careful. It's getting late. You know the crazies come out after dark."

Andrew looked at his watch and smirked in amusement. It wasn't all that late. "We'll be fine, Mom. Stop worrying."

***

Thursday, 9:00 P.M.

I exited the drugstore with a bag of medication and bandages tucked safely under my arm. "All I'm saying is that it's a little freaky. I don't want to live next door to a crazy person."

Andrew, who was strolling along next to me, shook his head in amusement. "You are quite the humanitarian," he said with a smirk. "I'll remember never to tell you if I'm having any out of the ordinary thoughts. You'll stop speaking to me."

"You're lucky I talk to you now," I teased. "You get any weirder, and I'm disowning you." Instead of the sarcastic response I expected, Andrew had grown quiet. Glancing in my brother's direction, I found his mouth pinched in a grim line and his eyes shadowed with tension. "Drew..." I studied him with confusion. "I was only joking about disowning you."

He waved me off, his eyes riveted on something across the street. "Do you see that guy over there?" he asked under his breath.

I glanced in the direction he was staring toward so fixatedly. There was a man walking parallel to us across the road. It was getting too dark to see much else besides the fact that he was stumbling around as if drunk. "Yeah. He looks sloshed. What about him?"

"He's been following us since we left the store."

Alarm welled inside of me, and I suddenly wished we'd

taken a car instead of walking the half mile to the small shopping center. "Like he wants to mug us?"

"Yeah, like he wants to mug us. Or worse." Andrew reached out and gripped my elbow, pushing me to walk faster. "Right now, we're still near the shopping center. There are store owners and a few shoppers relatively close by, but in a couple minutes, we'll be on roads with no streetlights, no stores. We've got to get some distance between us and him before we are."

My heart was in my throat as I bobbed my head vigorously in agreement. "Right. So walk fast. Got it."

"Mmm hmm," Andrew said distractedly. He continued to push me, his hand a viselike grip on my arm. Glancing over his shoulder, he grimaced. "He's crossing the road."

I shot a quick look over my shoulder and, sure enough, the man was shuffling across the street in our direction. He passed underneath a streetlight, and I caught a good look at him. His clothes hung in tatters; his skin was dirty and swollen. Spinning back around, I quickened my pace, speed-walking while trying not to look as if I was panicking.

We'd barely gotten half a block when there was a horrible screech of tires followed by a dull thud. Andrew spun around, and his face paled.

I'd never seen him look so frightened in my entire life, and it was starting to unnerve me. "Drew?" I asked, afraid to look at what had him so spooked.

"A city bus just hit him," he said on a whisper. "He..." Andrew trailed off, his voice wavering. He took a moment to collect himself before he turned and gave me a push in the back. "Walk. We need to get home right now."

"Drew, we can't just..." I spun to look at the bus, but Andrew put himself in my way.

"You don't want to see that. Trust me. Just...just walk, okay? For once in your life, just listen to me." My brother's tone was practically a plea, and it amped up my anxiety level.

"We can't leave! He might need help!"

"He was going to mug us, Rory." He glanced behind him. "The bus is stopped. There are about twenty people right there who can get help. We'll just get in their way."

Something in his tone chilled me to the bone. "He's dead, isn't he?" I asked softly. When he didn't answer, I let out a strangled sob. "Oh, God. He's dead." Unable to help myself, I peered around him to see the man lying on the ground in front of the bus.

There was blood smeared across the dented grill of the vehicle, and its left headlight was smashed, glass littering the street. The man's body was mangled in a way that left little doubt as to whether or not he would survive.

I quickly turned my back to the scene as my stomach threatened to upend my dinner all over the sidewalk.

Andrew put a comforting hand on my shoulder. "We're not going to be of any help."

I nodded my head, letting him guide me away. All I wanted to do right now was curl up in bed and forget this entire day ever happened.

***

Thursday, 9:30 P.M.

I entered our house, Andrew hot on my heels. My hands were trembling, and I could barely keep my voice lowered as I hissed angry words at him. "We shouldn't have just left, and you know it!" Now that there was distance between us and the dead man, and I'd had a little time to think on the situation, I was fired up about Andrew's decision to just walk away.

He opened his mouth to reply when my mother called from the kitchen. "Drew? Rory? Are you two home?"

Andrew spun on me, his voice a harsh whisper. "Don't say anything to Mom. It will just freak her out. She's had a hard enough day as it is."

My mother entered the room, and I bit back any retort I'd been about to make. He was right. Telling her would only get her upset. "We're back," I said, forcing a smile.

My father, home from work, followed her into the room. "You just missed all the fun," he said dryly. "The cops were here."

My mom sent him an affectionate grin. "It took both of those poor police officers to convince your father not to go over there and have a few words of his own with Mrs. Smith. After they got Dad cooled down, they went next door. Did you see the squad car in front of her house?"

Andrew took her arm and gently pulled back the towel he'd placed there earlier. He tried to politely act as if he didn't notice the blood that welled instantly to the surface, but I saw his grimace. "Yeah, we noticed," he said. "Hopefully, they'll take care of everything. We should concentrate on getting you bandaged up and leave Grace to the police."

His eyes shot to me with a pointed expression that I didn't understand. After a moment of silence, with his voice carefully neutral, he asked, "How about you hand over those bandages? You know, the ones we left the house to get?"

After everything that had happened, I'd completely forgotten about the bandages. "Oh. Okay." Feeling as if I was moving in slow motion, I pulled them from the shopping bag. When I looked up again, my father was holding a hand out, waiting for me.

"You okay, Rory?" he asked in concern as he took a roll of gauze I placed in his outstretched hand.

Andrew's head shot in my direction, and he frowned in disapproval.

"I...I'm fine," I said, lying. "Just worried about Mom."

"Your mother is fine," Dad assured, giving my shoulder a quick squeeze.

As my father lowered his head over Mom's arm, Andrew's annoyed expression turned to concern. "Rory, why don't you get to bed? You've had a long day."

My eyes met his, and the warning look he sent me spoke volumes. Breaking eye contact, I gave a small nod. "I am really tired. Perhaps it's for the best..."

"Go," he said, gently urging me to head upstairs to my room. "Get some rest. We can talk tomorrow, okay?"

His voice was much gentler now, and I could hear the compassion his words held. With a nod of agreement, I started up the stairs to my bedroom. "Night, Mom," I said quietly. "Night, Daddy." Without waiting for a reply, I shuffled to my room, leaving them so they could fix up my mother's injured arm.

Chapter 2

The Day the World Ends

Friday, 3:40 P.M.

"You even make spandex look good," I said to my reflection as I checked myself out in the mirror. I had just finished getting ready for my latest "self-defense" class, so I was decked out in black Yoga pants. Hot pink, fuzzy leg warmers came up to my knees, complementing my hot pink top with the word "Sexy" written in black glitter across the chest.

I always enjoyed wearing splashy outfits to class because Geneva loved her dull, tranquil shades, saying they brought her peace. I was an instigator, but at least I admitted it.

Giving myself a wink, I exited my bedroom and bounded down the stairs to find my mother in the kitchen staring intently out the window. "Hey, Ma!" I said in greeting, trying to sound upbeat. I was feeling much better now that I'd gotten a good night's sleep and had time to get over the traumatic events of the previous evening.

As reluctant as I was to admit it, Andrew was right. My mother was probably worried enough about the situation involving our neighbor. There was no reason to worry her over something else, especially when it was after the fact when there was nothing to be done about it.

When she turned to me, I noticed with concern that Mom's eyes appeared almost glassy. It looked as if worry over the dispute with Mrs. Smith had resulted in a sleepless night for her.

I opened my mouth to ask about her injured hand, but she distracted me by leaning closer to the window. "There's a police car in front of the Smiths' house. It must have arrived early this morning, because it was here when I got up to see your father off for work."

"Drew said the one last night was still there when he went to bed. She's definitely in some serious trouble if they came back this morning. Maybe she'll be on *Cops* or something." I leaned across the counter to turn on the small television that sat on the windowsill. Switching on my mother's favorite soap opera, I grabbed an orange from our fruit bowl and started peeling it. "You forgot to turn on your show," I said. "You're slipping."

My mother swallowed slowly before answering. "I...I guess I did." She was staring at me, her eyes gaping vacantly somewhere below my chin.

I frowned and rubbed my neck self-consciously. "Are you feeling all right?"

She licked her lips, as if to wet them, and opened her mouth to answer. She didn't get any farther than that. She suddenly gripped her stomach and lunged toward the sink.

The sound of vomiting reached my ears, and I cringed at how violent it seemed. "Mom!" I rushed over to place a hand on her heaving back. "Are you okay?"

Her head whipped in my direction, and there was ferocity in her eyes. "Get away from me," she growled.

With a gasp, I backed away from her, afraid of my own mother for the first time in my life. "What's wrong?" I asked, frightened.

She grabbed a towel from the counter and pressed it to her mouth. "I'm sorry, honey," she said after a pause, her voice going soft as she lowered the towel. "I guess I'm not feeling very well. My stomach didn't agree with my lunch, but I'll be fine. You go ahead to class. I wouldn't want you to be late."

"Are you sure?" I asked uncertainly. "I can stay home with you, take you to a doctor."

She shook her head, gripping the counter tightly. "No, just go to your class."

I stared at her pale face and couldn't help but notice how sickly she looked. I decided to try one last time. "Are you sure?"

"I said go!" She broke into sporadic coughing and put the towel to her mouth. "Please," she said, her tone beseeching around the cloth. "Just go."

I nodded in agreement, not wanting to argue with her

when she wasn't feeling well.

She pulled the towel away from her mouth and stared fixatedly at a small spatter of blood that blemished the pale cotton fabric. "I'm going to lie down," she murmured, her voice sounding distant. "I'm sure this will go away once I get some rest. I'll be fine when you get home."

"You're the boss." I conceded reluctantly, glancing toward the television as a news report interrupted the show.

The reporter on screen looked alarmed, and he kept glancing over his shoulder as he described the scene behind him. Another local woman had been attacked by what the reporter was assuming to be a pack of wild dogs. He explained that the dogs had eaten the victim alive, leaving appendages strewn across a park not five miles from our home. Police hadn't notified the family yet, so they were keeping the victim's identity a secret.

The camera flashed to the bloody background behind the reporter, and my mother paled further. A moan escaped her lips, and she squeezed her eyes tightly closed.

I reached up and turned off the television with an aggressive jab of a finger. "You don't need to see this, especially if you're feeling queasy. You go take a nap, and I'll see you when I get back from class."

My mother nodded. "I think that's a good idea." She turned and awkwardly stumbled toward her bedroom. Her socks shuffled on the carpet, and she looked unsteady on her feet.

With one last look of concern, I watched as she disappeared into her bedroom. I wanted to stay and help, but she'd made it quite clear that she wanted some time alone. I needed to go anyway. I had to hurry if I was going to make it to Geneva's class on time.

***

Friday, 3:55 P.M.

I pulled into a parking space just in time to see Damian step around the truck next to my car. As I put my car in park and pulled the keys from the ignition, he opened my door with what he thought was a charming grin.

"Wow," I said sarcastically. "I almost gave you permission

to put your hands on my car." It was the first thing that came to my mind and I just said it. I hadn't intended to be mean, but worry over my mother had brought bite to my words. I'd effectively used Damian as an outlet for my frustration. "How long have you been waiting there? You're like a stalker."

Damian's grin grew as if he enjoyed my insults. "Actually, this is my truck," he said, nodding to the heap of junk next to my flawless sports car. "You know, the one you almost hit when you pulled in?"

This back and forth game of cat and mouse was just what I needed to alleviate some stress. I don't think Damian ever took my attacks personally; he merely saw them as a challenge. Venting at him would go a long way in soothing my anxiety.

"I wasn't even close," I said flippantly. I marched away from the car, leaving my door open. If he liked touching my car so much, he could shut the door as well.

I grinned, my back to him, as I heard the door swing closed. He was just like a dog. You could train them to do good things, but they still humped people's legs...not that I thought he humped people's legs.

I glanced back at Damian as he hurried to catch up with me. I couldn't keep the grin from my face. Just like a good dog, he hurried obediently after his master. "Why are you walking with me?" I asked in a callous manner.

He shrugged. "Because we're going to the same place. Last time I checked, this was a public parking lot. For once in your life, can't you just be civil and walk with me?"

I sighed deeply, as if he was asking the biggest favor in the world. "Fine."

He chuckled deep in his throat, sounding more amused than aggravated at my reluctance to cooperate. "It's that hard to be nice to me?"

I felt a blush creep up my neck. I didn't like being called out on my less than civil conduct. "It's just that you...that you..." I broke off. I had no specific reason as to why I didn't like him. I just didn't. "If you just wouldn't..."

"You don't know why you don't like me," Damian said, interjecting as if reading my thoughts. "But I do."

"Oh? You do?" I asked, crossing my arms over my chest with a sound of disbelief. "Do share." I would love to know what it was about him that rubbed me the wrong way. I couldn't put my finger on it. If he knew the answer, I wanted to hear it.

"You're spoiled," he said simply. "You're a pampered little daddy's girl who doesn't like people who don't treat you like you're God's gift to the universe."

"That is not true!"

"Let me finish. You date your preppy boy-toys who are too immature to be in a serious relationship. You've never been with a real man, because you might start to care about someone other than yourself. You prefer your men to be un-intelligent and self-absorbed. It's easier to keep it casual that way. You'd be too tempted to fall head over heels if you dated a man who thought of something other than how good his hair looks or how much money he has, and you're too scared to risk your heart like that. You hate me because I tempt you on a level that makes you nervous." His voice grew low and husky. "I make you weak in the knees."

If I wasn't so pissed, I might have done just as he'd ac-cused and gone weak at that tone. Unfortunately for Damian, I was pissed. I spun on him, my face flushed with anger. "First off, a real man? Please. You mean an *older* man. You're far too old for me."

"I'm twenty-four—"

"And even if you weren't, you wouldn't have a shot in hell at me. I don't like men like you. You're nothing but trouble." I took a step closer to him, my finger poking into his chest. "You radiate trouble. I can almost feel it, like it pulses off your skin."

Damian's ever-present grin suddenly fell, and he took a step away from me. "What did you say?"

"I said you radiate trouble. No girl in her right mind would want to get mixed up with that." Turning away from him, I entered the building with a smug smirk on my lips. I waited a moment for him to follow, arguing in his defense, but the door never opened.

Turning back around, I watched through the glass doors of the building as he walked briskly back to his truck. There was tension in his shoulders as he climbed into the driver's seat and slammed the door shut behind him.

Maybe I'd gone too far this time...or maybe he was just

being oversensitive. I hadn't said anything excessively offensive. In fact, I'd said far worse before. I would never admit it
to him, but deep down, I was feeling a little guilty. I secretly
enjoyed the banter between the two of us, and the fact that
Damian had given up so easily bothered me. My stomach
turning with anxiety, I took one last look at his retreating
truck before joining the assembled group for another tedious
session with Geneva.

***

Friday, 6:10 P.M.

Class had just gotten out and I was delighted at the fact
that I could actually enjoy the rest of my evening. I had a date
with Eric Welsh, an old friend from high school who was also
home for the summer. I was meeting him in fifteen minutes at
Sandy's Shack, so I needed to hurry. Hopping into my car, I
grabbed my cell phone and called home. Before I did anything, I wanted to see how my mother was feeling.
    Andrew picked up on the third ring. "Hello?" He sounded
distracted and more than a little frazzled.
    "Drew!" I cried, relieved I had gotten a hold of someone.
    "What's up, Rory?" he asked breathlessly.
    "I wanted to know how Mom was doing. She wasn't feel-
ing too good when I left the house this afternoon."
    "Well, she's not feeling any better. She's been complaining
that she's freezing, and she can't keep any food down. She's
got this really eerie, dazed look in her eyes, and she keeps
snapping at everybody. She slept for a little bit, but mostly,
she's been lying in bed moaning and mumbling to herself." He
paused, and humor leaked into his voice with his next sentence. "And she says Dad overreacts when he's sick."
    Though I couldn't see him, I just knew on the other end
of the line, he was grinning and rolling his eyes.
    I gave a soft laugh in reply. "She was in rare form this
morning. She scared me a little."
    "You're lucky you missed the moaning then, because it's
definitely creepy. She sounds like she belongs in one of those
Exorcist movies." He tried to sound light about it, but I could
hear the concern in his voice. He was trying to keep me from
worrying.

"I was meeting a friend for dinner, but I think I'm going to cancel and come home."

"Don't do that," Andrew said. "You shouldn't cancel your plans because Mom's sick. There's not much you can do for her anyway. She's just going to have to wait it out. Hopefully, whatever this bug is, it will be out of her system by tomorrow morning and she'll be as good as new."

"Are you sure?" I asked with indecision as I turned onto the back road that would lead me to the restaurant.

"Positive. Go have fun."

I heard a loud, inhuman-sounding shriek in the background on Andrew's end of the line.

"Listen, Rory," he said hurriedly. "I have to go. I'll see you later tonight."

The connection was suddenly broken. I stared at my phone in concern, hoping the horrible noise hadn't been my mother. I briefly considered going back home, but Andrew had insisted I go out as planned. Besides, I was already turning into the restaurant parking lot as I tucked my phone away. I might as well stay for dinner.

I pulled into a parking space and looked up at the building. Regardless of the fact that I was pushing myself to stay, I wasn't sure if I was in the mood for burgers anymore. My stomach was in too many knots over the phone conversation with Andrew.

As I was once again contemplating on whether or not I should cancel on Eric, a tapping on my window pulled me out of my troubled thoughts.

To my disbelief, Damian stood outside my door.

I let out a frustrated sigh. I did not want to deal with him right now. This was the second time he'd shown up outside my car today, uninvited, might I add. I was honestly starting to wonder if he *was* stalking me. Resigned, I climbed out of the car and faced him, ready for whatever onslaught of insults he was preparing to give. "Yes?" I asked, annoyance strong in my voice.

I was startled to see that his expression looked something close to vulnerable. It was a change from his usual cocky demeanor. "I, uh..." He stopped and ran a hand through his thick hair. "I wanted to know if you meant what you said earlier. Do I really...radiate trouble?"

"Since when do you care about my opinion?" I asked tiredly.

"Since right now. Just answer the question."

Taking my frustration over the events of the past couple days out on Damian, I snapped. Glaring up at him, I gave him my exact opinion of what I thought about him. "Yeah, I meant it when I said you radiated trouble. You're bad news. I would never go out with a guy like you. Ever. Get that through your thick head. I date men who actually have a future. The guys I date know how to treat a lady instead of stalking and harassing them."

"God, you're a bitch," Damian said under his breath.

I gave him the cutest, brightest smile I'd ever given. I wanted him to know what he was missing. "Thank you," I said sweetly.

He shook his head, his anger practically dancing across his skin, bringing a heat to the air between us.

The hair on my arms stood up, and it had nothing to do with being cold. I took a tiny step away from him, instantly wishing I hadn't been so nasty.

Damian took a menacing step closer, his six-foot-two frame towering over me as he closed the short distance I'd put between us. His eyes darkened with fury.

"Don't threaten me," I whispered with a slight tremble to my voice.

"When I threaten you, you'll know it." He glared down at me a second longer before turning and stomping into the building.

When the door slammed shut behind him, I let my breath out in a shaky exhale, really wishing I'd just gone home. I forced myself to push that thought to the back of my mind. Eric was waiting for me. Besides, I wasn't going to give Damian the satisfaction of ruining my evening. I straightened my shoulders, and with my head held high, I marched into the restaurant.

It didn't take me long to spot Eric. He was seated in the center of the dining area, perusing a menu he'd probably memorized during our high school years. When he noticed me approaching, he smiled. "Aurora!" He stood to greet me. "You look absolutely breathtaking. I swear you get more gorgeous every time I see you."

I gave him a smile in return, some of the tension easing out of my shoulders. Eric's family was old money. Before he was even a teenager, he'd been to a dozen etiquette classes. Due to this, he always had an aristocratic politeness about him that set a person at ease. "You look good, too." Suddenly feeling eyes on me, I glanced up to find Damian staring darkly in our direction from across the room.

His face was in the shadows, but there was no mistaking the look of loathing he sent my way. He hated me. Yet, underneath all of that hate, I knew he still wanted me. I could see it in his smoldering, dark eyes.

Making my way through high school as part of the popular crowd, I was familiar with receiving such mixed emotions. People hated the popular crowd, mostly because they were jealous, but given the opportunity, they would have dropped anyone and everything to be included.

I suddenly had the urge to return the teasing he'd done to me with Brooke. I leaned across the table, feeling the short skirt I'd changed into after class slide high up on my thighs. I put my hand flat on the table as I leaned over and placed a soft kiss on Eric's cheek. I pulled back and stared at Damian, a triumphant grin on my lips.

Disgust was plain on his face. His jaw was set in anger, and I could see his shoulders rise and fall harshly in aggravation.

The expression on his face made me shiver. Instantly, it reminded me of the intimidating incident in the parking lot. I realized it probably wasn't the best idea to screw with someone who frightened me. I quickly sat down, lowering my head so I wouldn't have to see the rage in his eyes.

Eric, misinterpreting the kiss to be more than it was, gave a low chuckle. "Well," he said, drawing the word out, "it's nice to see you again, too."

I mumbled in agreement, my stomach in knots over the situation with Damian. I could feel his glare on me almost as if it had a physical presence, and I was afraid to look up and meet his gaze.

Eric, apparently taking my bowed head for shyness instead of the fear it actually was, leaned back in his seat with a pleased expression and fiddled with his silverware. "So," he said, not even attempting to keep his voice from being smug at the affection I'd just lavished on him, "what have you been up to these past couple months?"

I shrugged, distracted by a slightly raised voice coming from the front of the restaurant. "Not much." I glanced behind me toward the entrance of the building. There seemed to be a small commotion going on at the doors. One of the waitresses was trying to turn away a customer.

The man was dirty and his clothes were shredded. He was probably a homeless guy trying to weasel some food out of her.

I turned back to Eric, suddenly nervous as memories from the night before came crashing back. I blinked, trying to force away the invasive images of the mangled and bloody bus fender. "I've been busy getting ready for my first semester, signing up for classes and packing. It's been taking up most of my time," I said, my voice distant.

Eric grinned, seemingly unaware of how edgy I was. "Don't exaggerate. You were always a party girl. I know you—" He broke off as someone by the door started yelling.

I turned to see five more scraggly men pushing their way into the building. One of them was bleeding from his temple. Blood poured down the side of his head, dripping onto his stained shirt. "What are they doing?" I asked with puzzlement. I cringed as a few drops of blood spattered to the ground. "That one guy is bleeding." My heart sped up as the bleeding man continued to lumber toward the waitress who was waving them back.

The man suddenly lunged at her with alarming quickness, digging his teeth into her shoulder.

I stared in abject horror, too frozen with fear to even move. "Oh my God," I whispered.

Someone screamed, and in the blink of an eye, the atmosphere turned into chaos.

The rest of the ragged men rushed forward as if driven by the screams. They grabbed at people, teeth gnashing at the air as they stumbled toward the diner's customers.

As people rushed past us scrambling for cover, I jumped out of my seat and turned fearful eyes to Eric, looking for guidance as to what we should do.

His eyes were wide with fright, and I realized he wasn't going to have any brilliant suggestions to offer. Someone jostled him from behind, and he took a staggering step away from me. I went to say his name, to call him back to me, when he took off. He ran for the front door, barreling toward what he thought was safety.

"Eric!" I screamed. "Eric! Don't leave me!"

He didn't even turn around. He raced toward his escape, leaving me behind to fend for myself.

I saw another one of the bedraggled men to the left of Eric in the shadows. I tried to yell out a warning to him, but it was too late, and he was no longer listening to me anyway.

The man grabbed Eric around the shoulders, yanked him close, and bit into the side of his face. Blood gushed, and when the man pulled away, he took a large chunk of flesh with him.

I screamed, my voice echoing off the walls and mingling with the shouts of other patrons.

Eric's hand flew to his head, his fingers fumbling over his torn skin.

The man didn't even waste a second before diving onto Eric. He dug his fingers into Eric's skin, gnawing on pieces as he ripped them away.

As soon as Eric went down, another one of the men dove on top of him. Together, the two of them bit and chewed, tearing away meat nearly down to the bone.

Eric let out screams of agony and terror as they devoured him, his voice near hysteria. One of them sunk teeth violently into his throat.

The screaming suddenly stopped, and I knew Eric was dead.

I whimpered fearfully as I watched the psychotic men eat pieces of my date. I didn't want to watch, yet I was unable to look away. It was hard to comprehend that the bloody mess underneath them had been talking to me only moments ago.

Another one of the men was lumbering toward me, making grunting noises deep in his throat. He was like an animal with his wild eyes and uncomprehending gaze. There didn't appear to be any conscious thought to him, only the primal instinct to kill.

I stood frozen as he advanced on me, unable to make my feet move, though I knew I should be running. I felt bolted to the floor, unable to budge, while inside I was screaming.

I was suddenly grabbed from behind and yanked backwards. I thought at first it was one of the crazed men, but no further attack came. I was shoved behind whoever had grabbed me, removed from the homicidal man's path. I stumbled on my feet, my hands reaching out and steadying myself on the person's waist. Shocked, I glanced up to see who had risked their life to save me.

Damian stood facing the man who had intended to assault me. He had a chair in his hands, trying to keep distance between the man and us.

I watched in horror as every single one of the things turned to look at Damian in what felt like slow motion. I resolved to think of them as things now, because they weren't men anymore. Men didn't eat people. Monsters ate people.

The things all snarled, their lips pulling back to reveal bloody and blackened teeth. They made a noise I could only describe as a growl and started advancing on Damian.

"Oh shit," he said under his breath. "Aurora?"

"Yeah?" My voice trembled as I slowly backed away.

"Run." With that, he dropped the chair, pushed me in front of him, and did as he instructed me to do. He ran.

I went as fast as I could, but with his six-foot-two frame, it didn't take him long to catch up to me. We both turned simultaneously down the hallway, sprinting for our lives.

"Is there a window in the women's bathroom?" he hollered.

"What?" I yelled back breathlessly, having a hard time hearing over the pounding of my heart and the pursuing monsters.

"Fast! Is there a window in the women's bathroom?"

I scanned my mind, trying to remember the layout of the restrooms, a hard thing to do when being chased by a psychotic monster that wants to eat you alive. "Yes," I said uncertainly, my answer sounding more like a question.

"You better be damn sure, or we're both dead," Damian came back gruffly.

At his somber statement, I really concentrated, picturing the arrangement of the bathroom interior. "Yes! Yes, there's a window."

"Good."

Before I had a chance to take another step, I was thrown

to the side. I went barreling into the women's room, forcing the door open with my body as I went.

Damian was a step behind me. He lurched into the room, his tall frame slamming into mine and knocking me off balance.

As the door swung shut behind him of its own momentum, we both collapsed to the floor in a pile of tangled arms and legs. The air rushed out of my lungs as his full weight was thrown on top of me. One of my knees slid dangerously between his, and I accidentally caught him in the ribs with an elbow. "Damian," I groaned, pushing against his chest with my free hand. "You're squishing me."

With a grunt of discomfort, he rolled to sit next to me, breathing hard. His hands ran through his dark hair, and his fingers trembled with shock and adrenaline. While I struggled to a sitting position, he touched a hand to his jaw and winced in pain.

With his weight no longer on me, I was able to convince my lungs to start working again. I sucked in deep gulps of air, my throat feeling raw.

As we both tried to collect ourselves, the door flew open, and three mutilated faces stared in at us.

I stopped complaining. Scrambling to my feet, I threw myself against the door. It closed for a moment before being smashed into from the other side, forcing me backwards.

It opened enough for one of the men to get his arm into the room. I spun around, pressing my back against the door, trying to dig my feet into the floor to give me extra leverage.

Damian was on his feet in an instant. He hit the door hard, his hands on either side of my head, the front of his body slamming into the front of mine. He was jammed up tightly against me with my nose practically in his chest. His head was lowered toward me, and I could see his jaw clench with effort.

The door slammed shut on the thing's arm, and it gave an inhuman screech.

I glanced to the side to see the arm dangling limply next to my head. Blood poured down torn skin and dripped to the floor.

I opened my mouth to scream when Damian pulled back and slammed into the door again, knocking the air, and the scream, out of me. There was a sickening wet noise as the arm detached, landing with a thud at my feet. Without the arm blocking the door, it closed.

Damian reached above my head and clicked the lock into place. With a shaky sigh, he leaned his head against the door just above my shoulder, his body still pressed flat to mine. His breath was hot against the side of my neck, and his body covered me completely. I could feel him all the way down to my toes. He was just a little too close for a casual acquaint- ance, especially for one I didn't like all that much.

I brought my hands up and pushed on his shoulders. "You can get off me now."

He pulled his head back and looked down at me through his hair, his eyes glinting with amusement. "If I must." He lingered a second too long for my taste before moving away from me.

With him no longer crushed up against me, I was able to put a hand to my chest and suck in a deep gulp of air. "You almost killed me. I think you collapsed one of my lungs."

The look he gave me was one of disbelief. He seemed to be thinking about how to respond to that. Finally, he an- swered. "I could have let them eat you. Would you have pre- ferred that?"

"No, but..." My sentence was drowned out by the sound of something slamming into the door. There was a moment of silence and then another thud followed. "They're trying to break the door down," I whispered fearfully.

Damian gripped my arm at the elbow and took a wary step away from the door, pulling me with him. "Where's that window you promised me?" He tried to sound casual about it, but I could hear the strain in his voice.

I jumped as the door rattled once more in its frame. "Over here." I rushed to the window and pointed at it. It was at shoulder height for me, making it impossible for me to see anything beyond the glass unless I was to stand on my tip- toes to peer through. The window was big enough for me to slide through comfortably, but I couldn't see any way to get it open. "How are we going to get out? I don't see a latch."

Damian's fist suddenly went crashing through the win- dow, sending shards of glass flying everywhere.

"Guess that's how," I said in amazement as I watched

blood appear on his knuckles. I quickly got over the shock when something slammed into the door hard enough to crack it. The door started splintering down the middle. It had a large enough hole in it that I could see one bloodshot eye staring in at me.

I forgot all about the glass as I lunged toward the window. "Get me out of here!" I grabbed onto the windowsill, the remaining glass sinking into my fingers. I barely registered the pain because I was so desperate to get out.

"Don't worry, honey," Damian said as he helped lift me up to the window, assisting me so I could get my feet through to the freedom on the other side. "They'll eat me first."

I thought he was joking, but when I glanced over my shoulder, I saw one of the things peering from the other side of the door. It was staring at Damian with crazed eyes. Trying to force its way through the door, it made frantic howls of excitement.

That was the last thing I saw, because Damian hefted me out the window. I collapsed to the ground with a thud, unable to stay on my feet. At the sound of splintering wood, I craned my neck up toward the window with a gasp of fear. They had broken through the door.

I was a crumpled heap of terror in the grass, my ears straining as I awaited the sounds of Damian's agonized screams. I might not have liked him, but I didn't want him to die either. My breath came out in an exhale of relief as Damian suddenly pulled himself through the bathroom's shattered window.

He landed in a crouch next to me, his movements almost catlike and oddly graceful for such a big man. "Are you okay?" he asked, voice low.

My elbow ached horribly from where I'd jarred it when hitting the ground, but I was still alive. I couldn't complain. "I'm fine," I said, assuring him.

He reached into his pocket, grabbing for his keys. "Let's make a break for my truck and get the hell out of here."

Being the bullheaded person I was, I felt the need to argue with him. Why would I want to argue with the man who had just saved my life? Because he was Damian. There was no other reason than that, plain and simple. "I'm not leaving my car here to get stolen. We can run to my car."

"Do you think that soft leather roof is going to stop one of those things? They broke down a door in under two minutes. They'll just tear the roof off of that pretty little car of yours and eat us." He glanced at me in the dark. "Besides, do you really think there's anyone left alive in there to steal it?"

Faced with those unsettling probabilities, I had to agree with him. It looked like we'd be leaving my car behind. I didn't get a chance to inform him of my compliance, because a gunshot rang through the night. Blood and bone suddenly exploded around us. I let out a gasp of shock as blood soaked into my hair and ran down my arms.

Damian shook blood from his arms as he glanced behind us and whistled at the sight that greeted him. "Shit," he said softly.

One of the cannibalistic men was hanging from the window we'd just exited. His head was completely gone, leaving behind a stumpy mess that had once been a neck. Blood and chunks of meat fell down to the ground around us.

I whipped my head back around in awe to look at the person who had fired the weapon.

A tall black man stepped out of the shadows and marched over to stand a few feet in front of us.

The moment my eyes fell on him, I wanted to scream. There wasn't anything blatantly wrong with him, but just the sight of him chilled me to the bone, making my body tremor with fear.

His skin was a deep brown. What made it odd was that it seemed to almost gleam in the moonlight instead of blend in with the darkness. Silver hoop earrings traveled up his left ear, reflecting in the dim lighting and making his skin seem even more unnatural. His eyes were what frightened me the most. They were a pale gray that glowed, the light coming from everywhere and nowhere at once.

I gazed up at the seven-foot monstrosity in front of me, and my lips trembled.

"I've got a live one here!" He called the words out into the night. His voice was a deep rumble that made him seem even more intimidating.

Another voice hollered from the darkness behind him. "Aldrich found one!"

Five men suddenly surrounded us. They all had guns

raised and pointed as if they were ready to fire on command.

I scooted closer to Damian as they circled us, my fingertips brushing against the sleeve of his shirt as if to reassure myself that I wasn't alone.

The man named Aldrich took a lumbering step toward us. "Have either of you been bitten?"

"Wh...what?" I asked, my voice wavering in my uncertainty.

"Have either of you been bitten?" he repeated. His voice was even and lacking any sign of warmth.

"You mean by one of those things?" I asked, feeling slightly confused at his question. "N...no. We're okay."

He eyed us suspiciously before nodding his head. "Good. We're going to take you somewhere safe. Keep up if you wish to stay alive." He took off at a brisk walk, striding away from the building toward the dark, imposing road.

Damian climbed to his feet and pulled me up with him. He trailed slowly after Aldrich as if he didn't want to follow, but didn't see any other alternatives.

I moved closer to him and whispered under my breath. "I don't trust him."

Damian walked in stony silence before finally speaking. When he did, his voice was low and guarded. "You shouldn't."

Aldrich turned around, flashing a set of teeth so white and shiny I couldn't believe they were real. It took my mind a minute to comprehend that he had two of his teeth sharpened to points. I gripped Damian's arm, my heart frozen in fear. The way Aldrich had looked over his shoulder and grinned made it seem as if he'd heard me talking about him, yet that was impossible.

Aldrich suddenly stopped, turned, and put himself directly in our path. He towered over both of us, and his attitude portrayed that he was completely aware of this fact. There was intimidation plain in his body language. "Kieran and Banning will escort you to safety while we search for other survivors." He looked over his shoulder and let out a deep, almost mocking laugh.

Something in his tone let me know that this wasn't going to be the rescue I'd been hoping for. These guys weren't the military, and we weren't nearly as safe as it might have first appeared.

Chapter 3

Aldrich called out toward the wooded area surrounding The Shack and two men stepped out of the tree line. As a unit, they sauntered over, giving a quick nod to Aldrich as he instructed them to take Damian and me to safety. One of the men was tall and sinewy; the other was small and difficult to see in the shadow of the first.

The taller, thin man reached us first. He licked his lips as he assessed me, his eyes roving over my body in a way that made me uncomfortable. His dark red hair fell to his shoulders, and his eyes were green, the green of a cat's eyes. I had thought Aldrich was the scariest thing I'd ever seen, but this man beat him on the creepy scale. This man stared at me as if I was a mouse and he was a very big, very evil cat. I knew just by looking at him that if he got his hands on me, he would tear me apart.

The second man stepped up behind his partner. This man was tiny. I was taller than him by nearly two inches. He appeared to be around five-foot-five with brown hair a little longer than shoulder-length. It was pulled back in a ponytail, but tiny wisps had fallen loose to trail across his pleasant-looking face. He didn't seem half as scary as his cohort.

I took a nervous step away from the red-haired man, silently trying to convey to Damian my opinion of our two guards. This put me closer to the second man, but he seemed like the lesser of two evils.

The dark-haired man suddenly reached behind him and pulled a giant sword from a back holster. The sword had to be four feet long, its blade glinting in the moonlight.

How he held it was beyond me. The thing was almost as big as he was, and I couldn't keep the fear out of my eyes as

I watched him wield the weapon. I had just made the mistake of stepping into killing distance.

He seemed to notice the panicked look in my eyes, because he raised an expressive eyebrow. "Do you want me to protect you or hold your hand?"

Against my better judgment, I opened my mouth to give a sarcastic reply, but I was suddenly grabbed from behind and yanked backwards into someone's chest. I whipped my head to peer over my shoulder in concern.

Damian had a tight grip on my shoulders as he held me back against him. His jaw was clenched with tension and anger.

I gave him a puzzled look, and he nodded to where I had been standing only moments earlier.

The red-haired man stood with his fingers curled in the air, as if he had been about to grab something. His head slanted toward Damian, and a growl emanated from deep within in his throat.

"Kieran," said the man with the sword, clearing up their names. "We're not to harm them. You know that." There was a low warning in his voice, and his dark eyes held the other man's with intensity.

Kieran targeted Banning with an irritated look. "I wasn't going to kill her. I just wanted a taste of the sweetness she has to offer." He tilted his head in my direction, and the expression on his face was downright unnerving.

I was quickly beginning to think that having him look at me like that meant nothing good. I felt as if my blood had turned to ice as a result of his emerald stare.

Aldrich stepped between Kieran and me. "You won't be tasting anything," he said with a voice so low and dangerous it brought goose bumps to my arms. "You know what Alexandro would do to you if even a single drop of her blood is missing."

"Then I'll kill *him*," Kieran said, nodding to Damian.

"No." Aldrich's voice was a severe command. "We need him. Get them to Alexandro as you were instructed." He turned to Banning, his shining eyes targeting the smaller man with an intense stare. "Make sure he behaves himself. Keep him from doing anything he'll regret."

Banning nodded with a small sigh. "Why does it feel like

you are always giving me mission impossibles?"

Aldrich's brows furrowed with confusion.

"*Mission: Impossible*?" Banning asked. "Tom Cruise?" He gave another sigh. "Forget it." He turned to Damian and me. "We'd better go before you guys get eaten. We're sitting ducks here, and they will come find us."

"Question," I said, keeping my eyes glued to Banning because I was afraid to even look at the others. "What are *they*, and why are *they* trying to kill us?"

"*They* are zombies, the living dead," Banning answered. "And they don't just want to kill you. They want to eat you. That's all their brain is programmed to do."

I couldn't hold back my derisive snort. "Zombies? You expect me to believe those things back at the restaurant were zombies?" My voice grew quiet, as I was having trouble denying the proof I'd just witnessed. "Zombies don't exist." My voice sounded meek and unconvinced even to my own ears.

Banning laughed as he ambled toward the road, motioning for us to follow. "Oh don't they?" He shook his head, swinging the sword agilely in his hand. "You've got a lot to learn. There are plenty of other terrifying things that exist, things you have no clue about. Zombies are only the beginning."

He sounded so sure of himself it made me falter for a second. "You're lying. You're just trying to frighten me."

"No, he's not," Damian said softly.

I turned to look at him in surprise. "What?" I couldn't believe he would so easily accept what they were telling us without questioning it even a little. I'd never thought him to be exceptionally bright, but even he couldn't be that naïve.

"Did you not see those things, Aurora? They were eating people. They were mindless...well, zombies. They weren't looking to negotiate. They had no reasoning behind their attack. They were just looking to eat."

I swallowed nervously at his rationalization. The evidence all pointed to one thing, only that thing wasn't possible. I spun to face Banning, looking for any hint that he was lying to us. "If you're right, and that's a big if, why don't you look more worried? They'll eat you, too."

"Will they?" Banning asked with a coy grin.

Kieran suddenly spoke up from behind us, causing me to jump at his close proximity. "They'll only eat us if it's their last resort. We're too stale, too cold."

"*We*?" I asked. "What's with all the mysterious *we/they* garbage?"

"Save your questions for Alexandro. He'll tell you everything you need to know," Banning said, sending Kieran a dirty look.

"And what if I don't want to go see Alexandro?" I asked, suddenly feeling very much like a hostage. "Did you ever think of that? Maybe I want to go home. Maybe I want to check on my family."

"You don't have a family anymore," Kieran stated calmly. "They're all dead."

"What the hell is wrong with you?" Damian asked in a harsh voice. He turned to me, blocking me from Kieran's view. "Come on, Aurora. I'll take you home." He nodded to Banning and Kieran. "Thanks for the offer, but we're going."

Banning looked at the ground for a second, then back to us. "As rude as Kieran might be, he's right. We've been searching for survivors for an hour now, but we've been one step behind the infection. You two are the only uninfected survivors we've found so far. It's been total chaos out there. The city is overrun with these things. I wouldn't suggest going home. You're not going to find anyone alive, and what you do find, you'll probably wish you'd never seen. Believe me, you want to stay with us."

My family flashed before my eyes—my mother, father, and Andrew. I sucked in an unsteady breath as I pictured those things doing to my family what they had done to Eric.

"Our teams are out there," Banning said gently. "If there's anyone out there still, we'll find them. You're safer coming with us."

"You have no choice," Kieran said cruelly. His gaze shifted to Banning. "Quit catering to their sensitivities and let's get moving." His eyes shifted back to me, and he gave a snort. "The only two left, our Adam and Eve, don't have a say."

It seemed Kieran enjoyed confusing people as much as he did terrifying them. Leaning against Damian for support, I narrowed my eyes at Kieran and his perplexing statement. "What the hell does that mean?"

Banning sighed, glancing cautiously into the darkness around us. "What he's saying is that this thing is bad. We've known it was coming, could see them bumbling around in the shadows. We killed the ones we found, but there was no way of knowing how many they infected before they were neutralized." He ran a hand over the top of his head, wielding the sword one-handed. "We tried to prevent it, but the disease spread too fast. It felt as if they all attacked at once, all over town...all over the world," he admitted softly. "They simply spread the disease faster than we could keep it under control. Whatever the cause, they overpowered everyone. Their numbers were too many for us to handle. If you've ever heard of that last man on earth scenario...well, this could very well be it."

"You're joking, right?" Feeling stunned, I pushed off of Damian and followed Banning as he began walking again. I was desperate to hear more, but I was terrified of what he would say at the same time.

"I wish I was."

I sent him a skeptical look as I quickened my pace to fit his, trying to stay at his side. I was eager to prove his cynical prediction wrong. "How can you be certain this is all over? You said yourself that you only just started looking for survivors."

Banning glanced at Kieran as if looking for his opinion. He rolled his eyes with a little laugh as if mocking himself for even caring what the other man thought. His attention returned to me. "Trust me. I know." His voice held no ounce of question in it. "We have our connections. Just believe me on this. It's bad." He looked as if he was about to say more, but he suddenly tensed and his dark eyes flicked to Kieran. "Did you hear that?"

Kieran nodded and pulled two guns from holsters at his shoulders. "I heard it." He walked ahead, Banning falling in step behind him. He held the guns pointed up into the air, his gaze sweeping the tree line. "I don't know how you use that sword," he said conversationally, as if everyone's life wasn't suddenly in danger. "A gun can do so much more damage. You'll never paint brains all over a wall with a sword."

"Guns seem too impersonal," Banning said as a counter argument. He adjusted his grip on the sword, holding it loosely at his side as he moved at a measured pace away from Kieran, scouting the area.

"Yeah, because when I kill people, I like it to be personal," I said, sarcasm dripping from my voice. Using sarcasm when faced with crazy men wielding weapons probably wasn't the smartest idea, which was testament to the fact that I was using it as a coping mechanism. If I stopped to think about the irrational events that had happened over the past few days, I would have a nervous breakdown.

Instead, I tried to concentrate on something I could possibly wrap my mind around. "Who *are* you people?" I didn't get an answer because someone came stumbling out of the woods toward us, mumbling pitifully.

Kieran brought his arm down, even with the man's face.

"I'm...sorry..." The man barely managed to get the words out, his tone nearly incomprehensible. His next garbled attempt at speech faded into a growl as he lumbered toward us.

"Gotta hit 'em in the head," Kieran stated, his voice sounding almost delighted. "That's the only way they stay down."

"No!" I yelled, realizing what he was about to do. I wasn't sure anyone even heard me, because my scream was drowned out by the sound of Kieran's gun firing.

The bullet hit the man between the eyes, and he collapsed to the ground.

The only sound that filled the air in the next moment was the echo of Kieran's shot. The sound rang through the trees, bouncing back at us as if in accusation.

Unable to help myself, I rushed at Kieran, grabbing at his arm. "Stop it! Stop it!"

He looked down at me with wild eyes and a giant grin on his face. "Why?"

"He was alive! He was talking to you, and you just shot him. You...you killed him."

"He was one of them," Kieran said calmly.

Another person came rushing at us from the trees, much faster than the now dead man had been.

"They don't stop," Kieran said. "Unless you shoot them in the head, they'll keep coming." He raised his gun and shot this man in the knee.

The beast that had once been a human screeched and collapsed to the ground.

I yelped with a startled jump when the gun fired. It was

just so loud, and I'd never been around such senseless violence before. Recovering, I went to demand that Kieran stop shooting when the man began climbing to his feet.

He shuffled forward on his damaged leg, not even seeming to notice that he was injured. He dragged the slower leg slightly behind him in his determination to get to us.

"See?" Kieran asked. "The sons of bitches will keep coming." He raised the gun up again and, this time, shot the man in the shoulder.

The man staggered back for a second before starting toward us once again.

"You don't want me to kill him?" Kieran's voice held a mocking tone of enjoyment. He unloaded three more rounds into the guy's chest. "Fine. I won't kill him until you beg me to."

The man continued to move forward, not at all fazed by the gunshots or the black, sludge-like blood that ran down his chest, staining his clothing.

Kieran's lips curled into a cruel smirk. "He's only going to keep coming, you know. He won't stop until he tears his teeth into that pretty little throat of yours."

Damian moved toward Kieran, his face full of outrage. His fingers balled into a fist, and I knew that when he reached the other man, he would hit him.

Kieran swung his second gun up and pointed it directly in Damian's face. "Don't even fucking think about it."

Damian froze in his tracks, staring down the barrel of Kieran's gun with wide eyes.

"Kieran!" Banning's voice cracked through the air. His expression clearly showed that the situation was quickly getting out of his control.

"She needs to see," Kieran explained as if his actions were justified. "She needs to understand exactly what those things are capable of."

The man continued toward me, arms outstretched and reaching. Just because the rest of us were at a stalemate didn't mean he had a need to halt his progress.

I shot a nervous glance to Kieran as I took a step back. "Stop it," I whispered. "Make him stop."

Kieran held his gun up to the sky, not even making a move to stop the man as he lumbered past him on his unerring course to me. "What was that?" he asked in delight. "You want me to kill him?"

I stared at Kieran in silence, refusing to answer. My attention stayed on the man, who was getting too close for comfort. My feet shuffled on the gravel as I took small steps backward to stay out of his grasp. "Please," I said as the man drew closer, finding no other choice.

"Please, what?" Kieran prodded.

I gave a small whimper of terror, my voice trembling as the man grabbed for me. One of his hands brushed my shoulder and slid off, but it would only be seconds before he had me. "Kill him! Kill him!" I screamed the words, and they echoed through the night air. I felt a part of me break as I begged Kieran to kill another human being. Was that what he'd wanted, to crush both my spirit and morals in one single blow? If so, then he'd succeeded.

Two things happened at once. Risking a bullet, Damian lunged, snatching a gun from Kieran's ankle holster. He knelt, aimed, and fired. The bullet hit its target—the back of the man's head.

At the same time, Banning shoved past me and swung his sword around. Damian's bullet hit first, and an instant later, Banning's sword cut the man's head clean from his shoulders.

Damian had shown no hesitation whatsoever about shooting the man. He'd been forced to make a choice, a stranger's life or mine. I was extremely grateful he'd chosen mine, yet I was horrified by what he'd just done. I gave a strangled cry as I watched blood gush from the man's neck, blood I had instructed to be spilled.

Damian lunged to his feet and quickly made his way to my side. He grabbed me, pushing me behind him. He then brought the gun up, pointing it at Kieran's chest. "Don't you ever fuck with her like that again."

Kieran laughed, seemingly not at all perturbed by the gun pointed at him. "I'll fuck with her in whatever way I desire. It's none of your business, pup."

Damian glared at Kieran with violence in his eyes, and the muscles in his forearms flexed with rage. "Don't push me," he warned, his voice low and dangerous.

"What are you going to do?" Kieran asked tauntingly.

"Shoot me? Go ahead. I dare you."

"Kieran, knock it off," Banning said, voice thick with irritation. His eyes flashed with anger as he wiped the blood from his sword on the dead man's shirt. "The last thing we need—"

Without warning, Damian pulled the trigger.

I jumped, a yelp escaping me before I could stifle it. My hands reached out to Damian's shirt, and I clutched the fabric desperately between my fingers.

Kieran shrieked as the bullet tore into his shoulder. His gaze snapped down to look at the wound as it oozed blood. After the initial shock wore off, his head lifted and he glared at Damian. "It won't kill me. It can't."

"No, but I know what will," Damian said, a pleased look on his face. Though his words were confident, his voice was shaky. "And I would bet that still hurts like hell."

Eyes locked menacingly on Damian, Kieran dug his fingers into the bullet wound. A slight frown on his face was the only indication that he was in any pain. He tugged and pulled at his skin, stretching out the hole in his flesh. He dug his finger in past the knuckle. Then his eyes lit up, and a moment later, he withdrew his hand.

My blood ran cold as I realized what he held between two bloody fingers. It was the bullet Damian had put in him.

Kieran tossed the crumpled bullet to the ground at Damian's feet. "Don't make me decide you're expendable." He brought one of his guns up, the barrel pointed between Damian's eyes.

I felt panic race through me. *Please don't let him kill Damian*, I silently prayed. *Don't leave me alone with these lunatics.*

Banning stormed over to Kieran. The skin on his hand was a pale white from clutching his sword so tightly, and he was practically seething. Kieran had to be at least a foot taller, but Banning radiated dominance. Whatever it was, dominance or perhaps rank, it made Kieran hesitate. "Don't make me decide *you're* expendable," Banning said threateningly, tossing Kieran's words back in his face.

Kieran glanced at Damian as if considering his options. Finally, he lifted the gun to point skyward, removing its aim from Damian's face. "I was just having a little fun. That's all."

His gaze slid to the gun in Damian's hand. "Give it back."

"No," Damian said flatly, his voice letting Kieran know there would be no compromising. He was keeping the gun.

Banning sheathed his sword. "It's better that he's armed. He can help fight off those things the next time they attack." He sent Kieran a glowering look. "And thanks to your antics, they will attack. Fresh blood is going to attract them like flies."

Kieran made a face at Banning as he clicked the safeties back into place and slid his guns into their holsters. "I didn't shoot myself, you know."

"No, but you asked for it." When Kieran went to reply, Banning cut him off. "Start walking." He took off in the direction we'd previously been going. He didn't even look over his shoulder. He just assumed the rest of us would follow.

I scurried after him, not wanting to be stuck behind with Kieran. As I walked, I studied my surroundings, anticipating the next attack. If Banning said there would be more of those mutant people, I believed him.

The building we escaped from was a popular place. Its popularity came from the fact that it was secluded. It was set back into the woods, miles away from civilization. There was only one road to get in, and it was long and enclosed by trees. It was not a road someone wanted to break down on, not even on a normal night.

Tonight, running for our lives, it was terrifying. One of those things could be hiding behind any tree, any bush. If one of us was pulled off the road, God only knew if we'd be found. I was just waiting for one of them to snatch me away before anyone noticed. The thought sent a shiver of fear down my spine.

What frightened me most was that Banning said this was happening all over. Kieran claimed my family was dead, that everyone I knew was dead. I refused to believe it. Until I saw proof against it with my own eyes, I would hold on to the hope that my family was still alive. Maybe they had escaped, gotten free of this terror. What if they were at home waiting for me, worrying about where I was?

I reached for my phone and cursed under my breath. I had left it in my purse. I'd left my purse at the restaurant. "Does anyone have a phone? I want to try to get in touch with my family."

Damian shook his head sympathetically. "Mine was in my truck."

"A phone no longer serves purpose," Kieran said with annoyance. "There's no one alive to answer them. They're all dead." He paused thoughtfully. "Or they're one of the infected now, one of those."

The thought of my family becoming one of those mindless creatures frightened me. "Infected? This thing...it's an infection? How...how does someone get infected?" My voice came out a meek whisper. I wasn't certain I truly wanted an answer to that question.

"The disease is contracted through bites," Banning said gently. "Anyone who gets bitten by one of those things is infected. Most join their attacker's ranks after they expire from toxins associated with the disease, while a slim few never get back up. It all depends on how badly they were mauled during their attack. The lucky ones suffer enough brain damage to keep their bodies from being reanimated. Those people just die. Others..." He trailed off. "The worst kinds are those who get a small bite and survive the attack. They suffer. As the poison travels through their veins, they can feel it. At least if you die instantly and rise, you don't suffer."

He looked at me as if considering whether to continue or not. With a nod of his head, he added, "If a person gets bitten, the effects will kick in within hours. They'll get clammy and start sweating. Their temperature will rise. Most people will think they've got the common flu. In a few hours, they'll get shaky. Their nerves will begin to twitch and jump. They'll start vomiting and become ghostly pale." He frowned as if seeing it in his mind, like it was something he'd witnessed before. "They'll start coughing up blood, a lot of it. Their body is dying, going into a meltdown inside. The virus is like an enhanced cancer, spreading faster than you can imagine. Then the chills start. The person will begin having seizures. Then comes the moaning..." He stopped, seemingly unable to continue.

Kieran jumped in where Banning left off. "They'll go in and out between human and zombie mind. In zombie mind, they'll screech and thrash around, trying to eat their friends and family. Then their regular minds will snap back. They'll cry and apologize and promise it won't happen again, but it will. They fade in and out until, toward the end, the person they were is completely annihilated. Then they'll fully be one of those things. After that, you shoot them in the face. Bam! You put them down like a dog."

Banning had a stricken look on his face at Kieran's harsh words.

"Is there any cure?" I asked Banning, trying to ignore Kieran.

Banning shook his head sadly. "No. Once you're bitten, you're dead." He ran a hand over his face. "What's sad is that people's ignorance is what gets them killed. The media has been blaming this outbreak on wild dog or wolf attacks. They know damn well it wasn't dogs. Now people fear the wrong thing. They're getting bitten by friends, family members, neighbors, co-workers, you name it."

The instant he said neighbors, I felt my knees go weak, and I would have collapsed to the pavement if Damian hadn't grabbed me under the arms.

"Aurora!" Damian cried. "Aurora, what's wrong?"

"My mom," I said, feeling my head swim. "My mom...she...our neighbor bit her. Last night." My mind went to my mother's odd behavior this morning. Her eyes had been glassy, her temperament off, and she'd coughed up blood. Damn it, she'd coughed up blood! Why had I ignored such a glaring sign that something was wrong?

"Yeah," Kieran said with a chuckle. "She's dead."

Damian held me with one arm and lifted the gun with his other. He aimed it at Kieran's chest, his index finger twitching over the trigger. "I think you want to die," he growled through clenched teeth.

Kieran looked as if he was going to say something snide in return, but with a quick glance to his bleeding shoulder, he seemed to think better of it. He shrugged and ambled off toward the woods, his gaze sweeping the tree line.

Banning put a hand on my shoulder. "I'm sorry about your mother." His next sentence was a lie, and we both knew it. He said it anyway, but the optimism never reached his eyes. "Maybe she's okay." He looked away with a guilt-ridden expression and then started walking again.

I guess he didn't want me to know he didn't believe the hopeful statement he'd made about my mother. Trouble was,

I already did.

I pulled away from Damian, trying to regain my composure. I squeezed my eyes shut for a moment, determined not to cry. If the situation was as bad as Banning said, crying would only make things harder for our little group. If I didn't keep a straight head, I might get myself killed, and I personally didn't want to know what it felt like to be eaten alive. I swiped at my eyes, then straightened my shoulders with purpose before marching after Banning.

"Aurora?" Damian sounded surprised at my sudden determination to keep moving. He followed after me, gently touching my elbow. "Hey, slow down. Are you okay?"

I spun on him, my blonde hair whipping about my face. "Of course I'm not okay," I snapped. "My entire family is probably dead, and these lunatics are more or less kidnapping us. I've also got bone fragments and brain tissue in my hair." As I spoke, I picked a shard of bone free and dropped it to the ground with a shiver. "So no, I'm not okay. I'm far from okay." I took a deep breath before continuing. "It's none of your concern, though. Stop acting like we're friends, because we're not."

I wasn't really angry at him. Deep down, I knew I was taking my frustration out on Damian because he was the only person I felt safe enough to do it to. Honestly, I was relieved he was here. I did not want to be left alone with Kieran. Hell, Kieran or Banning.

Banning seemed harmless to the eye, but I had seen what he could do with that sword. He'd decapitated a man with a single swing of his weapon. That wasn't something a nonviolent man knew how to do. Plus, judging from the crowd he was hanging with, I doubted I could trust him very much.

Damian was the only ally I had at the moment. Pissing him off did not seem as good of an idea as it had this morning. I watched with regret as his eyes darkened and his shoulders tensed.

"Fine," he said, voice low. He turned his back on me and stalked angrily up the road to rejoin Banning and Kieran.

I suddenly felt vulnerable and exposed without him by my side. I'd made a mistake in ostracizing him. I *did* need his friendship. I needed it very badly. "Damian!" I called out and took a small, tentative step in his direction.

He spun back around, hostility all over his face. He didn't say anything. He just waited for me to talk.

"I—" I broke off, almost unable to finish my sentence. I'd spent so much time and energy being rude to him that I didn't know how to do anything else. "I'm sorry," I said softly, my voice barely audible. "I'm just scared." My eyes welled with tears, and I fought them back.

Damian continued to stare at me, his eyes narrowing. After what felt like an eternity, he gave me a tense smile. "You must be really terrified to apologize to me." Though his tone was teasing, there was truth to his words. I'd been so horrible to him in the past, and both of us knew it.

I nodded tearfully, admitting to my own faults because I had no other choice. "Just don't leave me alone with them, okay?"

Damian nodded his head, keeping his eyes glued to the men in front of us. "Don't worry. I won't." He motioned toward Kieran. "He creeps me the hell out. There's something about him that makes me want to run screaming."

Kieran glanced over his shoulder and gave us a wicked grin, as if he could hear our hushed voices. He licked his lips and turned back to the direction he'd been walking.

I shuddered, goose bumps rising on my arms. "Can't we just go home?" I asked miserably, though I already knew the answer.

Banning turned to face us. "Home doesn't exist anymore. Don't you understand that? There's nothing left. Everybody in this town is dead. You are the only two people we've found alive so far."

"That can't be true," I said in a strangled voice when I was finally able to speak. "There has to be someone still alive. You've got to be wrong."

"I hope I am," Banning said. "I really hope I am. I pray that we start finding people who went into hiding, people who didn't die, but so far, that isn't happening. We've had search teams split up all over town. We haven't found a single soul, at least not any we could save. The other search teams have stopped radioing in because the only news they were transmitting was bad. They said they'd wait until they had some positive information before they checked back in. The radios have been silent ever since...except for when Aldrich found the two of you." He shook his head at that grim news. "Until we have evidence to prove otherwise, we need to start accepting that the two of you may be it. This town is dead. That whole 'last man on earth' thing might be more accurate than we want to admit."

I buried my hands in my hair, gripping it in stress. "You said your teams have been searching for over an hour. Twenty minutes ago, there was a restaurant full of living people back there. What took you so damn long to get to us?"

"We forgot about it actually," Banning admitted. "It was so secluded and hidden...I think that's why it took them so long to get here as well. The rest of town has been under siege for much longer."

"Great," I grumbled. "Absolutely great." I dropped my hands to my sides in frustration. "What about neighboring towns? Can't we ask them for aid?"

Banning sighed. "Don't you understand what I'm trying to tell you? There are no more neighboring towns. There is no aid. There's nobody anywhere."

I went to argue with him again, to tell him he had to be wrong, when Kieran started yelling.

Damian and Banning joined in, and I was suddenly thrown roughly to the ground.

The sound of screeching metal invaded my ears as my hands collided with the harsh pavement of the road. I found myself face down on asphalt with Banning on top of me, shouting orders for Kieran.

A loud crash followed the original screech, echoing oddly in my ringing ears. I couldn't see what was going on from my downed position, but I could still hear the yelling. I squirmed underneath Banning, trying to catch a glimpse of what had everyone so frightened. His elbow was digging uncomfortably into my back, and his sudden weight on top of me had my breath coming in shallow gasps. "What's going on?" I managed to ask.

Banning scrambled to his feet. He grabbed me by my wrists and hoisted me to stand next to him. Grabbing my chin, he turned my head to our left. "That's what happened."

A small, blue Pontiac had smashed into one of the trees, a tree I had been standing close to only moments before. The front end of the car had been crumpled in, completely crushed by the impact.

The passenger door of the damaged vehicle flew open, and a teenage girl stumbled out. Blood ran from a cut on her forehead into her eyes. "My mother...she's hurt."

Kieran stared at the girl as if in a trance. He watched the blood as it fell, his emerald eyes seeming to follow individual drops as they dribbled down the front of her face. "Have you been bitten?" he asked breathily.

She put a hand on the car bumper, trying to steady herself. "What?" she asked, sounding dazed.

"Have you been bitten?"

She blinked and pushed hair away from her face, blood making it stick persistently to her skin. "Yes," she said on a whimper. "On my arm. It's really not that bad, though. I'm more worried about my mother. She was disoriented due to her injury and turned down the wrong street. If we could just get her to a doctor, she—"

Kieran's gun was out and raised in an instant. He pulled the trigger before the girl could even finish her sentence.

The bullet hit her between the eyes and sent her flying backwards into the trunk of the car. She slid down the metallic surface into a crumpled heap against the bumper she'd been using for support only moments before.

A scream tore from my throat at the sudden and unexpected display of violence. My hands began trembling and my eyes flitted frantically over the hole in the girl's forehead as I tried to make sense of what had just happened. My entire body began to quiver, and I feared I would never be able to stop. "You killed her!" My voice was raspy and horrified.

"She was already dead," Kieran said coldly, marching to the driver's side of the car. He held the gun out in front of him and threw open the door.

A middle-aged woman sat in the driver's seat, her eyes glazed and unfocused. A large chunk of glass was lodged into the side of her neck, causing blood to trickle down her throat to stain the collar of her white cotton shirt.

It took me a moment to recognize her through all of the blood. Her name was Tammy Barker, and she was a friend of my mother's. The two of them had taken a cooking class together a few years back, and she'd become a semi-permanent fixture at our house. She was one of the nicest people I knew. She was always chipper and never had a bad thing to say about anyone.

Seeing her like this made my stomach turn. I knew just by looking at her that she was grievously wounded. She was bleeding to death, and there was nothing I could do to help. I knew some basic first aid, but I wasn't this good. I almost suggested taking her to the hospital, but if Banning was right, there wouldn't be anyone left alive there to help her anyway. Besides, it didn't look like even a trip to the hospital was going to save her now.

"My daughter," she said weakly. "Did you help my daughter?"

Kieran ignored her question. "Have you been bitten?"

"Kieran, no!" I yelled the words as if my opinion weighed in at all on his decision. I knew he was going to do whatever he wanted, whether I protested or not.

He sent me a dark look before turning back to Mrs. Barker. "Have you been bitten?"

I braced myself for her answer, fearing what I knew would come if she answered in the affirmative.

"No," she said shakily. "But my daughter—"

The relief I'd felt when she said she hadn't been bitten was suddenly snuffed out.

Before she could finish her sentence, Kieran lunged at her. He tore the glass violently from her throat and tossed it to the ground behind him. An evil grin spread across his lips as blood cascaded down her neck and she gave a holler of pain. With lightning speed, he dug his teeth into the wound and began to gulp big mouthfuls of blood. As he drank, he tore at her throat with his incisors, ripping the already split flesh.

I screamed, and it echoed through the trees. As I watched Kieran, I knew what he was, what they all were. My mind rejected what my gut was telling me. It refused to accept what I saw before me, but deep down, I knew. I didn't believe it, but I knew.

He was something I had grown up knowing was fiction. Kieran was a vampire. Only, vampires weren't real. They were creatures made up just for a good scare. Yet, here one was, draining the life from someone I knew.

I didn't realize I was still screaming until Damian's hand

clamped over my mouth. "Don't scream," he whispered in my ear. "He wants you to scream. That's what this show is for. Your fear is egging him on."

I cowered back against Damian and fought to stay silent as Kieran spun toward us, blood trailing from his mouth all the way down his chin.

He dropped Mrs. Barker to the ground, not even glancing twice at the woman he'd just murdered. He walked slowly toward us, a low, predatory growl escaping his throat. He stared at me with those glowing eyes turned nearly yellow, hunger written across his face.

I straightened my shoulders and stared back at him. I was more terrified of him than I could ever put into words, but I wouldn't give him the satisfaction of seeing any more of my fear. Damian said he wanted me to scream, so that was the last thing I would give him. "I'm not afraid of you."

"Oh, but you are." Kieran's words were hissed around fangs that gleamed in the moonlight. "And you should be." He stared at me with an intensity that made my skin crawl. "I know I frighten you. I can hear your pulse quickening in your chest. Thump-thump. Thump-thump. Thump-thump."

I gave up trying to deny my fear and went with another angle. Blame. "You killed her. You killed an innocent woman."

"She was dying anyway. Would you have preferred me to leave them both? Let the girl turn and eat her own mother? Would that have been better? More humane?"

"You didn't have to be so violent about it," Banning said darkly, his voice leaking anger.

"I had to drain her," Kieran said in his own defense. "If someone wouldn't have shot me, I wouldn't have needed the blood." His head never moved, but his eyes rolled to look at Damian. "This is your fault. *You* killed her."

Damian tensed behind me.

Spinning to face him, I saw in his eyes that a part of him believed Kieran. He felt responsible for what had just transpired. "Don't you dare listen to him," I said firmly. "Don't believe anything he has to say, not for a second."

Banning stepped between us and Kieran, his frustration practically thickening the air. "Enough! I would like to get back to the safe house without being eaten alive. Our van is about two minutes from here. If you," he said, directing a look at Kieran, "weren't screwing around, we would have been there by now."

Kieran turned casually to Banning. "All right. Calm down. I'm just giving them a taste of what the world is going to be like from now on." He turned and nonchalantly walked away as if nothing had happened.

Banning looked as if he were about to argue, but stopped and shook his head. Silently, he followed after Kieran.

It frightened me that he didn't deny Kieran's claims, that he didn't say life wouldn't be like this. What did I expect, though? The zombies weren't just going to disappear. Mrs. Barker wasn't going to come back to life. This was it. This was life now. There was no going back.

I felt my hands begin to quiver at the thought of what that meant. To have Kieran be my future, to know I might have to see him day in and day out, terrified me. The fact that I would probably never see my family again wasn't too comforting either. I took a step closer to the only thing that was still familiar in my life, the only person I had known before this tragedy. I grabbed Damian's arm and held on as if he was a lifeline.

He glanced down at me questioningly. He must have seen something in my eyes, because he slid his free hand down my arm until it reached my trembling fingers. He then took my hand in his and laced our fingers together, squeezing comfortingly. He gave a small, solemn smile before following Banning and Kieran. His hand tightened on mine, making sure he kept me close to his side as we walked.

If you would have told me this morning that I would be holding hands with Damian and following two psychopaths with weapons, I would have said you were crazy. But here I was.

I was pulled from my grim thoughts when Banning came to a stop in front of a large, black van. He slid the back door open and motioned us inside. "We'll take this back to Alexandro's. It's not far from here."

With Damian's hand still clutched tightly in mine, I made my way over to Banning and the ominous black van. I was frightened of disappearing into that van and never coming back out, but being left out here wouldn't be any better. I was halfway inside when, from seemingly out of nowhere, a zombie grabbed Banning from behind.

Before he could move to defend himself, the thing sunk its teeth into his shoulder. He hollered in pain, trying to shake the deranged man off of him. His sword came out, and he stabbed backwards into the man's gut.

The zombie shrieked, but didn't relinquish its grip. It worried its teeth even farther in and shook like a wild animal as it attempted to rip flesh from bone.

Damian raised his gun, but the struggling pair was close enough that they knocked into him and jarred it from his grasp. It clattered to the ground and skittered away from him across the roadway.

I scrambled out of the van in what felt like slow motion, but I reached the weapon before Damian could recover from being knocked backwards. I grabbed the gun and raised it with shaking hands to point at the zombie. I held it up to the man's head, pressing the barrel to his skull. I froze with my finger on the trigger. I couldn't do it. I couldn't kill him.

Banning gave another cry of pain as the zombie doubled its efforts, gnawing rabidly at his shoulder.

He looked pleadingly into my eyes, and I couldn't not do it. I couldn't leave this thing to attack him, possibly eat him alive. "God, forgive me," I said raggedly. Then I pulled the trigger.

The sound echoed through the darkness, momentarily deafening me. The gun jerked in my hands, sending tingles of pain up both my arms. I watched as blood poured in thick, blackish rivulets from the large hole I had created in the man's head. I watched with wide, horrified eyes as his body fell suddenly and unceremoniously to the ground. With quivering hands, I dropped the gun to the pavement. I was on the verge of collapsing myself when I looked at Banning.

Blood cascaded down his shoulder to drip on the ground. He was holding a hand over the wound and hissing in pain.

I didn't want to ask the question, but I blurted it out anyway. "You're not going to need to drink someone now, are you?"

Banning looked at me for a moment before tearing away the bottom of his shirt. "No," he said, wrapping the cloth around his wounded arm. "Some of us have more control than others." He narrowed his eyes at his supposed comrade. "By the way, where were you back there while I was getting mauled?"

Kieran gave an uncaring shrug. He didn't even bother with an excuse. He simply didn't give a shit if we got killed or not.

On Banning's comment about some of "them" being stronger than others, I had to ask. I had to hear it from one of them to fully believe it. "You're vampires, aren't you?" I asked with a slight tremble in my voice.

Banning stared at me in silence for a moment, his hand clutching his injury. Finally, he nodded. "Yeah. We are."

A silence fell over the group as we stared at one another. Vampires and humans, we were from completely different worlds.

Damian picked the gun up from the pavement and tucked it into the back his jeans. His hands moved to my shoulders, and he drew my attention away from Banning. "We should get inside the van before any more of those things show up."

Banning nodded his agreement. "I'm not fit to drive." He pulled the keys from his pocket and handed them to Kieran. "And I don't trust you in the back with them."

Kieran gave him a dark look, but silently took the keys.

I climbed into the van, taking a seat in the back to be as far from Kieran as I could possibly get.

Damian followed, sitting next to me, and Banning took the bench seat in front of us, stretching his legs out with his back against the window.

I stared at Banning's shoulder, watched as blood already began to seep around his makeshift bandage. "I think you might need stitches. That looks pretty bad."

He pressed his hand to the wound again, trying to staunch the flow of blood. "I'll be fine."

Blood seeped through his fingers, and I couldn't help but argue. "I really think you might need stitches."

He shook his head in disagreement as Kieran started the van and pulled it onto the road. "I'll heal." Before I could argue again, he said, "I heal faster than you do. By morning, you won't even know I was bitten. If it was you, by morning, you'd be dead. Just be thankful it was me."

He said the word "bitten" and it jogged my memory. "If you've been bitten..." I trailed off, my mind going to the man

I'd just shot. "Won't you become one of them?"

He laughed dryly and let his head fall back against the window, his eyes closing. "Not possible. It doesn't affect us. The virus, or whatever it is they have, doesn't mix with whatever keeps us alive. Can't turn us into what we already are, the living dead."

I nodded, unsure of what to say to that. Banning admitting he wasn't human freaked me out a little bit. Walking, talking corpses was going to take some getting used to.

A thought occurred to me as I tried to rationally understand the two diseases he spoke of. "What happens to a person if you try to make them one of you after they've already been bitten? Can you save any of those people out there, make them like you instead?"

Banning glanced up at Kieran before answering. "Once they're like that, they're too far gone. Sometimes, in the beginning stages, it's possible. Getting the results you wish is unlikely, though. Usually, the person simply dies. Both...poisons," he said for lack of a better word, "will fight for control over the person's body. It's violent and painful. The diseases will fight until they kill each other and, more often than not, the person who is their host. In very rare instances, one side wins." He sat in silence for a moment, and then said, "And depending on which side wins, sometimes it's better to have died."

I wondered if he knew this from experience. The tone of his voice hinted that this had happened to someone he'd known.

"It's not a pretty sight," Banning said in conclusion. "It's better to just let people die. Learning to let go is easier than watching someone you care about go through hell."

Kieran's voice cut in from the front. "I hate to break up this wonderful conversation, but we're here."

I looked out the window to see a giant gate looming in front of the van. I recognized the road immediately. It was a turnoff from the main road just outside of town. It was a dirt path that led to nowhere but this gate.

For years, I'd wondered what lay beyond these gates. No one seemed to know. It was speculated that some rich extraordinaire lived out here. Before, I was curious as to what I would find past the heavy iron fence. Now, I dreaded the answer.

Kieran slowed the car to a stop and rolled down his window. Just outside the entrance, there was a small black box elevated on a slim pole. He punched a code into a pad, and the gate in front of us slid open.

The van started forward. As soon as it cleared the gate, the doors closed behind us, sealing us in. Nervously, I scooted closer to Damian on the seat. I looked out into the darkness and saw nothing but trees. It looked as if there was nothing but woods for miles.

An owl hooted overhead. Small red eyes hid amongst the trees, but it was impossible to see what type of animal they belonged to. It frightened me to think about what kinds of animals these people might have trapped in here with them.

The van continued down the dirt path that seemed to have no end to it.

I had known there was a decent chunk of land back here, but I never guessed it would be so vast. As we progressed, I peered into the darkness and finally found what I was looking for. Off in the distance, I could see lights. It took my mind a moment to comprehend what I was seeing.

The house was huge, towering over the van as we got closer. "House" wasn't even the right word for it. It was as big as a college campus, able to house a few hundred people easily. It was made of sturdy-looking stone, giving it the appearance of a castle with its thin, arched windows.

Kieran pulled around a circular driveway and came to a stop at a set of stone steps that led to large double doors. "Everybody out."

Banning climbed slowly to his feet and opened the side door. He wobbled a moment as if dizzy and then steadied himself. "This area is completely secured by our enclosures. You don't have to worry about coming out here by yourselves. If by some chance, one of those things penetrates our fences, an alarm will be triggered inside. One of our guys will go out and handle the problem before any danger has a chance to get near the house."

I knew by the way he spoke that the intruders wouldn't get a stern scolding. They would get a bullet between the eyes. Oddly, this made me feel safe. It also made me glad I'd been invited in.

Damian climbed out of the van. He never relinquished his hold on my hand, keeping us joined as we stepped out to face the vampire safe house. He waited for me to get clear of the van before pulling me close to his side. Apparently, I wasn't the only one who was nervous about what was going to happen next.

We were about to come face to face with Alexandro. I didn't know anything about the vampire leader, but I already didn't trust him. To be the man in charge of all the monsters probably meant he was the biggest monster of them all.

"I'm going around back to park," Kieran said. With that, he drove off, leaving Damian and me with Banning.

The dark-haired vampire gave us a look of encouragement. "Well, guys," he said with false sanguinity. "It's time to meet the boss."

Chapter 4

Banning opened a door to the lavish mansion and stepped aside. He held it open, motioning for us to go ahead of him.

I tentatively entered the foyer and gaped around me in awe. The place seemed even larger from the inside. The wide and spacious front hall connected to a living room larger than a small house. There was a winding staircase at the back of that room, and two floors above could be seen from where we stood. A giant chandelier hung above our heads. It sparkled, sending dazzling prisms of light to dance across the hardwood flooring. It was so astonishingly beautiful that, for a moment, I forgot where I was.

"Alexandro is waiting for you in his office." The words were hissed from the shadows behind us.

I jumped. One of my hands flew to my chest, and I gave a gasp of startled surprise. We'd walked right past someone on our entrance, and I hadn't even realized he'd been there.

My reaction made the owner of the voice jump in return. The man inched forward, slowly revealing himself to us. The first thing I noticed was short, spiked black hair—the blackest I'd ever seen. It was the color the sky gets on nights when the moon is completely blocked out by clouds, the kind of black you can't see your hand through.

My gaze quickly shifted down to his face. His eyes were a light blue that shone with that otherworldly light I was beginning to associate with vampires. The light from the hall seemed to reflect off of them, making them appear even brighter. His skin was a creamy olive that seemed void of a single flaw. There was only one word to describe him, and that was breathtaking. He was absolutely beautiful, a word not normally used to describe a man.

"Thank you, Orion," Banning said brusquely, and started off down the hall.

Orion sent me a timid, curious look.

I stared back at him. It was hard not to. He was just so pretty. I couldn't seem to take my eyes from his.

He broke eye contact first, looking down at the ground.

Banning stopped and spun back around. "Alexandro does not like to be kept waiting." There was a warning to his voice that had my shoulders reflexively tightening.

"Y-yes." Orion gave a slight bow of compliance and fell into step behind us.

It was my turn to give him a curious look. Of the group I already met, none of them had been timid in the least. I had watched Kieran and Banning kill without batting an eye. Aldrich also killed without any noticeable remorse. None of them appeared to be too concerned with the infected people's loss of life.

Orion was the first of them I'd seen who had anything other than absolute self-assurance, and it intrigued me. What made him different? Why wasn't he slavering at the mouth to get a taste of us?

Now wasn't the time to be inquisitive, I realized. I was being marched to what could possibly be my death. Orion's odd mannerisms shouldn't be high on my list of concerns.

Looking away from the timid vampire, I followed after Banning, trying to keep my priorities in line. I was about to meet Alexandro, and I was betting *he* wasn't shy.

Orion shadowed us, his footsteps so light I could barely even hear him moving. It was like he was trying to blend into his surroundings.

Apprehensively, Damian tightened his grip on my hand and glanced over his shoulder.

I wanted to assure Damian that I didn't think Orion would give us any trouble, but my attention was diverted to Banning when he walked into a room on our left and held the door open for us to enter.

I stepped into the room behind him and froze.

A man dominated what appeared to be an office. He stood in front of a massive oak desk, his arms crossed over his broad chest. By his intimidating appearance, I had no doubt in my mind that the man in front of me was Alexandro.

He towered over me, staring down with an unpleasant scowl on his face. He had long, straight black hair that fell nearly to his waist. He used it like a curtain; it seemed to shield him, protect him. He was at least six and a half feet tall, closer to seven by my guess. His shoulders were broad, but I'd seen bigger. I think it was the look on his face that frightened me so badly. He was looking at me as if I was the scum of the earth.

"I see our guests have arrived," he said, tone void of emotion.

Orion nodded emphatically as he entered the room and wrung his hands together. "Yessss." He hissed, the sound whistling through his teeth. It seemed a nervous habit of his. "As soon as they entered your gracious home, I instructed them to come."

Alexandro turned to stare silently at him.

Orion cringed and backed against the wall, looking as if he were trying to sink into the paint.

Alexandro turned to look at Damian, and his already less than friendly expression turned to contempt. "I was hoping your kind would have become extinct with the apocalypse."

I glanced at Damian in confusion. His kind? Was he speaking of humans? If Alexandro wished us into extinction, then why were we here? "That's kind of harsh." I couldn't help but interject my surprise at his statement. "You want humans to die out completely?"

Alexandro sent me a look of disbelief. He seemed to find it preposterous that I, a lower life form, was speaking to him. "I did not mean *your* kind, though I wouldn't really mourn the human race much. Beyond a food source, your race is comprised of a pointless people. I meant *his* kind," he said with a nod to Damian.

I glanced at Damian in confusion. I wasn't sure of his nationality, but I was guessing Italian. It was kind of harsh to wish death on all Italians...or did Alexandro mean men? Either way, it was an unnecessarily hostile statement. Despite my opinion, the aggressive look I'd received for my first comment was all the encouragement I needed to stay silent now.

Alexandro's look grew darker. "I hear you shot one of my men, one of the rescue team."

"He deserved it." Damian's voice came as a growl, and he

didn't shrink back against the accusation.

Alexandro stepped forward and raised his hand as if he was going to strike Damian when Banning spoke up, coming to Damian's defense. "He's right. Kieran put on quite a show. He drained a mortally wounded woman in front of them and made a spectacle of killing the infected. He scared them shitless. I would have done the same thing in such a situation. The gun was fired in self-defense."

Kieran suddenly rushed out of the shadows deeper in the room. "Had I not been shot, I wouldn't have needed to feed."

My eyes widened with surprise. Kieran had gone to park the car. Yet, somehow, he had beaten us to the office and had time to explain himself to Alexandro. It didn't seem possible that anyone could be that fast.

"Silence!" Alexandro roared. "I've heard enough."

As he bellowed, I suddenly realized why he was so terrifying. He wasn't breathing. There was no rise and fall of his chest, no exhale with his infuriated words. When he became still, his face reminded me of cold, hard marble. There was nothing in the depths of his eyes. He was as motionless as death, no more than an empty cavity.

"Just take them to their rooms. I want them out of my sight." His words were spat out with disdain.

I tensed next to Damian. I really didn't like the idea of us having separate rooms...not that I wanted to be sharing a bed with him either. I just didn't want to be shut off by myself. Damian was suddenly a pivotal part of my survival, and I didn't like the thought of being divided from him.

Alexandro's mouth curved into a wicked grin. "I've arranged for our female guest to stay with Ariel."

I let out a small breath of relief. A woman couldn't be half as terrifying as the rest of them. I wouldn't mind bunking with a woman. They were always easier to reason with, and they tended to feel compassion more easily than men.

Banning frowned, and it made me second-guess my assumption. "Ariel?" he asked in surprise. "Are you certain? Ariel has—"

"Ariel will do whatever I instruct to be done," Alexandro said sharply. "The girl is to be guarded at all times, and Ariel is the best person for the job."

Banning nodded, his expression one of defeat. "Whatever

you think is best." Without another word, he turned and walked from the room.

Instinctively, I raced after him. I followed him because I didn't want to see any more of Alexandro or Kieran. Whoever this Ariel was, she couldn't be worse than those two.

Orion rushed out of the room as well, scuttling after us. "I'll show the man to his room."

"It's Damian, not *the man*," Damian said grumpily.

"You're right," Banning said with an impish grin. "*I'm* the man."

I rolled my eyes behind his back, unable to help the smirk that stretched across my lips. I was quickly learning he had a crush on himself.

Instead of smiling like the rest of us, Orion ducked his head as if in shame at Damian's harsh tone.

I didn't know Orion, yet I wanted to assure him he had done nothing wrong. I hated the way his shoulders slumped, the way his eyes darted about as if he was afraid to concentrate on any one thing for too long. I was quickly getting the impression that any fight had been beaten out of him long ago. He looked as if he was afraid of his own shadow.

His submissive behavior only fed my anxiety. He was proof that we were living amongst monsters. No human being should be this fearful in his own home.

Silently, we started up the lavish staircase to the second floor. At the top, we took a right down a hallway dimly lit with small bulbs attached to wall sconces every few feet. Shadows clung to the spaces between each lamp, leaving parts of the hallway in total darkness. It looked like the set of a horror film.

As if sensing my discomfort, Damian squeezed my hand. I squeezed his in return, wanting to lend him what little comfort I could...which wasn't much knowing we were about to be separated from one another.

As we walked further down the darkened hallway, Banning revealed that behind each door was something similar to an apartment. Each living quarter had its own bathroom, bedroom, and living room, though some occupants had remodeled theirs to make living arrangements more to their liking. "There's no need to be nervous," Banning said as he spoke of our sleeping arrangements, his tone assuring. "We're not separating the two of you for long. It's late. We're showing you to your rooms so you can get a good night's sleep. You can see each other when you wake."

Orion stopped in front of a door on the left side of the hallway and looked soundlessly at Damian. He wrung his hands together fretfully as if trying to build up the nerve to speak.

Across the hall, Banning came to a halt at a doorway slightly adjacent to the first. "Besides, you'll be right across the hall from each other." He gave me a lopsided grin that would have been cute if it weren't for the fangs.

Orion held the first door open with an air of desperation as he waited to see if Damian would accept the living arrangements. There was fear in his eyes, and I knew then that if we disobeyed orders, Orion would be the one punished for it.

Making a decision, I nodded to Damian, letting him know it was okay for him to go. "It's all right."

He squeezed my hand again. "I'll see you in the morning," he said, his words a promise. He then entered the room Orion was ushering him toward. He gave me one last look over his shoulder before the door closed behind him, shutting us off from one another.

As soon as Damian was inside, Orion quickly retreated. He continued down the hallway at a swift pace before disappearing into another room. This left me alone with Banning.

He was leaning against the doorframe of the second apartment, grinning like a maniac.

"What?" I asked in uncertainty.

"You," he said with a shrug, the grin never leaving. "You're so cute. You're so...human. None of us have really seen that for a while. It brings back memories." He frowned at my outfit for a second, eyeing the short skirt and knee-high boots. "The styles have changed a bit."

I looked down at myself, unsure if I should be insulted or not.

"It's been a long time since I've been able to sink my teeth into someone as gorgeous as you. I'd say a couple hundred years easily." He upped his devilish grin "Interested?" His tone was teasing, but underneath the humor, there was true intrigue. "I'll let you bite me too if you like. Let's just say you don't have to be a vampire to enjoy some naughty nibbling."

I was astonished at his age. He'd casually admitted to being at least two hundred years old. It was hard to remember when staring into the face of a man who barely looked old enough to vote, that I was looking at someone much older than myself. When I finally recovered, I protested his insinuations. "There will be no sinking of teeth," I said firmly. "At least not with me there won't be."

He winked. "We'll see."

"No, we really won't." I squinted at him as a thought occurred to me. "Wait. You said you don't have to be human to enjoy that sort of thing... I didn't know S and M was that old. I thought a few hundred years ago, people were sort of prudish."

"You'd be surprised what people were into when no one was looking," he said with a wicked chuckle. "People just didn't become so open about it until recently."

I stared uncomfortably for a moment, then cleared my throat. "So...how about this Ariel? Maybe you should introduce us now."

Banning let out a small chuckle and put a hand to his chest, pretending to be insulted. "That hurts."

"I'm sure not as much as your fangs would."

He gave a small nod. "Okay. I can live with that answer." Conceding defeat for the moment, he opened the door to the apartment and peered inside. "How did I know you'd be in here like this?" he asked, addressing someone inside the room.

I stepped around him to see who he was talking to and was engulfed in darkness. There wasn't a light on anywhere. There was no soft glow of anything electronic, just perfect darkness. "It's so dark," I said before I could stop myself.

"I don't need light to see."

The voice stopped me in my tracks, made me gasp. The voice that answered me was deep and rugged. The voice belonged to a man, and that man sounded pissed off.

"Please, Ariel," Banning said pleadingly. "She's had a traumatic night. Don't frighten her any further."

The man laughed, his tone half angry, half sarcastic. "So she's met Kieran."

I heard the sound of a match striking a book, and a red

glow interrupted the darkness. Through the soft light from the match, I could see long, blond hair that framed his face like a halo. The hair shimmered in the glow. It was a soft golden color that made me want to reach out and touch it, run my fingers through it.

Ariel inhaled on the cigarette and blew out a cloud of gray smoke.

"I thought you guys didn't breathe," I said as I watched him do just that.

"We breathe. We just don't need to." He took another drag on the cigarette. "When one of us stops breathing, it's usually because we want to scare the living."

My mind went back to Alexandro. It was true that his lack of breathing had been unsettling, and it was no surprise that he'd intentionally done it to frighten us. More unsettling was this total darkness and my new male roommate who looked like he wanted to hurt me. I took a tiny step toward Banning, suddenly knowing now what could be scary about a person named Ariel. I did not want to be left alone with this man any more than I did Kieran.

As if sensing my unease, Banning flicked the lights on, filling the room with brightness.

I could see Ariel better now. My eyes landed first on the boots he had propped up on a table. They were a pair of black lace up combat boots that looked as if they belonged to the Army. No. They looked like they belonged to an assassin. Those boots alone were intimidating. They disappeared into a pair of black jeans. My eyes traveled up a broad chest covered with a sleeveless black shirt. The muscles in his bare arms rippled as he lifted his cigarette to his lips.

From the stories I'd heard about vampires, all mentioned supernatural strength. The muscled body seemed a little redundant to me. Why did he have to look like a body builder when he could bench press a Jeep without breaking a sweat?

He brought his hand back down from his lips, and my eyes were drawn to his face, more specifically his eyes. They were a deep shade of blue that was so dark it almost looked purple. But unlike most eyes that blue, there was a luster to them. They looked almost liquid, like the deepest part of the ocean. It wasn't until he blinked that I could look away.

His eyes flicked to Banning. "Why is she here?"

"Alexandro sends her to you for protection."

Ariel's eyebrows rose ever so slightly. "And what makes Alexandro so sure I won't eat her?"

"He knows you, Ariel. He knows you wouldn't harm her. Besides, you're the best we've got. If anyone can protect her from the dangers within our walls, it's you."

Ariel frowned but didn't disagree. "He knows how I feel about them." He said "them" like humans were nothing more than creatures to be despised.

"Maybe I should just stay with Banning..." I didn't know Banning all that well, but at least he didn't seem to hate us poor mortals.

"You'd be less safe there," Ariel replied. "Attacks wouldn't be the only thing you'd need to shield from."

Banning's face broke into a grin. "Hey, I never give the ladies any unwanted attention." His expression suddenly grew serious. "Does this mean she can stay here?"

Ariel gave a small nod of his head.

"Well, I guess I'll leave you two to get acquainted," Banning said. He gave me an encouraging look before gently guiding the door shut behind him as he stepped into the hallway. "Goodnight!" He yelled this from the other side, from the safety of the hallway.

I watched the door he disappeared through, longing to follow him. With a nervous exhale, I turned to look at Ariel.

"The bed's through that doorway," he said gruffly. He nodded toward an open door across the large expanse of the living room, not even bothering to get out of his seat.

I stared at him in awkward silence. It didn't feel right to me to just run and jump into some strange man's bed, especially after the traumatic day I'd been having.

"I'm not your grandmother. I'm not tucking you in." He took another drag on his cigarette and stared at me, those blue eyes full of hostility.

I quickly lowered my eyes to the floor and scurried through the doorway. Anything was better than having him look at me like that. Wanting to hide my head under the blanket and hope this terrible mess would go away, I pulled the comforter back, kicked my shoes off, and glanced down at my clothing. "I've got blood on my clothes," I said with a whisper. I didn't want to dirty his bed by crawling in covered in blood and dirt. When I looked back up, I found him staring at me. I saw the hunger flicker behind his eyes.

"I don't mind a little blood in bed." His voice was a low growl, almost sounding more animal than human. He caught himself and shoved the hunger back down. With his voice under control, he said, "I'm sure Banning will show you the showers and have clothes waiting for you close to sunrise. I'll have the sheets changed before you need to use the bed again."

I gave a small shiver at the mention of sunrise. Living with vampires meant they disappeared to die at dawn. It was a grim, frightening thought. I quickly slid into the bed and pulled the blanket up to my chest. I didn't pull it completely over my head, because I didn't trust Ariel. Then again, leaving my neck exposed didn't seem like a good idea either.

Like a child hiding from monsters under the bed, I pulled the blanket up and over my head to envelope myself in a comfortable cocoon. At least it held the heat in. I was shivering uncontrollably, so I welcomed the extra warmth. I think it was partially the chilly temperature of the room, but mostly, I think it was shock.

"Do you mind if I turn the lights back off?" His voice broke through the silence. It sounded as if it killed him to ask nicely.

"I don't mind," I said slowly. I supposed if he could bring himself to ask politely, I could bring myself to let him turn the lights out. I tensed as the light suddenly went out, throwing us into darkness. I squeezed my eyes shut and counted to ten.

Panicking wasn't going to do me any good. Odds were Ariel wasn't going to do anything to hurt me. He was assigned to protect me, so eating me in my sleep probably wouldn't constitute a good job. Besides, from the sound of things, if he decided not to protect me, I was as good as dead anyway.

I forced myself to relax. It was already late, and Banning would be in to wake me before dawn. If I wanted to be able to protect myself at all, I needed to rest.

As I lay there trying to fall asleep, visions of the horrors I'd witnessed a few short hours ago ran through my mind in flashes. I saw Eric as the zombies tore into his flesh. I saw Mrs. Barker as Kieran sank his fangs into her neck. Instead of sleeping, a sob wrenched its way up my throat. Clinging to Ariel's pillow, I cried until my throat was raw and my eyes burned. I knew he could probably hear me, but grief beat out my humiliation. It felt like hours before I finally drifted off into a fitful sleep.

Chapter 5

I crashed through the woods behind my parents' house. My pulse was pounding in my throat, and my lungs burned with exhaustion. I'd been running so long I didn't think I could make it much farther. My legs quivered in protest. I ignored the pain and pushed them harder. If I stopped, I would die. Glancing over my shoulder, I glimpsed the group of diseased people who were chasing me.

Some stumbled awkwardly after me, arms outstretched. Snarls and growls escaped from their bloody mouths. Chunks of flesh hung from their teeth, and they clawed at each other like rabid dogs in their efforts to get to me. They were tripping over each other in their frenzy, hindering their own progress.

These slower ones weren't what I was concerned about. It was the fast ones that worried me. The recently deceased who hadn't been torn apart too badly during their own infection were a bigger threat. They hadn't had time to decay as much, didn't have as many injuries. There were about a dozen like this, and they were closing in on me.

My foot caught on a root, and I tumbled to the ground. A twig jabbed into my palm, but I pushed the pain to the back of my mind. I had bigger problems than a stick. I rolled onto my back, my muscles tensing for what I knew was coming.

My would-be attackers had nearly closed the distance between us. The closest face came into focus, and I recognized Eric a second before he jumped on me. I screamed and kicked at him, trying to keep him from wounding me.

He fought against me, leaning in to claw with gore-encrusted fingers. His bottom jaw was completely gone. Blood and mucus dripped onto me from the gaping cavity.

I struggled and finally got a good kick in at his face. My foot sank into the soft tissue where his jaw had been. I gave a disgusted cry and pulled my foot away from the gooey con-

tents. Kicking him backwards had given me the few seconds I needed to get back to my feet.

I stumbled over a pile of leaves, but caught myself on my hands. My already injured palm screamed in protest. As I scurried to my feet and continued to run, I had one thought on my mind. I had to get home. If I could only make it back to my house, my parents would fix this. My parents always knew how to fix things.

I reached the lawn and took off in a sprint. I could still hear the mass of people behind me desperately trying to get to their meal before it escaped. Looking over my shoulder, I could see they were closer yet, more of them joining the ranks as I ran.

I nearly tripped over something before I realized it was my next-door neighbor. Most of the flesh on both of her legs had been eaten away, so she was just dragging herself through the grass, unable to get to her feet. A low, inhuman groan escaped her lips as I leapt over her as if she was a track hurdle.

I took the steps of the back porch three at a time, then lunged for the door. My hand closed over the doorknob, and I wrenched it open. Running inside, I slammed the door shut behind me and leaned against it, my lungs heaving as I struggled to catch my breath. "Mom! Dad!" Making sure the door was locked, I took off down the hallway. On my way past, I skidded to a stop in the living room doorway.

A figure was hunched next to the couch, shoulders heaving in a way that didn't look natural.

I recognized those shoulders, that blond hair. "Drew?" I whispered, wondering what he was doing.

My brother scrambled to his feet and spun toward me.

I gave a shriek of terror when my eyes landed on his face.

The first thing I noticed was the chunk of meat that hung from his lips. He snarled and shoved it fully into his mouth. It was then that I saw his hands. Blood was caked under his nails and clumps of hair hung from his fingers. His arms had deep, angry scratches down them.

I heard a small squeak at his feet, and my eyes flicked to the ground.

His girlfriend, Christine, lay on the floor, gasping for air. A large chunk of her neck had been ripped away. Every time she sucked in a breath, blood would bubble in the wound and then gush out as she exhaled. She was dying. She was dying and there was nothing I could do but watch. "R...r..." Swallowing down some of her own blood, she finally managed to get the single word out. "Run."

I looked back up at Drew with horror, and he growled. My blood ran cold when I realized what had happened to Christine. More accurately, who had done this to Christine. My brother had killed his own girlfriend.

I took off running down the hallway, moving as fast as I could.

Drew was an athlete, or had been, so he caught up to me quickly. Even in death, he was faster than I was. He lunged and grabbed me around the waist. We both toppled to the floor, him on top. He leaned in, his teeth gnashing.

I managed to roll to my back and attempted to hold him off as best as I could, but he was so much stronger than I was. "Drew!" I screamed, but he didn't halt, didn't even waver. If he recognized me as his sister, it didn't show in his feral eyes. I had my hands pressed against his throat, trying desperately to keep him from biting me, from killing me, but I was slowly losing that battle.

He abruptly overpowered me and forced his way past my arms, his teeth going automatically for my jugular.

I managed to jerk to the side enough so he didn't get my throat. Instead, his teeth dug into my shoulder, and my screams turned from fear to agony.

I woke suddenly with a gasp, my eyes flying open. Waking from my nightmare did nothing to relieve my anxiety.

A set of fangs dangled in my face, saliva dripping down them.

I would have screamed, but I couldn't catch my breath. I had a fleeting moment in which I realized I was about to die, but the teeth never closed the remaining distance. My eyes traveled up the writhing, spitting vampire, and I saw Ariel behind him.

Ariel had the vampire by the collar of his jacket, holding him inches from my face. His expression was slightly amused. "Did your buddy Kieran honestly think this would work?"

The vampire stopped his thrashing and looked up at Ariel, his abnormally dark eyes widening as if just realizing the trouble he was in. "He did not send me." The vampire's voice was thick with a Spanish accent and filled with fear of the man restraining him.

"You do nothing without his orders," Ariel said with disgust. "Save me the crap and just tell me why he sent you."

The vampire's eyes flicked back to me, roaming over my body in a way that made me uncomfortable. "He always has his reasons."

Ariel yanked him backwards and tossed him to the floor. "I don't wish to see Alexandro execute you, which you know he would do if he discovered you here. Go back to Kieran and tell him to move on. He isn't getting this one."

The vampire climbed into a crouch, watching Ariel intently. "Alexandro would never kill Kieran."

"Probably not, Salvador," Ariel admitted. "But he wouldn't think twice about killing you.

Salvador flinched. "Lies."

Ariel shook his head, advancing toward the crouching man. He bent down, putting himself at eye level. "Even if he doesn't, you try this again, and I will." The mere tone of his voice was so threatening, it had me trembling. I did not want to be on the receiving end of his aggression. Ever.

Salvador scurried backwards, trying to put some distance between himself and Ariel, until he bumped into a dresser. "Alexandro would punish you. He does not take it lightly when one of our own is murdered."

Ariel pushed to his feet, towering over the other vampire. "He wouldn't dare punish me for protecting the girl. Not when it was what I was instructed to do. Panthea would never allow it."

Salvador froze and his expression turned to one of terror. "You would bring Panthea into this?"

Ariel nodded solemnly. "I would."

Salvador scrambled to his feet, his eyes flicking anxiously toward the door. "My apologies," he said quickly. "We did not wish to hurt her, only to shake her up a bit."

"Well, you succeeded. Now get the hell out before I change my mind about not killing you right now."

Salvador nodded, bowing his head low. His long, thick, black hair fell over his shoulder to nearly sweep the floor. "Gracias."

"De nada," Ariel said. "Now get out."

Relief filled the man's face. "Perdón for this little misunderstanding."

As I watched Salvador grovel, I couldn't help but throw in a sarcastic comment. I was feeling brave with Ariel on my side. "Do you always speak Spanish when you're nervous?"

His eyes darkened in annoyance and flicked to me. "Sí..." Then his eyes darkened for a different reason as he fully took me in. I was fairly certain this time his eyes were full of sexual interest as he examined the blood still speckling my outfit. "And for other reasons."

I swallowed nervously and pulled the blanket up around me in a protective manner.

Salvador's gaze moved to Ariel. "I do not get how you can stay cooped up with her in this room and not have even a little taste. Her fear is causing her heart to pound so wildly beneath her breasts that her blood is roaring through her veins. I almost cannot stand it. I can feel it in my throat, practically taste it."

"I have more restraint than that," Ariel said with a growl. He fell silent, his gaze boring into Salvador with heated anger. His expression was evidence that he was finished with this conversation and wished the other man to leave.

Salvador took the hint and excused himself. "Perdón."

Ariel waited until the vampire was at the door. "Salvador," he called out. When the other man spun around, he said, "If you ever even look at her in a way I find inappropriate, I will kill you. There are no more chances after today. I will rip you limb from limb and then toss the pieces out for the sun to devour."

Salvador paled, his skin becoming blotchy as his face took on a look of fear.

"Get out," Ariel said darkly.

Salvador rushed from the room, the sound of his footsteps echoing down the hallway.

Ariel shook his head with disgust. "He's always sorry."

I slowly crawled out from under the blanket and placed my feet gingerly on the floor.

The second my feet touched the ground, Ariel turned to look at me as if he'd heard them. "You were pretty brave for someone about to be eaten." His voice held a touch of sarcasm, as if he was mocking me.

I faltered for a second before replying. "I didn't think you'd let him hurt me."

Ariel stared at me for a moment. He took in my tousled hair, my blood-stained clothing. Finally, he said, "It's probably best you did not scream when you awoke. It would have given them something to work with." As an afterthought, he added, "I'm sorry I even let him get that close to you. I was in the kitchen, and he is an extremely fast bastard. It won't happen again. I underestimated Kieran's fascination with you."

I almost admitted that I'd tried to scream upon awakening. Looking at his harsh expression, I decided admitting I'd been scared stiff wouldn't go over well. He seemed the type to frown upon weakness. Instead, I asked, "Who is Panthea? He seemed pretty terrified of her."

Ariel left the bedroom. Making his way to the living room, he sat down in his chair and was silent for a moment. "Panthea is Alexandro's twin sister. They were turned together. She is the only person he will take orders from. She's basically his voice of reason."

I followed him into the living room and took a seat on the couch next to his chair, curling my feet under me. I stayed silent, hoping he would elaborate. I wasn't disappointed.

"Panthea would be running this place if she wasn't so damn wild. I don't think she'll ever settle down enough to be a true leader to those who need her," he said, regret thick in his voice.

"I don't understand why Alexandro is in charge," I interjected. "If he's so awful, why is he the one everyone is taking orders from?"

"He's not in charge. He merely owns the house."

I stared at him in shock. I refused to believe that a tyrant as horrible as Alexandro could be allowed to rule them merely because of a deed to a house. "All he did was buy the place?"

"He offers shelter. He opened his home to our kind. He protects them from the outside world. It is his home. If you do not follow his rules, he will force you to leave. Look outside and tell me you wouldn't do anything he asks to stay, especially if you were one of the young ones."

"Like Orion?" I asked.

"Like Orion." His eyes flicked to me, his expression thoughtful. "How did you know Orion was young?"

I contemplated that for a moment. "I don't know. He just seemed...unsure of himself. He seemed weak."

"Weak and insecure are not qualities reserved for the young. I've known vampires a century old who still were incapable of existing on their own. I've watched them throughout their entire existence, waiting for them to gain enough power to maintain their own lives, but sometimes, that moment never comes."

"You're over a century old?"

He gave a small nod. "Yes. I'm over a century old. I've seen many things in my time, things you've only read about."

"Bet you've never seen anything like this," I said softly, referring to the unbelievable events that were taking place outside.

"You'd be wrong," Ariel said, his voice just as low as mine. "Very wrong."

I felt my heart skip a beat at such an admission. "This has happened before?"

His blue eyes clouded with unhappiness, and his shoulders stiffened. "More than once."

"When?" I asked breathlessly. "How..." I watched Ariel's face darken, his eyes harden, and I trailed off. I could see him throwing up defensive walls. He was shutting me out, and I couldn't fathom why.

"I'm through discussing this," he said coldly.

"But..."

"But nothing. Those things?" He pointed toward the window with a violent jerk of his hand. "They are not my problem. I wouldn't care if they ate your entire race if it wouldn't drag me down with it. My only concern is keeping you alive to ensure I have a food source in the future. That doesn't require the two of us socializing."

I recoiled at his sudden coldness. "I didn't mean to offend you or bring up a bad topic..."

"And I didn't mean to accept this job. It was a mistake."

I scooted as far away from him in my seat as I could. "I-I'm sorry." I couldn't understand what I'd done to make him so angry. I just wanted to know what was happening. I had a right to know. My family and friends were the ones dying out there.

"Everyone's always sorry." He reached inside his shirt

pocket and pulled out another cigarette. He lit up and put it to his lips in stony silence.

"You know those things will give you cancer?" I asked the question haughtily, unable to keep my frustration with him to myself.

Ariel's lips tugged into a slight grin. "Will they?"

He had me there. Could vampires get cancer? I wasn't sure if it would have an effect on him at all. "Well, it can give me cancer."

Turning to look at me, he blew a thick line of smoke into my face. "Pity."

I coughed and waved a hand in front of me. "Thanks," I said sarcastically. "I really appreciated—"

There was a knock at the door, and it cracked open. Banning leaned his head into the room. He nodded to Ariel before turning to address me. "It is nearly sunrise. I need to get you freshened up and reacquainted with your friend. He will guard you while we are...indisposed."

I felt tension ease out of my shoulders. I wanted nothing more than for these guys to go hide in their coffins, or wherever they retreated to, and to see Damian. We needed to discuss what we were going to do. I didn't particularly want to stay here with our new vampire friends, but outside didn't seem to be any better.

From what we had seen and heard, the town was overrun with zombies. Banning claimed the rest of the world wasn't fairing any better. I didn't know if there was anywhere safe left, yet I had my doubts as to whether this place was any less dangerous than outside. It was something we would need to discuss.

Climbing to my feet, I walked over to Banning, feeling like a prisoner being ushered from one place to another. I didn't say anything to Ariel, because I wasn't sure if a farewell was appropriate in this situation, and he didn't seem to like me very much anyway.

Banning led me out of the room and guided me down the hallway. "You seem silently somber this morning," he said. "Are you okay?"

"Well, in the past few hours, I've had an attempt on my life and was verbally assaulted by the man who is my supposed protector."

"The verbal assault I believe. Ariel can be a little...harsh, but he wouldn't try to kill you. I can assure you of that. He's very professional about his job."

"I never said Ariel was the one who did it," I snapped.

Banning's eyebrows rose. "Already? I figured some of the newbies would start to get a little desperate, but not so quickly. For those of us who are old enough, we can last long periods of time without blood, and if necessary, the blood of an older vampire can do the trick. Some, those as old as Alexandro and Ariel, we're not even sure if they need it at all anymore. The youngest of us, though? They depend on human blood to survive. They'll start to go insane without it in their systems. A few hours ago, we discussed searching St. Augustine Hospital downtown for donated blood, but no one's in a hurry to do that." He opened a door that led into another hallway.

"If you know they need it, then why are you putting it off?"

Banning turned to me, his eyes haunted. "Do you know what a hospital is?" Before I could answer, he pressed on. "All of those sick, bedridden people, people barely able to walk, unable to defend themselves." He glanced down at his feet for a moment before returning his gray eyes to me. "It's a bloodbath."

I felt the realization sink in. All of the patients were dead. They couldn't pick up a weapon and try to defend themselves. They had laid in their beds and screamed while being eaten alive. The ones who hadn't been killed first were forced to lie and listen to others get devoured while awaiting their turns. My mind traveled to the extensive baby unit our hospital housed, and I suddenly felt sick. "Dear God..." I whispered.

"We'll have to go in. The young ones won't be able to stay sane more than a week. Without that blood, we'd have to start slaughtering our own."

I stared into his troubled eyes and asked the question that was nagging at my brain. "Ariel said this has happened before. You've seen it too, haven't you?"

He nodded. "I have. More than once." He gave me searching, questioning eyes. "Ariel told you this?"

I shrugged. "Only that it happened. When I asked for more details, he got angry."

"This is not a subject you should bring up with Ariel," Banning warned.

"Why?" I asked a little stubbornly. "All I wanted to know was how this has happened before without anyone knowing about it."

Banning glanced around us. Giving a little sigh, he pulled me into a room and eased the door closed behind us. "People do know of it."

I raised my eyebrows skeptically.

"They do," he said persistently, "but people today are so easy to write things off or ignore the unexplainable. All of those ancient civilizations that up and vanished, what do you think happened to them?" Before I could answer, he continued. "I'll tell you what happened. I saw firsthand that they didn't just disappear. The citizens started eating each other. They ate each other until there was nobody left except zombies. Very few vampires unlucky enough to be in those cities made it out with their lives. I lost friends in more than one of those ghost towns," he said quietly. "You have no idea how hard it is to go in on a straggler cleanup when you know you're probably going to find the bodies of friends while you're there."

A chill traveled down my spine. "How can that be true? How did this stay such a secret until now? If things have been fine for so many hundreds of years, what changed everything? Why now? What protected us from such a widespread outbreak before?"

"Medicines," Banning said. "Medication has improved greatly over the years. Everyone's so much healthier now than they were back then. Your immune systems are so much better. Every once in a while, someone would get infected, the disease would slip through, but we've always taken care of it before it became a problem. This is the worst it's been in centuries. I honestly don't know how things went downhill so fast. Maybe the disease mutated in some tiny, minute way, and that small change was something the human immune system couldn't fight like it could the old strain. I don't know. I wish I had the answers, but I don't. I'm sorry."

The way he said they would *take care* of any of the infected they found let me know without him coming out and saying it that they'd killed anyone they found with the disease. They took care of it before anyone discovered its existence. It was horrifying to know this had been going on behind everyone's backs for so long, but it was also a relief. If they had been able to control the disease before, they would be able to get it back under control again. If we survived before, surely we'd survive now. "But we'll live through this, right?" I asked hopefully. "It destroyed places before and we survived."

Banning shook his head with a sardonic laugh. "Before, it destroyed civilizations, civilizations that were like today's cities. The disease took out one here, one there. We're not talking cities, Aurora. We're talking global. This is all over. And with today's mass population and easy travel, there's no way to contain it."

I had to put a hand out to the wall to keep from sinking to the floor. In the midst of my terror, a thought occurred to me. "All of those ancient civilizations that practiced cannibalism..."

He nodded. "They were diseased. Not all, but many. Many people who were in the early stages of infection were half human, half zombie. They'd talk to you like a normal, everyday person, then turn and rip someone else's throat out with their teeth. Others started to copy because it made their enemies fear them, but its roots started with the disease. The history books don't tell you that most people who participated in cannibalism had to be...put out of their misery shortly after. They went mad. They stopped attacking just their enemies and started eating their friends and family, too."

"My mom," I said softly. "She was bitten by my neighbor. I think...I think..." I stared intently into his gray eyes as the true horror hit me. "I need to get home. I need to see my family." I could hear the desperation in my voice, and I hated it.

Banning shook his head. "Our first priority is the hospital. Besides, you don't want to see your family." His voice became low and apologetic. "You might never recover from it."

"I need to see for myself. If there's any chance one of them is alive and I leave them out there on their own, I'll never survive it. The guilt of knowing I did nothing while the people I cared about were turned into one of those things would haunt me for the rest of my life. Not knowing is worse than seeing firsthand what happened to them."

Banning gave a small sigh. "As I said, the hospital is our

number one priority right now. I can't change that, but I will have a team sweep by in the next couple days if I can. It's really up to Aldrich. We share leadership of the teams. We don't do anything major without the other's consent."

I relented, knowing this was the best I was going to get. "Okay," I said. "Thank you for at least trying. It means a lot to me."

He gave a sheepish shrug before turning to look toward the door. "The sun is rising. We should hurry back."

I nodded. "Can I ask one more thing?"

"Yes, but please, make it quick. I must get to my resting place."

"Why can I not bring the subject up with Ariel?"

Banning sighed once again. "How did I know that would be your question?" His eyes flicked to the door. He then took a step closer to me, nearly pressing the front of his body to mine. "I do not have the time to go into it now. It is a very sensitive subject among vampires. I will tell you when we have the luxury of complete privacy. Such a topic is better discussed behind the soundproof walls of my apartment. Vampires hear far too well for us to be talking about this out in the open." He handed me the clothes that were draped over his forearm. "I promise I will talk with you, but not now. It isn't safe."

With a nod, I took the clothes and followed him back out into the hallway. I stared at the sweatpants and gray silk shirt. "Where did you find clothing to fit me on such short notice?"

Banning shook his head with a chuckle. "Actually, they're mine. Most of the people your size were either tucked away for the morning or unwilling to cooperate. Kieran isn't the only one around here with a less than favorable attitude toward mortals."

As sobering as living with irritable undead creatures was, I couldn't help but give a small smile at Banning's open generosity. "Well, thank you."

"Don't mention it." He stopped in front of another door and turned to face me. "Really. Don't mention it. It makes me look very unmanly that a petite girl such as yourself fits comfortably in my clothes."

My smile brightened. "It'll be our little secret."

He wiped his hand across his forehead and gave an exaggerated sigh of relief. Grabbing the knob, he swung the door open. "Here's the community restroom. Can you find your way back to Damian's on your own?"

I nodded. "I think I can manage."

"Good." He looked out the window next to us and glanced up into the sky. "I really must go before I burst into flames." He then pulled a heavy-looking, floor-length drape across the window, closing out the sight of the lawn below.

"You would think on the off chance of one of you guys getting caught in front of a window when the sun comes up, Alexandro would have made sure there were none in his safe house," I said thoughtfully.

Banning paused with a frown, thinking on that as if it had never occurred to him before. "You really would."

After a moment or two of silence, where I'm sure we both were envisioning the poor vampire that suddenly bursts into flames in the hallway because he didn't get safely tucked away in time, Banning shook his head as if to clear away that mental picture. "I'm going."

I nodded again. "I'll see you tomorrow...night."

Banning grabbed my hand tightly in his and forced me to look at him. "Watch your back, darling. Even though the dangers of our kind will be locked away with the rising of the sun, there are other things you need to guard against. Be careful." He leaned down and kissed the back of my hand. "Do not let your guard down."

"What else do I have to guard against?" I asked warily.

Banning patted my head softly as if I were a child. "Gnomes." His voice held humor that wasn't exactly appropriate for the seriousness of the moment. Without giving me a real answer, he turned and walked away.

That annoyed me, but more than being an annoyance, he had scared me. His warning sent a chill down my spine. What kind of life could I possibly have here if I had to constantly watch over my shoulder, waiting to see who or what would try to kill me next?

With that parting warning, Banning and I went our separate ways, him to go into a coma-like sleep with the waking of the sun and me to try to clean blood and gore from my body.

Chapter 6

I stood outside Damian's room staring at the door, rubbing my hands nervously against the front of the sweats Banning had loaned me. I tried to convince myself to knock, but my hand seemed to be fighting the order from my brain. I couldn't figure out what had me so on edge. I'd just spent the most awkward night of my life in Ariel's room. This couldn't be worse than that. This was the most normal thing in days. This should be a breeze. I should be excited to be reunited with Damian. Using that knowledge to dredge up an ounce of bravery, I knocked on the door.

It took a moment, but Damian answered. Upon seeing me, his lips curved into a friendly smile. "Hey," he said in greeting. He stood wearing only a pair of blue jeans. The front of them still had blood dried to the front. His bare stomach was bronzed and rippled with muscles. His thin waist made his shoulders appear even broader. He looked good, really good, but I fought not to notice. My overwhelming anxiety helped with that.

As I looked up at Damian, I knew why I had been afraid to see him. Around Banning and Ariel, I could hold it together, keep myself composed, because I didn't know them. Around them, I had to be tough.

Now, I only had Damian around. It gave me the leisure of breaking down. Seeing him was like a reminder that this wasn't a dream, that the horrors of last night had actually happened. The two of us had been through enough together, become familiar enough with each other, that I could relax around him. Relaxing meant I would finally come to terms with everything I had witnessed. I felt my face crumble, and the first sob escaped before I could stop it.

Damian stood frozen, his brown eyes wary, as if he was unsure of what to do. After a moment's hesitation, he held his arms out.

I fell into them, my sobs muffled by his chest. My shoulders heaved with every gulp of air I took between outpours of tears. I couldn't even concentrate on one certain thing to be upset over. Instead, I cried over the general disarray that had become our lives. I clung to him as if he was one of my closest and most trustworthy friends, not the distant stranger he truly was. We'd been through a lot together, but we still didn't know much about each other.

Damian's arms stayed awkwardly out, as if he was afraid to move. "Come on, Rory. Don't cry."

This only caused me to cry harder. "That's what my brother used to call me," I wailed. My brother, who was now probably a member of the walking dead, would never call me Rory again.

Damian finally brought his hands in, one rubbing my back, the other running over my hair. "Hey, it's okay. Maybe he's okay. You don't know for sure."

I felt my shoulders tense as he said it. He didn't believe a word of what he was saying, and it was obvious by the strain in his voice. With a sniffle, I pulled away from him, feeling silly. "I'm sorry. I need to get a hold of myself."

"You're allowed to cry," he said soothingly. "You've been through a lot in the past twenty-four hours. You deserve a good cry. I won't think less of you. I promise."

I looked up at him, still loosely holding onto his waist. "I'll think less of me," I admitted. "I can't sit around crying. I need to be coming up with a plan to get home so I can find my family."

"Honey, that is not an option," Damian said with warning in his voice. "You step out those gates and you're zombie food. Leave the search and rescue to the vampires."

I didn't respond, because it wouldn't be worth the argument it would cause. Instead, I pulled farther away from him and looked down the length of his body. Now that I was done crying, it was painfully obvious he wasn't fully clothed. "And, wow, you're really naked," I said, exaggerating. It was best to change the subject, and this should distract him nicely.

Damian quickly moved away from me, running a hand

sheepishly along the back of his neck. "Sorry. I wasn't expecting you yet. I figured you'd sleep longer. I didn't take the sunlight factor into consideration. I guess the vampires kicked you out after only a few hours because it came time to hide for the day." He rolled his eyes. "I'm not used to going by a vampire's schedule." He walked over to a chair in the small, open kitchen to the left and picked up his t-shirt. "Also," he said, pulling the blood-spattered shirt over his head, "I feel terrible about calling you R—" He stopped suddenly, catching himself. "By your nickname," he said, correcting himself. "I had no idea that's what your brother called you."

"Don't worry about it," I said with a shrug. "I like the name. It makes me feel safe. And I don't think he's going to be calling me that anytime soon. You may as well."

Damian smoothed the shirt over his stomach, avoiding blotches of dried blood as best as he could. "Good. I like Rory." He gave me a soft grin. "It sounds nice."

He didn't comment on my brother never calling me by my nickname again, but I didn't call him on it. I knew I wouldn't want to hear his honest opinion, so I left it as an avoided topic.

Letting out a sigh, I plopped into a chair at the kitchen table. "This apartment's pretty nice," I said. I looked out into the living room with appreciation. It was elegantly furnished with items that looked like they weren't from this century. The tables were made of a heavy wood, possibly oak, and were varnished to perfection. The quality of the furnishings was of a high standard, something I could tell even at a glance. They were pricey antiques no doubt worth more than my car. No cheap Wal-Mart items to be found here! The couch had a wooden base and clawed feet, the cushions made of a soft-looking maroon color. The floors were hardwood with lavish oriental throw rugs littered about. The whole place was magnificent, like stepping back in time a century or two. The only thing that gave away the modern age was a large television that took up most of one wall. "You've got a kick ass television," I said optimistically.

Damian plopped into the chair across from me, putting his back to the living room. "Can't make it look too much like prison."

"It's better than anything outside," I said. When he didn't

comment, I asked, "Do you have any roommates?"

His expression grew dark, and his hands balled into fists on top of the table. "No. They knew better. Besides, it's not *me* they want under constant supervision. You're the one they're concerned about keeping alive."

It was as if he was saying the vampires wouldn't be overly upset if something happened to him. I didn't understand why. We were both in the same situation. His survival seemed just as important as mine. Perhaps he was being just a tad bit touchy. I understood the situation sucked, but he was being excessively grouchy with me. It was a role reversal.

Since the topic of roommates didn't seem to be going any better than the subject of how nicely furnished his apartment was, I tried once again to change to a conversation that wouldn't receive any angry comments. "Didn't they give you any new clothes? Banning gave me something new to wear a few minutes ago."

Damian shrugged. "Orion said he'd hook me up with something at nightfall. He was making damn sure he was hidden before the sun rose." Damian gave me a sly look. "Though it's almost a bummer they gave you something new. I have to admit, I miss that little miniskirt you were wearing. It's a shame you got it all messy."

My eyes automatically narrowed. "Pervert." I, for one, was happy to be rid of the skirt. Last night would have been easier to deal with in sweatpants and sneakers. I'd been forced to survive the end of the world in a skirt and a pair of knee-high boots. I don't know how I even kept up. Maybe it was the possibility of death looming over my head.

Whatever the reason, I had survived and was glad to be out of the skirt and into something more practical. Lord only knew how many times I'd flashed everyone while fighting for my life last night.

With that in mind, a thought suddenly occurred to me. "Last night, did you look up my skirt?" Accusation was strong in my voice. I couldn't help it. We had a history that led to my distrust of his ability to be chivalrous.

"What?" Damian asked with a chuckle. He had a boyish grin on his face and an expression of wolfish pride.

In that instant, I knew the answer, but I had to ask again anyway. "Did you see up my skirt? When you helped me out the window last night, did you look?"

"No," he said with a teasing note to his voice. "I didn't see the red, lacy thong you had on."

I felt my face turn red, as red as my undergarments. "I can't believe you! Even then! Even then you couldn't behave yourself."

Damian held up a hand. "Now don't go getting all riled up. I wasn't looking for my own perverse fun. I was trying to get you out the window. It wasn't my fault your skirt was so damn short. You practically threw it in my face. I almost expected to see a blinking sign that said, 'Look. Here's my ass.' And I'll have you know, I was more concerned about getting out of the building alive than finding out what kind of panties you had on."

My lips protruded into a pout. "You still shouldn't have looked."

Damian gave a laugh. "I think you're more upset about the fact that I didn't want to look than the fact that I did."

My eyes widened in indignation. "I don't think so."

His grin turned devilish, and he slid lower in his seat. "Whatever, darlin'." His tone clearly said he thought I was lying.

I rolled my eyes. "Whatever."

Changing the subject to something less likely to get him into trouble, Damian asked, "So, what do you want to do today? We should be vampire free for a good while. Let's not waste it."

I sent a glance to the living room, more importantly, the television. "Maybe we should turn on the television, see if we can catch the news," I said hopefully. My anger dissipated at the thought of hearing word from the outside. "Maybe they'll have something good to report. Maybe the military is getting things under control out there."

Damian shook his head with an apologetic look. "Tried that earlier. None of the stations are working anymore. Two of them had an emergency message running on a loop, but other than that, it's dead air."

I felt a cold stab of fear run through me. None of the stations were operational? Reporters put their lives on the line for a good story. For no one to be even attempting to cover this meant things were extremely bad. And most stations didn't even have time to put up an emergency message? Just *poof*, everyone was gone? This was very, very bad.

"Is there something else you'd like to do?" Damian's voice interrupted my thoughts. His tone was gentle, as if he was trying to keep me from thinking too hard on what the lack of news coverage meant.

I'd already come to the horrific conclusion, though. The world was in total chaos outside. I felt irritated that he was trying to baby me as if I was a child who couldn't handle how bad things really were. I gave him an annoyed look. "What is there to do?" I snapped. "We're trapped in this God forsaken building with the fang gang, and you ask what I want to do. Let's go to the movies," I said sarcastically. "Oh wait! We can't. They're not open, because the people who run it are all dead."

Damian ignored my outburst and leaned over, grabbing a deck of cards from the kitchen counter. "Okay. Do you want to play cards?"

"No. I don't want to play cards," I said with an agitated huff. "Cards are boring." I knew I was being unreasonable, expecting him to find a better way to entertain me in this place, but I was still a little annoyed over being treated like a fragile china doll, not to mention the whole thong conversation was still fresh in my mind.

"Well…" Damian drawled the word with a wicked grin, not at all perturbed by my sudden attitude. "Back in the old days, they only had one way to entertain themselves. I personally find it to be the best option."

"What is that?" I asked, unable to hide my interest. "What did they do?"

"They had lots and lots of…" He broke off with a laugh. "Sex," he finished.

I sent him a look of disgust. "You're a pig."

"And you're the one who's too good to play cards." He began shuffling the deck in his hands, an amused glint in his eyes.

"Give me the damn cards," I snapped, yanking them out of his hands. I could tell by the look on his face when I took the cards that he was going to give me some smart-ass comment.

"The game is strip poker," he announced, not disappointing my assumption. "We don't quit until there's a winner. Though, honestly, in this game, I feel we all win."

"Nice try. Too bad I don't know how to play poker."

Damian frowned. "Well, we could play strip gin."

"I'm not playing strip anything." I shook my head at his look of disappointment. "Let's just play a game of war. It's simple and seems fitting. We play war in here while our hosts play war outside."

"Fitting," Damian agreed with a slight grimace. He grabbed the cards out of my hands and started dealing them out. "Only they're not out there now, because they're asleep in their coffins. Though when the sun sets, they'll be right back out there, killing and maiming with glee."

"Banning said they're going to the hospital tonight. They plan to take all of the donated blood and give it to the younger vampires. He said it will keep them sane."

"Makes sense," Damian said with a shrug as he dealt out the last card. "It's not like anyone else is going to need it."

I gave a small, exasperated sigh. "Don't you think they should be searching for other survivors right now?"

"No. The hospital should come first." Damian could see I was about to start protesting, so he held up a hand. "As much as I would love for them to find someone else alive, they have to protect those who *are* alive first, meaning us," he said in explanation. "Being the only humans left, you and I have big targets on our backs in the eyes of the younger vampires. If some of those younger vampires don't get that blood from the hospital, they are going to go looking for it somewhere else, and by that time, they'll be half-crazed. You saw how violently Kieran fed, and he was sane."

I shuddered at the thought. "I don't think he's sane."

"You know what I mean," Damian said, flipping a card over. "He has something there, some little bit of consciousness. When the blood lust takes over the young ones, they'll be like those mindless zombies outside, only more agile and battle trained."

"How do you know all this?" I flipped over my card and gave a small grin of delight that my number was higher than his. I grabbed both cards and put them at the bottom of my pile.

Damian made a face that let me know he was unhappy

telling me what he was about to say next. "It was made per-fectly clear to me by one of Alexandro's stooges that if I didn't follow every instruction given to me, I would be locked up with a crazed vampire and left to be eaten alive. I was made un-comfortably aware, in graphic detail, of what a young vampire who is deprived of blood will do to someone." To further ex-plain this, he added, "The older ones can last a long time without needing blood. Some of them can go years without taking in a single drop. The newly undead, though? They'll tear a man to pieces. They will rip out your throat without a second thought, because they are consumed by the need to feed themselves. Nothing else matters but the desperation to have fresh blood pouring down their throats. The older vam-pires usually have willing donors. They can make the experi-ence enjoyable, or so I've been told. The newly dead never have anybody stepping up to be donors because of how vio-lently they feed. People don't usually survive after feeding one of them. They need *victims*, because there won't be much left of a person once they're done...which is what was promised to me if I didn't follow orders."

My eyes narrowed in outrage, my next card frozen in the air. "I can't believe they threatened you." I smacked my card down onto the table in anger. "Someone tried to kill me, sure, but they didn't threaten me with such horrible things. Who told you that?"

"Someone tried to kill you?" Damian asked. He sat up in his chair, suddenly at attention. Concern filled his features.

I gave a shrug. "Yeah, but it's not important. Ariel took care of it."

"Not important? Aurora, someone tried to kill you."

"Technically, I don't think he really wanted to kill me. He just acted like he wanted to. Kieran sent him to scare me. I'm more concerned over the threats you received. Though I wouldn't put something that terrible past Alexandro. That guy creeps me out."

Damian went to argue, but changed his mind. "Okay. Both are bad, very bad. We really need to watch out for each other. I don't want to realize a couple hours too late that you've gone missing."

"Agreed. We'll watch each other's backs." I paused thoughtfully, wondering if I should tell him what had been churning in my mind since my talk with Banning. "Since we're on the subject..."

Damian's eyes automatically filled with suspicion. "What?"

"I'm going to follow them."

His expression went from suspicious to confused. "Follow whom where?"

I grew excited as I revealed my plan to him, leaning forward in my seat. "I'm following Banning's team to the hospital tonight. I think you should come with me."

Damian stared at me for a long moment, his expression portraying that he wasn't sure if I was being serious or joking with him. "You're going to go with them?"

I nodded. "Yep."

"You can't. They would never allow it."

"That's why they won't know I'm there."

Damian gave a laugh of disbelief. "How do you think you're going to pull that off? You'd be the only person with a pulse, and you stick out like a sore thumb."

"I saw that some of the members of the rescue teams were wearing police or SWAT helmets. I'm going to wear one. They won't even know I'm there."

"And where are you going to get a SWAT helmet?"

"I saw one in Ariel's room."

"So you're going to steal it." He made it a statement instead of a question.

"I'm not going to steal it. I'm going to borrow it. I'll put it back."

"Not if you get killed you won't." Damian sighed and flipped over another card. "Aurora, I can't let you go."

"You can't stop me," I said, challenging him to disagree.

"I can, and if you force me to, I will."

"You don't have the right," I said angrily. "You are not my parent."

"No, but I'm the only thing you've got left. I'm not going to sit back and let you get yourself killed."

I decided to try another angle. "Damian, I have to go. They're not going to be looking for survivors. They are going in for food."

Damian shook his head. "I'm sure they'll keep an eye out for survivors. They want us to become extinct as little as we do, though for less honorable reasons."

"Do you honestly think they are going to care one bit about survivors? They aren't going there looking for people. They are going with one thing in mind. They are looking to stock up on their blood supply. If it's not in a neatly packaged bag, they are going to shoot. They are going to go through that hospital like a tornado, killing anything and everything in their paths." I felt tears of desperation well in my eyes. "With me there, someone might stand a chance."

Damian's face softened and he leaned forward, grabbing my trembling hand. "Listen, Rory, there isn't going to be anyone left to save. They've been searching the entire town and haven't found a soul. The hospital isn't going to be any different."

"They did find a soul, two actually. They found us."

"You can't go," Damian said firmly. "Leave rescuing survivors to Banning. He seems decent enough. He got us back here alive, didn't he?"

I gave a small nod. "Yeah." I couldn't deny that Banning seemed like an honest enough guy...for a vampire.

"So you'll let Banning take care of things?"

I had a split second to make my decision. If I told him I still planned to go, he would stop me, going as far as physically restraining me. I believed he would. If I wanted to keep both of us happy, I could just lie and sneak out when he wasn't paying attention. "Yeah. I'll leave it to Banning."

He smiled. "There's my girl. Don't you even worry about what happens tonight. Everything will turn out okay. You just worry about your own survival."

I gave a small nod, pulling my hands from his and picking up my cards. "I will."

He gave a satisfied nod and flipped a card over. "Good." He leaned back in his chair again, visibly relaxing. "Now, let's try to spin this thing into a positive deal. We may be trapped here, but think of all the responsibilities we get to miss out on."

Laughing, I shook my head. "How can you see something positive in this?"

Damian shrugged. "It's better than sitting around feeling sorry for ourselves. Just think," he said, scooping some cards up. "I was supposed to get my truck inspected at the end of the month. Guess it doesn't matter now, huh?"

I flipped over another card. "I guess that's a good thing."

"Don't you have anything you're glad to not have to do?"

I shrugged, thinking on it. "Well, there's my college education I won't have to worry about paying back the loans for." I gave an unhappy sigh. "There's my brother's wedding. I won't have to save money to buy a bridesmaid's dress for that either. I suppose I won't have to worry about where to spend the riches my father set aside in a bank account for me that I couldn't touch until my twenty-first birthday. That's a relief." The next thought that occurred to me, brought to the surface by the mention of my birthday, made my eyes narrow in annoyance. "There's my birthday party I've been planning for two months. Now I'll never get to have that."

Damian laughed in disbelief. "Are you serious? You still have birthday parties?"

I gave him an angry scowl. "Yes. I was having a birthday party, and it was going to be great. I probably spent more on my party than you make in a year."

"Ooh, la-ti-da," Damian said sarcastically, rolling his eyes. "Aren't you just so damn special?"

"It *was* going to be special," I said with a pout.

"You know," Damian said as he stared at my protruding lip. "I don't think I've ever met someone as superficial and self-centered as you." He held a hand up before I could fight with him. "But whatever. Your party was going to be special, and I'm sorry you had to miss it."

"Me too," I said softly. "My family always made such a big deal over birthdays. Now it won't mean anything but surviving one more day." I shook my head and gave another sad sigh. "I bought a fancy dress and everything."

Damian was trying to hide a smirk, but wasn't doing a very good job of it. "You know what I've noticed about you?" He answered before I could reply. "You're a very moody individual. Your mood swings are worse than anyone I've ever met."

I scowled at him, and he pointed to my mouth. "See right there?" he asked. "You're happy one minute, sad the next, and then totally pissed off an instant later. I can't keep up with you. You're a man's worst nightmare."

"You're the reason I'm like that," I said accusingly.

"Me? You're blaming me for your psychotic tendencies?"

"They are not psychotic. And yes, I'm blaming you. I'm not like this with anybody else."

"There's nobody else left."

"I meant before." I glowered at him. "You make me moody. I'll be in a terrific mood, and then you'll do something to totally piss me off. It's amazing the skills you have. You could piss the Pope off."

"The Pope's probably dead."

"You know what I mean," I snapped. "One day, you're going to piss the wrong person off, and they're going to eat you."

He let out a deep, booming laugh. "Guess you wouldn't have to worry about me bothering you anymore then, would you?" On my horrified look at the causal joke of his death, he added, "I'm just messing with you. You need to chill out a little bit."

I looked down at my cards, feeling slightly embarrassed. I couldn't help my reactions around him, nor could I control them. Damian had a raw energy about him that always set me on edge. "I guess I'm just a little tense."

"It's cool," Damian said casually. "I'm used to women being nervous around me. It's the sexual tension."

My head jolted up, and I looked at him with incredulity. At his teasing grin, I gave in and rewarded him with a laugh. "You never quit."

"Not until I get what I want," he said softly.

Chapter 7

I sat in a van surrounded by unfamiliar men. The only people I recognized were Banning and Aldrich, and the latter wasn't much of a comfort.

Earlier, I'd left Damian's apartment with the excuse I wanted to take a nap before nightfall. Of course, Damian had offered for me to stay in his room, but I'd offered him the pretext that I wanted some time alone.

He hadn't liked the idea of me being by myself, almost as if he didn't trust me. Smart boy. Eventually, he gave in and let me slip away to my solitude.

Yeah, I was on my own—on my own with a group of bloodsucking vampires in a van that was going on a vacation to hell. Against Damian's wishes, I'd snuck out, my helmet hiding my identity.

In the hall, I'd found a closet with shelves full of black clothing, the kind of clothing one would wear when going on a trip to create destruction and mayhem. It was the same sort of clothing the group that rescued Damian and I had been wearing. Though I was starting to wonder if rescuing was the right word or if it was more along the lines of kidnapping.

After monitoring the closet and finding big, bad assassin-type men pulling outfits from that very closet, I thought it would be a good idea to take one of my own. I was lucky enough to find an outfit that seemed fit for a woman. It was small enough, tight enough. I'd been concerned my high-heeled boots might give me away, but I'd been lucky enough to find a pair of black combat boots in my size at the bottom of the closet. I just had to hope Damian was wrong about the pounding of my very human heart betraying my identity. So far, I'd been lucky enough to blend into the massive group. I was still pleasantly shocked by this, but I wasn't going to complain. I just had to keep staying out of direct sight of anyone who might peg me as a fake.

Presently, Banning knelt at the front of the van between the driver and passenger seats, facing those of us in the back.

Aldrich was on the closest bench seat facing Banning. He was turned sideways, leaning against the window on the left. I think he was turned that way so the others could see Banning around him. He was tall enough that he needed to slouch against the window to sit comfortably and keep his head from hitting the roof. He was one of the biggest men I'd ever seen. He had to be at least seven feet tall, and every inch of him was intimidating.

"Try to stick together, save breaking off to investigate rooms," Banning said as he loaded ammunition into the weapon in front of him, bringing my attention back to his instructions. "Aldrich's team will take the ground floor. My team will take the second floor."

Aldrich gave an unhappy growl. "The ground floor." His lip curled in disgust. "Zombies don't climb steps very well. You gave yourself the easier floor."

I made a mental note to stick with Banning's team. Not only would they be on the less dangerous level, but I also felt safer with him.

Banning tried to hide the grin that was threatening to spread across his face. "Once both areas are secured, we will meet up and divide the third floor in half. Make sure you have your weapons on you. Those of you using firearms, make sure you have extra rounds. You will need them. Everyone should have a knife or comparable weapon on hand in case things degrade to close quarters, hand-to-hand combat. We are searching for blood, but remember, keep survivors in mind." He turned to look at Aldrich as the van slowed to a stop in the hospital parking lot. "Do you have anything to add?"

"Yeah," Aldrich said, slinging his AK-47 over his shoulder. "Kill anything that fucking moves."

"Cute," Banning said in response. He opened the sliding door on the side of the van and climbed out, gravel crunching under his feet.

The rest of the men exited after him, checking their

weapons and ammunition to make sure they were prepared. Once the others were out of the van and I was left alone, I scrambled along the floor, looking through the extra weapons that had been left behind. There were guns, a few knives, an alarming number of swords, and a canister of mace.

I let out a triumphant cry as I found a gun I actually knew how to use. I silently thanked my father for the monthly trips to the shooting gallery as I scooped it up and opened the chamber. It was loaded. Five rounds, the sixth bullet missing, possibly already used. I searched the ground for extra rounds. There weren't any. Shit. If we got into a real showdown, I was up a creek, as the saying went.

I gave a thoughtful look to the other guns lying on the floor. I considered grabbing one, but I wouldn't know what to do with it anyway. Using a firearm I was unfamiliar with could have dangerous results. I looked to the canister of mace. If bullets didn't stop zombies, mace definitely wouldn't even slow them down. I did scoop up one of the large hunting knives and tucked it into my pocket as a last resort. With a nervous sigh, I glanced down at its handle. "I better not need you."

I exited the van, glancing awkwardly at the strange men around me. It was hard to act casual when I was the outsider. I didn't want to do anything stupid and give myself away, so I stood as still as could be, waiting for instructions.

Aldrich and Banning were side by side, discussing details of the raid. Standing next to Aldrich, Banning looked tiny. Aldrich towered over him by at least two feet.

I had to fight back a giggle at Banning's diminutive size as I watched them confer over rendezvous points. The only thing that held my nervous laughter in check was the fact that it would give me away. Somehow, I didn't think vampires giggled.

"Okay, listen up," Banning said, addressing the assembled group. "We're going in the side door here as opposed to the main lobby. We expect less activity because it's a less congested area on a regular day. Hopefully, we'll be able to work our way through with less risk of being overrun. Once we get inside, my team to the right. Aldrich's team head to the left." He pulled his sword from its sheath and took a few test swipes at the air. "Let's rock 'n' roll."

Everyone paused and blinked at him in confusion.

Aldrich's eyebrows furrowed. "What?"

Banning gave a disheartened sigh and his sword drooped a little. "Rock 'n' roll. It's…well it's…never mind. Let's just go." He gave a shake of his head in disappointment. Then he started in the direction of the side entrance.

The man next to me leaned into my shoulder. "What does rock 'n' roll mean?"

I shrugged, not wanting to draw any unwanted attention my way.

"Must be some of that crazy modern lingo he loves so much," the man said with a chuckle.

I simply shrugged again. I couldn't believe none of them had heard of rock and roll. How long had these men been dead and oblivious to the outside world?

I worried the man next to me would continue with our one-sided conversation, but the second Banning threw open the hospital doors, everyone fell silent. You didn't need to be inside to know it was exactly what Banning promised—a bloodbath. A bloody handprint stretched along the inside of the doors, attesting to the violence that had transpired within.

Aldrich raised his weapon, suddenly on alert. A frown marred his lips as he entered the building behind Banning. No shots followed, so I assumed this side entrance was clear for the moment.

Banning nodded to the left and Aldrich quickly split off. He headed down a dimly lit corridor, and half the men broke off to follow him.

To those of us remaining, Banning motioned with his sword to the steps just off to the right. He led the way, and we fell in line behind him, loyally following our leader. The men in front of me started up the staircase in groups of two, weapons drawn and ready. Each subsequent person, when reaching the bottom of the stairs, stepped over something before ascending the first step.

I strained to see what it was, but the other men were too big for me to get a good look around them. I didn't find out until I was on top of it.

"It" was a man, at least it used to be. What lay at my feet now was just a shadow of a human being. His throat gaped open with a bloody wound at its center, and judging by the way he lay crumpled on the ground, he had fallen down the stairs, probably while trying to get away from whatever had injured him. One of his legs was broken and bent at an unnatural angle. There was a puddle of blood underneath his body that let me know more injuries would be found if I turned him over.

I faltered, unable to just carelessly step over the evidence of such violence. This man had been someone's father, someone's grandfather. He deserved better than this, better than being just a broken corpse at the bottom of a staircase.

The man beside me stopped as well and stared down at the body at our feet. "Poor bastard." He shook his head. "You're still so human, Kenya. Even after all this time, you care." He grabbed my arm and assisted me in stepping over the body.

I swept my gaze over the man at my side as we made our way up the stairs.

The only thing visible through his helmet was a pair of blue eyes. In those eyes, I could see trust. Shit. This guy thought I was someone else, someone he trusted with his life. I felt as if I was betraying him. His eyes sparkled when he caught me looking, and though I couldn't see his mouth through the helmet, I knew he was smiling.

"Why do we wear these stupid things?" I asked of the helmet. "It's starting to make me feel claustrophobic." I mentally kicked myself for speaking. Luckily for me, the helmet muffled my voice, keeping my identity a secret.

"You know why," he said gently. "Zombies love to go for the neck and face. They'll attack someone without a helmet before they attack someone wearing one. They like the easy access to the throat. With the helmet, they'll falter for a second, and that second could mean your life."

Ah. So that explained it. The people in the helmets could get over their egos enough to admit they wanted to lower their chances of dying.

"Yo! Diego, Kenya."

Banning's voice drew my attention to the front of the group. He stood with the tip of his sword resting on the floor as he leaned on its handle. "You two take the back rooms on either side of the hall. Five minutes tops." Then he turned away, spouting out instructions to other groups.

I assumed this meant me, since I had been mistaken for this Kenya once already.

"That's us, babe," the man beside me said, turning toward the door on our right.

I guess that cleared up his name, at least. I turned and followed Diego, my heart pounding frantically in my chest. I did not want to go off alone with a stranger. I did not want to have to use the gun I'd snatched from the van.

Diego slid inside the room, holding the door open for me with his foot to keep his hands free.

I was barely inside the doorway before a burst of rifle fire sounded from the hallway behind me.

Diego glanced over my shoulder with a chuckle. "Sounds like they got one."

I felt my blood run cold, knowing that gunshot had killed someone who'd been an innocent victim of this disease, possibly someone I knew. I didn't have time to think on that horrid awareness long, because a snarl from inside the room brought my attention back to our assignment.

A woman in a nurse's uniform crouched on the bed closest to the far wall. She let out another inhuman growl and lifted her head in our direction. Blood dripped from her mouth, trailing down her neck to stain the top of her once-white dress.

I could guess what she was doing by the way the bed closest to us looked. It held a patient at one time. Now all it held was meat. I couldn't think of that bloody blob as a person or I was going to throw up. The smell alone caused my stomach to turn. It reminded me of the time a raccoon got trapped in our storage shed. My brother hadn't found it until it had been dead at least a week. Magnify that odor by a hundred, and that's what this room smelled like.

Flies circled what was left of the body, buzzing excitedly. My stomach clenched again at the sight, and I reached out to grab the wall, breathing raggedly.

Diego brought his gun up and shot the nurse between the eyes.

She fell backwards on the bed and lay still.

We both stepped forward to peer down at her. I really didn't want to look, but my eyes disobeyed my brain's orders.

She was terrifying. Her left arm was bent and mangled,

the skin torn to shreds and hanging grotesquely. One of her eyes was missing, and mucus trailed down her cheek. Her fingers were bloody with chunks of meat and skin hanging from them. I didn't think most of it was hers.

Maybe Damian was right. Maybe I wasn't ready to handle this. Maybe I should have left this to Banning and his team.

"Nasty little fuckers, aren't they?" Diego asked, bringing me out of my panicked thoughts. Walking across the room, he kicked in the bathroom door. It seemed a little unnecessary to me, but whatever. He was the trained professional. "Bathroom's clear," he called out.

I gave a small, sheepish nod as he rejoined me. I wouldn't have to see another one of those things at the moment. It was a relief. Though to get back to the vampire safe house, I would need to continue my trip through the hospital, and I would bet this wasn't going to be the last one we found.

Diego stepped back into the hallway, and I followed closely on his heels. He went to step over a fallen body that was victim to one of our group's bullets when he froze in his tracks. "Shit."

I glanced down at the body. It was a zombie, not a great thing, but it wasn't any different from the rest we'd seen. At least not that I could tell. "What?"

"He's old."

I'm sure there was some significance to that statement I was supposed to get, but since I wasn't who he thought, I was clueless. I stared at him, waiting for an explanation.

"Kenya, he's old. The disease has never been able to manifest itself in the elderly before. Their bodies weren't strong enough to host the virus, so it just killed them. The same thing applied for children. Their bodies weren't mature enough, weren't strong enough to handle the disease." He shook his head. "These humans with all of their medications... If the virus is now affecting the elderly, they've doubled the amount of zombies we're going to be seeing."

So that was the big deal. More zombies meant more chances of getting overrun and killed. "Great," I said sarcastically.

"I know," Diego said. "Like it wasn't bad enough to begin with. They had to go and make things worse."

In grim silence, we moved to the second door. Diego

threw it open to reveal a linen closet. It was clean and tidy, all the towels a fresh white, as if untouched by the end of the world. With a pleased sound in the back of his throat, he pulled the door closed. Then we walked around the corner, catching up with the rest of the group.

Banning gave a nod of acknowledgement, but didn't bother to ask us what we'd found. Judging from the unhappy looks of those without masks, I'd say they were finding things similar to us. Corpses, zombies, and not much else.

My brother's girlfriend, Christine, worked at this hospital. I was praying we didn't find her mangled body at the bottom of some flight of steps. I couldn't for the life of me remember if she'd worked yesterday or not. It was as if it was blocked from my mind. I think I was purposely forgetting. I didn't want to think about the people I cared about being victim to such violence, or worse, becoming one of these reanimated monsters.

I was suddenly dragged from my thoughts by a plea for help. My hopes soared, and I eagerly stepped into the doorway of the room it came from.

A girl was inside, on her knees. Her hands were held in front of her pleadingly and she was crying. She stared up at the vampire in front of her and begged for her life. "Help me. Please help me. Those things..." Her voice lowered, and a whining growl escaped. Her eyes turned feral for a moment before returning to their natural soft green pigment. "Once they bite you, they make you do things...things you don't want to do."

The vampire's shoulders sagged for a moment, and then he slowly raised his gun.

The girl's eyes grew wide with terror. "What are you doing?" She shrieked in fear, but made no move to get out of the way. She was obviously too stunned to fathom what was happening. "You're supposed to help—"

I quickly turned away, squeezing my eyes shut. The gunshot echoed in my ears a moment later. I pressed my face against the wall next to the door, taking a deep breath. There was no hope here. Damian had been right. I peeked my eyes open when I heard the vampire rejoin us in the hallway.

He gave Banning a soft nod, letting him know his assigned room was clear.

Banning nodded back, his expression grim. Visibly steeling himself, he turned to the assembled group. "We're coming up on the second floor's main waiting room. Expect to see a decent amount of zombies in there, and expect them to be lively."

I grimaced. I could have done without the last comment. The livelier the zombies, the more likely they were to kill me. Wonderful. I wasn't even going to think about how many of them there might be. It would just freak me out even more.

I crept closer to Diego, gun trembling in my hands. As we stepped into the waiting room, I could see Banning's guess was correct. The room had more than a dozen zombies inside. I tried twice to count them, but at fifteen, I lost track of which I'd already tallied.

Banning whipped his sword out, and with amazing speed, beheaded the one closest to us. The cut was clean, the blade going completely through in one swing.

The zombie collapsed to the ground, making no other movement.

Diego leaned in close to me as we watched Banning move on to a second victim. "The man prides himself on being the only one of us who is modernized, yet he's never upgraded his weapon."

As I watched Banning with his sword, I realized he didn't need a gun. He was excellent with his weapon of choice. He made it look effortless. I guess a few hundred years of practice could do that.

I quickly forgot about Banning as one of the zombies shambled closer to me than I was comfortable with.

Diego raised his gun and fired before I could even think of raising my weapon. His eyes flicked to me and sparkled behind his helmet. "Either I'm getting faster, or you're off your game tonight. You usually beat me to the draw." He snorted. "You usually beat everyone to the draw."

I refrained from commenting. Why did they have to mistake me for some weapon-crazed assassin? Why couldn't I have been mistaken for an average vampire soldier? That still would have been a stretch, but it would be easier to fake that than pretending to be the best of the vampire best. They thought I was the vampire with the fastest draw of the undead. In reality, I would probably have trouble shooting an elephant standing still from a few feet away. Shooting crazed human beings on the move was a tad difficult for me. Looking around the room, I seemed to be the only one with that delinquency.

The zombies who'd been trying to kill everyone moments ago now all lay on the ground. It didn't look as if they would be getting up again any time soon.

Banning didn't even pause to think. As he wiped his blade clean on the clothing of a now headless zombie, he quickly pointed to groups with his free hand, barking out assignments.

Diego and I were assigned to a set of rooms down the west wing hallway.

Everyone was split up between the four corridors, making me feel exposed at being so spread out. The less people around me, the more likely I was to come into contact with a zombie.

Banning was down east hall, the furthest from us. I didn't like that fact much. I didn't feel very secure being this far from him.

Diego had killed two of those things without blinking. I should feel safe with him, but there was something about Banning that was relaxing. Maybe it was because all of vampirekind was trying to bite my head off, some of them metaphorically, and literally for others. Banning was the only who hadn't tried to harm me. Diego hadn't done anything offensive yet, but he believed me to be someone else. If he knew I was just some mortal, frightened girl, he might be acting differently. I glanced sideways at him as he crept closer to the rooms we were assigned to inspect.

He held his gun up, ready to shoot at the sign of any movement. His eyes flicked from side to side, ever watchful. He moved slightly ahead of me, taking the lead. When he reached the doors we were assigned, which were across the hall from each other, he made an annoyed noise in the back of his throat. "Look at this."

I peered around him to see both doors hanging loosely from their hinges. They were barely connected to the frames, and I was pretty sure I could guess what had done the damage.

"Well, let's start with the left," Diego said, seemingly

picking at random. He kicked what was left of the door in, the wood easily splintering away from the lock.

The instant the door broke away, the moaning of zombies could be heard from within.

Diego strode into the room as if there was no reason for concern. He started firing his weapon before I even cleared the doorway.

Upon entering, I could see at least seven of them in the main room, all of them equally horrifying.

A woman was dragging herself along the tile flooring in Diego's direction. Both of her legs were broken. Parts of them had been torn away, leaving bone to glisten wetly in the light.

Diego was so busy concentrating on the ones rushing him, he didn't even notice her. He just kept emptying shells into the skulls of the others.

With a trembling hand, I moved in closer to the woman on the floor to make sure I didn't accidentally shoot Diego in the leg. I leveled my gun with her head, mentally running through all of my father's instructions. I stared into her face, looked at her rotting mouth, and pulled the trigger. The gun kicked, sending a tremor up my arm, but it did the job.

Her head exploded because of how close I'd been when pulling the trigger, and as her head fell lifelessly to the floor, I could see slivers of bone in her hair from where I'd shattered her skull. It was hard to look at, but not as hard as it would have been yesterday. Knowing I had lost a certain amount of innocence made me sad.

"Shit. Thanks," Diego said, pulling me out of my self-pity. "Damn, there's a ton of these guys." As he said this, four more shambled in from the connecting bathroom. He began stepping backwards, retreating from the advancing throng.

I followed his lead, not wanting him to trip over me. I knew he needed my help, that if I didn't do something, he'd be overrun and we would both die.

Throwing my morals completely out the window—no use having them if you're dead—I raised my gun two-handed and fired. I was surprised when the bullet hit my target in the forehead. I didn't have time to celebrate, though, because another zombie stepped into the fallen one's place.

As I was taking aim, I was distracted by the sound of

growling from behind me. I spun with a gasp to see the zombies from the room across the hall stumbling through the broken door as they made their way toward us. "One, two, three..." I counted them out loud as they came forward. "Four, five..."

At five, I rushed to our door. Diego had kicked it in, making it wobble on its hinges, almost as if in invitation to the extra zombies. I threw my body against it, closing off the route of the zombies moments before they reached us.

Unfortunately, the door had been in shambles even before Diego kicked it in. Now it was so bad that it wouldn't close, and there was a large, splintering hole in the center.

A zombie reached through the hole at face level in an attempt to grab me. Its grimy nails raked the side of my helmet, and I gave a holler of disgust and yanked my head away. It took a second swipe and managed to catch the edge of my helmet this time. With prying, cracked fingers, it pulled the helmet askew, causing some of my hair to fall loose. It took a third grab at me, and a chunk of hair caught in its grasp.

I pulled back sharply, letting it tear away a clump of blonde hair.

The zombie seemed satisfied with the hair, because it shoved it into its mouth, biting away pieces of its own hand as it chewed.

Another one reached for me, and I had to jump away to keep myself out of its clutches. As I did, the door creaked open, its busted latch refusing to catch.

I gave a frustrated cry and threw myself at the door again. I held myself as far away as possible, my arms outstretched to keep distance between the gaping hole and myself. Still, they reached through the door, barely missing me with their desperate snatches at the air.

Dropping to the floor, I pushed my feet against the door to keep it shut while still staying out of harm's way. I fixed my helmet with fumbling fingers, tucking my hair back underneath, and glanced over my shoulder at Diego.

He was shooting wildly, no longer working on killing, but simply on slowing them down. There were too many to take the time to aim.

I slouched down further on the floor, my back pressed to the ground for better leverage against the door. I arched my neck, trying to see Diego while looking upside down.

I raised my gun over my head, arms extended, trying to steady my sight on one of them. I was already insecure about my aim. Upside down, I was nearly panicking.

I was pretty sure I was steady on one of them, so I pulled the trigger. My aim was off. It hit the zombie in the shoulder instead of the head, but it did enough damage to stagger it backwards.

Diego glanced over his shoulder while he was reloading and saw me on the floor. His eyes traveled upward to the zombies attempting to force their way into the room. "Shit."

He didn't have much time to worry about the door situation because a zombie grabbed his arm, inadvertently spinning him around. Diego ducked the zombie's second grab at him and brought a foot up into its chest, forcing it back.

I attempted to get another shot off to help, but I was drawn back to the door as a rotting glob of meat splattered down onto my chest, spraying across the visor of my helmet.

My eyes traveled upward to see a zombie attempting to crawl through the hole in the door. Its entire upper body was through, and it was in the process of wiggling its lower half to the other side as well.

"Oh fuck!" I screamed, my voice shrill with terror. I brought my gun up and aimed at the mangled face. I pulled the trigger, and the head exploded, sending blood and rotting flesh cascading down on me. I held my breath, not wanting to breathe in any of the goop that was still dripping onto me, splashing out when it hit my chest.

I tilted my head back up to look at Diego and felt some of the blood run down my neck as I moved.

He was staring at me with a very confused, almost frightened look. A zombie reached for him, and he ducked it, having no choice but to return to combat.

I'd seen the look, though. I think my cover had just been blown. Regardless of whether or not he still believed I was Kenya, now wasn't the time to be troubled about him finding out my true identity. I pushed that concern to the back of my mind and brought my attention back to the door.

A few zombies were fighting to move the corpse out of the door, while others tried to crawl over it.

I fired into the group, hitting one in the chest and forcing it backwards.

I pulled the trigger again, my blood running cold as the chamber clicked empty. I tilted my head up to Diego just as a zombie took him to the ground.

He gave a holler of pain as the zombie tore into him, teeth gnashing and fingers raking.

I lay frozen in fear, unsure of what to do. If I went to Diego's aid, I wouldn't be able to hold the door closed, and more of those things would get in. If I didn't help him, I would be alone. Without him to hold off the ones in the room, I was dead anyway. "Damn it!" I made my decision quickly. I had to.

I let go of the door and scrambled to Diego's side. I stared in horror at the zombie that was attacking him, watched as it tore into his flesh. It was at that moment I remembered my gun was out of bullets.

Knowing it was useless, I tossed the gun to the side. Then I pulled out the hunting knife I'd taken from the van. I'd hoped not to have to use it, but I was out of options. Lifting the knife over my head, I gave a predatory scream as I brought it down into the top of the zombie's skull.

The blade sank into tissue and bone. I managed to crack through the skull, but apparently not deep enough. While the knife stuck comically from the top of its head, the zombie continued to tear away at Diego as if it didn't even notice.

I needed that blade in deeper, and I needed something to force it down with. I searched the area, looking for anything that I could use as a weapon. It would have been nice if I could get to Diego's gun, but it was trapped in the scuffle between him and the zombie.

I spotted a bedpan lying carelessly to the side in the right corner of the room. It was large enough, and I could probably get a decent amount of force behind it. I ran for it, ducking the clutches of another zombie. I skidded to a stop, scooped it up, and spun around, waiting to see what followed me to the corner.

One zombie stood between Diego and me. I walked slowly toward it, waiting for it to make a move first.

It stumbled toward me, growling as it did. It's feet shuffled and staggered along the linoleum. It was barely able to keep itself upright, but that didn't seem to hinder its determination.

The minute my eyes landed on its face, my breath was stolen away. I recognized him. He worked on Christine's floor. The two of us used to flirt back and forth on occasion, but nothing much came of it. From the way he looked now, a date with me was the farthest thing from his mind. Instead of my company for dinner, he looked like he'd prefer me as the main course.

I hadn't known him well, but seeing someone I knew as one of those things threw me. It made me realize that if he was wandering around, Christine might be as well. I did not want to see Christine like this. I silently prayed she was safe at home, alive and well. I stared at the man, Kevin, and my hands trembled. He made such a gruesome sight as he shambled forward, drool dribbling from his mouth. His entire nose was gone, and mucus ran down to mix with his drool.

In that instant, I hated him. I hated that he'd allowed such a thing to befall him. I hated that he'd forgotten who I was, and I hated that he'd suddenly made this situation all too real for me. I figured hate was better than falling apart, though. Hate would keep me going.

I crinkled my nose, unable to control my look of disgust. "About that dinner," I said, raising the bedpan. "I think I'm going to have to pass." I pulled my makeshift weapon back and swung it at his head, hitting him in the temple.

It didn't kill him, but it stalled him enough that I could get past.

I raced to Diego's side, trying to concentrate around his shouts of pain. Lifting the pan over my head, I let out a nervous breath and brought it down as hard as I could onto the knife.

It sank deep into the zombie's brain, sliding in to the hilt. The zombie fell away, but as it did, it tore the front of Diego's throat away with it.

I let out a horrified scream that bounced off the walls as I watched blood spurt from Diego's torn throat. Blood sprayed out every couple of seconds as if forced out by the beating of his heart...but that was impossible, wasn't it? Vampires didn't have a heartbeat...right? The blood drenched his shirt and the floor in front of him, spilling from his body at an alarming rate.

Diego slowly raised his gun and pulled the trigger, his aim still perfect despite his wound. Behind me, a zombie collapsed to the ground, suddenly harmless.

Diego's arm fell back to his side, and the weapon slid from his grip. He suddenly yanked the helmet from his head and tossed it to the side. Then his head fell back against the wall he was leaning on, as if he was too injured to hold it up any longer.

I finally saw the man I'd been with the entire evening. He had short, spiked blond hair. His eyes were a soft blue that, at the moment, were filled with pain. I dropped to my knees in front of him and, without thinking, ripped my helmet off as well.

He sputtered around blood for a moment before he managed to gurgle out a few stilted words. "You're the human." He coughed, and blood spurted from the hole in his neck. "I...I knew you weren't...Kenya does not curse."

So that was how he'd figured me out, my foul mouth. I was going to have to start working on that. "I-I'm sorry," I whispered.

For fear he might bleed out, I scrambled to a drawer a few feet away and yanked out a towel meant for patients. Returning to his side, I pressed it against the wound in his neck, attempting to stop the bleeding. It was useless, though. The towel was practically filled before I put it fully against his throat.

I gave a helpless cry and pressed down even harder. "I don't understand. I thought you guys didn't have heartbeats."

"Usually," Diego said around the pain. "Only when we are greatly frightened or excited."

I knew which category he fell under without having to see his widened, terrified eyes. I wondered with dread if it was possible for him to bleed to death. I quickly tossed that thought from my mind. I was panicked enough as it was. I did not want to think about him dying in front of me.

"Hold on, Diego," I pleaded. "You're—" I didn't get to finish the sentence because a gun fired, drowning out my words. The next thing I knew, there was a wall of blood cascading around me. I gave a surprised gasp and spun around, getting a glimpse of gray brain matter clumped in my hair as

I moved.

Ariel stood behind me, a sword covered in blood in his left hand and a shotgun in the right. His right arm was aimed toward us, and it took my eyes a moment to realize what he had his gun trained on. Kevin's body came into focus a few feet to my right.

It looked as if Ariel had shot him from point-blank range in the back of the skull. The closeness of his weapon had caused the back of the zombie's head to explode, the spray of metal tearing out the front of his face.

The shot left my ears ringing. I was lucky I was off to the side of the now fallen zombie. Otherwise, I might have been hit with the outskirts of the buckshot.

Kevin had snuck up on me while I tended to Diego. It was his blood I was wearing. The only way I could even tell it was Kevin anymore was by the plastic name tag on his uniform. There wasn't enough of his face left to identify him.

Who would have guessed when I met Kevin that one day I would be standing in a pool of his blood with bits of his brain stuck in my hair? Even more disturbing was the fact that I was relieved he was dead.

Ariel's other arm was aimed toward the door, ready for any more zombies attempting to enter the room.

I realized that his sword had killed the mob trying to swarm us, slicing through them with its razor-sharp blade. Many of the zombies were now headless, others cut in half. It looked as if he'd used the sword on all of them, saving the shotgun until he got to Kevin. He'd probably done it to scare the shit out of me. Either way, Ariel had committed a tiny massacre while I was distracted by Diego's bleeding throat.

As I watched in disbelief, Ariel jerked his arm, effortlessly dropping the empty shell out of his gun. He then slid the shotgun into a back holster and pulled a pistol from his thigh holster.

As soon as he finished, a zombie came shuffling out of the bathroom. Its leg was horribly mangled, explaining why it had taken so long to join in on the bloodbath.

Ariel swung the pistol around and fired, the bullet striking the zombie between the eyes.

It flew backwards into the doorframe before collapsing in a heap on the ground.

I stared at Ariel in wide-eyed shock.

"You're in an awful lot of trouble, little girl." Shoving the pistol back into its holster, he marched over and grabbed me around the arm. His hand fit all the way around my bicep, closing around it, and he yanked me roughly to my feet.

I gave a cry of pain and stood on my tiptoes to keep him from hurting me too badly. "Help him," I begged through the pain. At that moment, I wasn't concerned for my own safety. I was more worried about Diego.

I was suddenly hit from behind as something forced its way past me, and my knees gave out. I collapsed, but Ariel held me up by my arm, getting another cry of pain from me. My eyes fell on what hit me, though it was more like whom.

A woman of Asian descent was kneeling in front of Diego. Her black hair swayed as she moved, brushing across her thin shoulders. She turned back to look at Ariel. "What happened to him?" she demanded. She climbed to her feet and stormed over to us. "What was she doing with him? Why would Banning send her off on an assignment?" Her black eyes glared angrily into Ariel's. "I wasn't aware we were sending humans to do our job."

"We're not," Ariel said darkly, his teeth gritted in anger. He looked like he was going to drop the subject, but then decided to come to Banning's defense. "She deceived Banning into thinking she was you. He was too busy doing his job to notice the switch. Besides, nothing bad happened."

"*Nothing bad happened*?" She shrieked, pointing wildly. "Look at what she did to Diego!"

"Kenya, calm down," Diego said, his jaw clenched.

I could hear the pain in his voice, but he sounded better than he had only moments before. I looked at his throat. To my amazement, I saw that it was healing. It was still bloody and raw, but where there'd only been a gaping hole before was healing skin. It looked scarred and painful, but it was no longer just a bloody mess. He was healing in front of my eyes. "That wound was much worse a second ago," I said, pointing to Diego's throat.

"Thanks to you," Kenya spat.

Diego held a hand up to silence her. "It wasn't her fault. There were just too many of them."

"Too many for her," Kenya said with a sneer, nodding

toward me. "If you were with a trained professional, this never would have happened."

"She held her own," Diego replied, climbing very slowly to his feet. He stumbled and just about fell, an unfocused look in his eyes.

Kenya grabbed onto him, steadying him when he nearly toppled over. She held him around the waist, supporting most of his weight.

He rested his arm on her shoulder for balance. His eyes quickly regained their focus, and he shook his head as if to clear away his momentary dizziness.

Kenya was looking at me with disbelief in her eyes. "A human? She held her own? I'd like to see that." She said it sarcastically, and I knew she blamed me for what happened to Diego. Hell, *I* blamed me for what happened to Diego.

"If I would have been here from the beginning, you never would have ended up like this," Kenya said to Diego with an angry glance at me.

He didn't argue, piling on more guilt. He was trying to be nice, but the way he avoided looking at me said it all. He knew he'd have been better off with someone who knew what they were doing. I could have gotten him killed.

Kenya gingerly brushed her fingers along Diego's throat, getting a hiss of pain from him. "You should have watched her better than this!" The words were directed at Ariel, and she targeted him with a look of rage. "She never should have gotten here in the first place!"

Ariel's eyes flashed with anger, but he let the comment slide. Suddenly, he released my arm. "We better get moving. The rest of the group has proceeded to the third floor. I told Aldrich to have them move on while I trailed behind to supervise Diego and our assassin in disguise." Sarcasm dripped from his voice, letting me know his opinion of my actions.

"You've been following us?" I cried incredulously. My mind whirred as I realized he'd known. He'd known we were here, and he left us to defend this room on our own. He didn't step in until the last possible second. "You knew," I accused in disbelief. He'd known I was in here, fighting for my life. He'd known and just stood there watching like it was some kind of game.

He gave a short nod. "Kenya came to me when she realized her clothing for this evening went missing and that she'd been left behind. She was trying to figure out who would steal her clothes, and then I noticed the helmet on my dresser was missing as well." His eyes slid to Kenya. "Kenya went to Damian while I loaded up an extra van with weapons. Our suspicions were confirmed when she didn't find you with him. Damian told Kenya about your little plan to sneak along with Banning, so the two of us left right away. We made good time getting here. We arrived just as you were entering the hospital." He eyed me for a moment, a snide look crossing his features. "If you think I'm pissed, you should see Damian. Kenya said he looked ready to kill. He wanted to join us, but besides him being a hindrance to me, I was concerned he was going to tear you apart when we found you. Kenya told me she had to practically use force to convince him to stay at the safe house."

I ignored the comment about Damian. I could deal with him later. Right now, I wanted to deal with the man in front of me. "You knew I was in here, and you waited to help us." It was a statement, not a question. We both knew he hadn't come rushing in to save the day as soon as he could.

"I'm here, aren't I?"

"Now," I said. "Why weren't you here earlier?"

"Because I was teaching you a lesson. Hopefully, it scared some sense into you. You're not in junior high anymore. You can't just sneak out when you please and assume you'll come back alive."

"I don't know why your child," Kenya said, narrowing her eyes at me, "had to learn her lesson at Diego's expense. You should have let me come in here the moment we found them."

Diego's eyes widened as he realized Ariel had left him to suffer just to teach me a lesson. "Yeah," he asked, "why at my expense?"

Ariel took a lumbering, threatening step toward the pair, his eyes flickering between them both.

I was to the side of him, so I could barely see his face, but I didn't need to be head-on to be terrified by the look he gave them. It threatened violence if they continued to argue.

"You do know why, Kenya," Ariel said darkly. "I explained it to you on the drive here. If she didn't come close to dying, she'd never learn. We had to trail them from a safe distance until she realized she was in over her head and learned better than to disobey me ever again." He gave Diego an unconcerned look. "It is unfortunate that someone had to get hurt in the process, but he will live."

Diego took a step back and became silent as Ariel towered menacingly over him.

Kenya didn't step back, but she lowered her eyes to the floor. "You know it's not right," she said softly.

"I am sorry about Diego, but I did what was necessary to show her. I would not have let him die."

"It was a painful lesson," Diego said jokingly, but there was a hint of accusation in his voice.

Ariel turned deep blue eyes to him, staring silently.

"What?" Diego asked. "It was."

Ariel's eyes flicked back to Kenya. "We should get back." He turned back to me, his expression angry.

He stomped over, and I involuntarily cowered back from him. My left hand went to my upper arm, holding it in the spot where he'd used it to yank me to my feet.

Something that looked like guilt filled his eyes, but as quickly as it appeared, it was gone. "Stay with me." He lifted his sword and pulled his gun back out.

I nodded silently. I was afraid to be next to him, but even more afraid to be without him. I was once again caught in the dilemmas of this new world. It was hard to know what the greater danger was.

He pushed past the broken door and glanced over his shoulder. "Everybody keep up."

Kenya sent him a glowering look. Wrapping one arm around Diego's waist, she helped him take an unsteady step forward. With her other hand, she pulled a gun from the waistband of her pants. She held the gun up and clicked the safety off, as ready as she could be with her limited mobility.

I stepped out into the hallway after Ariel to find it empty except for him.

He caught my surprised look. "As I said, everybody has moved on. The floor was cleared with only minimal problems." He made his way down the long hallway to the stairs at the end, his back to me.

Lucky for him. Facing that way, he missed the dirty look I

sent him. It was a good one, too. I knew exactly whom he meant with that last comment. We were *the minimal problem*. Well, not we. I think he meant more along the lines of me. Screw him. There was a hell of a lot of zombies. How many had Mr. Big Shot taken out?

"Are you going to hurry up, or are you going to stand there and pout?" Ariel asked. He didn't turn to look at me, so it was pretty amazing he could tell I was pouting.

That pissed me off even more. "I am not pouting."

"No?" He glanced over his shoulder with an amused grin. His eyes flicked to Kenya, who was struggling to help Diego maneuver around a corpse. Apparently feeling a moment of compassion, Ariel said, "You can take him back to the estate. He is in no condition to be here."

I glanced over my shoulder to see relief flooding through Kenya's eyes. "Thank you," she said softly.

"Take the van we came in. I'll squeeze in with the teams that are still here."

"Thank you," Kenya said again, her voice thick with emotion.

Ariel nodded, turning away from the still bleeding Diego to look at me. "Are you done pouting?"

I stamped a foot. "I—" Gunshots from above caused me to stop mid-sentence.

Ariel cocked his gun and gave a growl. "It's time to join the party, wouldn't you say?"

I wanted to leave with Diego and Kenya. I really, really did. I didn't ask to for a couple of reasons, though. The first was that I was the one to sneak out so I could be here. I came because I wanted to find survivors. That hadn't changed.

The second reason was that I didn't think Ariel would let me leave. He said he wanted to punish me, teach me a lesson. There was no way he was going to let me skip out in the middle of that lesson. He would make me see this mission through to the end. Also, Kenya scared the crap out of me. If she decided to kill me for what I'd done to Diego, he was in no condition to be of any help to me even if he wanted to be. I did not want to face off against Kenya by my lonesome.

I frowned as Ariel handed the shotgun over to me. I looked at the weapon in my hands, surprised at its bulky weight. "What the hell am I supposed to do with this?"

"You aim it, then pull the trigger," Ariel said as if talking to a child.

"No shit," I spat back. "I meant because of the kick. It will knock me on my ass."

He had an amused look on his face. "I guess you better hope for carpeting then." With that comment, he bounded up the stairs.

I gave a long, aggravated sigh at his lack of concern. Not having much choice, I followed him at a slower pace. My movement was hindered due to the heavy, awkward gun. I reached the top of the steps to see Ariel pulling his sword out of a zombie's skull.

"They left a crawler," he explained.

My eyes lowered to the man who had been dragging his way across the floor, leaving a trail of blood behind him.

Ariel pushed past the downed zombie as if he didn't even notice the gaping hole he'd left in the man's head.

I stepped gingerly around the body. I'd seen one of them keep coming after serious injury before, so I wasn't taking any chances.

Ariel turned down a corridor with intent. I didn't know how he knew where the group was. I didn't hear any gunfire at the moment, and there were bodies littering every corridor. It couldn't be the body count he was using to find them. It must be vampire hearing.

I shivered at that. The fact that he could hear things I couldn't freaked me out big time. Right now, he was probably listening to the frantic pounding of my heart and enjoying every terrified beat. I wouldn't put it past him to get a sick thrill from it.

He scared the poor human nearly to death. Yippee for him, that sick bastard. I sent him another dirty look I was glad he couldn't see. I followed him around another corridor, and the group came into view. They were standing in the hallway, talking quietly.

Banning looked up from the group, and his eyes widened when they landed on Ariel. "What are you doing here? Aren't you supposed to be…" His words trailed off the second he saw me. "Holy shit."

Ariel nodded. "Yeah. You sent her off with Diego."

"No, I sent Kenya with Diego."

"You sent Aurora with Diego," Ariel said firmly. "You left Kenya at home."

Banning glanced around in concern, apparently searching for Diego.

"Diego was attacked. The two of them ran into a bit of an ambush, but he'll be fine. Kenya's taking him back in the van we brought," Ariel said.

A bit of an ambush? He'll be fine? I never considered having your throat torn out a minor injury. Ariel didn't seem all that concerned about what had happened to Diego. Not that Ariel ever seemed concerned. About anything.

Banning shot me a questioningly look before turning back to the group. "We've only got this last wing. Aldrich's group found blood on the ground floor and sent a group back to the van. We're already up here, though. We might as well make sure there's nothing else we can use." He started assigning different rooms to everyone.

I was shocked when he gave Ariel a room at the end of the hallway. He knew that I was to stick close to Ariel. Essentially, he was giving me an assignment as well. Feeling a bit proud about that, I followed after Ariel.

"Have your weapon ready," he said darkly. His eyes were narrowed, and he wouldn't even look at me.

I sighed. So he was still being pissy. Not a big surprise. With a little bit of effort, I lifted the gun up, feeling my arms strain with the awkwardness of such a large weapon.

Ariel stalked forward, his boots crunching on pieces of shattered glass that littered the floor. He reached the door assigned to us and brought his foot up, kicking it in.

I avoided the broken door, which was now swinging loosely on its hinges, as I entered the room. I shook my head as I surveyed the damage to the hinges. "Do all of you guys like breaking things unnecessarily?" I teased.

"Yes," he responded dryly, no hint of humor in his voice.

I rolled my eyes behind his back.

He suddenly stopped in his tracks and stepped to the side, revealing a zombie that was pounding repeatedly at a thick, metal door. "You wanted to come along and be a hotshot assassin. Now's your chance. Go ahead." He nodded toward the zombie, lowering his weapon. "Kill it."

If this was his idea of testing me, testing my limitations,

he was going to be disappointed. I'd killed too many today to feel anything anymore. "Fine," I said, aiming the weapon at the back of the zombie's skull. I angled myself so that if the bullet went clear through the zombie's head and ricocheted back, it wouldn't hit me. Then I pulled the trigger without a second thought. The kick of the gun forced me backwards a few steps, but I quickly regained my ground. I glanced at Ariel through blood-streaked hair. "Happy?" I asked coolly as the body fell to the floor.

His lips tugged into a slight smirk. He said nothing, and his expression quickly returned to its usual annoyance. I'd seen the smirk, though. He was happy. He got a thrill from watching me kill. Wonderful. "Let's go," he said darkly.

I turned to leave when a thought occurred to me. "When we first came in here, that zombie wasn't going after us."

"And?"

"What was he trying to do?" I looked at the large storage closet the zombie had been clawing at. Unlike most of the other doors, it was metal, and it was also firmly closed. "There's somebody in there," I said optimistically, "somebody alive."

Ariel looked skeptically at the door. "There's probably a half-changed in there. They were probably bitten and crawled in there to hide while they still had some of their sanity."

"You don't know that."

He gave a shrug. "Go ahead and open it." As I moved for the door, he added, "Let me do the talking." He lifted his gun.

I gave a sigh at his attitude and slid the door open.

A woman sat cowering on the floor, her eyes wide with fear. She wore a pair of pink flannel pajamas, and a matching pink hat covered her head. Her eyes focused on me, and she whispered, "You're not one of them." Relief flooded her face, and she leaned her head against the wall of the closet with a sound of disbelief.

I guessed her to be in her mid-forties. There were tired lines around her eyes and her face was dull with exhaustion. She looked unwell, her skin a sickly pallor.

"How long have you been in here?" I asked

Her eyes opened again, and she looked at me with a haunted expression. "A day...maybe two." She looked behind us in fear, as if expecting an attack. "Too long. I couldn't stand hearing those things out there trying to get in. It almost seemed worth it to let them have me. At least then it would have been over."

"Have you been bitten?" Ariel's voice broke into the conversation, all business.

I held my breath, fearing her answer.

"No," she said adamantly. "When I saw what these things started doing, I hid. You couldn't even trust the nurses. One minute they were helping a patient, the next they were eating them. I've seen enough zombie movies to know better than to let them bite me." She waved a hand at the closet she'd been hiding in. "I carefully searched the hospital for a strong, secure door and shut myself in."

Someone cleared their throat, and we all turned to see Aldrich standing in the doorway.

"We've finished clearing the floor. There was nothing left up here but the maternity ward." He shook his head, his earrings sparkling in the moonlight coming through the window. "What a mess that was." His eyes flicked to the woman in the closet. "Take care of her, and let's go. I'd like to get home before sunrise."

The way he said "take care of her" let me know exactly what he meant. I stared at him in disbelief. "What? Why?" I felt panic creep up my chest. "She hasn't been bitten."

Aldrich's face darkened as he looked at me. "I know that."

"You know? Then why would you..." I trailed off, unable to finish the sentence. Aldrich didn't seem to have a problem discussing killing someone to their face, but I did.

"She's of no use to us," Aldrich said as if it made perfect sense. "She's too sick to bear a child or be used as food. She'll just take up needed space in the van."

"So you just leave her here?"

"No," Aldrich said ominously, reminding me of what he wanted Ariel to do.

"Just because you can't use her doesn't mean she shouldn't be saved!"

"She'll slow us down. She is in no condition to move quickly."

"So carry her." My voice had become pleading. I begged for the life of the woman before me. I couldn't allow them to kill in cold blood when there were alternatives.

"I need my hands free for my weapon," Aldrich said, his tone dismissive. He'd obviously already written the woman off and was not going to compromise.

"I'll carry her," I offered, desperation creeping into my voice.

"You've slowed everyone down enough already," Ariel said.

I stared at him in astonishment. I couldn't believe he was going to take Aldrich's side on this. Stubbornly, I stepped in front of the woman. "I won't leave without her."

Ariel, angered by my defiance, took a menacing step toward me. "You will if I tell you to."

"You can't make me."

"I can. And I will."

In that moment, I knew I had him. He'd just walked himself into a trap. "And how would you do that?" I challenged.

"I'll toss you over my shoulder and carry your ass back to that van if I have to."

"For all that effort, you might as well carry her. At least she won't try to kick and punch you."

Ariel realized what I had done and shook his head in disbelief.

Now was my only chance. Being nice now might mean this woman's life. "Please, Ariel," I said beseechingly. "Take her with us." I threw in an added bonus, trying to convince him. "I'll do whatever you say. I'll listen to every command, and I won't try to run away again."

"Getting you to listen is going to be a lot harder than that." He was being sarcastic and perhaps a bit rude, but he bent over and lifted the woman out of the closet. That was all I could ask for.

She gave a shuddering sigh of relief, and her eyes met mine, full of gratitude.

"Thank you," I said, placing a hand on Ariel's arm in gratitude. "Thank you so much."

Aldrich rolled his eyes and left the room.

Ariel followed after him, an unhappy scowl on his face.

That was fine with me. He could be as angry with me as he wanted as long as he kept that woman with us. I glanced up at her thin frame, which Ariel carried with ease. When our eyes met again, I asked, "What's your name?"

"Ginny," she said softly.

"I'm Aurora," I replied.

"Enough of the chit-chat," Ariel grumbled. "Pick up your weapon and be ready."

I gave him a dirty look, but did as instructed.

"And wipe that shitty look off your face, little girl."

This order was more challenging than the first, but I did my best. Who was he calling "little girl" anyway? Just because I wasn't some centuries old badass didn't make me little.

As we entered the hallway, Aldrich shook his head, and a smirk curved onto his lips when he saw Ariel still carrying Ginny. Aldrich was being an asshole over the fact that Ariel listened to me. I knew if it was up to him, he would have simply shot Ginny and threatened to leave me behind. I wouldn't have had a choice but to follow, not if I wanted to live. He was mocking Ariel, purposely letting him know that he thought Ariel was letting me walk all over him.

Ariel growled deep in his throat, the sound carrying across the expanse of the hallway.

Some of the other men cringed, and even Banning turned our way, concern on his face. Ginny gave a frightened whimper. She looked white as a ghost, fear evident in her expression.

Banning was suddenly at Ariel's elbow, trying to diffuse the situation. "None of that," he said, his voice light and conversational. "We need to get out of here. It's been a stressful couple of hours for everyone. Both of you just cool down."

"Hey," Aldrich said, backing up and holding his hands in the air. "I'm cool." He waited a moment, his eyes shifting to Ariel. "Besides, laughing isn't a crime."

Ariel just stared at him, his face chock-full of aggression. Finally, he turned to Banning. "I'm taking them down to the van." His eyes flicked to the men waiting around for instructions. "I suggest you round up the troops and do the same." He turned and marched swiftly for the stairs.

My eyes met Banning's, and I couldn't help but let my fear show. These men nearly killed a helpless, infection-free woman. What would they do to me if they decided I was more hassle than profit? I was threatened and manhandled enough while I was considered to be an asset. At that moment, I couldn't think of anything I wanted to do more than get back to Damian.

"Aurora!"

At the barked command from Ariel, I spun on my heels and hurried after him like a frightened dog. I was afraid not to. Besides, I wanted out of this hospital. I'd seen enough death and violence for one day, for a lifetime actually. I followed after Ariel, having to nearly jog to keep up with him.

He didn't speak, didn't look over his shoulder to see if I was even with him.

"Wait up," I said, scurrying forward as quickly as I could in heeled boots. I would really have to ask Banning for a pair of sneakers.

"Keep up." He sounded as angry as I'd ever heard him. Granted, I hadn't known him long, but in that time, he'd been in some really crappy moods.

I went to complain again, but something in his voice warned me I shouldn't. The aching in my right shoulder was a sign to just leave him alone. Silently, I followed, thinking on the fact that I should not be terrified of my protector.

We reached the base level, still walking at a quick pace. On the ground, one of the zombies was left alive, a crawler, as Ariel called them.

As we passed by, it reached out and grabbed onto my leg. I gave a cry of shock, jumping frantically out of its clutches, heart pounding in my throat. I quickened my pace, keeping as close to Ariel as I possibly could without touching him.

"Frightened?" he asked, a hint of amusement in his voice.

I didn't answer him, because what was on the tip of my tongue he wouldn't like. It rhymed with…okay, screw the rhyming. I wanted to tell him to fuck off, plain and simple. Instead, I said, "No. I just need a damn pair of sneakers."

This finally got him to look over his shoulder. "I guess if you didn't dress so—"

"So?" I asked, anger on the edge of my voice.

"Scantily clad," he said, finishing his sentence. "Women today dress like they just walked out of a brothel."

"A *brothel*?" I shrieked. "You're saying I dress like a *whore*?"

"I said it nicer than that."

"You still said it!" I yelled, my voice rising.

Ginny was starting to look a bit uncomfortable with the argument. I couldn't blame her, yet I couldn't stop. "You're not so perfect either." I spat the words at him, my tone biting.

"Yes, I am," he said confidently. We reached the vans, and he opened the door, setting Ginny down inside.

I was stunned for a moment by his comeback. He really did think he was perfect. It wasn't just an act. "I'll have you know that your hair is just one of your many imperfections. You look like a woman with your hair that long." I was lying, of course. His hair was breathtaking, and there wasn't a feminine thing about him. I decided to go with a different approach. "And what kind of name is Ariel anyway? That's a woman's name."

He spun on me with a growl, his fangs showing. "I've about had it with your mouth. And Ariel is a man's name. It wasn't until that fucking mermaid—" He broke off with a frustrated snarl. "If I wasn't forced to keep you alive, I would snap you like a twig." He reached out, grabbing me by the arms, yanking me toward him.

"Don't threaten me," I said through clenched teeth. I struggled to get free of his grip, but he was too strong, too angry.

"You're in no condition to be making demands." He shook me, jarring the arm I'd hurt earlier.

I let out a cry of pain, and my attempts to get free of him became almost frantic. The realization that he could seriously hurt me hadn't truly clicked in my brain until I felt that white-hot rush of pain down my arm.

"You're hurting her," Ginny cried, speaking up for the first time.

Her words seemed to break the spell, because Ariel suddenly released me, and I stumbled back.

I gripped my arm and rewarded him with half a sob. I hated myself for it. I hated letting him know he'd hurt me, that I was afraid of him. I looked up into his face with a few unshed tears making my sight waver.

His expression was a mix between horror and guilt. His expression changed as quickly as always, his face suddenly heating with anger again. He raised his gun up even with my head, and my heart skipped a beat at the sight of his barrel aimed right between my eyes. He shifted the gun at the last second and fired just over my left shoulder.

A zombie shrieked and fell to the ground, its body bumping into the back of my feet as it hit the cement.

I stared at it in horror. How close had it been to grabbing me? How close had I just come to being bitten? We'd both been so preoccupied with our argument that we hadn't even noticed its approach.

"Aurora, please get in the van," Ariel said tensely.

I scrambled into the vehicle, taking a seat at the far back, crossing my trembling arms over my chest. I was ashamed I'd let Ariel make me cry. Just as quickly as I'd crossed them, I uncrossed my arms and wiped angrily at my eyes. I didn't want the other men to get here and see me while I had tears threatening to tumble down my cheeks.

Ariel climbed onto the middle bench seat, keeping himself at a distance, yet putting himself in a position to keep an eye on me.

We sat awkwardly in the van, waiting for the others to return. No one spoke. We were each distracted by our own gloomy inner turmoil.

After what felt like an eternity, the van door slid open, and Aldrich's face appeared. His eyes went to Ginny as he climbed in and sat next to Ariel. He made a huffing noise in his throat, a show of his displeasure.

Banning entered after him. He sent me a bright smile as soon as his eyes landed on me. "Hey, girlie. Nice find." He slid down into the seat beside me, kicking his feet out so he could stretch his legs.

I didn't get Banning; I couldn't figure out how he had gotten into a position of power. He was the only one of them that wasn't dark and scary. He seemed like a nice guy. How did a nice guy come to be in charge of the death squad? Easy. He wasn't a nice guy. Nice guys didn't lead a group full of assassins. That meant his chipper persona was fake, yet I'd still rather be near him than Ariel.

Banning reached his arms out, resting them on the back of our seat, putting one behind my shoulders. "I can't believe you snuck along. That was a bold move, sweets." He leaned up at Ginny. "I guess it was worth it though, huh?"

"It was," I said darkly, my voice lacking the light tone of his.

Banning brought his hand down and squeezed my shoulder. "Don't be so hostile, cutie. You should be thrilled with this outcome."

I stared at the arm he put around me, a slight glare on my face as a thought occurred to me. I spun in my seat to face him. "Let me see your arm."

He blinked in confusion. "My arm?"

I grabbed the edge of his shirt, pulling on it. I couldn't see what I was looking for, so I nodded toward the shirt. "Take it off." My tone was demanding, my words to the point.

Aldrich made a whistling sound that I think was meant to be a catcall. "Are you going to screw? Because that might be fun to watch."

I sent him a dark look. He may be a vampire, but even he backed down to the evil bitch look.

"Do you really think this is appropriate?" Ariel asked, a hint of fury in his voice.

"Do you think I care?" I snapped at him, my eyes full of hostility. Turning back to Banning, I spoke in a low voice. "I need to see something."

Ariel went to retort, but Banning held a hand up. "If she wants to see, then I'll give her a show." Grabbing the waistband of his shirt, he pulled it up over his head.

My breath caught at the sight of his flawless body. Muscles moved on an immaculate set of deeply tanned abs, making me take notice of the flirtatious vampire in a whole new way. I was curious as to how he was so tan. Legend told that vampires hated sunlight. It tended to make them burst into flames. I was sidetracked from my original task with wondering how he kept himself so dark.

He tossed his shirt to the seat, spreading his hands out to better show off his body. "Did you find what you were looking for?"

Anger quickly snapped me out of my stupor. "Yes." I grabbed at his bare shoulder, having to touch it to believe it. "You're healed."

His shoulder, which was as flawless as the rest of his body, had been in shreds only yesterday. I'd watched a zombie tear into him, ripping away pieces of his flesh. Had he been human, he would have died. No one should be able to survive having large chunks of meat ripped from their body without seeing a doctor.

I shoved his chest, my voice raw. "You inhuman asshole." I wasn't really angry with him. I was just shaken over the events of the past few hours, and once again, seeing the reality of the things that go bump in the night was terrifying. Diego was a stranger to me, so it was easier to accept his healing abilities. Secretly, I was starting to think of Banning as one of the good guys, maybe even a friend, and seeing the proof of his immortality was unnerving.

He caught my hand, pulling me against his chest. I could see by the look in his eyes that I'd insulted him. As he leaned toward me, his hair brushed my cheek, giving me goose bumps. His voice stayed lighter than his eyes as he whispered, using a modified line from the Big Bad Wolf, "The better to protect you with, my dear." His breath was hot on my face, causing my stomach to tighten in ways that made me uncomfortable.

I stared up at Banning through my lashes. My eyes first traveled up his chest, taking in his perfect physique. Then they landed on his eyes.

There was no hidden agenda in their depths. He just looked hurt that I'd called him an asshole.

"I'm sorry," I said with a breathless whisper. My voice caught in my throat, and my heart fluttered in my chest. I had to take a step back to clear my mind. "Could you..." I waved to his shirt.

With a slight grin, he pulled his shirt back over his head. "No problem." I couldn't tell if he was talking about the whole situation or simply about the shirt.

When he broke eye contact to pull on his shirt, I could think more clearly. "You're not the one who hurt me. You've been nothing but nice to me. I shouldn't have said that."

He pulled his hair out from underneath his shirt, the chestnut color of the thick strands gleaming in the artificial light. "My job is to protect you, not hurt you." He sat back down, motioning for me to follow suit.

I flopped down next to him. "I know that. It's a few of the others who don't seem to know what it means to be a protector." I avoided eye contact with Ariel. I wanted him to know he was among that group, but I didn't want to look into his hateful eyes.

Banning put his arm back around my shoulders.

I let him this time, not taking my anger at Ariel out on him. I would just have to remember to avoid confrontations with Ariel. I couldn't avoid him altogether, because his assignment was to protect me. Though *protector* was such a loose term to use for him, because a true guardian would never lay his hands on the person he was supposed to be keeping safe. I needed to stay away from his temper. My arm couldn't take any more violent outbursts.

As everyone else slid into the van, I scooted closer to Banning on the seat, deciding that not speaking to Ariel might be the best approach.

Chapter 8

I let out a shaky sigh as we trooped into the entrance hall of Alexandro's mansion. I didn't realize how good it would feel to be back inside and away from the zombies.

"I'm going to go get a room set up for Ginny," Banning said, placing a hand on my elbow.

I spun and looked into his gray eyes. Staring at him now, I knew I trusted him. I didn't have any doubt he would take good care of Ginny, making sure she had everything she would need for the day. All of my uncertainty came from the others. Vampires like Kieran, Alexandro, Salvador, Kenya, and even Ariel were what had me feeling so overwhelmed with living here. Looking up into Banning's eyes, I realized I trusted him with my life. "Thank you," I whispered.

His hand tightened on my elbow, giving it a quick squeeze in acknowledgement of my thanks.

It sent a chill up my arm, and I had to take a step back, forcing him to let go. "Can you let me know where you have her?"

Banning nodded, gave me a brief smile, and then headed off down the hallway.

The second he was out of sight, I let out a hiss of pain and bent down to take off my boots. I silently scolded myself for how I had dressed for my date with Eric. From now on, it was tennis shoes for all occasions, even dates. I rolled my eyes at that. Who was I kidding? There probably wasn't such a thing as dating anymore.

As I was bent over, fighting with the zipper on the boot, a shadow suddenly fell over my field of vision. I glanced over my shoulder and let out a silent groan when I saw Ariel.

"I need to speak to you," he said, voice low and gruff.

I abandoned the shoes and stood, not saying a word. I had my back to him, but I didn't turn around. I didn't want to look at him, didn't want to let him see the hurt in my eyes over the way he'd treated me.

He took a step closer to me, and I automatically tensed. The memory of him yanking me around was too fresh, too imbedded in my mind for me to feel at ease around him.

"Damn it, Aurora." Ariel sighed, and out of the corner of my eye, I saw him run a hand along the back of his neck. "Listen, I'm sorry about your arm." Though there wasn't much distance between us, he closed it with inhuman speed. He had a hold of my arm before I even realized he'd moved.

I let out a gasp of surprised alarm, but didn't pull away. He was inhumanly strong. If he didn't want me to, I wouldn't be getting away from him. There was no use struggling against him unless he decided to get rough with me. I would only embarrass myself.

From behind me, he slowly rotated my arm around in its socket, testing the joints as if looking for any permanent damage. "I didn't mean to hurt you," he continued, massaging lightly. "You just scared me, and I reacted. I'm not used to being around anyone so fragile. It's been a long time." He stopped speaking, his voice thick with emotion.

I didn't say anything in return. I didn't know how to take Ariel. One minute he was so cold toward me. The next, I felt like I was almost seeing the gentler version he kept hidden deep inside himself. I was afraid to speak now, afraid for him to shut me out again. He seemed on the verge of opening up to me, and I didn't want to ruin it.

His hands moved up to my neck, slowly rubbing, causing chills to race down my spine.

I could feel his breath hot on the back of my neck and knew it was for effect. He didn't need to breathe. He was only doing so to appear more human. His thumbs pressed into the skin between my shoulders, smoothing away the tension there.

Here I was with a vampire's arms around my neck. I should be telling him to stay away from me, but I didn't want him to stop. I closed my eyes and leaned into his touch. I knew then that part of the vampire legends must be true. They had a very sexual vibe to them. Between Ariel and

Banning, my hormones were going crazy.

Taking a shallow breath, I spun and looked up into his deep blue eyes.

He stared silently back at me, his blond hair surrounding him like a shining halo.

My breath caught at how absolutely beautiful he was. Sometimes it was hard to remember the gruff, disgruntled man when looking into his soft, emotion-filled eyes. I had to force myself to take another deep breath.

As suddenly as he captured me with his eyes, it was over. "You need a shower," he said, his voice lacking any intimacy.

I glanced up, seeing the blood caked in my hair. "Yeah, I guess I do." My gaze returned to his, and I already knew the answer to the question I was about to ask. "You'll be gone when I get out, won't you?"

Ariel nodded. "I must go soon."

I returned the nod. "I figured as much." I looked into his eyes and wanted to say more. I hesitated, though, and the moment passed me by.

"Banning is finding your human a room and will retire for the day once he's done."

"Her name is Ginny." I paused, looking down at the outfit I was wearing. It was totally destroyed. There were tattered holes in both knees, and blood was splattered all the way down my right leg to my toes. From the knee down, my entire left pant leg was red instead of gray. "Do you know where I can get some more clothes?" I asked timidly. I had thrown the clothing Banning lent me earlier into the hamper. I hadn't exactly planned on being covered in blood when I returned. I was sure the outfit Banning lent me was long gone by now. These vampires were a tidy bunch. Everything seemed in perfect order, any mess cleaned the moment it was discovered.

In hindsight, I probably should have kept Banning's clothes no matter what. If I'd been lucky enough not to be discovered at the hospital, someone would probably get suspicious that I was running around in assassin clothes right after they returned from a blood raid. Another dumb thing I'd done in a string of many.

Ariel just stared at me in silence for a moment before saying, "I suppose I could lend you something before you go running off to steal from other unsuspecting people." He looked down at the clothes I had on in disgust. "Though the way disaster follows you, I shouldn't say lend. I'm giving you an outfit to destroy." He turned and started toward his room.

I rolled my eyes and started after him. Great. Sarcastic and grumpy Ariel was back. As we made our way to his room, I couldn't help but think what a challenge it was to get along with him.

Ariel cracked the door and entered his apartment, not bothering to turn any lights on.

"Damn vampires and their good night vision," I complained under my breath, fully aware that Ariel could probably hear me. I stepped into the room, unable to see a thing once I moved past the small sliver of light shining in from the hall. I held my arms out in front of me, blindly searching my way through the room. "I bet you guys save a ton of money on the electric bill," I said teasingly, hoping he would get the hint and turn on a light. No such luck.

"We don't pay for electric. We generate our own," he said, voice bored.

I continued moving slowly in the unfamiliar room until I collided with something solid. I assumed that the something was Ariel's chest when his arms reached out to steady me.

I had my hands pressed flatly to his chest and could feel his pulse underneath them. It still amazed me that they even had a pulse, but there it was, sending a shocking tremble down my arm. Everything about Ariel was so intense, so extreme. The fact that his heartbeat could send an electrical shock through my body didn't seem odd. I felt my own heartbeat pick up speed due to the pulsing Ariel radiated. I turned my face up to him and could only dimly see his features in the darkness.

Blood was splattered in his hair, but it didn't seem out of place. He looked like some ancient warrior fresh off the battlefield. His shirt was sliced through across the abdomen, revealing a section of pale flesh. The slash must have happened at the hospital before he'd revealed himself to me, probably while he carved up the horde hell bent on eating me alive.

My hand reached out and ran over that smooth expanse of skin.

Ariel leaned down, his face near mine. He inhaled softly, his nose brushing my ear ever so slightly. His face moved to my hair and he smelled that as well, barely touching it with his lips.

My eyes closed and a shudder ran through me at the tender way his fingertips caressed along my back. It was hard to remember I was mad at him when he behaved like this.

The door suddenly swung open and the lights glared to life. Ariel jumped away from me as if burnt.

The second my hand was gone from his chest, I felt a chill wash over me. It was like being unexpectedly doused in ice water. I turned sluggish eyes to the door to see who had intruded upon our private moment.

Alexandro stood in the doorway, his face a mask of disgust. He stalked into the room, his long black trench coat brushing the carpet as he went. "I can see we are keeping this relationship strictly professional."

Ariel let out a soft, barely audible growl, which made my arms prickle with goose bumps.

"The way Kenya talked, you nearly ripped her arm clean from her body," Alexandro continued. "I hope she did not lie to me. You know how much I hate it when people lie to me."

"She didn't," Ariel said darkly, his teeth clenched.

"How did we get from that to this?" Alexandro asked. He tilted his head to the side, his black hair falling to curtain his face. "Are we feeling conflicted already?"

"It was nothing," Ariel said, his voice a snarl.

"One would think you should have learned from past experiences. These humans aren't worth the effort, Ariel. They aren't worth anything besides a good meal." His black eyes stared into me with hatred, boring deep, as if his gaze could touch my soul. "Betrayers and whores is all they are." Alexandro's eyes flicked back to Ariel. "And they die so easily."

Ariel rushed at him in a blind rage. Grabbing Alexandro by the collar of his jacket, Ariel threw him out of his apartment and into the hallway, sending him crashing into the far wall.

The blow to the wall would have broken bones if Alexandro were human. Instead, he climbed to his feet, seemingly uninjured. "Watch yourself, gladiator. You don't want to be cast into exile." He dusted himself off, brushing pieces of plaster from his jacket sleeves. "I simply wanted to tell Aurora that her little *guest* is settled in on the third floor."

He said "guest" sarcastically, to make certain I knew he was unhappy with Ginny being here. "I am retiring for the day." He turned as if to leave, then paused. "By the way..." He took a menacing step back into Ariel's apartment, his cold gaze locked on me. "If you ever run off like that again without your watcher's permission, I will make sure you are sorry. Maybe a couple hours of alone time with Kieran would correct your discipline problems." He spun and stomped out into the hallway. Looking over his shoulder, he said, "He does love to be locked up with pretty girls. Your job is to breed, not make waves. Keep that in mind."

My thoughts went into panic mode at his parting words. *I was here to breed*? I think someone forgot to give me that memo, because this was news to me. I wanted to argue with him, but I didn't want Alexandro showing me any more attention than he already had. I stood still, not letting out my shaky breath until he turned the corner. I looked up fearfully at Ariel. "What was that about?"

Ariel silently shoved a clean outfit into my hands.

He didn't answer my question, so I pressed on. "Why does he hate humans so much?"

Ariel still ignored me, pushing me toward the door.

"Ariel, what's going on?"

His hand tightened on my arm almost painfully.

"Ariel...I'm sorry." I didn't know what I was apologizing for, but I just wanted him to speak to me. He pushed me out into the hallway, and I felt tears of frustration brimming in my eyes. "Ariel, don't leave me. Tell me—" The door slamming in my face was the only answer I received. I let out a sigh, and my shoulders sagged. Living here like this was going to drive me insane.

I pushed my hair away from my forehead with one hand and started toward the bathroom. I couldn't get any answers until the sun went down, so I might as well clean up and get some sleep. Though when the sun went down, all bets were off. Someone was going to explain to me why Ariel and Alexandro seemed to have a grudge against one another, not to mention the entire human race.

Chapter 9

I was clean and comfortably wrapped in Ariel's clothing a short while later. I might not be with him, but just being in his clothes made me feel a litter safer. I was still angry with him for his actions at the hospital, but his admission of only doing so because he was afraid for me made things a little better. Lifting his shirt to my nose, I breathed in the scent of him. There was a mixture of fragrances, including his shampoo and musky cologne.

Giving a small, involuntary shiver, I let go of the shirt and turned reluctantly in the direction of Damian's apartment. I knew he was going to be mad at me for sneaking off behind his back, but I wanted to see him anyway. I was banking on the odds of him not holding a grudge against me when he found out about Ginny. I just wanted to curl up and relax after the stressful events of the evening. To do that, I had to face Damian first.

Upon reaching his door, I held my breath nervously, wondering how long he would stay pissed. Only one way to find out. Exhaling shakily, I reached out and tapped lightly on the door.

It was immediately yanked open, swinging inward violently, and Damian glared out at me. "What the hell were you thinking?" His voice was practically a snarl, his anger evident on his face.

I gave a sigh as I threw out the impractical hope that he might have cooled off while I showered. I didn't want to argue with him. Ignoring his question in hopes of him dropping it, I stepped past him into the room.

The door slammed shut, rattling in its frame. "I asked you a question. What the hell were you thinking?"

"I was thinking I wanted to save a life, and I did." My words were clipped and short as I fought not to return the wrath hurled my way.

Luckily, my statement seemed to deflate his irritation. "You did?" he asked in disbelief.

I gave a slight nod, feeling pride well inside of me. "Yeah, I did. If it wouldn't have been for me, they would have killed her."

Damian's brow furrowed in confusion. "How? Why?"

"She...she was sick," I said softly. At the time, I'd been able to hold my fear in. Now, looking back at how heartlessly Aldrich had behaved, I felt my voice waver. "Aldrich said she was too sick to have children or to be used as food. He said she served no use to them." I broke off, my words catching in my throat. "He told Ariel to kill her. I had to beg Ariel not to do it. If I wouldn't have been there..." My voice stopped wavering, and I looked up at Damian, my gaze strong. "I did it, though. I saved her."

"Where is she?" Damian asked quietly.

"Banning was fixing her a room. Alexandro said something about the third floor."

"Alexandro creeps me out." Damian blurted this out as if unable to help himself. "I'm glad I haven't seen him around much since yesterday."

My mind wandered to Alexandro's threats. I had no doubt in my mind he would do as he'd said. I would definitely agree that he gave me the creeps as well.

Damian paced forward into the room, then turned to look at me, his earlier hostility gone. "I still can't believe you lied to me."

"If I would have told you the truth, you wouldn't have let me go," I said matter-of-factly.

Damian shook his head with a slight laugh. "That's true." He put his hands on his hips. "Just don't do that again, okay? You seriously scared the shit out of me."

His hands drew my attention to his waist. That, in turn, took my eyes to his pants.

He was wearing a pair of gray sweatpants that were so tight you could see his thigh muscles bulge as he walked. They were also a few inches too short, only making it to mid-calf. They pulled tightly across the front of his body, not leaving much to the imagination.

Despite the seriousness of the conversation, I gave an unexpected bark of laughter. My eyebrows arched in question, and I looked up into his eyes. "Nice pants."

He stiffened at my observation with a look of embarrassment. "Orion lent me something to wear. It was the best he could do for the time being."

Orion was small. He wasn't as short as Banning, but he was barely as tall as I was. He was also very thin. He had narrow hips and a tiny waist. He was on the verge of being scrawny, but he had just enough weight to look fit.

Damian had a much larger frame than Orion. Damian was built more like a football player where Orion had a gymnast's body. Damian was nowhere close to Orion's size, as was evident by the fit of his sweatpants.

Damian shifted uncomfortably on his feet. "It was either this or wear something covered in blood."

"I had to borrow some clean clothes, too," I said sympathetically. "I got an outfit from Ariel a couple minutes ago."

Damian's gaze traveled to my pants.

They were practically falling off of my body because they were so huge. The cuffs dragged the ground. They were meant more for Damian's build than mine.

"Switch me," he said insistently.

"No," I said, just for the sake of arguing. "I happen to like these pants." Apparently, even the end of the world couldn't stop me from pushing Damian's buttons. It was a habit that was nearly impossible to break.

"Come on, Aurora," he begged. "These pants are tight enough to prevent me from ever having children."

"And that should bother me why?"

"You may want to have children one day. Do you think any of these vampires are going to get the job done? Doubtful. I'm your only hope."

I felt a blush creep up my neck. "I don't think we'll have to worry about that."

"Never?" Damian asked in surprise. "We've got the whole last man alive thing going on, and it's still a no? That hurts."

He said it jokingly, but it made me stop and think. At this moment, as far as we knew, we were the last two people left alive who were able to reproduce. For mankind to have any type of future, I would have to have a baby. That thought frightened me.

Alexandro had already pointed this out, but he was being cruel about it. It was easy to ignore the words of someone exaggerating just to frighten me. Now, looking at it from a reasonable perspective made it all the more unsettling. Rationally coming to the same conclusion as the terrifying vampire in a trench coat made it seem so much more dire.

"Aurora, please."

"Alright," I conceded, too freaked out by my realization to continue to bait him. "But you owe me." I quickly slipped out of the sweatpants. Ariel's t-shirt hung nearly to my knees, so it wasn't like I was exposing myself. I held my hand out for the sweats he had on.

"If you think I'm taking these off in front of you, you're crazy." He grabbed for the sweatpants in my hand. "Gimme those and I'll change in the bathroom."

I suddenly had a thought. I tightened my grip on the pants and kept them just out of his reach. "No. You'll do it here."

His eyes widened in disbelief. "*What*?"

I plopped down into a chair, picking my feet up to curl them into the soft cushion as I stubbornly settled in. "You thought it was funny last night when you were staring at *my* underwear."

His mouth fell open, and he stared at me in surprise. "That was different."

I propped my elbows on my knees and leaned my chin on my hands. "Was it?" I asked, my voice full of curious innocence.

He huffed in annoyance and shifted his weight, his expression turning to one of unease as he realized I might actually make him strip in front of me. "Come on, Aurora," he pleaded.

I held the sweats up and waved them in the air. "If you want them, you'll strip."

While I was holding the pants up just out of his reach, Damian's eyes traveled downward. Instead of looking at the sweatpants, he was ogling my legs.

The shirt I was wearing had ridden up when I plopped down, leaving the majority of my thighs bare.

Damian had an almost wolfish expression on his face as he eyed my legs. His mouth slowly slid into a wicked, mischievous grin.

I stared at him with a look of annoyance. It took nearly a minute for him to realize I was no longer talking and I'd caught him gawking.

He gave me a guilty yet pleased grin. "Sorry. I got distracted." Before I could realize what he was doing, his focus returned to the sweatpants. He grabbed for them, trying to yank them out of my grip before I could react.

With an exclamation of indignation, I yanked back. I pulled so hard, I nearly knocked him off his feet.

Damian stumbled forward, half falling on me in the chair. It forced him to relinquish his grip so he could keep himself from crushing me.

I took this opportunity to hide the sweatpants behind my back, tightening my grip on the fabric. "You sleaze!" I accused, unable to hold back a laugh. "How dare you try to take them by force."

With a laugh in return, Damian slid his arms behind my back, rooting for the sweatpants. "I never claimed to be a gentleman."

"No kidding!" I slid down in my chair, practically lying on top of the sweatpants and my hands to keep him from getting a hold on the pants. I knew if he really wanted to, he could take the pants from me without much problem. This was his not so sly way of flirting with me. I didn't care, though. This was the first time I'd laughed in days. I needed this moment of silliness to keep me from losing my sanity.

We wrestled for a moment more with me giggling and Damian's low chuckle sounding next to my ear. Then he gave up and pulled back. As he stood, his fingertips grazed along the sides of my breasts, causing a shiver to shoot straight down to my toes.

I gave a yip and smacked his hands away. "Pervert." I could feel a blush tingeing my cheeks pink.

"Says the girl who just asked me to take my pants off in front of her," Damian said with a sly grin, seemingly not bothered by my accusation in the least. He inhaled as if trying to catch his breath after our tussle. His hair was mussed, tangling to hang in front of his left eye. I hated to admit it, but he looked absolutely adorable.

"Quit stalling." I knew exactly what he was trying to do. He thought he could get me to back off if he distracted or embarrassed me enough. He would get his way as well as get to pretend he'd *accidentally* touched my breasts. He was wrong.

I wasn't going to let him get away with the way he'd behaved last night without any repercussions. "If you're too afraid to take your pants off, then I'll just keep these." I stretched out a foot and placed the pants in front of me as if preparing to don them.

Damian laughed and grabbed the drawstring on his sweats. "I'll do it," he threatened. They were too tight to be tied. Messing with the already untied string wasn't much of a threat. His teasing grin slipped a little. "You're really going to make me do this, aren't you?"

By the look on his face, I knew he'd hoped I would back down if he threatened to actually strip. Wasn't much of a threat, though, since I was the one who told him to do it in the first place.

"Payback's a bitch," I said angelically in reply. My lips curved into an impish grin. "Start stripping."

"You're evil." Damian grumbled a few more complaints under his breath that I didn't catch. Then he grabbed the waistband of his pants and pulled them down.

I gave a howl of laughter at seeing him in his boxers and clapped my hands in delight at my victory. Catching my breath, I said, "I'm not evil. Vampires are evil. I'm just mischievous."

"You're something alright." Damian threw his sweats at me, hitting me in the head.

I peeled them away with another round of laughter. "Just keep in mind that you did this to yourself." I lifted my hips off the seat and shrugged into Orion's sweats.

Damian's eyes followed my movements, watching intently as I slid the pants up over my hips.

I didn't even bother to say anything. He would just give me that fake innocent look and act like he wasn't doing anything wrong. Picking Ariel's pants up from next to me on the seat, I tossed them to Damian. "Cute boxers," I teased, settling my feet under myself and curling into the arm of the chair.

If he wanted to catch a glimpse of my undies, I should have every right to acknowledge his—which depicted the face of one of the Smurfs.

Damian rolled his eyes, quickly sliding into Ariel's pants.

As he situated his clothing, I gave an involuntary yawn that made me realize I'd only gotten a few hours of sleep in the past two days. The only sleep I'd managed to get was in Ariel's room before Salvador woke me up by trying to kill me. Besides being woken up to fangs in my face, I'd also dreamt my brother was a ravenous zombie. To say the least, it hadn't been a peaceful sleep.

"I'm sorry my little striptease bored you," Damian said dryly.

I yawned again. "I'm sorry. I can't help it. I haven't gotten more than a few hours of sleep in days."

"Me either," Damian admitted.

"You didn't sleep last night?" I asked curiously.

"I would have been nervous enough trying to sleep while those things were awake. When I realized you'd snuck out, I freaked. I was afraid you weren't coming back. I couldn't sleep until I knew you were okay. Instead of sleeping, I spent the entire night pacing."

I gave him a soft smile, melting slightly at his concern. "I'm glad you would have missed me." I stifled another yawn. "You didn't have to worry, though. Ariel took care of me."

I realized then that as much as Ariel frightened me, he protected me that much more. He was probably telling me the truth when he said he had been scared. I snuck out and put a lot of people on edge, not to mention put myself in danger. Though I would do it all over again if it meant saving Ginny's life.

"The chick you're staying with?" Damian asked in confusion, bringing me out of my thoughts.

I gave a soft laugh, realizing Damian had made the same assumption as me. "Ariel is a man," I said. "Go figure, huh?" I motioned toward his legs. "Do you really think that is a woman's pair of pants you're wearing?"

Damian glanced down at himself with a frown. "I just thought Ariel was a hefty girl." He looked back up at me, his eyes narrowing. "They have you staying with a man?"

"He's harmless."

"He's a vampire. There's no such thing."

"Okay, so he's not harmless," I admitted, "but he's not going to kill me either. He may be terrifying as hell, but he's kind of like my bodyguard. His entire job is to protect me. From what I've heard, he's the best."

Damian gave in a little, visibly relaxing. "He's not going to try to rape you or anything, is he? Rape isn't killing. Neither is breaking bones or torture."

I gave a sigh that turned into a little laugh. "No. He's not going to rape me. He's much too cranky for that. I'm not sure he even thinks about that kind of stuff. He is totally into the whole 'Kill zombies, grump at girl' thing."

Damian gave a shrug. "Whatever. Just watch your back, okay?"

"Of course I'll watch my back. We're living in a house full of vampires. I'm watching my back and my neck." I yawned again, unable to stop myself.

Damian caught the yawn. "Hey, why don't we both catch a few hours of sleep? When we get up, we can get something to eat and sit out in the sun for a bit if it's still up."

My stomach rumbled at the thought of food. "I haven't eaten in days." My mind went to the restaurant the night before. I hadn't even gotten anything to eat before the zombies crashed my date. That felt like a lifetime ago. "Isn't outside dangerous?" I asked, jumping back to the situation at hand.

"Surprisingly, no. Orion told me that fences surround all of the property. He said it's safe as long as we don't try to go beyond them."

I perked up at this idea. "Outside, sun, and food. I can't wait. We'll have to invite Ginny to go with us."

"Sounds like a plan. We'll get some food, relax, and spend a little time with Ginny. I'm sure she wouldn't mind breathing fresh air for a change."

My head, which was drooping tiredly, popped up. "We're not going to be sleeping together, are we?" I was tired, but I wasn't *that* tired.

"You always have to think there's an ulterior motive, don't you?"

I shrugged. "It's in my nature."

"Well, for your information, Miss Priss, I was giving you

the bed and taking the couch."

I climbed to my feet with a sweet smile. "I was just checking. I can't say that I could trust a person who gives someone they barely know a striptease."

Damian's eyes narrowed. "Very cute."

I dusted my hands across my sweats and pushed to my feet. I made my way back toward the bedroom and climbed into his bed, pulling the blankets up around me. "I know."

Damian had followed me to the bedroom. He stood in the doorway, watching me with intense eyes the color of rich chocolate. "Speaking of the striptease, I was wondering if you would switch me shirts, too. This one is way too small."

I looked at the shirt he had on. It was stretched tight across his chest, making his muscles stand out. I had to admit, though not to him, it was pretty damn sexy. His dark, tanned skin made it all the more delectable. "Nope," I said with a grin. "I gave you the pants. I'm keeping the shirt."

"You know, for someone about to steal my bed from me, you're not very nice."

I gave him one of the grins I had specifically saved for him. "I think you look...cute," I said, throwing his word back at him.

Damian looked down at himself. "So you like guys in this kind of get-up?"

I laughed, unable to help myself. "Yep. That is what my dream man wears, tight shirts and Smurfs boxers. Hey, maybe you should see if Orion has a pair of leather pants, because that would be really hot."

"You really want me to never have sex again, don't you?"

"Your sex life isn't my concern," I said, curling up in the sheets. "Besides, who do you think you're going to be having sex with anyway? In case you haven't noticed, there's no one alive left."

"Who knows? I may hook up with a sexy, undead vampire." Damian's face suddenly fell, presumably as what I said about no one being left alive finally sank in. "I may never have sex again," he said, and groaned in disappointment. "I'm talking good human sex, not cold vampire sex. It has to be like having sex with a corpse." He shuddered at the thought.

"In my opinion, when it comes to sex, you're not missing anything anyway."

"Not missing anything?" Damian asked incredulously. "You're so not doing things right if that's your outlook."

"I just don't see the big appeal, okay? That three-minute adventure in the backseat of some rich boy's car isn't that big of a thrill. I can do without it."

"Three minutes in the backseat of a car?" Damian asked in disbelief. "That's not sex, at least not good sex. I'm talking an hour and a half of pleasure. You've renewed my interest in sex, because I'm hoping you'll let me show you the fun of it one day. You'll forget all about backseats. Instead, you'll be remembering silk sheets and mind-blowing orgasms."

Heat rushed to my face, and I wished I wouldn't have opened my mouth. Looking at Damian now, I could see myself giving in to him, letting him demonstrate all of the pleasures he claimed to be capable of showing me. I could practically feel his big hands sliding along my skin.

I forced myself to snap out of it. My father had raised me better than that. I was not going to just throw myself into Damian's arms and let him have his way with me. My father might not ever know about Damian or the things he wanted to do to me, but I couldn't throw aside one of his life lessons for a man I wasn't sure I even liked...though sometimes it was temping, more tempting than I wanted to admit.

Every once in a while, when Damian would toss me one of those adorable, boyish grins of his, my stomach did somersaults. I could feel my resolve weakening. I found myself wondering what it would be like to run my hands through his hair to see if it was as soft as it looked. I caught myself wondering what his lips tasted like, and I was more than tempted.

I felt my chest tighten in panic. What was wrong with me? More importantly, what was it about Damian that made me want to toss caution to the wind? Here I was practically trying to talk myself out of a lifetime of morals because Damian made a casual, teasing comment about showing me that sex wasn't always a negative experience.

That's what frightened me the most. Something told me he could make sex very enjoyable. I frowned, not liking where those thoughts were going.

"Rory," Damian said, interrupting my internal struggle. "I was just messing with you. I figured you deserved it after the whole striptease thing. You can stop yourself from getting pissy, because I don't expect you to sleep with me."

"I know," I said softly. And that made it all the more alluring. He wouldn't push. If we slept together, it would be because I wanted it to happen. He was joking, but there was a hint of truth to his words. He would enjoy showing me what an adult relationship was like.

I rolled onto my side and buried my head into the pillows, attempting to fall asleep. The nagging thought in my mind as I drifted off was that I wondered if I might enjoy it, too.

Chapter 10

"Damn it!"

I awoke with a start at the sound of a loud clatter. My initial response was alarm, but the voice that had spoken sounded frustrated, not terrified. I forced myself to calm down and observe my surroundings.

Once again, the person cursed softly from somewhere within the room, and then an odd squeaking sound followed the hushed outburst.

I slowly opened one eye to find Damian kneeling near the foot of the bed. He was rubbing his thumb over a nonexistent smudge on a plate. "What are you doing?" I asked tiredly, yet intrigued.

He spun hastily, fumbled with the plate, and nearly dropped it. "Did I wake you?" he asked apologetically. He continued on, not waiting for an answer. "I'm sorry. It's just these plates. I cracked two of them together and thought I may have chipped one. Seeing as they belong to a vampire, God only knows what century they came from and how much they're worth."

I stared at the plate in bewilderment. "Where'd you find a plate?"

"In the kitchen."

I sat in silence for a moment as that sank in. There was a kitchen in a house full of vampires. Go figure. "The vampires have a kitchen?" I asked, just to make sure I hadn't heard him wrong.

Damian shrugged. "I know. Weird, isn't it? It's a pretty big kitchen, too."

"Did you find anything to eat in there?" I tried to keep my voice from sounding too hopeful, but I was starving. Almost anything would be acceptable at this point.

"Yeah," Damian said, sounding surprised. "I found some steak. I made that and whipped up some mashed potatoes for dinner."

"Vampires that stock up on steak. Interesting." I thought about that for a moment. "You're sure it's steak?" I sat up, intrigued by his discovery. I really didn't want to eat it and later be informed it was people chunks.

He gave a quick nod of confirmation. "It was in its original packaging. Straight from the vampire butcher." He shook his head with a wry expression. "The whole concept of them having their own butcher is creepy, but the packaging definitely says steak."

I shrugged in return. "Steak it is." I looped my arms around my knees, staring up at him as he straightened to his full height. "Now, how do we find out where Ginny is so she can join us for dinner?"

Damian produced a piece of paper from his pocket and held it up. "I found this on the door this morning. I guess Banning put it there. It's directions to Ginny's room."

"That was kind of risky for him to stop by here, don't you think? The sun was nearly up when we got in."

"Guess that's why he didn't stay to chat." He shoved the paper back into his pocket. "Either way, it saves us time."

I slid out of bed, stretched my arms over my head, and yawned. "Is our picnic ready?"

Damian seemed frozen in his spot for a moment, his eyes lingering a little too long on my body as I stretched. He swallowed thickly before dragging his eyes back to his plates as he set them in a packing crate. "Yep. All we have to do is get Ginny."

Deciding not to rag on him about his obvious interest in me, I instead looked at the old crate he was stacking things inside and laughed. "Love the picnic basket."

"Hey! I was lucky to find plates. Vampires may need to use plates for some reason or another. Picnic baskets are stretching it. They can't go out into the sunlight, so they're not going to be heading out on any picnics."

"Maybe moonlit picnics," I said. "That's kind of romantic." I grinned at the thought. I could almost picture Banning out on the expansive lawn with the moonlight shining across his face as he wooed some girl.

Damian rolled his eyes. "I spent my morning cooking for you. I planned this entire outing while you slept, and I get nothing. It's merely mentioned that the vampires might do it at night, and it's romantic." He picked up the crate. "They get rewarded for having a severe case of photodermatitis. To me, catching on fire and the smell of burning flesh is just gross. I don't find anything romantic about that at all."

I laughed at the affronted expression on his face. "Come on. You know girls go for that moonlit stroll stuff. Just because I'm not swooning doesn't mean I don't appreciate your efforts. I do. Very much. Now will you please quit pouting? It's very unbecoming, and I want us to enjoy the sunlight instead of pondering over vampire allergies to it."

With a chuckle of easy amusement, Damian hefted the packing crate onto his shoulder and followed me out the door. "I think I can do that."

We walked to Ginny's room in silence. I think we were both anticipating seeing the sun again and were lost in our own thoughts. It had been two days, and I yearned to feel sunlight on my face. I'm sure he did as well.

When we reached Ginny's room, I knocked on the door and went in when she called out in invitation.

She was sitting on her bed, face pale and lined with weariness.

I didn't give her tired state too much concern, though. I couldn't blame her for being weary. Her entire life had been turned upside down. All of ours had. Being a little overwhelmed was expected.

She slowly scooted to the edge of the bed, looking as if she were concentrating hard on that simple movement. She gave a cringe of pain as she finally stood. "I'm just a little sore," she said.

Damian and Ginny shared a look, and he rushed to her side. He held the crate of picnic supplies with one hand and helped her walk with the other.

The look they shared indicated to me a previous, private discussion, something I was not going to be let in on. "Have you guys met?" I asked, trying to keep my tone from sounding too suspicious.

Ginny shuffled her feet forward. "Damian brought me a

cup of soup earlier. He told me about your picnic. I don't remember the last time I was out to see the sun. It's been months," she said wistfully.

"You've been there, at the hospital, that long?" I asked in surprise. I couldn't imagine being shut up and unable to leave for months. It was a horrible thought.

She gave a brief nod. "It's been a long time, hon." Her movements grew better as she walked along, getting to see the outside world seemingly her motivation.

We reached the front door, and I anxiously threw it open. I was eager to breathe fresh air, to get a glimpse of what our new home looked like in the daylight.

I was stunned to the point of speechlessness when I saw the massive yard that stretched out before me. Yard wasn't even the right word for it. The property went on for miles. When we'd arrived a few days ago, everything had been dark. I'd been unable to tell how much land there was for us to use. Now, I stood frozen in shock. It was beautiful here, absolutely beautiful.

"I have everything set up in the back," Damian said, breaking through my trance. He started off around the side of the mansion, moving with a confidence that conveyed he wasn't as spellbound with this place as I was.

I followed him around the side of the building, and an Olympic-sized swimming pool came into view. Farther off, I could see tennis and basketball courts. "My God," I whispered in awe.

"I know," Damian said. "This place is like prison for celebrities."

I rolled my eyes at that. He still considered it a prison. To me, it was more like a sanctuary. I had seen the hospital. I desperately did not want to go back out there where the dead walked the streets.

Damian nodded toward a large pink blanket. "Here we are."

"Wow," I said teasingly as I noticed a bottle of apple cider chilling in a wine bucket on the edge of the blanket. "You really put some thought into this."

Damian set the crate down on the blanket, and Ginny slumped down next to it, her breathing labored. "I knew I was entertaining a spoiled, pampered daddy's girl," Damian said with a teasingly sardonic lilt to his voice. "I had to pull out all the stops."

I flopped down next to Ginny, a pout on my face. "You shouldn't talk about Ginny that way."

Ginny gave a soft laugh at my joke as she attempted to catch her breath.

Damian gave a surprised chuckle. He stared down at me for a moment, an amused grin on his face that had a hint of affection hidden under the surface.

"What?" I asked, patting my hair self-consciously. Sometimes when Damian looked at me, there was a tenderness in his expression that unnerved me. Banter and snarky comments I could take from him. Affection, not so much. It was too confusing.

He shook his head, his expression becoming almost self-deprecating. The moment of warmth was quickly over, and he simply plopped down across from us. Reaching into the crate, he fished around for a moment, then pulled out three plates. He handed one to me and kept two in front of him.

I looked at the plate in my hands with mock criticism, trying to return the mood to its light and playful air of earlier. "I hope this isn't the one you fingered up."

"I saved that one especially for you," Damian said with a wink. He then pulled out a few containers of food, and my mouth watered.

He handed me the container of finely chopped steak, which I eagerly opened. "This smells delicious," I said, breathing in the scent. I couldn't remember food ever being so appealing. "Where did *you* learn to cook?" I asked accusingly as I shoveled a gracious spoonful onto my plate.

Damian laughed and scooped mashed potatoes onto one of the plates in front of him. He then handed the plate to Ginny, sliding a fork to her. "I'm a good cook, thank you very much." He gave me a sly grin as he proceeded to grossly over exaggerate my old life. "I wasn't pampered. I didn't have a personal chef giving me my wildest desires." He popped a small chunk of a roll into his mouth. "I had to learn to survive on my own."

I stuck my tongue out at him and helped myself to some of the potatoes. "You're just jealous of the extravagant life I led."

Damian rolled his eyes in response.

We sat in silence, enjoying our first meal in days. It was the best meal I'd ever eaten. I didn't know if it was because I was half starved or if Damian was that good of a cook. It was probably a bit of both. I had to give Damian credit, though not audibly, because it would boost his already soaring ego. The food was great.

As I scarfed down a big forkful of potatoes, I noticed Ginny was barely picking at hers.

She was making a face with every bit of food she put into her mouth. She only gummed at the potatoes, never chewing. She looked like she was having a hard time swallowing, her face scrunching as if she was going to be sick.

"You okay, Ginny?" I asked.

She nodded slowly. "Yeah...I'm just a little tired." She set her plate down. "I'm also kind of full."

"Already?" I asked in surprise. "You barely ate a thing."

Damian cleared his throat. "Hey, Aurora, would you like to go for a walk?"

I tossed the last piece of steak on my plate into my mouth. "Yeah. I guess so." It wasn't like we had anything better to do, and I wanted to stay outside for a while. It was nice not to be cooped up inside the mansion.

"We can check out the land, see how much space we have. Ginny can rest her eyes for a moment while we do that."

Climbing to my feet, I brushed a few wrinkles from my pants. "I suppose I would like to see how big this place is." I turned to Ginny, who was already lowering herself to the blanket. "Will you be okay alone?"

She nodded her head. "I'll be fine. The vampires can't come out into the sunlight, so I shouldn't have to worry about anyone bothering me."

Her casualness surprised me. I didn't realize she was even aware we were living with vampires. She accepted it so calmly. It was amazing really.

If she was going to take it so smoothly, I guess I could try to do the same. "Okay," I said, swinging my arms back and forth in a carefree manner. "If you need anything, just holler."

Ginny nodded her head, her eyes already closed.

I spun to face Damian. "Now what?"

He grabbed my elbow and guided me toward the wooded area of the property. "I want to see how much space we're working with here." As we entered the trees, he moved through the thick brush as if being in the woods was second nature to him. He was pulling branches out of the way for me and looking at the sun as if it was a compass.

I tried to hide my entertained grin when he took my hand and helped me step over a fallen tree. Sometimes, he was kind of sweet...when he wasn't being a giant pain in the ass. Not that I'd ever let him in on that little secret. It would make him unbearable. "I didn't know you were the woodsy type."

"Kind of hard not to be when once a month I—" He broke off abruptly, clamping his mouth shut.

"You what?" I asked, ducking under a large branch.

"I...go camping." Damian averted his eyes, kicking a fallen branch out of his way.

His sudden discomfort had the hair on the back of my neck standing up and my senses tingling. He was lying. I was positive of it. I narrowed my eyes at him, studying his face for signs of the truth. "That sounded like a lie. I've told enough of them in my time to know when someone is averting the truth."

"It's not a lie," Damian said defensively. "Being outdoors soothes me, okay? Let's just leave it at that."

I rolled my eyes, deciding not to press the issue. He'd probably been about to say he took women camping every month. He said it soothed him. Great sex with strangers tended to soothe many a man. Personally, I couldn't imagine rolling around in the dirt getting leaves stuck in my hair. There were better ways to enjoy a man's company than behaving like cavemen.

I'll admit the trees we moved through now were gorgeous. Thick, green leaves hung from their branches, and colorful flowers speckled the ground. I was an inside girl, though. I didn't see the thrill of rolling around in the grass. It just didn't do it for me.

Damian brought me out of my thoughts with a question. "Do you notice anything weird?"

I took a look around, then turned to him, eyebrows

arched. "Do you notice anything that's not weird? We're living with a group of vampires who have an Olympic-sized swimming pool and a tennis court in their backyard. What the hell does a vampire need a tennis court for? They can't even go out during daylight hours."

Damian shrugged. "They supposedly have exceptional night vision. Maybe they play after dark." After a slight pause, he added, "Also, I think I saw spotlights around the outside of the court. They could always just turn the lights on." He shook his head. "That's beside the point. I didn't mean generally. I meant specifically. Do you notice anything specifically weird?"

"Yeah. I find it specifically weird that vampires have an Olympic-sized pool."

Damian gave an exasperated sigh. He grabbed my hand and halted me in my tracks. "Listen."

I paused and waited a moment. "I don't hear anything," I said, slightly annoyed.

"Exactly," Damian said with a snap of his fingers. "There's nothing. My best guess is that we are either close to the highway or that little shopping center right off of it." His eyes nervously glanced further into the woods. "There's absolutely nothing, though. I don't hear any cars, people, or life in general. There's just a void of sound."

I stayed absolutely silent for a moment, straining to hear anything, any noise at all. He was right. There was nothing. "We could go to the edge of the property. Banning said there's a fence. We could try to look through to the shopping center."

Damian nodded his head in agreement, hair falling into his eyes. "That's a good idea. I'd like to judge for myself just how bad it is out there."

"If it's anything like the hospital, it's bad."

Damian glanced at me, a grimace on his face. "Let's hope not."

We both walked in silence. I was lost in thought over what might be lurking on the other side of the fence. His thoughts were probably the same. Odds were, it was a disaster zone beyond this safe area.

My mind wandered to my nightmare from two nights ago. I had a sudden flash of Andrew, blood and hair embedded into his fingernails, snarling. I pictured Christine lying on the floor, gasping for her last breath. I shivered at the next image from the nightmare. It was Drew as his mouth inched toward my throat, his teeth piercing flesh.

"There's the fence!"

Damian's exclamation caused me to jump. Grabbing my wrist, he raced toward the high, wired fence that separated us from the outside world, pulling me along behind him.

I stared warily at the fence in front of us, not sure if I even wanted to see anymore. Before I could decide to turn away, Damian lifted a low hanging branch out of our way. About fifty yards out from where we stood was the shopping center.

With a gasp at the sight before me, I went to the fence. I placed my hands flat against it and peered out.

The shopping center looked as if it had been through a natural disaster. I guess in a way it had. Shopping carts were tipped on their sides. Cars were left abandoned, their doors hanging open as if their owners had been so hurried they couldn't stop to close them. I could see blood smeared across the glass doors of the small grocery store. The entire area was deathly silent. There was no sign of life for as far as I could see.

Suddenly, I heard a pitiful moan from the ground on my left, just beyond the fence.

A woman, or what was left of her, lay writhing on the ground. Another piteous moan escaped her throat as she thrashed against the earth underneath her. Her skin had a light layer of smoke rising from it, and she tossed about as if in agony.

I realized in horror that the sun was burning her. There wasn't enough left of her arms or legs to pull herself to shade. Her appendages had been too damaged from the at-tack that made her what she was. She was trapped where she'd fallen in death, forced to endure the sun's burning rays without any mercy.

Her eyes landed on me, and she pulled her lips back in a hiss. She chomped her gums together as if trying to bite into me from her place on the ground. Even with her suffering, her brain was programmed for one thing— killing.

Damian's hands wrapped around mine and gently pulled them away from the fence. "Safety precaution," he said soft-ly. He pulled me away from the fence and back against his chest, his hands never letting go of mine.

I stayed there, letting him hold me for a minute.

We stared at the woman on the ground. We stood together, hand-in-hand, as the last chance of survival for our race.

I stared at the suffering creature in front of me and didn't want him to let go. "I didn't know the sunlight burnt them."

"Neither did I." His voice was low and full of pain. "I guess their...allergy," he said for lack of a better word, "isn't as severe as a vampire's, but...apparently it's still enough to—" His voice trembled on his next words, his tone filled with disgust. "It's enough to cook them."

"She has to have been lying there since the sun came up," I whispered in horror.

"She's probably been here for days," Damian said, his voice full of remorse.

I gave a shudder and clung to the protective arm he had wrapped across my chest. I could feel his arm shaking and knew he was just as terrified. I couldn't imagine ever leaving the safety of Alexandro's home without being under vampire protection. If this was the sight that awaited us any time we ventured past his gates, we would never be safe out there. That thought chilled me to the bone. We could never leave. We would no longer be able to survive without the vampires. Yet, some of Alexandro's vampires frightened me just as much as the outside world. Sometimes, I felt less safe inside the walls than I did at the hospital.

In that instant, I realized Alexandro would never let us leave, even if we wished to. He wouldn't allow his only hope of repopulating his blood supply to just walk away. He would hunt us if we ran. He would hunt us down and drag us back to his house of horrors. We were helpless against him. We were prisoners.

Fear welled inside of me to the point that I wanted to collapse to my knees and weep. Instead, I forced Damian's arms off of me. "I want to go back inside now." I turned from the fence and began walking briskly back to the blanket. I wouldn't let him see me lose control. I couldn't.

Damian wisely chose not to ask what was wrong. He merely followed at a respectable distance, giving me a moment to collect myself.

Upon reaching the blanket, I started angrily throwing

things back into the crate. It was easier to be angry at our situation than terrified.

Ginny's eyes flew open at the violent way I shoved the containers of leftovers into the crate. Her eyes filled with concern as she asked, "What happened?" She saw the expression on my face and sat up in concern. "Damian didn't...he didn't...make an unwanted pass at you, did he?"

I shook my head vehemently. Her statement almost made me laugh. When wasn't Damian making a pass at me? If that was all I had to worry about, life would be easy. "No. I just have to get out of here. I've seen enough death to last a lifetime."

"So have I," Ginny said, her voice low.

Damian reached us and grabbed my hand, stopping me from breaking invaluable vampire china. "Hey," he said gently. "Don't worry about this. I can get it and bring Ginny inside once I get everything cleaned up. You go ahead."

"Ginny's not a dog," I snapped.

"It's fine," Ginny said in reassurance. "I'd like to stay out here a bit longer, and the help getting inside would be appreciated."

I let Damian peel my fingers from the plate. "Are you sure?" I asked uncertainly as much of my anger faded away. I felt kind of bad leaving him with the clean-up. He'd prepared this entire afternoon. The least I could do was help him take everything inside.

"Positive." Reaching up with his free hand, he tucked an errant lock of hair behind my ear. "I don't mind. Honest."

"Thank you." The appreciation was mumbled and I ducked my head in embarrassment so he wouldn't see the whirl of emotions swimming in my eyes.

Damian's grip tightened on my hand, squeezing my fingers comfortingly. When I looked up, he stared into my eyes, searching them for an answer to my sudden disquiet.

I pulled my hand back and leaned away from him. It was just too personal for me. I couldn't deal with the horrifying thoughts monopolizing my mind while looking at the worry in his eyes. I jumped to my feet and marched toward the house. I felt as if I would lose my sanity if I didn't leave now.

I was jogging by the time I reached the front of the mansion. I pulled the heavy oak door out of my way, slipped inside, and gave a sigh of relief as it closed solidly behind me.

I started walking slowly down the hallway, uncertain of where to go. I didn't have a room to call my own or a place where I could find privacy. Everywhere I knew, someone would think to look for me there. Most of the mansion wasn't even familiar to me. I could easily make a wrong turn and get lost. I so did not want to find myself in an unfamiliar place and faced with one of the less than friendly vampires I'd met.

I was so immersed in my thoughts I didn't see the person coming toward me until he was nearly on top of me.

He didn't see me either, because his eyes were locked to the ground.

When I finally saw him, I jumped in surprise. "Fuck!" I cursed, unable to stop myself.

"Shit!" The expletive escaped his mouth just as harshly, as if he hadn't expected to run into me.

Our eyes locked and we stared at each other in shock.

Ariel stood in front of me in nothing but a pair of boxers and a knee-length bathrobe that hung open and loose around his body. "Watch your mouth, little girl!"

"You watch your mouth," I contested. After those comments, we fell silent, staring at each other.

It was impossible. It was absolutely impossible! The sun was blazing down outside, and here was Ariel standing in front of me as if not affected in the least. Here was badass Ariel in a lavender bathrobe. "What are you doing?" I asked accusingly.

"What are *you* doing?" He shot my words back at me with an angry hiss.

"I'm not the one who's supposed to be locked up in a coffin."

"I'm not supposed to be locked in a coffin," Ariel said testily. "How would I get out if I locked myself in?"

"I don't know," I said, tone sharp and reproving. "I'm not a vampire. I've never locked myself in a coffin before."

"We don't..." Ariel stopped his argument, and I swear I could see him mentally counting to ten to calm himself. "That's not the point."

"No," I agreed. "It's not. The point is that you're up. During the day. While the sun is out. Why are you up?"

"I had to piss," Ariel said simply.

"But the sun is out." I was practically whining, but his presence defied everything I knew. It made life a whole lot scarier if vampires could wander about during the day. "I thought you guys went into a coma or something when the sun comes up."

"Tell that to my bladder," Ariel said, grumbling under his breath. With a sigh, he glanced around to make sure none of his dead friends were in hearing range. "Come here." He led me the short distance back to his apartment, moving automatically into his bedroom, where he leaned against a worn dresser and crossed his arms insolently over his chest.

As soon as I entered the room behind him, my eyes landed on his bed. I gasped, feeling almost betrayed. His bed was unmade, the black silk sheets tossed to the side. "You weren't even sleeping in a coffin!"

Ariel motioned for me to quiet down. "I never said I slept in a coffin."

Every vampire legend I had heard spoke of coffins. None of them mentioned king-sized beds with silk sheets. "I thought all vampires slept in coffins."

Ariel sighed and ran a hand over his face. "Alright. Let's get all of your vampire questions out of the way now, because I have a feeling you know close to nothing about us. I'm warning you. All the vampire lore you've heard is probably wrong."

I gave a nod, happy get some answers, even if he was just appeasing me so I would stop continuously badgering him. "Okay. No coffins."

Ariel nodded in confirmation. "No coffins. That stereotype got affixed to us long ago. Back when this country was first forming, there weren't many uninhabited homes. When someone came to a town, a home was built for them. Being vampires, we traveled from town to town seeking prey. There weren't places for us to stay like there are today. There was no such thing as a hotel. When the sun would rise, many times we would be forced into mausoleums or crypts. Because of the chance a crypt door might be opened by a human while we were sleeping, we shut ourselves in coffins to protect ourselves from the light." He thought about that for a moment, lost in thought. "That is one thing that holds true. The sun is not kind to us."

I took this information in, picturing Ariel hiding in a crypt from the sun. It seemed almost scary to me. If anyone had suspected them of what they were and knew where their daytime hiding spot was... I shuddered at the thought of how vulnerable they were in such a position. Looking back up at Ariel, I enthusiastically asked, "Does Dracula exist?"

Ariel gave an angry grunt. "No. Dracula does not exist. Well...not really."

"Not really? What do you mean by that?" My eyes were wide with interest, my expression no doubt far too eager. I was finally getting some answers, and from Ariel no less!

Ariel rolled his eyes, seemingly disgusted by the thought of it. "Dracula never existed. Dracula was Banning's creation."

"Banning is Dracula?" I asked in shock. I knew my eyes had to be as wide as saucers, but I couldn't help it.

"Banning *created* Dracula, if that's what you mean. Dracula was a big joke to him, a way to make a reputation for himself with women. It worked so well that long after he stopped using the alias, people were still telling the tales. In fact, it was almost two hundred years since he'd gone by that name before the book was ever published. Banning used to tease mortals with his tales of Dracula. He would confuse them with his powers."

"His powers?" I asked, feeling mystified. I'd never heard of Banning possessing any powers other than the obvious.

Ariel gave another sigh as if this conversation was extremely tedious. "All vampires have a power. It's something every human who is born has that stays dormant until after they've been turned. Some choose to strengthen it. Others choose to ignore it. Even the most submissive vampires have something special about them. They're just too afraid to develop their skills." Ariel shook his head as if he didn't wish to continue.

"What is Banning's power?" I urged, anxious to know what he could do.

"Sex."

"Sex?" I asked, disappointed. "He's really good in bed? That's not a power. It's more like a talent."

"It's not sex exactly," Ariel said with annoyance. "It's more along the lines of sexual attraction. He can mesmerize people, steal their breath away."

"So? I've had plenty of human men steal my breath

away. I think you're giving yourselves way too much credit."

"I don't think you're giving us enough credit. I'm not simply talking about taking your breath away. He steals your breath. Have you ever been so mesmerized that you forgot to breathe? If he would not instruct a woman who was deep under his power to breathe, she would die."

"No one has that kind of power."

"Banning does," Ariel corrected. "You've heard of stories where Dracula turns into mist and disappears into thin air?"

I gave a nod, picturing Banning in a long, black cape, throwing it over his shoulder and vanishing.

"Well, he can't disappear or turn into a bat. He would use this form of mind control to keep his victims held in a dazed state. He could slip away and be out of sight before letting them snap out of it."

"You said women. His powers don't work on men?"

"Only those that would fall victim to his charm." Ariel's face tugged into a smirk. "Only men that preferred..."

"Ew," I said, letting him know I caught his drift. "Guys who were into guys. Got it."

"Banning hated that. Sometimes when he was young and didn't have his powers under control, he would inadvertently capture a man."

I couldn't help but laugh at the thought of Banning freaking out because he had men hitting on him, had men sucked under his power. "What other tales did he tell?" I was wide-eyed and excited to know what legends Banning had created. I was seeing him in a whole new light.

"The thing about garlic. Not true."

"No?" I asked in amazement.

"No. When Banning was human, he had an allergy to garlic. His face would swell up. He would break out into hives. It was a learned behavior for him to avoid it. The rest of us eat it."

"So you do eat?"

"Of course we eat. Would you give up the taste of food simply because you didn't have to eat it? Blood keeps us alive, but it is not a meal. Nothing beats a good steak."

"So that was your steak we ate?"

Ariel's eyes darkened, and he stared at me, trying to determine if I was lying.

"Sorry," I said, offering a grimace.

He shook his head. "I don't know how you do it, but somehow, you manage to piss me off in every way possible."

"We were hungry," I said meekly. "What did you want us to do, starve?"

"I wanted you to leave my steak alone."

I sighed and decided to move the subject away from food. "What is your power?"

"Don't think I don't know you're trying to change the subject," Ariel said, a smirk touching his lips. He then fell silent. He seemed to be thinking, trying to find a way to describe his power to me. "I think intensity is the best word to define my power."

"Intensity? How is intensity a power?" I asked, confused. "Doesn't seem like there's much you can do with that."

Ariel gave a low, almost evil chuckle. "Oh, there's plenty I can do. I can take any emotion, any feeling, and intensify it...my emotions or emotions of those around me," he said, adding to the explanation.

"How's that going to help? I like you. I really like you. I hate you. I really hate you. It's all the same emotion, just different levels of it."

"It helps in a fight. If I know an enemy is frightened of me, I can make him so terrified his heart will simply give out from fear. I have the ability to kill a foe without ever drawing a blade. I could kill someone yet be a mile away."

"You can't scare somebody to death just by wishing it to happen. It's not possible."

"It is possible for me. It doesn't work all the time, mind you. Some people can control their fears, and others simply aren't frightened of me." He laughed arrogantly at his last comment. "Though that rarely ever happens."

The thought of someone not being afraid of Ariel seemed ridiculous. Ariel would have Batman quivering in his rubber suit.

"I can intensify the physical world as well as things of the mind. Imagine for a minute," Ariel said, "that I injure an enemy in a fight. I can multiply the pain, make them suffer so much agony they can't think around it."

I shuddered at the thought. Being wounded was bad enough without having to worry about having your pain increased by supernatural means.

"And there's my personal favorite," Ariel said, voice low. "I can use it for sex." He moved toward me, reaching a hand out to touch my hair. "Imagine every touch, every caress being intensified until you think you'll lose your mind from the pleasure, and still I give you more." He circled around me as he said it, his hands the lightest touch on my arms.

I shuddered again, but this time, it wasn't from fear. I spun to face him, chin turned up so I could look into his deep blue eyes.

His finger curled around my chin. He tilted my head back, lifting until my neck was as straight as it could be.

His gaze was fixed on my throat, and it made me wiggle with anxiety. Having a vampire studying my neck was a bit nerve-wracking.

He leaned his face down, putting his lips inches from mine.

All I had to do was lean forward a step and we would be kissing. I felt my heart speed up, thumping in my chest as if trying to escape.

"I need to get back to bed." His words were a breath against my lips, heating them. Ariel's eyes slid to his bed, and I couldn't help but picture him lying there, blond hair spread out across the pillows.

His eyes held a hint of suggestion to them as he stared at the bed. As quickly as it happened, it was over, something that was becoming a pattern with him. He pulled away and walked the short distance to the bed. "You can let yourself out."

I stood completely still, breathless for a moment as I stared at his half exposed body. I wanted him. I wanted to run my hands over his chest and rub against him like a cat. "Don't do that to me ever again."

"Don't do what?" Ariel asked, amusement in his voice.

"Don't use your powers on me." I tried to sound as angry as possible, though my breath still ragged from his touch.

Ariel slid out of his robe, leaving more of his pale flesh bare. "I didn't."

"You didn't?"

"No, but just imagine if I did."

I couldn't conceive him making me crave him more than

I already did. Any more and I don't think I would be able to control myself.

Ariel had one foot in his bed and was staring pointedly at me. I'd nearly forgotten he told me to let myself out.

With a huff, I spun on my heels. "Damn vampires," I said as I slammed the door behind me.

I could hear him chuckle as I stormed off down the hallway. I tried to ignore him. I had bigger things to worry about than Ariel and his stupid sexy powers. I had much more important things to occupy my thoughts with, like zombies.

Chapter 11

The day had gone, and the sun had set. The rest of the afternoon passed slowly but without incident. Damian, Ginny, and I had hung out in Ginny's small apartment playing nearly every card game known to man.

As soon as the sun disappeared behind the trees, I excused myself to go find Banning. He had promised me some answers two nights ago, and I wanted them.

By the time I got to his room, he was already gone. I realized with annoyance the house was enormous enough that it could take me all night to track him down. It was nothing more than luck that I ran into Orion, who informed me Banning tended to use the shower at the end of the hall as soon as he awoke.

After thanking him, I marched to the bathroom door and found it locked. Assuming Banning was inside, I leaned against the wall opposite the door and crossed my arms over my chest. I would wait for him if I had to. I had nothing better to do with my time now that the outside world was overrun with the walking dead.

Twenty minutes later, when the door opened amidst a cloud of hot steam, Banning jumped at the sight of me. Startling a vampire should have been harder than that. Didn't they have supernatural senses? "I've had stalkers before," he teased, "but this is kind of crazy."

I simply raised an eyebrow at him. "We need to talk."

Banning ran a towel over his head, drying out his long, thick hair. "That is never a good thing. Okay. I know you're not having my baby, and I don't owe you any money." His face brightened. "Are you horny?"

"No," I said darkly, feeling slightly insulted he thought I'd wanted him for a booty call.

Banning held a hand up to ward off my angry look. "It was just a joke. Sorry." He ran a hand through his still damp hair to brush out a few tangles. "What do you need?"

"I want some answers. You promised to tell me more the other night. You said we could talk, but it had to be alone."

Banning's lip curled into a wicked grin. "So you want to spend time alone with me? Sounds like a booty call in the making."

I stared coldly at him, daring him to continue. How did a vampire know the phrase booty call anyway?

Banning gave a sigh of resignation. "Fine. Let's go to my room so we can be alone." He said the last two words in a tone dripping with double meaning.

I fought the urge to give him another dirty look. I forced my countenance to stay impassive and followed after him. I wanted something from him. I couldn't afford to be so sensitive.

Banning's room was the next one down after Ariel's. Though room was an understatement. These rooms were more like large, very expensive apartments. Each dwelling had at least three rooms off of them that could only be reached through the main entrance.

Banning's place was amazing. It was the bachelor pad every man dreamed of.

Two black leather couches faced one of the biggest televisions I had ever seen. It had to be at least seventy-five inches, putting the fifty-five incher in my parents' living room to shame. A black marble table sat in front of the couches. I knew good furniture when I saw it. That table probably cost a small fortune.

There was a bar along the left wall made of the same marble as the coffee table. There was a light, hardwood floor by the bar, and the black carpet by the couches made me want to take my shoes off and sink my toes into it. There was a cozy, almost sexual feel about the room. It fit him perfectly.

Banning's hand on my back brought me out of my daydream. "Would you like a drink?"

I nodded, stepping forward and away from his hand.

He made his way to the bar and moved around it with

complete poise. Everything about him flowed. His movements were smooth and flawless. In no time at all, he spun
back around with two glasses in his hands full of a sparkling,
golden-colored liquid. He glided across the floor without spilling a drop.

"This is many years your elder," Banning said, handing
me the long-stemmed crystal glass. "Enjoy it."

I sniffed the contents tentatively and took a small sip. I
didn't often drink and didn't care for the little I'd tried. I
needed something to loosen me up, though.

Banning crossed the room and slid into the cushions on
one of the leather couches. He motioned for me to join him.

I was still standing awkwardly in the doorway, because
my high-heeled boots were caked with a mixture of blood
and dirt. I didn't want to track it across the carpet. I quickly
slipped out of the boots, leaving them at the door. I padded
across the thick carpet to join him. It felt as wonderful as I'd
imagined.

Banning patted the spot next to him.

I slid into it, noticing the soft leather felt like heaven.
"Nice place," I said. "All you're missing is a fireplace."

Banning gave me a look that clearly said he found my
suggestion absurd. "We don't like fire. Why risk immortality
for show?"

"That's right. You guys don't like fire...among other
things."

"Like sunlight," Banning offered.

"And garlic," I said, wanting to see his reaction.

His shoulders curled up like a cat about to hiss. "Vile, evil
thing, garlic is."

"For you anyway," I said casually.

Banning's eyebrows rose in surprise at my offhanded
comment. "Yes. For me." He took a sip of his drink, watching
me over the glass, waiting for an explanation.

"I asked Ariel about Dracula. He told me about your antics." I took a sip from my glass, the alcohol sliding down my
throat like silk. It was absolutely delicious. I waited for his
comeback, anxious to hear the truth.

"Ariel's been a busy boy," Banning said softly, "telling all
of our secrets."

"Not all," I corrected. "That's what I came to you for."

"It is dangerous to give away our secrets. There are some things better off untold, things that others will kill to keep hidden."

"No one is going to kill me over a little gossip."

"Are you so sure?"

"Right now, I'm the human race's only chance at survival. I'd say odds are good that no one will kill me."

Banning gave a half shrug that I took as an agreement. "What do you wish to know?"

"You told me zombies are a bad subject for you guys, especially Ariel. Why?"

Banning sighed. "You ask the questions most painful to answer."

"Painful? What's so painful to you guys about zombies?" I gave him a puzzled look. "Especially Ariel. Why would Ariel be bothered by something he seems to have no trouble killing without mercy? He's so gruff and unaffected by everything."

"It wasn't always this way with Ariel."

"No? He's so good at it, I figured he was always unpleasant."

Banning chuckled. "It is not that he's unpleasant. I think he is afraid to care. He was hurt badly before. By a woman very dear to him."

"So someone dumped him?"

"No. It was nothing so painless as that. Let me start this tale at the beginning."

"How long ago is the beginning?"

"For Ariel, Rome."

"*Rome*? As in like gladiators and chariots Rome?"

Banning nodded with a laugh. "That Rome."

I sat in awe for a moment. Ariel's life started in Rome. I couldn't even imagine what it must have been like.

"Ariel was a renowned warrior, a prisoner to the Roman Empire," Banning said. "People came from miles around to watch him fight. He was unbeatable. He would defeat all monstrosities they threw at him, no matter what the odds."

I pictured Ariel in chained armor, a sword in hand, slicing at a lion. The image fit, and it gave me a glimpse into why he was so difficult at times. He seemed like a man who settled things by action, not by discussion.

"An Egyptian woman traveled to his town. She had heard the rumors of a great warrior. She paid a messenger to set up a secret rendezvous in Ariel's cell. She offered Ariel an out. Being a prisoner, he couldn't have much hope for a future. He was there to fight to the death. This woman gave him a chance for something different. Of course, I will mention that this was a midnight meeting because she was not very fond of the sun. I'm sure you can guess where this is heading."

"Of course," I said, getting the idea of what was about to happen.

"The woman's name was Electra. She was a beautiful goddess of a woman. Her skin was like gold, her hair like black silk. Dark perfection is what she was. Absolutely breathtaking...or so Ariel has told me. These are the very few details I've ever been able to drag out of him about her, and believe me, I've tried. He won't talk about anything that happened after Rome. All he said was that she rescued him. She wanted him for a specific purpose, and he graciously slid into that role."

"She wanted Ariel to be her undead lover?" I asked, feeling slightly creeped out by that.

"No. She did not choose Ariel because he was attractive. She chose him for his fighting ability. She wanted a warrior, not a lover."

"Lucky him," I said sarcastically. "If I was going to live forever, I would want it to be for love, not servitude."

"They loved each other. Just not the kind of love you speak of. Electra was like a sister to him. They were together many years, long after I was made."

"When was that?" I asked in awe.

"Medieval times. I was born in the year 1327. I was turned into a vampire in 1348 at the tender age of twenty-one." His voice had a playful tone to it, as if these memories were so far away they held no emotional attachment to him.

"Medieval times? Like with knights and horses?"

Banning nodded with a smirk. "That would be the one." He took another sip of his drink. "I was a knight. I rode horses and carried around a lance." He laughed as if it were ridiculous.

"Did you enjoy it?"

This question seemed to throw him. A look of vulnerability crossed his face. "No one ever cared to ask that of me."

"I care," I said softly.

He looked down into his drink, swiveling its contents around. "Did I enjoy it? That is a hard question to answer. I suppose, in the end, yes."

"The end is the smallest part of the journey."

"In that case, I would have to say no. I did not enjoy it. My father forced me into knighthood. I wanted to marry. I wanted to be a father. I wanted to do something...peaceful. Look at my size. I was not meant to be a knight. I was not meant for violence and battle."

I didn't want to be rude, but I interjected. "You are a knight, though. You fight like..."

"Like I've had a century of practice? I was not always as skilled as I am now. I had no choice but to learn when I was forced into my fate. I was a mere child. I was clumsy and unsure on my feet. The others would take advantage of my size. It made them feel better about themselves to injure me, to pick on the runt. I would cry myself to sleep every night, my body nothing but bruises. I would plead for my death. It took nearly a decade, but I got my wish."

My heart sank and I stared at the man in front of me with pity. He was not simply a creature of darkness, an empty shell. He was a man. He had feelings, not just a thirst for blood. "That's terrible."

Banning gave a half smile that held more sorrow than cheer. "That was a long time ago, little one. Don't feel so bad. I prefer these times to the time when I was mortal. I like what and who I have become."

"And just what is that?"

"A cowboy."

"A cowboy?" I asked incredulously. "A vampire cowboy?"

Banning gave a shrug. "I've seen stranger." He gave me that cute smile. "I am a cowboy like none alive today. I helped tame the Wild West. I can ride a horse frontward, backwards, sideways, and upside down. I know the prairie days are long over, but I still yearn for the thrill of a good ride. I've even got a horse on the grounds for when the mood strikes."

"What's its name?"

"Nightshade."

"Fitting, since you can only ride it at night."

"You'll have to let me take you out one evening. There's nothing more romantic than riding under a full moon, the stars sparkling overhead."

I envisioned what that would be like, the wind whipping through my hair. I could almost feel Banning's back under my cheek while I held tightly to him as the horse raced through the woods. It felt almost like something out of a cheesy romance novel, but I loved it.

"Let me return to Ariel," Banning said, interrupting my daydream. "I know you want to know all about us, but I think what you really came for today is him."

I almost protested, but held back. I *had* come to hear Ariel's story. Another time, I would ask to hear more about Banning, the immortal knight. Maybe in a few days, I would ask him to give me extra details about vampires, but right now, I wanted to know what made Ariel tick. He was my guard, so learning not to displease him was important.

Banning seemed to relax now that we had dropped the subject of his past. "Ariel and Electra planned to leave Rome, to explore the world. The night of their departure, they strayed from the road, drawn by screams."

"When they got within sight, a frantic man waved them down. His sister had been thrown from a horse onto pieces of a broken chariot. A metal rod had entered her back and gone completely through her stomach. She was bleeding to death while her brother stood helplessly by her side.

"The woman pleaded for death, welcoming anything besides the pain. Her brother, Alexandro, begged them to do something for her. He begged for her life."

"*Alexandro*?" I asked in surprise. "Alexandro...as in the man who owns this very building?"

"That would be the one," Banning confirmed.

"It was Panthea who had been thrown from the horse."

"It was." Banning paused and lowered his voice. "Panthea had been Ariel's secret lover."

I took in a shocked gasp of air. The relationship between Ariel and Alexandro was strained at best. To know that Ariel had been a lover of Alexandro's sister said a lot. There was bad blood between them. I was starting to have a hint as to why.

"Panthea is a wild creature who will never be tamed. Both she and Ariel were aware of this. They got from each other what they couldn't from others. Ariel was a prisoner, an outlaw. He was held captive in the dungeons to be called upon to fight whenever the whims of others held a desire for blood. Panthea was a noblewoman, high class. Her husband was a man of power, thus placing her in a position of power by association. Her husband was an evil dictator, a vile man. His mind was too filled with torture and violence to worry about pleasures of the flesh, more importantly the pleasures due to his wife. He would use her and toss her to the side."

A frown touched his lips, and he shook his head as if he couldn't believe the man's stupidity. "Ariel and Panthea had an affair they both knew would not last. It was built on need, not love. Despite this, when Ariel saw Panthea dying, he begged Electra to turn her. He pleaded with her, offering everything short of his own life. Being as young as he was, he did not know how to turn another. Even if he had known the mechanics of it, he was still too weakened from his own turning."

He shrugged. "Electra finally conceded. She did not want to start her relationship with Ariel on such a sour note. At first, Panthea protested. She refused to be turned without her brother. She wanted his protection, his companionship, because she knew she had lost Ariel. He would not be taking her with him even if she lived. Electra agreed, wanting only to leave with Ariel. She turned both Panthea and Alexandro that night. She and Ariel waited only long enough for the two of them to rise, then they disappeared completely."

His brow furrowed, his expression becoming thoughtful. "I do not know what happened to Electra after this. The version of this story I know was told to me by Panthea. Electra was never heard from again by anyone. We only know that she and Ariel spent a long time in each other's company. Only Ariel knows what happened after Rome, but he's never told. Getting information from Ariel is nearly impossible."

"So I've seen. He's very...silent."

Banning nodded. "Ariel enjoys his privacy. Most of it is due to events that I have not yet gotten to in this story, a tragedy that left Ariel unable to trust."

I tucked a foot underneath me and leaned forward eagerly. "What happened?" Ariel was such a mystery. I was eager to hear what had made him who he was.

Banning sighed. "No one saw Ariel for quite some time, an awful long time. By the time he returned, I was already staying with Alexandro in this very house. It must have been the late sixteen hundreds. It was a time when people went on witch hunts and strongly believed in the supernatural."

"You did so much to diffuse those rumors," I said slyly.

Banning gave a deep chuckle. "Life is not worth living unless you can enjoy it." He shrugged. "And who was to know back then that my tales would become so popular? I was merely entertaining myself...and my female admirers." He shook his head, laughing again. "It wasn't the wisest thing to do when witch and demon hunts were conducted on the regular. I'm sure we would both agree to this point." He sat in silence for a moment, as if remembering that time long ago.

With another chuckle at his past, he said, "Let me get back to Ariel's story. I was living here with Alexandro, as were a few others, Kieran being one of them. Panthea was off, as usual. She had left with her lover Sterling many years before.

"Ariel showed up on the doorstep one night, his clothes in shredded ruins and blood covering his body. As soon as Alexandro opened the door to him, Ariel collapsed. How he even made it to the door in the condition he was in is beyond me.

"Alexandro took him in and gave him a place to stay. He was grateful to Ariel for saving Panthea's life, so he offered him everything at his disposal. Ariel never spoke of where he had been or what happened to Electra. For weeks, a haunted look dominated his eyes, so we all assumed something terrible had befallen them. As time went on, Ariel and Alexandro grew close. Though Ariel did not always agree with many things Alexandro did, he stayed silent. Having a safe place to live was more important than how Alexandro ran his affairs.

"During the 1600s, both men grew interested in mortal girls from the nearby village. They would entertain them here, lavishing them with gifts and tales of their bravery."

"Wait," I said, unable to stay silent. "Alexandro had a human lover? Alexandro who despises mortals?"

Banning nodded. "As I said with Ariel, things happen that change people. Neither man was then as they are now. They were more open, more innocent."

"What happened to change all that? Alexandro and Ariel seem to hate each other now."

"They do. There is nothing left of their friendship. Too many lines were crossed. Too many horrible things were done to one another." He paused, his eyes filling with an expression of grief. "Let me get back to the girls, because this is where the hostility started.

"Ariel fell absolutely head over heels with a girl named Angelina. She was as sweet as could be. Everyone loved her. The reason Ariel was so swept away by Angelina was that she could sense things. She had minor psychic abilities."

"Psychic?" I asked dryly.

"Yes." Banning saw the look I was giving him and sighed. "People used to have psychic abilities before they stopped believing in anything but science. I'm not talking scary, floating, seeing the future psychics that appear in your horror movies today. Back then, they merely sensed things."

Banning leaned his head on his hand, his elbow resting on the back of the couch. "The thing you have to realize about us, vampires that is," he said with a wicked grin, "is that we are independent people. We broke away from most of our human dependencies. As you can tell," he said, lifting his other arm to wave at the lamp to his left, "we generate our own electricity. We have a vampire for everything. We have a plumber, an electrician, farmers, dentists, anything you can think of. The food you eat here came straight from one of our own. The clothing the same.

"It was Panthea's idea. She reached out to vampires around the world, saying it was for our own good. We shouldn't depend on humans in case of another period like the witch hunts and, well, this. Everyone thought the idea was kind of loony, but they feared her. Many would agree with anything she said just to avoid her wrath. We're lucky she pushed the issue." He took a deep breath and plunged back into the story. "Back then, we weren't as independent. We had to go out for human foods, clothing, and those sorts of things. There is more we need to survive off of than just blood.

"One night, Ariel and I were on one of these trips to get a few necessities. Angelina owned one of the few stores still open after dark. She was the only one there when the two of us came in. Angelina watched Ariel the entire time we gath-

ered the things we needed. She seemed completely en-
thralled by him. When Ariel went to pay her—" Banning
broke off with a sad laugh. "She stared into Ariel's eyes and
whispered, '*You're not human.*' It threw him for a loop. Hell,
it threw me, too."

I could tell by the affectionate look in his eyes this was a
fond memory of his, but the sad sound to his laughter worried me. I had a feeling things were not going to turn out
very good for Angelina in the end.

"Ariel was a bit startled by this. No mortal had ever been
so direct with him. He wasn't human, and she knew it. He
quickly paid her and left the store. He never said anything to
me about the strange girl behind the counter. In fact, after
we left the store, he was back to his old self, and I didn't give
it second thought. She wasn't pointing her finger and
screaming for the men with torches, so I figured we could
leave well enough alone. I assumed Ariel felt the same way.
I later found out he returned to that store, night after night,
wanting to know how she knew he was different. I'm sure
you can figure out the rest. They talked. They flirted. They
fell in love. The bond between Ariel and Alexandro grew even
stronger now that they both had human companions.

"Angelina and Alexandro's Colleta got along perfectly. It
was like one big, mushy, happy vampire family. It made me
want to vomit, you know?" He chuckled. "I loved Angelina,
though. She was a doll to every one of us. The only problem
was Colleta's father. He was a political man, always looking
to advance himself. He was big into witch hunts, vampire
executions, you name it. When he caught Colleta with Alexandro, he lost it. Alexandro was not highly ranked in socie-
ty. He wasn't a rich nobleman. Basically, he wouldn't be a
good political ally, which is what he wanted in a husband for
his daughter. Before the town could find out about Colleta's
involvement with Alexandro, her father accused him of being
a vampire. It was a wild, lucky guess, a stab in the dark.

"The town was in an uproar, ready to kill Alexandro.
What her father didn't see coming was Colleta's rebellion.
She ran to Alexandro, defying her father and the town. The
townsfolk accused her of being a witch and a vampire's fa-
miliar. For months, Colleta hid here under our protection.
The villagers could not get through our walls. Everything

would have been fine until Colleta decided to sneak out.

"She was feeling smothered because she wasn't able to leave this house. She couldn't take being with only vampire companions. She needed human contact. She needed someone to walk with her in the sunlight, someone other than Angelina. She missed her family.

"Once outside our protection, she was quickly captured and taken to the local prison. When her father visited her cell, she wept and begged for his forgiveness. She claimed Alexandro had captured her with his dark powers. She betrayed us all, giving her father names and descriptions of each of us. She told our vulnerabilities, our secrets. She spilled anything that would put her back into his good graces.

"He promised he would spare her and kill the demon that stole her innocence. He waged a war against us, killing those he caught outside the walls." Banning looked up at me, his eyes wide with past fears. "They would leave us to burn in the sun. They would tie our own outside our gates so we could hear their screams as they were tortured. There was nothing we could do but stand at the windows and watch helplessly while our friends burned."

Goose bumps formed along my arms at the thought. I couldn't imagine anything more terrifying than being trapped inside, waiting for death to come to any who tried to escape.

"We had to go out," Banning continued, his voice haunted. "We needed food. We needed clothing..." His eyes drifted down then back up to me, his intense and frightened gaze locking on mine. "We needed them." He stopped talking, his eyes glossy and unfocused as he remembered the horrors. "She told them our worst fears."

Never in my life had I imagined vampires as victims. They were supposed to be the bad guys. This story defied that logic. It made me sick to my stomach for them. I could see the anguish they'd suffered reflected in Banning's eyes and knew it was inhuman, the things that had been done to them.

"When he was unable to flush Alexandro out, he found the best way to hurt him." Banning's voice was low and had a slight tremble to it. "One night, just before sunrise, the whole town came marching to our gates. Of course, we all went to the windows to see what was going to happen."

Banning shivered, and I knew it had nothing to do with

the temperature of the room. "Colleta's father dragged her to our gates. He held her by the hair, shoving her face into the fence. He hollered up to Alexandro and told him to come rescue his dark bride. He tied his own daughter to a stake and threatened to burn her alive unless Alexandro came down and turned himself in. He dared him to stop it."

Banning paused for a moment, and I knew the tale was too painful for him to keep going. He needed a moment to collect himself, so I sat silently, waiting until he found the strength to continue.

"Colleta screamed and begged for her life. She cried out to Alexandro over and over again. Alexandro stood at his window and stared unemotionally down at what he claimed was the love of his life. He didn't even blink as they lit the wood around her. It was as if he didn't want to miss a moment of it." He shook his head with disgust at the memory.

His open distaste for Alexandro's actions made me once again aware of how evil the man was. How could he not care about Colleta? Sure, she'd betrayed him, but that didn't make love instantly go away. Had nothing lingered in his blackened soul?

"Ariel begged him to go to her aid. He pleaded with Alexandro to save Colleta's life. When Alexandro refused, Ariel said he would go down for her." His hand balled into a fist, and his eyes hardened. "Alexandro made it clear that Ariel was to stay exactly where he was. He was not to interfere. If Ariel was to defy this order, he would be banished from the home, forced to stay outside with the mob of angry humans.

"Angelina tried to reason with him as tears rolled down her cheeks. She grabbed onto his arm, trying to force him to listen to her. Alexandro backhanded her in the face, yelling, 'Get this human out of my sight!' It was at that moment his hatred for mortals started.

"Ariel was enraged that Alexandro had laid a hand on Angelina. The two of them had a dreadful argument, not only about Alexandro's violence toward the woman Ariel loved, but the heartlessness in leaving Colleta to die. In the end, it was apparent that there was nothing Ariel could do to save the condemned girl. He simply scooped Angelina off the floor and cradled her against his chest while she cried.

"Ariel made sure she kept her face buried into his shoulder so she couldn't see Colleta burning. Though he would not let Angelina witness such a horror, he watched the treachery with hatred for Alexandro brewing in his eyes. He covered Angelina's ears, but could not protect himself from Colleta's tortured screams.

"Throughout the event, the villagers cheered. What a great man Colleta's father was in their eyes. He would not give in to evil. He would punish his own daughter if it meant keeping them safe.

"We all stood by helplessly, unable to stop the injustice. We watched until there was nothing left of Colleta but ash." Banning sighed again as if he didn't want to continue. He shook his head, but pressed on. "The next night, Alexandro waged a war against the village. If you ever wondered how ghost towns came about, here's your answer. Alexandro took Kieran with him, and together they slaughtered the entire village. They killed women and children, murdering many in their beds. They took no pity on anyone. In a single night, they wiped out every living person. They reappeared at dawn on our doorstep covered in blood and gore. Alexandro had Colleta's father's head on a stake, which he stuck in the yard like a trophy."

"Kieran helped him?" I asked in disgust. "Why does that not surprise me?"

"Kieran was disturbed from the beginning of his creation," Banning explained. "Alexandro can't be blamed for all of his problems, but Kieran only followed what he was taught once he joined us here. Alexandro took an already demented mind and helped sculpt him into what he is today. He instilled his hate and murderous tendencies on someone willing to learn."

"He's evil," I said softly. "Anyone with a conscience would not be swayed to slaughter that many people so easily."

"I am not sure Kieran ever had a conscience. He was always a violent man. Alexandro merely helped him perfect his skills." Banning shifted on the couch. "We're about to get to the tragedy that changed Ariel forever." He took a long drink as if to stall the rest of his tale. "The morning after the slaughter, Angelina left the safety of our walls. She figured that since everyone in the town was dead, she would be safe.

"She went down to Colleta's ashes and dug out the necklace Colleta always wore. It was one given to her by Alexandro. Angelina's family was long dead before she met Ariel. She'd been alone really. Colleta was her only mortal friend and the only person of the town who she mourned. She wanted the necklace as a token of her friend's existence.

"When Ariel woke, he was enraged. He couldn't believe she had left without his protection. It wasn't until he realized she was unharmed that he calmed down. His concerns were warranted, because something happened to Angelina while she was in the village. It took him a few days to notice there was something wrong. He fawned over her, begging her to tell him what had happened to her while she was out.

"After a few hours of his prodding, she broke down and admitted she'd seen Colleta's little cousin, John. She'd stayed silent for fear that Alexandro would hunt John down and kill him if he knew. She finally spoke up, because she realized there had been something wrong with John. She pulled up the sleeve of her shirt..."

I groaned. I could guess what was coming next. "He bit her," I said softly. "Didn't he?"

Banning nodded. "Angelina pulled up her sleeve and showed Ariel a bite. Ariel went ballistic. He went out in search of Colleta's cousin to confirm his fears. He left Angelina in my care while he was gone.

"I knew even before Ariel returned that Angelina was infected. She had started to turn before my eyes. I had to sit and listen to her growl and cry and beg. She was so sick, too. She couldn't eat, couldn't sleep. I thought she was going to vomit out her organs she was so ill. It got to the point where I had to tie her down to keep her from biting me. When she was herself, she would weep and beg me to untie her. She would promise me she wouldn't try to bite me again.

"I knew she would be unable to help herself, so I had to leave her lying there. Her fear pushed at me, filling me with guilt. I almost untied her quite a few times." Banning shook his head sadly. "I sat with her for hours while she cried for Ariel. She knew she was dying and wanted him at her side."

He swallowed thickly. "Two nights later, I heard a clatter outside the room. I opened the door to find Ariel collapsed in the hall, blood covering his clothes. His face was in his hands, and his shoulders shook with inconsolable sobs. I touched his shoulder and told him he needed to be with Angelina. I knew he realized she was dying. I didn't need to warn him.

"He looked up at me, removing his hands from his face. He was a mess, Aurora. I will never forget the sight, the look in his eyes. The blood from his hands was streaked across his face. His eyes were bloodshot and had a completely hollow look to them. I could tell by the deadened look in his eyes that, when Angelina died, his soul would be dying with her. He wasn't ever going to be the same.

"He went to her bedside and collapsed to his knees in front of it. It was the worst thing I've ever had to witness. He cried and stroked her hair and…" Banning looked almost sick. "She tried to bite him."

He exhaled shakily, raw emotion on his face as he told me the horrors of Ariel's past. It wasn't his story, nor had he been the one in love with Angelina, but it pained him to tell it all the same. "When Ariel jumped back, I could see the anger and hatred in his eyes. I was afraid of what he was going to do. He yelled at me to hold her head still. I knew in that instant what he planned to attempt."

Banning took a deep breath and let it out slowly. "When someone is bitten, there is a very slight chance they can be saved. If a vampire drains someone bitten by a zombie and tries to turn them, they have a chance. The two diseases will fight over who gets claim to the body. They will fight until one side wins, zombie or vampire. Or they will battle until they kill each other, killing the person with them. It is a very violent, painful process. Even if the vampire side prevails, there is no accounting for the person's mind. It is torture for the person and not likely to work.

"Ariel's love for Angelina made him make that decision. If there was any chance that he could save her, he was going to take it. He made me hold her head down while he did it. She hissed and thrashed, trying to savagely tear into us." Banning shivered again. "Ariel knew if Alexandro heard what we were doing, he would have Angelina killed. Ariel jammed her mouth shut and covered it with a rag, forcing her silent. I thought he was going to suffocate her. It was at that moment when she turned back to herself. Ariel was blocking off her airflow while his teeth imbedded into her neck. She screamed in terror, causing Ariel to release her. Fangs dripping with her blood, he begged for her to trust him. He told her he was going to save her. Then he kissed her.

"Angelina trusted him wholeheartedly. She closed her eyes and turned her neck to him in silent offering. As he bent down to continue draining her, she whispered something into his ear. Ariel cried as he finished his task, tears sliding down to mix with the blood. To this day, I don't know what she said to him. I'm not sure I even want to. Whatever it was, it cut him to the core. I think a part of him broke there in that room, a part he never got back."

He fell silent for a moment, and it was only then that I felt the tears on my cheeks. My heart ached for Ariel, my reluctant warrior. I couldn't fathom how hard every day must be for him. Losing a love like the one he shared with Angelina was like a razor strap to the soul. It left scars and deep, unfixable wounds.

Banning shifted in his seat and continued. "Once Ariel finished, all we could do was wait. It took days. I've never seen anyone suffer as Angelina did." He closed his eyes, and when he reopened them, tears shimmered in their edges. "Somehow, Alexandro found out." He whispered this under his breath.

His tears looked so otherworldly. I wanted to reach out and touch them. They looked like pure crystals in his eyes, sparkling in shades and hues that shouldn't exist in a natural iris.

"Alexandro was enraged. He was furious that Ariel had turned someone in his home without his permission. I guess before I found Ariel in the hallway, he had been pleading with Alexandro to let him do it. He had begged for hours after finding John. To say the least, Alexandro was pissed when he found out Ariel had disobeyed him, had disobeyed a direct order. He had Ariel beaten. He joined in on the torture, helping punish Ariel for his so-called crimes.

"Ariel never fought back. Alexandro let Kieran do most of the damage. The two of them beat Ariel terribly. Had he been human, the blows would have been fatal, but he never fought back. They could do whatever they wanted to him as long as Angelina lived.

"I had shut myself in with Angelina against Alexandro's orders, protecting her while Ariel could not. Ariel, Aldrich, and I are the fiercest warriors amongst our group," he said. He didn't brag. It was merely a matter of fact. "No one would have overpowered me, save a group or Aldrich. Lucky for me, Aldrich took no sides. He stayed in his room, avoiding the conflict. And Alexandro did not wish to alert a group to Ariel's defiance. It would give the others doubt of his leadership and power. None of it mattered, though. After everything we risked, Angelina died anyway."

Banning's eyes darkened in anger. "No. It would have been better if she would have died. She turned into one of them, a zombie. Alexandro gave Ariel the worst punishment of all. He made Ariel kill her. He made it as horrible for Ariel as he could. Alexandro gave Ariel a sword and told him to take care of it." Banning paused and looked at me with disgust. "I enjoy using a sword more than anyone else here, but I use it for enemies. It isn't something you use on someone you love, and it was never Ariel's weapon of choice. What Alexandro made him do was cruel.

"At this point, I'd already been taken to the dungeon in the basement. I knew they planned to torture us both after he finished. They chained us up, trapping us in the dark and cold without food or water. Alexandro had us tortured every day for four months...until Panthea came home. She was outraged. Ariel had saved their lives, and Alexandro was having him tortured. She released us from our hell and had the doctors look us over. Many bones had to be reset, wounds stitched.

"She freed us from what could possibly have been our deaths. She told Alexandro we both had immunity from his rules, that we were to remain at the mansion and be left alone. Since that day, Ariel has excluded himself from everyone in this house and avoided all human contact...until you."

I thought of how much it must have affected him to accept protecting me, how much pain it must have resurfaced. He had avoided human contact for a few hundred years. It was a major concession for him to be doing what he was for me.

"And that is why Ariel is so disgruntled. Try to take some pity on him. He's doing the best he can. I thought knowing his past might help you. I thought it might make you see why he behaves—" Banning suddenly stopped talking and grabbed me behind the head. Before I could register what was happening, he pressed his lips roughly to mine.

I gave a squeak of protest before I realized what he was doing. There were footsteps right outside the door, and someone was entering. Banning had been so insistent upon no one hearing us. He really meant that.

Keeping up the guise, I leaned into him, returning the kiss. His lips were thick and warm, heat emanating from them. I knew the kiss was just a front, but my body responded to his touch. I clutched the front of his shirt with my fist and allowed him to part my lips with his own.

He pulled me into his chest, crushing me against him. His mouth devoured mine, and he kissed me with an intensity I hadn't ever experienced before.

"Wow. I walked in at a bad time."

Banning broke the kiss with a laugh. "Just covering my ass. We were discussing things I didn't want Alexandro or his cronies to hear."

"So that was a cover-up kiss? Damn. I have to start bringing up more taboo topics."

My eyes drifted lazily to find Diego in the doorway. I snapped back to my senses once I truly got a good look at him. He looked great. His blue eyes were sparkling with humor, his blond hair spiked up to perfection. You couldn't even tell that the night before, he'd had his throat ripped out. "Diego," I said breathlessly from shock. "You look...terrific."

Diego gave a sly grin. "Why thank you. Does this mean I get a kiss like that, too?"

I went to give a sarcastic reply, but Banning beat me to it. "Only if you want Kenya to rip her head off." Banning glanced at me. "Unless you want to die, Diego's off the market."

"I wasn't wondering," I said dryly. "I've got enough on my plate right now."

"I can see that," Diego said teasingly, nodding to Banning. "I think I might need to take a cold shower after that."

"I meant because of the zombies." I tried to look offended, but I couldn't keep the blush from spreading across my cheeks.

Banning casually crossed his foot over his knee, his arm stretching out behind me. He touched my hair playfully, almost possessively.

"Stop that," I demanded, scooting away from him.

"Vicious with a weapon and feisty," Diego said with a whistle. "We're all in trouble."

Banning nodded. "Trouble indeed." His grin fell, and he turned serious eyes to Diego. "I assume you are not here for pleasure. What did you need?"

"Alexandro wishes to see our guest."

I turned apprehensive eyes to Banning. I did not want to be alone with Alexandro. I wouldn't have before, but after hearing this story, I was downright terrified of the man.

Banning seemed to read my mind. "I'll find Ariel before I let you go. No way is he letting Alexandro near you without being there as a buffer."

I gave a nod, relief filling me as I got to my feet and followed Banning toward the hallway. It wasn't that I didn't trust Banning. It was just after the story Banning told me, I knew Ariel would never take any crap from Alexandro.

As Banning reached the door, I couldn't help but say, "I have one more question for you."

Banning stopped and turned around. "Yes?"

"How about mirrors? Legend says you guys cast no reflection. Is that another lie?"

Banning and Diego stared at each other for a moment before bursting into laughter. "We are far too vain to go without mirrors," Diego said between laughs. "Do you think we could look this good without mirrors at our disposal?"

"Who said any of you were good-looking?" I asked.

Banning spun toward me with inhuman speed and had me in his arms before I could even think about moving out of the way. The fingers of his right hand tangled in my hair as his palm cupped my face. "I know I am beautiful. A century of women telling me so is my proof." He pulled me against him, and my breath caught in my throat. "Even without my powers, I've had countless women throw themselves at my feet."

I stared up at him, my pulse beating rapidly, my eyelids drooping to flutter closed.

Banning leaned his mouth down to my ear and whispered into it. "The quickening of your pulse and the shortness of breath tells me all I need to know." He released me suddenly and swept out of the room before I could recover.

I was stunned for a moment, unable to think clearly. I

simply gaped at the spot he'd disappeared from.

"Man," Diego said with a whistle. "I wish I could do that." He shook his head. "It took me a hundred and fifty years of nagging to get Kenya to agree to go out with me."

I was about to come back with a snippy comment when my mind registered what he'd said. "It took you a hundred and fifty years to get her to go on a date with you? That's dedication."

"More like annoying persistence," he said with a guilty grin.

Banning returned a moment later with Ariel. "Didn't take long to find him. He was just next door."

I stared at Banning, studying the contours of his face, the perfect curve of his nose. He had pulled his hair back from his face, looking like the cowboy he claimed to be with his ponytail.

I watched him turn to speak to Ariel. His hips were narrow, his jeans fitting tightly across his perfect body. In that moment, I had never seen anything so sensual. Even the tiniest details about him made everything female in me stand up and take notice. I unconsciously licked my lips, watching the way his shirt clung to his muscled chest.

I hadn't even realized it, but Ariel had come to stand in front of me. His mouth was moving, but I couldn't hear what he was saying. It was as if I were deaf. I didn't care, though. I simply tried to look around Ariel so I could gawk at Banning.

Ariel shook my shoulders, jarring me roughly.

I ignored him. He was merely a distraction to what I wanted, what I craved. I craned my neck, trying to get around him to Banning. I seemed to be struggling through a fog. It was as if a thick haze had swept through the room, and only I could see it. It blocked out everything but Banning, the one light in all that gloom. I struggled, feeling sluggish as I fought against Ariel's grip. I kept losing focus on him, losing everything to the fog that clouded out the rest of the world.

The next thing I noticed was Damian coming into the room. My eyes strayed from Banning to him, the persistent fog suddenly lifting. As soon as my eyes left Banning, my thoughts began to clear, and my hearing returning.

"You took her under!" Ariel was screaming at Banning, accusing him of something I didn't understand. "What were you thinking?"

"I didn't mean to!" Banning's reply was frantic. "It's been so long since I've been near anyone my powers could affect. I didn't even realize what I had done until after you did. My control is not what it once was."

"What the hell did he do to her?" Damian demanded. His hands were balled into fists, the knuckles white as they trembled with anger.

Ariel was still shaking me, and it was starting to hurt.

"Will you let go of me?" I asked, annoyance in my voice.

All four men in the room turned to look at me in shock.

"What?" I asked self-consciously.

"You are no longer under his power," Ariel said in astonishment.

"No." I turned to Banning with an accusatory glare. "No thanks to you."

"Impossible," Diego said in disbelief. "Most people under Banning's spell cannot break it. It takes weeks of separation and Banning willing it so for a connection to be severed this thoroughly."

"He's as bad as all that?" I asked skeptically.

"He can be. Yes," Diego answered. "You are very fortunate he merely had a slip of power and did not intentionally try to enthrall you. You are fortunate to have broken out so easily."

"What made you come out of it?" Ariel asked. Suspicion was heavy in his voice, and his eyes narrowed at me. "What was the first thing you saw clearly?"

"I remember seeing...Damian." I admitted honestly to what they asked, not sure of the meaning behind their questions. "He came into the room, and my mind came out of its haze. It was like there was a fog so thick I could barely breathe through it. When Damian came in, it vanished."

The three vampires turned to look at Damian in unison.

Damian held his hands up in the air and took a step back. "Whoa. Hold on. I didn't do anything."

"Oh, but you did," Banning disagreed. "You broke my control over her."

"It has been many years since we have seen someone with the ability to dispel our powers," Ariel said, his voice sounding close to disbelief.

"I swear I didn't do a single thing," Damian said.

"You willed it," Banning murmured. "I felt it."

"Yeah. I was wishing that whatever was wrong with Aurora would go away, but…" Damian's eyes widened in shock. "You're saying I did that?"

All three men nodded.

"Shit," Damian concluded.

"Exactly," Banning said with a nod.

Someone cleared their throat from the doorway.

I looked up to find Alexandro.

His arms were folded over his broad chest, and his eyes were narrowed into angry slits. "When I say to bring someone to me, you do it." His eyes slowly lowered to look at Diego's neck before sliding back to his blue eyes. "Did having your throat ripped out yesterday affect your brain?" He curled his hands into tight fists, then slowly uncurled them. He repeated this action seemingly without realizing he was doing it, his knuckles turning white from the force with which his fingers curled against his palm. The repeated action seemed very threatening, as if he was only barely able to confine his rage to his hands. "Or wasn't that enough punishment for you? Are you trying to piss me off so I'll have you tortured?"

Ariel stepped forward, anger written on his face. "He was waiting for me. I was away from her, and he knew I did not want her alone with anyone I considered a threat without me by her side."

Alexandro gave a barking laugh, not at all offended he'd been deemed a threat. "You are taking this more seriously than I expected. I was almost positive your uncontrollable temper would have caused you to slip up and kill her by now, giving me just cause to have you executed. Even my sister couldn't argue with the punishment for such a crime, but it looks as if you are starting to have feelings toward our prisoner instead. I thought you would have learned your lesson from getting involved with mortal filth in the past."

I could feel everyone in the room tense. This was not going to be good.

"My human was not the one fickle enough to betray me. I was helpless to save Angelina. You watched Colleta burn. You are both betrayers. You deserved each other." Ariel's words were taciturn and hateful. I almost expected ice to linger on the air with how coldly he'd spoken.

Alexandro growled, deep and menacingly. "You know better than to speak that name in my home."

"And you know better than to think I would let you be alone with her," Ariel said. "Discuss what you want here, because you will not be taking her to your office."

Alexandro looked as if he was about to fight Ariel, but then he relaxed with a grin that meant nothing good. "Fine. I wanted to remind your human of her duties. She seems to have forgotten."

I narrowed my eyes. "What duties?"

"You are to be working on breeding. That is your sole purpose here at our safe house."

"Like hell it is!" My voice was full of outrage. I couldn't believe the audacity of him, the cruelty with which he delivered his statement.

Alexandro marched toward me, grabbing me by the throat before anyone could stop him. "You will do as I say, or I will toss you to the zombies outside." He pointed his other hand to Damian. "You will fuck him, or you will die. You are not to be a whore to the undead."

I knew I shouldn't run my mouth to a vampire who had me by the throat, but I couldn't control my outrage. "*Who are you calling a whore?*"

His hand tightened, cutting off anything further I might say. "Stop screwing my vampires, and worry about the human."

Ariel and Banning both rushed forward at the gurgling sound that escaped me as I struggled for air. They paused when Alexandro shot them an evil glare. I knew they feared he would kill me if they made a move against him. He had lightning speed and could snap my neck before they reached me.

Alexandro leaned in and put his face in mine. "Without a child, you are useless to me. I don't keep useless things around. Fuck him soon, or I will dispose of you." With that, he released me.

I dropped to the floor from lack of oxygen, giving a ragged gasp as I struggled to suck in air. I rubbed at my throat as a spasm-filled cough forced its way up.

"In two nights, you will go out and search for more survivors," Alexandro said to the vampires in the room. "Hopeful-ly, you will find some mortals better than these."

I glared at him, but kept my mouth shut. I didn't want him laying his hands on me again. Besides, I didn't think I could speak if I tried. My throat hurt too badly.

Banning's eyes widened at Alexandro's proclamation. "Some of our men are still injured from last night. All did not heal as quickly as Diego. It is careless to send them out again so soon."

"It is careless not to. Without more survivors to feed from, they will die anyway. The longer we wait, the less likely we are to find anyone still alive." He made sense. Damn him. "If you are too good to send your men out, I could always send mine." He made a sweeping motion behind him.

I hadn't even noticed until that moment that Orion knelt behind him in the doorway. He was hunched over on his hands and knees, his head lowered to the floor.

"I could always send Orion and others like him into bat-tle," Alexandro said with a sneer. "There are many living in this house who have never been on a battlefield. Perhaps it is time to make them earn their keep."

At the mention of his name, Orion looked up in terror. It was then that I caught full sight of him. His lip was gashed and bloody. His right eye was bruised black and purple. Someone had beaten the living hell out of him and recently, too. The blood hadn't even had time to dry. It explained why he was crouched on the floor instead of standing behind his so-called master. It didn't look like he even had the strength to get up.

I gave an involuntary gasp at the obvious violence that had been done to him. I was still kneeling on the floor, so we were at eye level with each other. We stared at each other with wide, frightened eyes, our terror reflected in the other's expression.

"Or we could send Damian with you," Alexandro contin-ued. "I'm sure the zombies would love to sink their teeth into his boiling hot blood." He paused a moment, giving everyone time to think that over. "You can make the choice, Orion or Damian."

Orion attempted to scramble to his feet. "Do not s…send the human. I will go. I will go." His voice trembled as he said this, and he collapsed back to his knees. Still, he repeated, "I will go."

"No," Banning said darkly. "You won't. Neither of you will. My team will be ready to go out."

With a pleased smirk, Alexandro turned on his heels and left the room. "Orion," he called with a dark warning in his voice.

Orion turned and started scrambling after him.

I climbed shakily to my feet, moving protectively toward Orion. "Leave him. Please."

Alexandro spun in the doorway to face me, hatred fueling his expression.

I took a step back in fear, but repeated my plea. "Let him stay with us. You've no use for him." I didn't know exactly what uses Orion served to Alexandro besides one. He was Alexandro's whipping boy. I couldn't let him disappear through that door. I knew what would happen to him once Alexandro got him behind closed doors. Orion would suffer for our diso-bedience. Orion would suffer for each and every one of us.

"You want him so badly?" Alexandro said. "You can keep the little curse. What's one more to the group when you're whoring yourself to half a dozen of them?"

I bit my lip to keep my mouth shut. I didn't want him to change his mind and take Orion with him. Let him think I was sleeping with all the vampires he wanted. It wasn't go-ing to affect his opinion of me. He hated me no matter what I did. Defending myself wouldn't change anything. His hatred for humanity stemmed from something far deeper than a simple annoyance at me. Because of what Coletta had done to him, he wouldn't trust any of us no matter what we did to prove ourselves.

As Alexandro stormed out and stomped his way loudly down the hallway, Orion put his head to the floor and wept. "Thank you. Thank you." He whispered the two words over and over again. His arms trembled, and his back heaved with sobs.

I stared after Alexandro and decided I didn't want him pissed at me. Look at what he had done to Orion simply be-cause he could. I needed to double my attempts to avoid Alexandro, because I think if he got me alone, he would hurt me in ways I couldn't imagine.

Chapter 12

I'd been sitting with Ginny the first few hours after I woke the next morning. She'd coughed into a handkerchief and mumbled tiredly through our card games. She didn't seem to be feeling very well, so I finally gave up and left her to get some rest.

I tried to spend some time with Damian after Ginny finally fell into a fitful sleep, but he seemed very distracted. I ended up spending most of the day with Orion.

He wasn't able to sleep, and after I assured him he hadn't spilled vital information by letting me stumble upon him during daylight hours, he agreed to give me a tour of the mansion.

I had never been anywhere quite so big. It looked like a private school with all of its mini apartments and different rooms. If I had to be trapped somewhere during the zombie apocalypse, I'd picked the right place...if I could ignore the murderous vampires, that is.

That's where I was now, wandering the massive halls of Alexandro's mansion. I glanced at Orion as we walked, taking in his features. He still looked like a boy to me. He was over a hundred years old, yet he didn't look a day over eighteen. He didn't fit in with the rest of them either. He was too quiet, too timid. I couldn't fathom how he had wound up with this group of characters.

"How did you get stuck here with Alexandro?" I couldn't stop myself from asking. I knew it was a personal question, but I had already learned parts of Banning's and Ariel's stories. What was one more?

"You want to know how I got here?" Orion asked in surprise.

I nodded, prompting him to speak.

He gave a boyish grin and looked down at his feet. After a moment, he looked back up at me in shy bewilderment. "No one has cared to hear anything from me in a long time."

"Well, I care. I want to know. How could someone like you end up with Alexandro? You're so nice and he's so...evil."

Orion shrugged. "There are people out there who take advantage of the weak, human and inhuman, mortal and immortal. They have this ability to pick us out." He gave an unhappy sigh. "My father was one of these men. He was a giant, a man made more of muscle than brain. He was a man accustomed to manual labor. I lived in a time where many children didn't have the opportunity to attend school. Many of them simply joined their fathers in work at home or found themselves other jobs that required nothing more than physical strength. My father understood nothing about schools or intelligence. On top of helping to run our farm, he wanted me to become an executioner for those sentenced to death by our court system. I was reaching adulthood during the witch trials, and my father wanted me to step up and do what he felt was my civic duty. He said it would turn me into a respectable man if I rid our God-fearing world of demon worshippers and other miscreants.

"I wanted to be a doctor, a healer, not a killer. I had neither mind nor body for killing. My father did not understand this. He thought he could beat me into submission. He would pummel and strike me almost every day. The whole time my mother insisted I be allowed to be schooled, he abused me. If he caught me with a book, he would burn it.

"One night, he was in a rage like never before. He beat me nearly to death. As I lay bleeding and broken in our yard, I begged for freedom of him. I almost hoped he would kill me. It would have been worth it to end my miserable existence." He paused. "An angel heard my pleading and answered my prayers. You can call vampires devils, but she was no devil. She got between us; she forced him away from me. She screamed that he was killing me. She told him she was a doctor and demanded that he allow her to examine me. As she bent over me, she whispered, 'If you want me to take you from this place, pretend you are dead.' I lay perfectly still. It was so hard, because I wanted to weep with joy. I was overwhelmed at the thought of being free of him.

"My merciful liberator screamed and accused my father of murdering me. She was in a rage. Somehow, she convinced him to let her take my body. I think he gave me to her to keep my mother from finding out what he'd done." He shrugged at this, as if the reason why truly didn't matter. "She took me away, somewhere out in the woods where we wouldn't be discovered. As I lay in a half-conscious daze, she told me her name was Sheridan and that she was going to save me. She informed me that I was in fact dying, but she could change that. I could live forever. With her. I guess in one of my moments of coherency, I gave my consent. She made me what I am." He paused, as if remembering the moment. "She was the best thing that ever happened to me."

He frowned sadly before pressing on. "For the next two years of my life, everything was perfect. Sheridan and I did everything together. She was the exact opposite of my father. She was gentle and sweet. She was loving. She was my guardian and protector. She was everything I'd never had before. She was...perfect.

"We were happy, but we lived in constant fear of witch hunters. We never killed when we fed, but townsfolk still saw us as a threat merely because we were unknown to them. A stranger must be someone dangerous. That seemed to be the theme in most places. Despite the hazards, it was the best time of my life. I wouldn't have given it up for anything." Orion gave an unhappy sigh. "Like I said, it only lasted two years. We had hunters in endless pursuit. One particularly nasty group caught our trail and were determined to see us dead. They chased us through two different towns. Sheridan wrote to Panthea, a trusted friend of hers who was staying at an inn a few towns west of us, and begged her for assistance.

"For five nights, no one came. We ended up surrounded in an abandoned farmhouse. Sheridan sobbed helplessly and swore that Panthea would come for us, that she would not leave us to die. When the hunters attacked, Sheridan hid me. She took them head on, hoping they wouldn't find me. Those terrible men set her on fire and left her to take the house down around her. They didn't need to search for Sheridan's companion. They were going to burn us both alive."

Orion shivered in horror at the memory, and I reached

out to gently touch his hand. He offered me a weak smile before continuing.

"I stayed hidden, too terrified to move. Sheridan was dead, and I was alone. I don't think I wanted to live. A voice called out to me through the smoke. For a brief, delusional second, I thought it was Sheridan. I should have known better. Sheridan's voice was soft and musical, like chimes. This voice was low and sensual, very sultry. It was calling to me, trying to find me. The next thing I remembered was a pale hand wrapping around my arm. With inhuman strength, my savior pulled me from the building, pulled me to safety."

"Panthea," I said, taking a guess.

Orion nodded ever so slightly. "Panthea. She pulled me from the burning building. Outside, all of the men who had attacked us were dead. Two other vampires stood in the middle of the carnage. One, Sterling, had fiery red hair to his waist and green eyes that seemed to shimmer in the moonlight. He was shirtless, with the blood of the fallen men traveling up his bare arms. The other, Sebastian, had short blond hair and bright blue eyes that shone with violence. His mouth was caked in blood, and those wild eyes... The pair was known for their prowess in battle. They were legendary." His eyes lifted to mine and he explained. "They were also Panthea's lovers."

I'd heard a little about Sterling from Banning, but Panthea's second lover was a surprise to me. "*Lovers*?" I asked, stressing the fact that it was lovers plural.

Orion nodded with a wry grin. "Yes. Lovers. Let me describe for you my first encounter with them. Panthea sauntered over to Sterling and Sebastian while they were covered in the blood of Sheridan's killers and ran her hands down each of their bare chests. She covered her palms in blood. Then she stuck her fingers in her mouth, sucking them clean. Leaning over, she slowly licked the blood off their chests, her eyes never leaving mine. It was the most provocative thing I'd ever seen. I was...shocked, to say the least. My time with Sheridan had been calm and downright virtuous. This was a side of vampires I hadn't known existed, the pure sexual bloodlust. Sterling grabbed Panthea by the hair and pulled her to him, kissing her in a way I'd never been witness to before. I was still much like a young boy. The only love I'd ever known had been gentle and innocent. Sheridan treated me like an injured child, which I suppose I was. She was like a mother to me, shielding me from the terrifying and abusive world around me. The three of them were using the horror I'd been protected from until this point as a stimulant for rough foreplay."

Orion shook his head, a blush of embarrassment touching his cheeks. "I'm sure by that description, you can guess I didn't last with them long. Panthea tried to make me feel included. She really did, but I didn't fit in with their lifestyle. Panthea was wild, adventurous. She was untamable. Everything the three of them did was dangerous. She tried to seduce me a few times, but I was never receptive. I didn't know the first thing about sex." His blush deepened, and he shook his head, not looking me in the eyes. "I just wanted to be left alone. The more she tried to seduce me, the further I receded into my shell. None of us were happy with the situation.

"I was holding them back. A few months with them, and I was on the verge of a nervous breakdown. Panthea could see it coming. She offered for me to stay with her brother Alexandro. She told me he was quiet and reserved like myself. She wasn't aware what was going on with him and his human love—" He broke off abruptly. He bit his lower lip, and his eyes darted around nervously as if afraid he might have been overheard.

"Colleta," I said, trying to ease his concern. He wasn't telling me anything I didn't already know with this part of the story. "Banning told me the story. Let me guess, Alexandro took losing Colleta out on you?"

He gave a quick nod, his surprise at my knowledge fading. "Yes. Let me tell you something about Panthea. There are only four beings in this world she truly cares about—Sterling, Sebastian, Alexandro, and Ariel. Out of respect for Sheridan, she stopped by a few months later to see how I was adjusting to life at the mansion. She discovered Alexandro was having Ariel tortured, and I was forgotten in her arguments." He shrugged. "I've been here ever since."

I shook my head in disbelief. "Couldn't you—" My sentence broke off as I was suddenly hit from behind. I slammed chest first into the wall. My lungs protested at the sudden impact, as did my wrist as I caught myself, barely keeping my head from crashing into the wall.

I was violently spun around to face Kieran. He slammed my back against the wall with enough force to rattle my teeth. My mind went into panic mode, and I struggled against him, a terrified squeak escaping me.

Kieran buried his face into my neck and inhaled deeply. "You smell of fear...and Banning." He narrowed his eyes at the second scent he'd picked up from me. This seemed to anger him.

Orion inched toward Kieran, hands shaking. "Let her go, p-p-please."

"When you can speak without stuttering over your words, then I'll consider listening to you," Kieran said snidely. "Let her go! L-l-l-l-let her go!" He yelled the words in a false voice, mocking Orion. "Why don't you come over here and make me?"

"I'll make you," said a voice from behind Kieran.

The red-haired vampire spun around to reveal Banning standing behind him. I was so unbelievably grateful he'd stumbled upon us.

Kieran gave a warning hiss before turning back to me. He pressed his body flat against mine and leaned down to whisper in my ear. "If you want to fuck vampires, maybe you should let me show you a good time. I'll make you scream in more ways than one."

I was really starting to get pissed. Why was I being labeled as the vampire call girl? I hadn't slept with a single person since arriving at Alexandro's, except for in rumor.

"Get away from her." Banning's tone was low and threatening.

Kieran tensed. Then, as if deciding it wasn't worth the fight, he backed away from me, hands held in the air. "I didn't hurt her. I was merely giving her an offer." He sneered at Banning. "Who made you her babysitter anyway?"

Banning gave a deep, throaty laugh. He walked past Kieran, turning his back momentarily on the other vampire in an arrogant fashion. He then leaned against the wall next to me, brushing against the side of my body with his own. He put his face an inch from my hair and rolled his eyes up to look at Kieran. "Why be a babysitter when there are so many more benefits to being something else?"

His breath was hot against my neck, and I couldn't help

but shiver and close my eyes for a moment due to the sensation. When I opened them, I saw Kieran falter.

He seemed at a loss for words. He gaped at the two of us, his jaw clenching until I thought he might break teeth he was grinding them so roughly. Finally, he just growled in frustration and stormed away, stalking off down the hallway.

I looked at Banning in confusion. "What was that all about?"

Banning gave a weary sigh and pulled away from me, the persona dropped. "His weakness." Banning looked a little overwhelmed. I'd never seen him so concerned before. "Aurora, listen to me. You cannot let Kieran catch you alone. I am serious when I tell you he will rape and murder you. Kieran has always had a thing for human women. When Colleta was killed, Alexandro forbade us human contact." He closed his eyes and shook his head. "It has been torture." He reopened his eyes, and their gray depths were haunted. "When Alexandro decided none of us were allowed to engage in human contact anymore, it was unjust punishment for most of us. For Kieran, it was a relief to everyone. He needed to be banned. He doesn't like women like the rest of us do. He used to torture them during sex. He liked to hear them scream. It wasn't just rape. It was mutilation. It's been three hundred years since he's had the opportunity to do these things. He's had three hundred years to think of what he'd like to do, and you may be his last chance."

I shivered at that. "Torture and sex, what a fun combination."

Banning's face slid back into its customary grin. "I'll just take the sex if you're offering." When I gave him a dirty look, he held up a hand. "I'm only kidding." He put his hand on the back of my neck and gave it a quick squeeze. "Damian was looking for you, by the way."

I gave a nod. "I'll head over to his place now. I think I'm done with my death threat tour." I glanced to Orion to see if he would be following me. "Orion?" I asked.

Banning stepped forward, clearing his throat. "Actually, there are some tasks that Orion's assistance is needed for."

I shot Banning a suspicious look. "You're not going to take him back to Alexandro, are you?"

"Absolutely not," Banning assured. "We told you last

night after Alexandro's childish scene we'd do our best to keep the two of them apart. He will be with me the entire time. I need his help with something."

I conceded to that. I didn't think Banning would do anything to hurt him. Besides, I wasn't Orion's mother. I couldn't tell him what to do. He was two hundred years my elder. "Okay," I said with a glance to Orion.

He gave me a brief nod, letting me know it was okay. "We should walk Aurora to Damian's," he said to Banning. "Just in case Kieran is still lurking about."

Banning nodded his agreement and put a hand to my back, ushering me in the direction.

I was wondering what the rush was, but didn't ask. Every time I asked a vampire a question about their actions, I never liked the answer. They were a screwed up group. Their answers either involved violence or mockery. To this date, I hadn't run into any gnomes, so I was assuming there weren't any actually running around the mansion. I'd been fairly certain Banning was just pulling my leg when he'd told me that, but it just proved that they could smile and skirt around questions.

When reaching Damian's room, Banning opened the door and pushed me inside. He nodded to Damian before quickly shutting the door.

I stared at Damian in puzzlement. "What was that all about?"

Damian laughed and shook his head. "Subtlety," he said in amusement. He turned and walked into his bedroom, motioning that I should follow. "I have a surprise for you."

I felt a grin spread across my face as Banning's odd behavior was pushed to the back of my mind. "Oh yeah?" I practically skipped back to the bedroom, eager to see what he had up his sleeve.

"Yeah." He grabbed a dress from his bedpost and turned to me with it. It was an aqua color with beading that sparkled in the light. It would bring out the blue in my eyes as well as show off a sexy portion of leg in the slit that ran nearly all the way up the thigh of the fabric. The dress was absolutely breathtaking, and I was itching for it to be mine.

"Where'd you get this?" I asked, trying to keep myself from reaching out and taking it from him.

"I made it."

"You made it?" I asked in shock. My eyes slid from the dress to him, and I surveyed him skeptically. "You made this dress?"

"Yep."

"You?" I asked again, just to make sure he'd understood the question the first time.

Damian laughed again. "Yes. It may be a shock to you, but I used to do this for a living. I designed women's lingerie in my home and sold the right to produce my patterns to large companies and department stores. I even handmade a few garments for rich ladies who wanted one-of-a-kind pieces."

I stared at him in astonishment. "Really?"

"Really. I have a...condition that keeps me from being...out and about sometimes. I had to find a job I could do at home when the need arose." He shrugged. "So I sucked up my manly uncertainty and went to school for fashion design."

I pushed aside my curiosity about his odd career choice as concern filled me. "What's your condition?" I asked in alarm. The whole time I'd known him, I'd thought Damian was just a slacker. I hadn't realized he had something wrong with him. I suddenly felt very guilty over the way I'd judged him.

He gave a nervous cough. "Don't worry about that. It's nothing important." He held the dress out to me, waggling it invitingly. "Hurry up and get dressed. The real surprise is coming."

I took the hanger from him with a coy grin, delighted that the dress was indeed for me. "What kind of surprise?" Living with vampires in a post-apocalyptic world did not offer many opportunities to get dressed up. I was eager to see what he had up his sleeve.

"Get dressed, and you'll find out."

I stared suspiciously at him for a moment more before giving in. If he had something fun planned, I wasn't about to argue. We could all use some fun. With an excited skip, I ran to the bathroom to get changed.

Chapter 13

A half hour later, I stood with my eyes closed, anticipation making my blood pump rapidly through my veins. Damian was guiding me purposefully as we walked to some undisclosed location in the mansion where his surprise was hidden, completely disorienting me after only one hallway. One of his hands was covering my eyes just to make sure I wasn't peeking. "You can open them," Damian whispered in my ear, finally removing his hand.

I did as instructed and gave a gasp of shock. There was a giant banner that read, "Happy Birthday, Aurora!" It hung over expensive-looking DJ equipment. A table in the corner held a tiered cake. There were balloons and glitter all over a giant dance floor in the center of the banquet room.

"How did you..." I trailed off in amazement, unable to believe what I was seeing. During a zombie apocalypse, he'd managed to throw me a surprise birthday party.

"Well, I made the dress. Orion made the banner. Banning supplied the DJ equipment and helped me decorate while Orion kept you away from here."

"Amazing." Tears sprang to my eyes, and I was completely overwhelmed with the effort they had put in on my behalf. "Absolutely amazing."

Damian pressed a button on the equipment and a song began playing through the speakers. He took me by the hand and walked backwards to the dance floor. Once there, he grabbed me around the waist and pulled me to him. "I know it's not as garish as what you had planned, but we did our best."

"It's perfect," I whispered. I gazed up at him for a moment in disbelief before I realized the music was still playing and he was grinning at me in amusement, patiently waiting for me to dance with him. He'd more than earned the first dance with me. He'd earned a million. I slid my arms around his neck and moved forward until my body brushed the front of his. Then I moved gently in time to the music, allowing him to lead our movements once a rhythm was set.

As we swayed slowly to the beat, I studied his face. I was seeing Damian in a new light. This was hands down the most romantic thing a man had ever done for me, and it made me realize what an unbearable bitch I'd been. Damian had been going out of his way for me since the moment that first zombie broke through the doors of Sandy's Shack. He'd saved my life. He'd protected me. He'd comforted me. He'd done everything in his power to make me happy.

Coming to the conclusion that I was done being difficult with him, I lowered my head to his shoulder and took comfort in the sheltered feeling of his arms around me. I felt safer with him than anywhere in the world.

He leaned down to my ear and sang softly with the music. The familiar words of some old love song by Al Green invaded my senses. I listened to the words in Damian's familiar tone, and they washed over me with an intensity that made me shiver.

Damian's breath was hot against my ear, and it brought goose bumps to my flesh, sending a tremor down my spine. I pulled back to look at him and felt my heartbeat pick up speed.

This was Damian. I shouldn't be feeling like this about him. Just because I was ready to call a cease fire did not mean I had to start having feelings for him. I tried to remind myself of our past, of all the reasons we hadn't gotten along before. He was obnoxious. He was rude. He was everything I didn't want in a man. Every little thing about him annoyed me.

Yet when he leaned down to kiss me, I stood on my tiptoes to help him reach.

He paused, his lips hovering inches from mine. He stared down at me with fire in his eyes that gave me chills. Just as he was starting to close the distance between us, the door flew open.

"I love you, baby!" Banning bellowed along with the music as he strolled into the room, a wicked grin on his face. "Is this a sappy love fest, or is this a party?"

Damian and I jumped guiltily apart. My eyes held his for a moment as I stared at him with something close to horror. I'd nearly kissed Damian. Thank goodness Banning had arrived and broken the romantic bubble we'd been trapped in. Of all the mistakes I'd made in my life, kissing Damian would have been the most dangerous. The zombie apocalypse was the last place a girl should go looking for romance. Despite that fact, I couldn't help feeling disappointed that he hadn't closed the remaining distance. "A party…I guess." I looked to Damian for confirmation.

He gave a quick nod and took another step away from me, his expression sheepish. "It is. I knew how bummed you were about not getting to have your party, so I had a few of the more approachable vampires help me throw this together."

"More approachable? Is that all I am to you now?" Banning asked with a *harrumph*. "I'll remember that next time you ask to raid my DVD collection."

Damian rolled his eyes with an entertained grin at Banning's comment, but his attention was still fully on me. He was examining my face with soft affection, watching my delighted reactions with obvious pride.

I held eye contact with him for a long moment. There was so much I wanted to say to him. A giant thank you would have been first on the list. Then perhaps if I was feeling weak, the finish of that kiss would have followed. None of that was to happen, at least not now. We had an audience. I turned to Banning, offering him a grateful smile. "This is great."

"And you haven't even gotten to your gifts yet," Banning said with a wink. He nodded to the doorway.

As if on cue, Orion came into the room, precariously balancing packages in his arms.

"Orion wrapped them all," Banning admitted. "I'm not good with wrapping paper. I was dead long before it came into existence. It just wasn't a skill I deemed useful, so I never learned to use it well. Plus, I'm just too manly to play around with pretty pink, flowered paper. It's not cool."

I looked around me in amazement. I couldn't fathom that vampires would throw a birthday party. How could they even understand the importance of getting older? They didn't age. When you're over five hundred years old, what's one more year? Yet, they had done a fantastic job. They decorated.

They brought gifts. They wore suits.

"You guys look great," I said, unable to keep from gushing.

"Well, with the rest of the world dead, I figured this might be my last time to get dressed up and wear fancy clothes," Banning said. "Besides, I'm not one to turn down a party."

"Of course not," I said with a laugh.

"I'm one of the first people here, and I'll be the last to leave," Banning said boastfully. He winked playfully in Damian's direction. "Might end up the drunkest as well."

"One of the first people?" I asked in surprise. "How many people did you invite?" I could count the people I knew here on my fingers, and half of those people I hoped wouldn't show.

"Everybody."

"Everybody?"

"There are a few hundred vampires living here. I slid memos under everyone's door," Orion said. "Many of them are very anxious to meet you. Alexandro did not allow them contact with you. He wanted all of your concentration on the human."

He paused at Damian's dark look at being referred to as *the human*. "He wanted you to concentrate on Damian. S-s-some can't wait to see the only human woman left alive, the one that softened Ariel after all these years. The two of you are like the new Adam and Eve of your species."

I could tell he was getting nervous with the topic. He was starting to stutter again, his tongue getting caught between his fangs causing him to hiss. "Well, it's about time I met everyone then. Alexandro does not control me. I'm not his prisoner."

Banning cleared his throat uncomfortably as if he didn't quite agree with that statement.

I went to continue my argument, but it got lost in my throat as Diego entered the room with Kenya on his arm. I was so startled by the change in her appearance, I was speechless. I could see why he waited a hundred and fifty years for her. She was breathtaking. From our short interaction at the hospital, I hadn't gotten to see just how beautiful she was. Being out of combat attire and not looking ready to murder the next person who spoke to her did Kenya miracles.

Glitter sparkled in her hair and across her heavily shadowed eyelids. Her dark hair was straight and fell just across her shoulder blades. Her frame was thin, and she had on a slinky, blue sparkled dress that accentuated her features. She was one of the most stunning women I'd ever seen.

Diego held a package up and out to me with a goofy grin. "For the birthday girl." He offered it to me with a playful bow.

I took the box from him with a grin in return. "Why thank you. What store did you buy this from?" I teased, knowing full well there were no stores open any longer.

"Kenya's closet."

Kenya turned dark eyes to Diego, eyebrows narrowed in warning.

"I'm kidding," Diego said, quick to defend himself. "As I think Banning mentioned to you before, we are independent people. We provide for ourselves. We buy and sell from each other. You would never catch us shopping at the likes of a Wal-Mart."

"So you have, like, designers? Exclusive vampire wear? Interesting."

"Very," Kenya said. "We have kept it out of human circulation. I suppose I don't see the harm now that you're the only one left."

I was glad to see she didn't hold too much of a grudge over Diego getting his throat ripped out. Last time I saw her, she'd wanted to hurt me.

I gave her a small smile before turning my attention back to the box. I was itching to see what they had given me. I wanted to see what vampire-made attire rested inside. Whatever it was, it would be that much better because a vampire designed it. I felt like I was being inducted into a chic, very exclusive club.

People, or should I say vampires, starting filing into the room. I didn't recognize the majority, but my eyes landed on Ariel as he entered.

He leaned against the far wall, arms crossed. He looked downright miserable to be here. I was guessing partying wasn't in his blood like it was Banning's.

As if sensing I was thinking about him, Banning grabbed my wrist and pulled me to him. "I came here to dance," he said. "And I came here to do it with you." Before I could protest, he had me in the center of the floor. He pulled me in tight against him and waggled his eyebrows. "You're mine now." His grin was a flash of fangs.

Oddly, after the sight of the fangs, I relaxed against his chest. "Okay, Mr. Party Animal, show me what you've got."

Banning made a motion to someone by the equipment, and the beat of the music picked up, the sound thumping through the speakers. "I'm about to rock your world, sweetheart."

I spent the next forty minutes with Banning. He was as good at dancing as he claimed to be. He wasn't stuck in the eighteen hundreds like some of his friends. We danced to rap, R&B, pop, everything modern, and Banning danced like he was in some happening club.

He had a way of being sexual with everything he did. He could stand unmoving and still be completely sexy. Dancing, he was almost too much to take. His hands ran over my hips and waist with a familiarity he shouldn't have. It felt like sex, not simply dancing.

When the beat finally slowed, Banning let out a breathless sigh.

I was contemplating whether the sigh was real or not. If you didn't need to breathe, you shouldn't be out of breath, right? Yeah, and I thought they slept in coffins too, so what did I know?

His hand stayed firmly around my waist, and he moved slowly to the music. "I think someone else would like to dance with you."

"Who?" I asked in confusion.

Banning nodded just over my right shoulder. He tipped me backwards, and I looked in the direction he had pointed.

Orion was leaning against the wall, nervously wringing his hands and looking our way.

"Poor little guy," I said.

"Poor little guy?" Banning asked, moving us toward him while we danced. "He's one of the four of us who has been permitted around you. *Four of us*," he said, "out of hundreds. Alexandro permitted Ariel, because it would be torturous to him. He permitted me, because I would be best after Ariel at keeping you safe. It was either me or Aldrich. Aldrich is neutral. He does not care what happens to you. Nor does he need the blood to survive. He is old enough to no longer require it. If you die, it would not affect him, so he simply does not care. Alexandro knew I would. I have been too long without mortal companionship. He knew I would do anything for the chance to be with a mortal woman again."

His dark eyes held mine for a long moment before he continued. "Diego became acquainted with you because of the hospital incident. Alexandro wasn't too upset by it, because, as much as Diego jokes, he is devoted to Kenya. And Orion... Alexandro did not see him as a threat. He is too weak, too timid. He hoped that none of us would distract you from Damian and what he wishes of you."

I didn't like that Alexandro just tossed Orion to the side as if he didn't really matter. Alexandro didn't see him as a threat because he didn't have the strength to defend himself. He should have realized that his tender personality was what would affect me, not how many people he had killed.

I wasn't attracted to Orion like I was to the others. We were forming a friendship that I hoped would continue to bloom. Still, it bothered me that Alexandro didn't consider him worthy of anyone's affection because he didn't take enjoyment out of making people suffer.

My eyes narrowed in agitation. "How about we let Alexandro sweat that decision out a little?" Just because nothing would ever happen between Orion and me, that didn't mean I didn't enjoy his company. It also didn't mean I couldn't annoy Alexandro with the possibility of a budding romance. I knew Orion wouldn't look too deeply into us dancing with one another. We were friends. We could dance and have a conversation without it meaning anything more than that. But Alexandro with all his prejudices couldn't see me without thinking I was seducing whoever I was with. Us dancing would irk him.

Banning made a face as if he wasn't sure provoking Alexandro was such a wise idea, but he walked me to Orion anyway.

Orion's eyes darted nervously about as if searching for an escape route.

I wasn't going to give him one. As we reached him, I gave a breathless sigh. "This man," I said, pointing to Banning, "is too wild for me. Do you want to take his place for a song or two?"

Orion quickly looked to Banning, afraid to accept without Banning's permission.

Banning gave a bow. "I want to see if I can piss Ariel off any more than he already is." With that, he strolled across the room toward the spot where Ariel still leaned against the wall.

With the way he glided as he walked, I could see how women fell for his Dracula tales. I could see him in a cape and top hat enjoying every minute of the chaos that went along with his alter ego's presence. He was just mischievous like that.

With a laugh, I turned back to Orion, holding my arm out to him.

"I don't know how Ariel hasn't killed him yet," Orion said thoughtfully as I pulled him onto the dance floor.

I slid my arms around Orion's neck, keeping a friendly distance between us, and glanced over at Ariel. His face had taken on an even more unpleasant expression. I hadn't thought it possible, but he managed. "I think he still might end up killing him," I said with a laugh.

Orion finally relaxed, letting his hand rest loosely on my waist. He held me with such innocence, his movements timid. He was the exact opposite of Banning, yet they both melted my heart.

Smiling up at Orion, I ran my hand over the shoulder of his suit. "You look very yummy," I said teasingly.

Orion's eyes clouded with confusion. "Yummy? I don't know this word."

I sometimes forgot they were hundreds of years old. None, except Banning, seemed up on any modern terms or phrases. "It's just modern slang," I informed him. "It just means you look good."

I could see relief in his eyes when he realized it wasn't an insult. "Th...thanks," he said shyly. "You look beautiful as well. Everyone here has been staring at you in awe." A faint blush touched his cheeks. "I don't understand why you would dance with me. There are many important people here that wish to meet you."

"I don't know them. They aren't important to me. I wanted to dance with you," I said. "You, Banning, and Damian put this together. That makes you important in my eyes."

We danced in silence for a moment as Orion seemed to

ponder my blunt statement. He looked on the verge of tears.

I gave him an inquisitive look. I didn't feel I'd said anything to deserve such an emotional reaction. I was merely showing him the common courtesy and respect any man deserved.

"In my entire existence, I have been happy no more than two years. Two years," he said, stressing the briefness of his joy. "I have not felt a single ounce of happiness in over three hundred years...until now."

I set him with a serious look, my resolve unwavering. "Well, you'd better get used to it. I'm not letting Alexandro anywhere near you, and I made Banning and Ariel promise they wouldn't either. If he even thinks about hurting you again, I'll make Ariel kick his ass, so you better get used to enjoying life."

He closed his eyes and let out a shaky breath. "I'm not sure if I know how," he whispered softly. "I'm afraid to hope for a better existence. I did that once, and it was ripped away from me."

"I can't guarantee you anything," I admitted, "but I promise I'm going to try to make life as good as possible for all of us." I realized in that moment I had a group of men who I would do anything for. I would do everything in my power to keep them from harm. All of them had suffered so much under Alexandro.

Ariel had lost Angelina. Banning had been tortured for standing up for what he believed was right and banned from the human touch he craved so much. Orion had been Alexandro's toy for three hundred years, taking punishment for everyone. Alexandro had given them pain. I was going to try to give them happiness.

"I think Alexandro might be jealous. The more he messes with me, the more he's driving me to band together with those of you who aren't evil. The more he hurts us, the more it brings us together. I think it bothers him to see me with any of you. He doesn't remember what friendship is like, and it kills him to see others happy. He did this as a punishment to Ariel, and it backfired."

"Who would not be jealous of you?" Orion asked. "You are the only living flesh left." His left hand reached up to gently touch the exposed skin at my wrist. "Many vampires crave human flesh. As much as they value their immortality, they crave the living. It is not just the blood that calls to us. It is the life. It's the warmth, the comfort it offers."

"It's just blood," I said grimly, not wishing to put more value on myself than I felt was due. I'd done nothing but survive. I was not special. I was not interesting. I simply wasn't dead.

Orion went to reply, but he was ripped violently away from me.

I gave a cry of protest as I watched him hit the floor. I didn't get a chance to see if he was okay because I was pulled roughly into someone's chest.

I looked up to find myself in Kieran's arms and nearly panicked. He probably wouldn't hurt me in a room full of witnesses, but I didn't know for sure. I squirmed against him, trying to loosen his grip on me.

Instead, he tightened his hold, pressing me flat against his body. "Did you think about my offer?" he asked, his lips near my ear. His words melted into a deep growl, and I feared he might bite my ear off.

"Drop dead." I kept a hard edge to my voice, refusing the give in to my fear.

"I already did," Kieran replied wickedly. "It's your turn." He swayed to the music, running a hand inappropriately down my backside. "Not before I have my way with you first, of course."

His left arm held me tightly against him while his right hand slipped inward to slowly run up my inner thigh. His eyes narrowed at the look of disgust on my face. "You didn't seem to have a problem when Banning was practically fucking you in front of everyone. Why be shy now?" His hand skimmed over my hip and slid up my stomach.

I wasn't sure how he had gotten his hand between us, because he had me pressed so tightly against him.

His hand continued to travel upward over my ribs. "I want to hear you scream." His fingers inched up, gently running along my breasts.

"Let me go," I said angrily, fighting against him.

"Beg me to," Kieran said breathily in my ear. "Beg me." His eyes flicked to something behind my head. "Scream for Ariel. I want to hear the desperation in your voice." His mouth lowered to my throat, and he licked along the skin. He then smelled along the path his tongue had just taken.

I was beginning to think this was a trait of vampirism, because he hadn't been the only one to smell me.

"The thought of your screams excites me," he whispered, straightening up to look at me. "Scream for him. Do it now. Scream for him!"

"She doesn't need to."

Hearing Ariel's voice helped me to relax a little. He had seen Kieran's assault and come to my rescue.

Kieran gave a hiss as he looked over at Ariel. "I did not do anything different than the others. I am merely dancing."

"And I'm cutting in." Ariel pulled me away from Kieran. "You are not to be near her again."

"I cannot help if she wanders into my path."

"If you harm her, I will kill you before you can run to Alexandro. He will not be able to hide you from me. I will torture you until the little sanity you have left cracks. You wouldn't be able to handle the pain I rained down upon you."

Kieran's expression stayed confident, but I saw the flicker of fear behind his eyes. I think Ariel saw it, too.

Orion was not as good at hiding his terror. He shivered from where he cowered on the floor, his eyes wide in fear of torment that was not even to be his. Ariel must be damn good at the art of torture to receive such a reaction.

Kieran's eyes narrowed angrily, but he didn't dare openly challenge Ariel.

"Leave us," Ariel said, his voice low with warning. "I don't want to see you again this evening."

Kieran gave a bow that was full of sarcasm. "As you wish. I did not mean to dampen *your* evening." He said "your" in a way that let me know he had fully intended to destroy mine. Kieran straightened from his bow, and his green eyes locked onto mine, darkening with malicious intent.

I gave a sigh of relief as he suddenly turned and disappeared into the crowd. I expected Ariel to leave as soon as Kieran was out of sight, but he stayed, tightening his grip on my waist.

I guess he could see the shock on my face, because he gave a deep chuckle. "You think that I do not enjoy dancing?"

"You don't seem like the dancing type," I said honestly.

"I'm even more surprised because I thought you didn't enjoy me."

Ariel laughed again and moved slowly to the music, guiding my body to follow his rhythm. "Sometimes I wonder. I truly do."

"Your life would be boring without me in it." I knew it was a ridiculous thing to say. He was a vampire. I don't think a single moment of his life had ever been boring.

His eyebrows rose in amusement. "So you're saying I wouldn't have people breaking into my place trying to kill its occupants? I wouldn't have to run out to a zombie-infested hospital to save a bullheaded, careless girl who doesn't know how to follow orders? Our men wouldn't be forced to put their lives in danger due to your recklessness? Is that all the excitement I'd be missing? I'll take the boring life."

"You'd miss me," I accused.

"What makes you so sure?"

"The fact that you're here." I smiled softly up at him, knowing in my heart it was the truth. Ariel had his demons, and they were awful ones, but he was trying. His presence here was proof of that. He should hate me for every horrific memory my mortality dragged up, but he didn't.

"It's my job to be here."

"No. It's your job to protect me, not dance with me. This you're doing of your own free will."

"Maybe I do like you," Ariel admitted. "But just a little."

"Just a little," I said in agreement, nodding my head with a wry smile.

"You have to make this as hard as possible on me, don't you?"

I gave a soft laugh and wrapped my arms around his neck, stepping closer to him. "You know me. I'll never let you do anything easily."

Ariel pulled me flat against his chest. "That's exactly how I like it." There was a growl to his voice that gave me chills.

I took a deep breath and stared up at him. "So does this mean you don't hate humans anymore?"

Ariel's grip lightened, and his face softened. "I never hated humans, Aurora." He still moved to the music, though he had slowed considerably. "I'm just frightened by your mortality. I loved..." He broke off and looked away from me. He swallowed and closed his eyes tightly. "I loved a mortal woman once."

"I know."

Ariel's eyes flew open in surprise, and he gave me a questioning look.

"Banning told me."

Ariel shook his head in slight amusement. "*Now* Banning really has managed to piss me off."

I could tell by the tone of his voice he was only joking. I don't think he held it against Banning. It was probably easier than having to relive the event again by telling it to me himself.

The mere mention of it seemed to have shaken Ariel badly. Unshed tears glittered in his eyes from just thinking about Angelina. "I can't do that again. I can't get...I can't lose someone like that again."

I knew he was about to say he couldn't get attached, but it was too late. Whether he liked it or not, there was a bond between us. He cared about me, and I cared about him, too.

"He made me kill her," Ariel said. "He made me dig a ditch and dump her body. He made me bury her right outside, so I will always walk over her remains, always remember."

His eyes held a haunted look that made my heart sink to the pit of my stomach. Alexandro had wounded them more than I ever imagined. How anyone could survive here with their sanity was beyond me.

Ariel looked down at me, his face a mask of misery. "I'll never forget."

I tightened my arms around his neck, trying to offer him a bit of comfort. "You shouldn't forget about her. You loved her." Resolve filled me at my next comment. "It's not going to happen again, though. I will never allow Alexandro to hurt me." I stared into the depths of his dark blue eyes. They had lightened with his tears, making him look more human.

My eyes then traveled over the contours of his face. By nature and without knowing a single thing about Ariel, any woman could see he was absolutely beautiful. This vulnerability made him even more irresistible to me. He was attractive in his arrogance, but when he looked down at me now with his uncertainty, he was truly beautiful. This was the real him. He'd finally cast aside the mask.

I brought my hand down to touch his chest, running my fingertips over the fabric of his suit jacket. His chest was firm and muscled to perfection. I wasn't aware of anything but the feel of his solidness beneath my hand. The rest of the world seemed to fade away.

As we swayed slowly to the music, surrounded by other couples, the fingers of his left hand buried into my hair, gently running through it, caressing my scalp.

It startled me a little, bringing my gaze back to his face. I took a sharp intake of breath as the back of his hand moved to run across my cheek. His skin felt like the softest silk. An idea began forming in my mind, and I closed my eyes against the intensity of his gaze. Leaning into his touch, I whispered, "Use your powers on me." I wanted to know what it was like. He could affect me so thoroughly with just a look. I wanted to experience, if just for a moment, what his true power felt like.

An instant after my request, my head swam. My skin felt like it was on fire where he touched me. That fire traveled and collected at a place just south of my stomach, filling me with a throbbing need. It was overwhelming, like nothing I'd ever felt before. I gave a soft gasp and collapsed against him, barely able to stay on my feet.

He didn't seem to mind this one bit. He held me against him, supporting my weight easily in his arms.

My head fell back as if by its own will, and I took a ragged breath. I hadn't been prepared for this, for how overwhelming his touch could be if he willed it so.

Ariel ran a hand down my throat that made my entire body tingle. I was feeling things in places I shouldn't from him simply running a hand across my neck. His fingers traveled downward, running softly along my collarbone, bringing a whimper from me.

I opened my eyes to look at him. I had thought he couldn't get any more gorgeous, but he was. It stole my breath away to look at him. His eyes were darkened by lust, yet his hair seemed to have lightened so much it practically glowed. I wanted to rip the front of his shirt open so I could feel his skin underneath my fingertips. I was desperate for him, desperate for his touch. I wanted him in a way that frightened me. I wanted him naked so I could caress every delectable inch of his body.

As quickly as it started, it was over. I could tell the instant he pulled his powers back, the instant he stopped what he was doing before things went too far.

I stared up at Ariel, and he was just himself. He was still very sexy, but I was able to get myself under control. The need to touch him wasn't as desperate as it had been a moment before. The urge to strip him naked had faded.

With a proud, almost smug countenance on his face, he leaned in to whisper in my ear. "And that was without any sexual contact. I didn't even kiss you. Imagine the pleasure I could give in the heat of intercourse."

I let my breath out slowly. "Wow."

Ariel lifted one eyebrow, his lip curling into a grin. "I know." With that, he let go of me and walked off the dance floor.

I stared after him for a moment in befuddlement. I couldn't seem to focus clearly after his sudden departure. I knew I was standing in the center of the dance floor gaping like a fool, but clarity had yet to return to my mind. I silently told myself to start walking. I needed to get off the dance floor to keep myself from looking like an imbecile, standing all alone without a partner, staring longingly after Ariel as if lovesick.

I stumbled toward the refreshment table, trying to avoid other couples with my unsteady steps while my mind was completely absorbed with Ariel. I couldn't even fathom the full extent of his powers. It was a little scary, yet I found myself wondering how pleasurable just a little more could have been.

My hand found the drink table, and I shakily poured myself a glass. The contents of the punch bowl were a deep amber color. I hesitated only a moment. Surely they wouldn't fill a punch bowl with blood. I brought the glass uncertainly to my nose and took a tentative sniff. As I smelled my drink, a woman on the dance floor caught my attention.

She stood by herself in the center of the floor, swaying to the music while everyone else made a pointed effort to avoid bumping into her. It was more like the music swayed to her, though. She had a thick mane of brown curls. Blonde highlights streaked through it, catching the light and causing her hair to practically shimmer. In the back of my mind, I contemplated the fact that they probably weren't natural highlights. Vampires didn't see sunlight for them to be real. She turned on the dance floor, her gold dress sparkling around her, and her eyes locked onto mine.

I stepped backwards and bumped into the table, feeling a stab of anxiety to have her catch me staring.

A coy grin crept up her lips, and she started making her way in my direction, never stopping her graceful dance. She looked like a supermodel on a runway. Everyone moved out of her way as she walked, staring after her in open admiration and awe.

I self-consciously tugged at my dress. I was usually very confident in my looks, but there was just something about her that made me second-guess myself.

She stopped in front of me, her eyes roaming over my attire. "So, you're the human," she said in a voice that was a sultry purr. "I guess I can see what the fuss is all about." She eyed me from head to toe, her eyes flicking restlessly over me. "The girl that finally softened my Ariel."

"*Your* Ariel?" I asked in disbelief. Ariel didn't belong to anyone. He was obstinately independent. He was a loner. "Not to be rude, but who are you?"

She tossed her head back, giving a deep, throaty laugh. "It has been a long time since someone here did not know who I was." She put her hands on her hips and her blue eyes stared piercingly at me. "You stay in my home, yet you do not know of me."

It suddenly dawned on me exactly who she was. "Panthea." The name sent a tingle of fear down my spine. Alexandro's twin. She was here, in the flesh.

"Very good," she said with a little grin. "Someone has been educating you."

I bristled, my fear amping up to a higher level. She was the woman vampires feared. Even Alexandro conceded to her.

"I see Ariel is not the only one you enthrall." She nodded casually behind me.

I turned, expecting to see Banning. Instead, I found Kieran staring at me from the shadows. I gave a shiver and spun back around. I was surprised to see her lip curl up in a bitchy sneer.

"Despicable creature," she said under her breath. "I should have put him out of his misery centuries ago."

I found it odd that Panthea hated Kieran. He was Alexandro's second in command. He was her brother's most trusted ally. "He does seem pretty evil," I said cautiously. "I think his vampire powers have gone to his head."

"No." Panthea disagreed. "Power has not changed him. He was the same alive as he is now."

"He was psychotic back then, too?"

She nodded. "He had himself in quite a predicament before he became a vampire. He had a pesky little habit of killing women. He might have gotten away with it had he killed the homeless or prostitutes, people no one would miss. Our boy had a soft spot for rich women, though. He loved to capture himself a debutante. He reveled in the fact that Daddy's money couldn't save them from him. He couldn't be bribed. He couldn't be reasoned with. He was unfeeling and unmerciful. He was also sloppy."

She gave a careless shrug. "Of course, he got caught. Not only did they catch him, they caught him in the act. They pulled him off of some snooty lass of high standing. She had been perfect before Kieran got to her. They saved her life, but they couldn't save her pretty face. She was mangled, beaten, raped. Kieran destroyed her. It might have been better for them to just let her die. It surely would have been more merciful." She waved this away as if it truly didn't matter. "Since Kieran only picked high-class women, when he was caught, people started putting things together and connecting all of his murders back to him. Like most serial killers, he had patterns that linked every last murder together. To say the least, he had many powerful enemies. There was no trial for Kieran. Things weren't how they are now when he committed his crimes. They were going to put him to death. His neck was on the chopping block, waiting for the guillotine to lob his head off when we swooped in and rescued him."

"Why would you save him when you knew how evil he was?" I couldn't understand why anyone would wish to save such a monster. The world would have been a better place without Kieran in it.

"We all have our reasons," Panthea explained. "Is it not worth it to have something wonderful if you keep the bad as well? Or would you give up the thing you loved most just to be certain that evil did not live?"

Her answer confused me. What about Kieran was good? Nothing that I could see.

"Like I said, we all have our reasons." Panthea stared at Kieran, and her eyes softened. I could see warmth and affection in her gaze, and it confused me.

She suddenly whipped her attention back to me, moving quicker than any human would have been able to. She'd only been looking over my shoulder, so she didn't have far to move, but her actions were too smooth, too swift. She didn't even seem to realize she had used supernatural speed. "Enough about him." She turned blue eyes to me. "I would like to talk about your little escape."

I felt threatened by her tone. She hadn't done anything specifically threatening. She was simply intimidating, and the topic was not one any of the vampires were happy with. I'd pissed off a lot of people by taking off. "I...I..."

"I heard you snuck out under Ariel's watch, had him in a panic." She raised a hand up to study her nails. Her casual air made it that much more frightening. I was afraid she was going to reach out and snap my neck without any warning. Kieran, I knew, would see punishment for killing me. Panthea could probably get away with it.

"Ariel is a very difficult man to deal with when things aren't going his way," she continued. "He gets rough." I could tell by the purr in her voice that she liked it when he got rough. "I heard he had your arm an inch from breaking the socket." She gave a delighted sigh. "It is an art he has perfected. He knows the exact point of break. It is a talent I helped him perfect over the years."

I pictured the two of them hovered over some poor mortal, testing just how far they could bend something before it snapped.

"When Ariel was still a warrior, he was rough in all things," she confided. It didn't take a rocket scientist to know what she was referring to. Ariel was rough in bed. Great. "He had such raw, angry passion. Sex with Ariel was fear-provoking. It was exhilarating. You never knew if he was going to go too far. It kept you on your toes...or any other way he wanted you. He was still that same violently passionate man when I met up with him years later, after we'd both become vampires." She gave a pout. "Then he met the human.

I did not see much of him then, for I was away, but I know he changed. He softened. Our kind is not meant to be so vulnerable. He took all of his rage, his wild passion, and turned it into love for his mortal. Everything was for her." She stopped, staring into space, lost in her own memories.

"Did you love Ariel?" I couldn't help but ask. It must have been terrible to watch the person you love be stolen away.

She looked at me with thoughtful eyes. "I loved Ariel. Not in the way you think, but I did love him. Ariel and I were never a couple. We did things when the need arose, but it was never out of love. I was not jealous of Angelina. I merely feared for Ariel. He was too swept away with such a fragile creature. When she was killed, Ariel's violent tendencies re-turned. Only, it wasn't a rage of passion. It was cold. He didn't kill because he was angry. He didn't drink for the thrill it brought. He just did it. That Ariel terrified me. He cared for nothing and no one." She paused and her eyes held mine, their depths full of intensity. "He has been that way until now. You have brought back some of the fire into his eyes. He had not used any of his powers for anything good since Angelina's death...until tonight. I am envious of you. To have the affection of such a creature..."

Her eyes suddenly darkened to anger, and I felt my pulse speed up in reaction. "To put you with Ariel was a very risky thing to do. With the disposition he's been trapped in, he simply might have killed you just to keep his heart protected from reminders of Angelina. You are very fortunate to be alive right now." She paused, letting that sink in before she added, "Sneaking off does not add to life expectancy either."

I tensed, unhappy to be on that subject again. "I...I'm sorry." I swallowed down my fear and changed my answer to fit closer to the truth. "I'm not sorry I did it. I'm sorry I did it behind Ariel's back."

She threw her head back, giving another deep, purring laugh. "Do not apologize to me, little one. I do not care one way or the other. I just know it takes great courage to defy Ariel. Not many have defied him and lived. I find it all quite amusing. I have to admit, I always loved to see Ariel sweat." The tone of her voice held sexual innuendo. She didn't linger on it, though. Instead, she pressed on. "Diego tells me you're quite the marksman, said you picked a few zombies off while lying flat on your back." She gave that velvety laugh again. "Vampires love a girl with talent flat on her back."

There it was again, that sly sexual undertone. I wasn't sure if it was directed at me or simply part of her nature. Orion had said she was very erotic. "I'm not sleeping with any of them," I said, defending myself just in case.

"Pity," she said with a frown. "You don't know what you're missing." Her eyes traveled across the room to Banning. "Especially with the little one. While some of us perfected the art of torture, he was busy perfecting something else." She took a sharp intake of breath, her breasts rising, crushed against the tight fabric of her dress. She tip-toed her fingers down her hips. "If I thought for one moment he would be happy to stay with me, I would take him for my own, but he craves the touch of human flesh too much. I settle for the few nights he gives me when he is in the mood for our cold bodies." She ran her tongue slowly along her lips, taking in the sight of Banning. She wasn't even under his spell, and he warranted this kind of reaction. I would have to remember to be cautious around him.

Panthea let out a shuddering sigh, then turned back to me. "Back to the story of you being a naughty girl." She gave me a casual grin. "Diego said you snuck to that hospital to save lives. You succeeded. We need that. Some of our men are too brass. If you can use a gun and you can persuade Ariel to do your will, you can do anything. I think you should go with the men tomorrow night. Ariel will be there to watch over you, as will I."

I was shocked for a moment. She wasn't here to punish me. She was rewarding me.

"I know you wanted to see for yourself whether your family survived or not. We can stop by your home. You need some belongings anyway. You can pack a few bags and help look for survivors." She smiled wryly. "Besides, it will thoroughly piss off my brother if I let you come along. I couldn't pass up that opportunity."

I didn't know what to say to that. She was letting me join them out of spite, but at least she was letting me join them. I couldn't believe what I was hearing. Panthea was letting me go home. I could see if my family was alive. I wouldn't forever be filled with unanswered questions.

"You must be able to handle what we will probably find. You need to be prepared. We have done multiple searches in town without finding anything positive to report. Are you prepared to see your loved ones as one of those things?"

I gave a quick, emphatic nod. "I just want to know."

"Then you will find out."

I let out a breath of relief. "You don't know how much this means to me. I didn't know if I'd ever get the chance to see if they were alive."

"Do not make me regret this decision. Find others as yourself, and come back alive. You've already saved one that the men would have left to perish."

I glanced around the room, realizing for the first time Ginny wasn't present. "Speaking of which, where is Ginny?"

"I heard she was feeling ill. A shame. Our kind was looking forward to meeting the only three humans known alive."

"Three," I said softly, my eyes wandering to Damian. It was quite obvious to me that the female vampires were looking forward to meeting him.

Damian had a flock of women around him. They all stared up at him in admiration while he told them some story. It appeared to me as if he was retelling the events of the restaurant the night our world was turned upside down. He was waving an invisible object at an equally invisible foe. The actions brought back memories of him brandishing a chair at a hoard of famished zombies, protecting me from certain death. He talked animatedly, seemingly loving the attention. His eyes suddenly landed on me, and he gave me that sly, seductive grin. He had caught me staring at him. Damn it.

I spun quickly to avert my gaze and ran straight into someone's chest. I gave an *oomph* and had to steady myself on the person's arms. I found myself staring into Banning's eyes. It was odd not to have to look up to meet his gaze.

He put his hands on my shoulders, helping to steady me. "Whoa there, girl. You've got to watch where you're walking."

I felt a blush creep up my cheeks. "Sorry, I was just…" I didn't want to admit I'd gotten caught staring, so I didn't finish the sentence.

"It's cool," Banning said casually. "It's not like you're going to hurt me. I've got that vampire strength. I was more worried about you. You're going to break your nose running face-first into things like that." He tapped a finger playfully to my nose. "Yours won't automatically fix itself like mine would."

I touched two fingers to my nose, feeling for imaginary damage even though I hadn't actually bumped it on anything. "No, it wouldn't."

While I was distracted with my nose, he slid his arm around my waist and pulled me firmly to his chest. "I'm not finished with you," he said, voice deep. "You owe me at least one more dance."

I laughed, relaxing into his arms. "You really are quite the party animal."

"I warned you," Banning said with a grin. He lifted my arm and twirled me in a circle, pulling me quickly back into his chest. "Don't deny that you want to go out there and show off with me."

I ran my fingertips over the shoulder of his suit jacket, giving him a seductive grin. "I didn't."

His eyes darkened, and I recognized the predatory look in them. It wasn't the look of a vampire wanting to sink fangs into a victim's neck. It was a look I recognized. It was the look a man gets when he's attracted to a woman.

I tilted my head, letting my blonde hair brush against his arm. "Are you ready to show me a good time?"

He pulled me in tighter against him. "I'm always ready to show a woman a good time."

"So I've heard."

Banning glanced at Panthea over my shoulder, an amused smirk on his lips. "Have you been telling stories?"

Panthea simply shrugged.

Banning leaned in toward my ear. "It's all true." With that, he pulled me onto the dance floor.

I glanced over my shoulder at Panthea.

She raised her eyebrows at me, a suggestive look on her face. The look was to let me know she was right. It would be pleasurable to just give in to Banning.

I quickly averted my eyes. I couldn't just sleep with someone because they were good in bed. As comfortable as everyone else around here seemed to be with sex, I wasn't.

Banning pulled me close to him, enveloping me in his arms. He swayed slowly to the music, guiding my body with his own. I could see the hunger behind his eyes. It wasn't just the hunger to be around mortals. It was for me.

As if sensing where my train of thought was, he said, "We are sexual beings. It is in our nature. I can't change what I feel. Nor can I change what I am."

I tightened my arms around his neck. "I never asked you to."

A look of surprise crossed Banning's face. It quickly turned into his devilish grin. He spun me around so that my back was to him. He pulled me in close to his body, placing one hand on my hip, the other flat against my stomach. He guided my body to move in rhythm with his. "I think we should have a little fun then." He breathed the words into my ear, seducing me with mere speech.

A tingle traveled down my arms, my entire body reacting to his touch. It would be so easy to give in to him, to succumb to his advances, to let him show me what a thousand years of practice could teach a man.

I took a deep breath and forced those urges back. I would not sleep with Banning. It wouldn't be right. That didn't mean I couldn't have fun with him, though. There was no harm in a little flirting or in dancing with a man. I spun to face him, pressing my body firmly against his, leaving no space between us. "Just dance with me," I said, voice low and husky with desire. I leaned into him, putting my lips inches from his. "We'll start there."

Banning gave a soft groan at the closeness of my lips. I could tell he wanted to close the distance between us, but he held himself in check. Good boy. "Sounds like fun." He didn't seem to be able to keep his hands to themselves despite his agreement. They ran slowly down my back and over the curves of my ass. He pulled my lower body roughly against his. "To start."

I looked up at him through my hair, my breath hitching at such blatant sexual contact. I might not sleep with him, but dancing felt damn near close enough when it came to Banning. At that moment, I really didn't care. I was going to enjoy myself.

Tomorrow might be the worst night of my life, depending on what we found at my old home. Tonight, I was going to relax and put everything else out of my mind.

Chapter 14

I stood inside the hallway of Alexandro's mansion, nervously wringing my hands together. Last night, when I'd discussed assisting the rescue teams on their search for survivors, it seemed like a great idea. Now, I was terrified.

What if we didn't find anyone alive? What if when we got to my house, my entire family was dead? I'd thought last night that knowing the answers would be better than wondering what had happened to them. Now, I was pondering if I'd been wrong.

I was so distracted I didn't notice someone approach me until they leaned in to whisper in my ear. The voice was cold and insensitive. "Having second thoughts, are we?"

I turned and found myself looking up into Kieran's catlike eyes. I fought the initial urge to cry out. There were too many people nearby for him to start much with me. Both Aldrich and Banning's teams were spread out in the hallway. All it would take was one cry for help and vampires would surround me.

Diego was helping Kenya tighten a shoulder holster for a knife, his hands moving affectionately over her arms. Banning was only a few feet away with his back to me, a ridiculously large map held up in front of him. He turned to the side, and the map in his hands became visible to me from the new angle. He squinted at it as if it was written in a foreign language. "This doesn't make any sense," he said, slapping at the center of the massive sheet full of roads and buildings.

Ariel was staring down at the map, an amused look on his face while he calmly tried to explain the directions to Banning. "That's called a side road."

"But it was never there before," Banning protested. "I've never seen this in my life. It's like it's a completely different town. It's like..."

"You haven't been to it for forty years."

"Well...yeah," Banning said sheepishly. "I haven't."

"Exactly."

"Don't ignore me." Kieran's voice lashed out in agitation, instantly drawing my attention back to him. "I asked if you were ready to chicken out yet. Is seeing the mutilated body of your mommy going to be too much for you to handle?"

My eyes slid back to his. I tried to tell my heart to control itself, to stop beating so frantically. There really wasn't much he could do but call me a few names. I was a big girl. A little name-calling didn't require me calling the cavalry.

Kieran's lip curved up into a grin as he studied my expression, watching hopefully for signs that he'd gotten to me. "I killed *my* mother. Hacked her to pieces. And I made my little sister watch."

"Kieran." Panthea's voice cut in as she stepped up beside him. "Fuck off."

Kieran gave her a long look of outright hatred. He backed up a step, though. Looked like he wasn't as tough as he liked to pretend to be. He was afraid to stand his ground against the woman of the house. "I'll leave you whores alone," he said darkly before melting into the shadows.

Panthea rolled her eyes and let out a little sigh. "He's always such a pleasure." She looked in the direction he'd disappeared to, eyes narrowed. "I keep hoping he'll sleepwalk into the sun. Haven't had any luck yet."

That was something I fully agreed with. If he were to accidentally stumble out into a fiery death, I wouldn't shed any tears over it.

"Don't you worry about him," Panthea said, patting me gently on the shoulder. "He's just pissy because I arranged for him to stay home this evening. I figured he'd do more harm than good. We wouldn't want him sneaking into your old bedroom and smelling your panties or anything now, would we?"

I shuddered at the thought of Kieran having access to anything that belonged to me, especially underwear. "Yeah...thanks."

"Don't mention it, babe. Us whores have to stick together," Panthea said with a wink before walking off. She sidled over to Ariel and Banning, slinging an arm over each of their shoulders as she engaged them in banter.

I was left staring after her, feeling a need to defend myself. She'd only been teasing, but I still didn't feel comfortable being labeled a whore, not even in jest. I wasn't as easy as everyone around here was making me out to be. Just because I was extremely attracted to three different men didn't make me a whore...right? It wasn't like I'd done anything about it with any of them, and I couldn't help the way I felt.

Banning had supernatural sex powers, and Ariel had ways to use his powers to turn me on as well. They had spent nearly a thousand years perfecting sexy. I was powerless against them.

And Damian...I didn't know where to start with that one. A few days ago, I'd thought I hated him. Yet, he was growing on me...in a big way. Last night, I had been mere inches away from kissing him. I had gone to bed mixed between relief that Banning had walked in and disappointment because I really, really had wanted to kiss him.

I'd thought the urge to kiss him was something I would be able to sleep off, but the moment I saw him this morning, my heart started pounding like I'd just run a marathon. I was in deep...way over my head. I'd never had a serious relationship before. I didn't date multiple men or get involved with such complicated circumstances, and now three men tempted me. Life was confusing sometimes.

As if sensing I was thinking about him, Damian appeared at my side. "You look nervous," he said quietly.

I spun to face him, anxiety on my face. "That's because I *am* nervous. I'm afraid of what I'm going to see...I'm afraid I won't come back."

"Banning won't let anything happen to you," he said reassuringly. "I already threatened his life if you get so much as a scratch."

I let out a laugh, relaxing a little at his joke. "Was he scared?"

"Terrified," Damian confirmed. "He promised to bring you back in one piece. He doesn't want to face my wrath."

"I'm sure," I said with a little smile. "What exactly are you going to do that's going to frighten a vampire with superhuman strength and speed?"

"I don't know," Damian said with a shrug. "I'll feed him some garlic or something."

I let out a loud laugh and covered my mouth to silence it. I glanced in Banning's direction and lowered my voice to a whisper. "Yeah, that would do it."

I had told Damian about the whole Dracula thing. I think he'd gained some respect for Banning after that. Men. Go figure. Banning makes up an identity to trick women into sleeping with him, and Damian is impressed. I shouldn't have been surprised.

"So, that's Ariel?" Damian asked.

My eyes moved from Banning to Ariel. The look of amusement that had been on his face only minutes before was completely gone. It had been replaced with annoyance. His expression was downright sour, though Banning still looked peachy as could be. "Yeah," I said to Damian, my voice full of amusement. "That's mister grumpy himself."

Damian nodded thoughtfully. "He doesn't look like a friendly fellow."

"No. He usually isn't."

With a shrug of dismissal, Damian turned back to me. "Promise me you'll be careful out there. I couldn't bear..." He shook his head. "I don't want anything to happen to you."

I nodded, my anxiety from earlier returning. "I know." I suddenly felt very cold, a side effect of terror. I wrapped my arms around myself, gripping my elbows tightly for warmth. "I'll be careful."

Damian grabbed my face in his hands. Leaning in, he kissed my forehead. "You come back home to me."

I looked up into his chocolate brown eyes, my breath catching anxiously in my throat. I felt tears start to well up in my eyes. Oh God. I was going to cry. I was going to start weeping like a baby because I was afraid and wanted him to take me in his arms and keep me safe. The only problem was that Panthea had forbidden him to come along. It was me or no one. I was on my own.

"Aurora!" Ariel barked my name, his tone hard. "Let's go!"

I lifted terrified eyes to Damian.

He brought my hand to his lips and kissed my knuckles gently. "They'll keep you safe."

I nodded numbly, gripping his hand tightly in mine.

Ariel suddenly grabbed me by the elbow and pulled me away from Damian. "We have to go now. Either quit stalling or stay home." Ariel wasn't happy about this arrangement. He didn't want to go with the rescue teams, and he really didn't want me going with them.

Damian shot Ariel a quick look of annoyance before putting his fingers to his lips. He then pressed his fingertips to my nose. "Bring us back some survivors."

"Because she's going to be so helpful on this trip," Ariel grumbled, pulling me out the door. He ushered me to the van like I was a dog he feared would take off if left unattended.

I climbed into the van, pulling my arm free of his grip. "He was just worried about me," I said as I flopped down and slid across the seat to the window.

"As he should be," Ariel said, sliding in to sit tightly against me. "You're out of your fucking mind. I think you want to die. I honestly do."

I rolled my eyes. "I think you're exaggerating just a little."

Banning jumped in next, taking the seat next to Ariel. He interrupted any defensive comment Ariel had been planning to say. "Hey, buddy. Good to see you in an excellent mood." Sarcasm dripped from his voice, and he grinned devilishly at me as he spoke.

Ariel sent him a dark look, not bothering to say anything.

Banning cringed. "Yikes."

I smiled and looked down at my hands. At least I wasn't the only one who thought Ariel was being a little too grouchy.

The van started to move as Banning closed the door behind him, and I completely forgot about who was being grumpy and who wasn't. My thoughts went to my family and what had become of them. I would hopefully know soon enough.

We drove in silence for less than five minutes before the driver pulled to the curb and stopped. It was night, but the moon was nearly full and bright, lighting the area like a giant, horrific flashlight.

Vehicles were overturned. Bodies lay strewn in the street. It was like a nightmare come to life. Looking at the damage, I didn't know how it was possible for anyone to still be alive out here. That grim fact hit me hard, making my stomach roil queasily.

Before I could even collect my thoughts, the door of the van slid open and everyone started jumping out.

"Everyone stay on alert," Banning said, hollering out instructions. "Ask questions before you shoot. We're looking for survivors here, not just cleaning house."

Aldrich climbed out of the van, stretching out his long legs. "I prefer the kill. You want questions asked, you're going to have to do it yourself."

"Thanks," Banning said sarcastically. "Thanks for all the help."

I slid across the seat and went to exit the van when Ariel's arm swung out and blocked my path. "Where the hell do you think you're going?"

I gave him puzzled eyes. "Out?"

He shook his head and pointed to the seat. "Sit down. Panthea said you could help search your old home. There's no way in hell you're getting out of this van until that point, so sit back and relax."

Sometimes, Ariel was an idiot. I don't think he realized how impossible it might be to relax while zombies shuffled around outside the vehicle, moaning to get in.

"What if the zombies tip the van to get to me?" I asked, fear racing through me at the thought of being left alone in the van while everyone else conducted their searches.

"You can't leave her alone," Panthea said in agreement to my worried thoughts.

Ariel's arm was blocking Panthea from exiting the van as well. "I'm not. You're staying with her." He gave her shoulder a little push, forcing her back down into her seat when she tried to stand.

"*Me*?" Panthea asked in astonishment as she half sprawled across the seat as a result from Ariel's shove. "You think *I'm* staying?"

A smirk crept up Ariel's lips, and he gave her a mock look of regret. "I know you are. You were the one who wanted her along. It's now your responsibility to babysit."

He slammed the door shut, cutting off any argument Panthea might have had.

With a huffy exhale, she straightened up in the seat, crossing her legs to return herself to the picture of elegance.

"Well….I…I can't believe the nerve…" Shaking her head, she said, "No one but Ariel." Settling back as if this was entirely her idea, Panthea gave me a bright smile. "I guess we get to have a little girl time."

I heard a shout, and then a gun fired. Through the window, I saw a body hit the ground and not get back up.

I turned worried eyes to Panthea, but she was still giving me that bright smile as if she hadn't even heard the shot. I knew she must have noticed. It hadn't exactly been quiet. This led me to the conclusion that she was a maniac. She'd seen one too many people tortured. She cared far too little about the men outside and the dangers they faced.

"Oh, don't give me that look," she said with a sigh. Leaning her head on her wrist, she added, "I've seen Ariel in action. A few zombies aren't going to get the best of him. Not in a million years." She arched an eyebrow. "I assume you've heard of our colorful past together. My husband threw an entire arena of bloodthirsty criminals and starving beasts at him, and Ariel prevailed. He's frightening when he gets a weapon in his hands. If an arena of men could not stop him when he was mortal, a street full of zombies won't even make him break a sweat now."

She turned to face the large window on the sliding door of the van. "You've just won a front row seat to watch a Roman gladiator battle. If you've never seen Ariel in action before…" She trailed off with a wicked grin, licking her fangs and squirming around in her seat anxiously. "This is a show you don't want to miss."

She seemed very confident in Ariel's abilities. Maybe I was just worrying too much. She'd seen him in battle many times before. I'd only had a few glimpses of what he was capable of. I would just have to take her word for it.

I turned wary eyes to the window. Even if I was totally confident in his abilities, that didn't mean I wanted to witness the damage Ariel was about to do. The hospital had been horrifying enough. I wasn't looking forward to a repeat experience.

The events going on outside the window were like a bad car accident. I didn't want to look, but somehow, my eyes found the bloodiest things going on, and I didn't have the ability to look away.

Zombies were shuffling forward from all directions. They were stumbling out of the open front doors of houses to add to the masses slowly surrounding the van.

Banning and Ariel were holding off their advancements, one slicing and cutting away appendages as the other fired round after round into the mob. While they did this, a small team of four vampires I didn't recognize kicked down the door of the first house on the street. The vampires disappeared inside as a second team moved forward to the second house, repeating the action.

Banning and Ariel stayed outside, trying to keep the vehicles from being overrun while the search teams did their thing. There were so many zombies, though. It seemed like every time Banning or Ariel took one down, three more appeared in its place.

I gasped in fear as Banning went down under three of them. For a terrifying moment, I was afraid he wouldn't be getting back up. Having Banning die would be bad enough. To be forced to watch him get eaten alive would be unbearable.

"Give him a minute," Panthea said calmly. "Banning is a sly little guy. He'll get back up."

I wished I had her confidence. All I knew was that someone I perceived as a decent man had just been tackled to the ground by abominations that wanted to tear his flesh from his body and consume it.

Ariel had a gun in his left hand. He was firing at zombies approaching from that side. With his right hand, he swung his sword in a wide arc at one of the zombies that had fallen onto Banning.

One handed, he managed to behead it while his bullet hit another between the eyes. He then brought the sword down viciously through the back of the second zombie on Banning. The sound of bones and organs being sliced through reached us in the van. He spun around in a blur of speed, firing directly into the throat of a zombie approaching him from behind. He didn't even wait to see if Banning got back up. He just assumed he had.

My eyes frantically searched the area where Banning had gone down. I let out a sigh of relief when he sprang to his feet, nipping up. He brought his fist up into the jaw of the third zombie.

While the zombie was recovering from the blow, Banning swung his sword around, catching it in the throat. He hollered something to Ariel that I couldn't make out, and Ariel smiled.

I furrowed my eyebrows in surprise. The expressions on their faces... It looked like... They looked like they were having fun. The instant I thought it, I knew it as truth. Son of a bitch, they were enjoying themselves! Each and every last one of these vampires were freaking maniacs.

Both continued to progress in silence, their movements as smooth and graceful as dancers. They glided over the ground, leaving a trail of death in their wake.

I'd never seen such destruction done firsthand in my life. They were vicious and swift, moving quicker than any human could. They moved in tandem with each killing blow.

Banning used his upper body to put more force behind his sword as he forced it down into a skull. As he ducked down to drive the blade home, Ariel's arm automatically raised to where Banning's head had been a fraction of a second before, and he fired his weapon without a single hesitation.

If either were off by even a millisecond, one of them would severely hurt the other. Their movements were so in sync, so perfect, I knew just by watching them they'd fought side-by-side hundreds of times.

A zombie came in close to Ariel. He brought a booted foot up to the man's chest and kicked him backwards onto the waiting sword of Banning. The sword skewered the zombie, slicing through meat with a sickening squish until it pierced all the way through the front of its chest.

When the man fell to the ground, Banning bent down to rip the sword out of his back. The moment he ducked, Ariel swung his own sword horizontally where Banning had been only moments before.

The sword sliced across the throat of a zombie that had crept up behind Banning. Blood sprayed in an arc through the air, splashing the pavement.

I cringed, unable to help myself. They were laying waste to more lives than I could even bear to count anymore. As much as I wanted both of them to be safe, it was hard to forget these zombies had once been people.

A few moments later, both teams returned from inside

the houses, all of them shaking their heads to the questioning looks from Banning and Ariel. The teams moved down the block, going to the next two houses.

"This neighborhood is beyond saving," Panthea said bluntly.

"Don't give up hope." I sounded desperate. Even I knew the odds of anyone surviving this nightmare were slim.

A woman screamed and came barreling out of one of the houses the rescue teams had gone into. She was clutching her arm to her chest. "I won't turn! I won't! It was just that one time. It was only a minute. I promise!"

Blood dripped from the arm she clutched, and I instantly knew she was infected.

Apparently, so did Ariel because he lifted his gun and unloaded a bullet into her skull before she even realized he was there.

She collapsed to the ground in a spray of blood and brains.

"There is no hope," Panthea said darkly.

I sat back in silence. I was starting to believe her. There were far too many bodies shambling in the streets for there to be anyone left alive inside the buildings. I didn't even know there were this many people in the area to begin with.

I sat in a stupor, watching Ariel methodically take out the entire neighborhood.

Panthea was right. Ariel showed no mercy. He drove his weapon into men, women, and children without the slightest appearance of regret on his face. He didn't even look like the man I knew. I didn't recognize the heartless, merciless creature in front of me. Sure, Ariel had been disgruntled, but this was devoid of even the usual anger he possessed.

Banning moved with the grace of a dancer, but Ariel moved like a warrior, like someone who thought of nothing other than the kill. At the moment, they were both scaring me.

"Absolutely breathtaking, aren't they?" Panthea asked, her voice full of admiration.

I turned to her with eyes full of concern. She worried me with the amount of psychotic tendencies she possessed. How could she find anything about this breathtaking? It was horrible! It was enough to make me sick to my stomach.

With a little laugh, she said, "Darling, think on it. Right now, there are many, many people out there who wish you harm." She pointed to Ariel and Banning. "Those two men out there have sworn to protect you. They will die before they let you come to harm, and they've made everyone very aware of that. You may find what they're doing out there to be grotesque, but if it was me, I'd be thrilled. With their skills, combined with the fact that they have no qualms about killing, you've got two people that no one will wish to challenge. The more death they deal, the more secure your life is. Do not judge them for this, respect them for it."

I sat in silence, thinking on that. As I continued to watch them kill, I found I wasn't as horrified as before. Panthea's statement rang true. The people they killed were far beyond saving. They were taking care of those they still could.

As I watched, Banning spun around and caught my eye through the window. He gave me a quick wink.

I smiled and blew him a kiss in return.

That right there proved to me that everything they did was part of a strategy to keep me alive. I might not like what they were doing, but they were doing it for a good reason.

I sat back, watching as they continued to rain destruction down on the unfortunate inhabitants of the neighborhood who had been robbed of their lives. I didn't want to see any more, but I didn't have a choice. Like it or not, I had made the decision to come along. I had to accept the things I saw and the way people behaved when confronted with violence. I should have known things were going to be bloody. I'd seen the hospital.

This was different, though. The hospital was across town. Right now, we were only a few blocks from my house. At the hospital, I had held out hope that things hadn't reached my family, that they were safe. Now, blocks away, I knew that wasn't true. This place looked like a natural disaster had swept through. It looked like a bomb had gone off, leaving a mess of bodies and debris. There was no way this area had suffered a tornado of violence and death while my block remained unharmed.

Dread was overwhelming me as we inched closer to my parents' house, closer to answers I wasn't sure I wanted anymore. Every time the van advanced a block, revealing more destruction, my heart sank a little more. When we were a block from mine, I squeezed my eyes tightly shut. I didn't want to see what had become of my childhood home. I wanted to remember everything how it was before I'd left, not how it was now.

Panthea ran her hand soothingly over my hair. "It will be okay, child. This will make you a stronger person. It will make you understand how important it is for you to live."

I listened to her comforting words and realized she was right. I needed to get past this. I needed to be strong. If I couldn't do that, I was as doomed as the zombies who moaned hungrily outside the window.

To survive, I needed to become tough. Just like Ariel. He swept his emotions aside and did what was needed of him. Steeling myself for whatever I was about to face, I opened my eyes. I was needed for the endurance of my species, and I would not hide from the challenges my survival faced.

As I took in my surroundings, I realized we were on my block.

Chapter 15

I stood outside the home I'd lived in before the world went to hell and swallowed back a sob. Tears sprang to my eyes as I gazed upon a structure that had once meant shelter and security. Now, all it meant was inevitable heartache.

All along I'd thought I wanted answers. I wanted to know if my family was okay or what had become of them if they weren't. Deep down, I wanted to curl up in my parents' laps and have them tell me everything was going to be okay. Looking at the neighborhood, I could tell it wasn't going to be okay. Most things would never be okay again.

The once spectacular houses that lined the street were in shambles. Body parts littered the lawns along with debris and the walking dead. Something had exploded two doors down from my old home and the house that once stood there was now a burnt husk of a building.

As I surveyed the damage, I noticed the overturned car in my neighbor's yard had someone underneath it. Their son, Billy, lay trapped under the bulk of their vehicle. His face was a mask of blood and exposed tissue, the features of the seven-year-old child barely recognizable.

He gave a pitiful howl as he tried to pull himself loose. His jaws snapped at the air, teeth gnashing. He turned dead eyes toward me and doubled his efforts.

It jolted a memory in my mind. His mother, Lila, only a few days before had been trying to get him into their car. He had been growling and yelling like a maniac.

She had given a slightly embarrassed laugh, telling me one of his playmates from school had bitten him and it looked to be infected. She explained he was afraid to go to the doctor, which was why he was acting up about getting into the car. When he grabbed for her arm and attempted to bite her, she had given him a forceful shove into the car, saying, "You know the age."

I realized now it had nothing to do with age and everything to do with zombies. Hands trembling, I was unable to move my eyes from Billy. It was tragic to look upon the face of a boy who'd been happy and healthy only a few weeks ago. What happened to him was unfair, and it made me sick.

A pair of comforting hands touched my shoulders, and I knew without looking they belonged to Ariel. He squeezed gently, comfortingly, but sent Panthea a sneer. "I told you she would not be able to handle it."

"Give her time to adjust," Panthea said sharply. "She needs to come to terms with the fact that this isn't her world anymore. It's theirs." She shook her head sadly at the image of Billy. "She needed to see."

I really hated it when people talked about me like I wasn't there. "I'm ready," I said darkly. "Let's get into the house already."

Ariel's grip on my shoulders tightened. "You are not ready."

I yanked away from him. "I said I'm ready." I marched up to the front door and turned to Panthea. "Kick it in."

Panthea's face took on a look of delight at my demand. I was starting to understand them a little. They had all of this suppressed power. It was fun to let loose sometimes and break things. Freaking psychopaths.

"Allow me," Panthea said, stepping around us. With an eager grin, she brought a booted foot up and kicked the door in. The wood gave way as if hit by a truck. It splintered as the lock busted away from the doorframe. It was amazing the amount of strength they all had, absolutely amazing. She strutted into the room, her curls bouncing. "Honey, I'm home," she said in her deep, sultry voice.

I rushed in after her, my breath catching in my throat. I wasn't sure what I expected to see, but the house looked untouched. Everything was in order, not a single thing out of place. That had to be a good sign. Unlike outside, there was no blood or evidence of violence.

I felt hands on my shoulders and looked up to see Ariel. His face was an unreadable mask that had doubts rushing to the surface of my mind. He looked farther into the house as if not trusting the calm of the hallway. He was searching for dismembered bodies, the bodies of my family members. He was cold and calculating in his perusal, as if the results didn't matter to him either way.

I could see the gun he held out of the corner of my eye and knew he would use it to gun down my family without blinking. I yanked away from him in disgust. "Get that thing away from me!" I marched away from him, moving down the hallway. I started up the staircase, taking them as fast as I could. "Mom! Dad!" I needed to find my parents. I needed for them to tell me this was all a dream. I needed this not to be real. I needed them to be alive and well more than I needed anything else. I reached their bedroom and threw open the door.

Both of my parents were lying in bed, their bodies completely still. "They're just sleeping," I said, trying to convince myself. "They're just sleeping." I tiptoed closer to them, my heart pounding in my chest. "Daddy?" I whimpered softly, my voice trembling. I made my way around the bed, my movements tentative.

My father became fully visible from this angle and horror filled me at the sight. His entire throat had been ripped out until the only thing remaining was a ragged hole. The wound was a few days old, so the blood had started to congeal, looking thick and jellylike. There was a bullet hole in the center of his head, execution style.

With trembling hands, I turned to look at my mother.

Her face was a bloody mess and it took me a moment to realize the blood wasn't hers. It went from her mouth, down her chin, and trailed nearly to her waist. Her hands were caked in blood and chunks of meat, flesh sticking out from under her nails.

I suddenly knew what happened to my father. His own wife, my mother, had torn his throat out with her teeth and nails. There was a matching bullet hole in her forehead, making the two of them appear a solid unit even in death.

I clamped my hand over my mouth to drown out the sound of my mournful wail. I spun to run from the room and slammed into Ariel's chest. "I wasn't ready." A sob burst from between my lips, and this time, I did nothing to cover it up. "I wasn't ready. I wasn't ready."

Ariel tensed for a moment before pulling me in against him. He never said, "I told you so," or asked any stupid questions. He simply held me. He ran a hand over my hair, his touch tentative, as if he wasn't used to comforting anyone.

I cried into his chest, clutching him around the waist. In that moment, I didn't care about tension that seemed to flare between us whenever we crossed paths. I didn't care that he could be such an ass at times. He was here now, holding me when I needed it. That was all that mattered.

He let me cry, his hand moving to stroke my back. After a few minutes, he gently started pulling me back into the hallway. He reached over me and shut the door, closing off the sight of my dead parents. He then peeled me away from his chest and stared down at me. "Aurora, I need you to be strong for me, okay?"

I gave a sniffle and my lip quavered in response.

His fingers dug into my shoulders, as if he could force my attention to him with pain. "I know this is bad. It's really bad, but you have to keep it together until we get back. We have to find more survivors."

I nodded. "Yeah...more survivors." Even to my own ears, my voice didn't sound convincing. It was hard to focus on finding survivors after the morbid sight I'd just witnessed.

Ariel's grip tightened. "You don't realize just how bad this is. Listen to me. If we don't find more survivors..." He broke off, unable to finish his sentence.

Something in his tone made me snap out of my despair. I took a moment to study his face, and what I saw frightened me. For the first time, I realized Ariel was afraid. He was afraid of what he knew.

"If we don't find more survivors soon, Alexandro is going to force you to get with child." His voice was low and full or regret, his deep blue eyes troubled.

"He can't," I said in horror.

"Are you going to refuse when he gives you the option of either sleeping with Damian or having him blow his brains all over the wall?"

Panic seized in my chest. "He won't kill Damian. He can't. He would be ruining humanity's chance at survival."

"He doesn't like Damian," Ariel said through clenched

teeth. "Once he does away with Damian, he will do everything in his power to find a replacement. Eventually, he will
find one, and there's a great possibility that person will do
whatever it takes to stay on Alexandro's good side, whether
you agree to it or not."

He was talking about rape. Alexandro would let someone
rape me until he got what he wanted. The thought alone was
enough to make me weep. Ariel was my sworn protector,
though. Surely he wouldn't stand by and let such a thing
happen. "Can't you..."

"He would not be trying to kill you. I don't think I could
interfere without breaking his rules. If I interfered, he would
send his followers after me. Even I cannot take them all.
That is why we need to find other survivors, so the burden is
not yours alone." His grip on me softened along with his
eyes. "I will do everything in my power to save you, Aurora.
I promise you that. But it is imperative that we find someone
else. And soon."

I let this information sink in, let it wrap around my mind.
Looking at my parents' door, the reality of my situation finally became clear. I didn't have them to protect me anymore. I
was not the young, naive girl I'd been merely a week ago.

I turned back to Ariel, my hands moving to cover his. I
might not have my parents, but I had Ariel now. He would do
his best to keep me safe. I now understood he needed me to
help him along the way. I couldn't fight him or be difficult.
We had enough stacked against us without bickering with
each other. I made sure my voice was steady when I said,
"We had better find some survivors then."

Ariel's lip curled into a partial grin. "Your strength is
amazing." His hand moved to my throat, and he tilted my
face up with his thumb. "We're going to be okay."

I closed my eyes, letting the cool feel of his skin soothe
me. My parents' bodies were only a few feet away, yet I
threw all of my attention at Ariel. Everything about him made
my body relax. He made me realize that though things might
be horrible right now, I still had people who would do anything they could to keep me alive. He made everything less
terrifying, made my anguish less debilitating.

Air brushed past me, and I knew someone was beside
me before their voice interrupted. "There's nothing down-

stairs. Not even an overturned lamp," Panthea said, sounding a little depressed. "Anything up here?"

Ariel held me to him as if shielding me from Panthea. "Nothing salvageable."

Panthea's eyes flicked to me as if to gauge the amount of hysteria I was in.

I knew she might judge me by this. If I freaked, she might never permit me to ride along on outings again. I pushed carefully away from Ariel and took a deep breath. "There's one more person unaccounted for. Let's just finish the upstairs."

Panthea grinned, licking her fangs. "She's got spunk," she said in approval. "I expected her to be falling apart at this point. I'm pleasantly surprised."

I sent her a dark look. I didn't enjoy being her human guinea pig. "Let's get this over with. I just had to look at my parents' mutilated bodies. I'm not in the mood for your damn vampire mind games." I marched past both of them toward Andrew's room. "I'm going to check out my brother's body, if you don't mind. Feel free to come and gawk, take a few pictures if you'd like. That way we can capture my torment for all eternity."

I knew getting snappy with them wasn't going to help me, but I couldn't contain my anger. I had just seen my parents' bodies, had been forced to see the horrors that befell them. I wasn't in the mood to listen to vampire bullshit.

The way the majority behaved, it was apparent they had no compassion, no feelings. It was just hunt and kill for them. The dead in this house weren't my parents or brother to them. They were simply target practice.

I yanked the door to Andrew's room open, preparing myself for the worst. To my utter shock, I found him conscious. I gave a sharp gasp of surprise, my hand flying to my heart at the sight of him.

Andrew was sitting on the floor, leaning against his bed. His eyes were wide and dilated, his breathing erratic. He was sucking in large, uneven breaths, the sound echoing around the otherwise silent room.

I took a tentative step toward him, half expecting him to jump up and try to eat me like he had in my nightmare.

His eyes slowly lifted to mine, their depths looking nearly

dazed. "Rory," he croaked, his voice full of emotion. "I-I thought you were dead. All of us dead."

I looked down at his hands and saw the gun lying in his lap, held loosely in his fingers. I suddenly knew who had put a bullet in our parents' heads. I felt my blood turn to ice, imagining what that must have been like. There was no recovering from such a thing. I went to shift my gaze back to his face when I noticed blood trailing down his wrist. I followed it up his forearm to a nasty gash.

He saw me gaping in horror and gave a sarcastic laugh. "Mom made me what I was before, and she made me what I'm about to become as well."

I choked back a strangled sob, clamping a hand over my mouth. He'd been bitten. Our own mother had taken his humanity, his chance of survival, and severed it.

"I would have done myself as well," he said weakly, "but I didn't have the courage."

This was worse than finding my parents. At least I hadn't had to watch them suffer. Andrew would suffer, and if one of the vampires found him, I knew what they would do.

Just then, I heard the door open, and Aldrich stepped into the room. He took one look at Andrew and started raising his weapon.

"No!" I screamed, the sound tearing from my throat, leaving it raw. I ran at Andrew and threw myself into his lap. My arms wrapped around his neck and I clung to him, desperate to cover him from Aldrich's view. "You can't kill him! Not him!"

"Let him do it," Andrew said, his voice thick with pain. "Let him end this."

I looked at my brother in horror. "Drew, no!"

Aldrich took a step in our direction, his boots thudding against the floor. "Move out of the way," he ordered.

I shook my head, my arms trembling in terror. "No."

Aldrich stalked forward in anger. He grabbed me around the waist in an attempted to haul me off of Andrew. "I said get out of the way." He gave another forceful tug.

I held on to Andrew's neck, fighting with everything I had, but I was no match for vampire strength. Aldrich pulled again and ripped me away from my brother. My already injured arm felt like it caught fire from the force of his yanking, and I was unable to hold back my scream of pain.

Aldrich tossed me unceremoniously to the side like a rag doll.

I landed on my arm and white dots flashed before my eyes. Tears poured down my cheeks, and a shuddering sob escaped my lips. "Please, don't kill him." I begged through tears, my vision swimming with black dots. I clutched my arm to my chest, fully crying now. "Don't kill him."

The door flew opened and Ariel burst into the room with Panthea on his heels. He took one look at me and spun on Aldrich. "What the hell is going on in here?"

"An infected," Aldrich said, his voice neutral. "She freaked out." He gave me a withering look, and his lip pulled back over his fangs in a snarl. "She's hindering our job. This is why we never should have brought her along to begin with."

Ariel turned to look at me, a question in his eyes. He should have been able to connect the dots, but I think seeing me sprawled on the floor as I was had shaken him.

"Don't kill him," I pleaded to Ariel, praying with everything in me he would heed my wishes, just this once. "Don't let him shoot Drew."

Ariel glanced at Andrew. Realization dawned on his face, but he quickly schooled his expression to something more guarded when he turned back to me. "Aurora, he's infected." He gave a weary sigh before squatting down in front of me. He leaned in close to me, his voice a whisper. "He will suffer more if we do not do what is necessary."

I pushed away from Ariel, shoving him in the chest. "I don't care." A thought occurred to me and I clung desperately to it. "Make him one of you!" I nodded, liking the sound of that. "Turn him." Panthea opened her mouth to speak, and I pointed a finger at her. "Don't tell me it's not possible. You've done it before. You can do it again."

Panthea's mouth snapped shut, and she crossed her arms underneath her breasts. Her eyes sought Ariel's and there was uncertainty in their depths. That meant she was at least considering my pleas. It was better than I'd expected.

Pain filled Ariel's eyes, and he seemed to have a hard time saying what came out of his mouth next. "Aurora, Angelina died. She suffered. I haven't done it before, not successfully."

I grabbed onto his leg, gripping the fabric of his jeans tightly in my grasp. "Please try. Please." I buried my face in his thigh, sobbing pitifully. I knew I was asking too much of him, but this was my brother. Lifting my tear-stained face to him, I whimpered, "Please."

He glanced at Panthea who shrugged. "You gave me my life. I can deny you nothing," she said quietly.

Ariel turned to look back down at me.

I clung to his leg. "Please. I will do anything you want. I will give you anything. Just please save my brother."

Ariel turned my face up to him, rubbing his thumb over my cheek. "You ask me for so many things I have a hard time giving you." A sad smile touched his lips that I didn't understand. "How many times have you promised to give me anything, everything?" He leaned forward, closing the distance between us. An instant later, his lips brushed across mine. His mouth caressed mine, kissing me with emotions he'd buried so long ago. With that, he stood and walked over to Andrew.

"You're going to be fucked if Alexandro finds out what you're doing," Aldrich said darkly.

"Alexandro does not rule me." Ariel spat the words, his contempt for their leader evident in his tone. He towered over Andrew, staring menacingly down at him. "Is this agreeable to you?"

"I get to live?" Andrew asked with a laugh that was more from stress than humor.

"No," Ariel said. "You'll die regardless. It's what you come back as that is up for debate. You will either live as we do or you will suffer tremendously before becoming one of those monsters."

Andrew shrugged. "I'm dead anyway, right? What have I got to lose?"

I gave a sigh of relief. They were going to save him. My brother might have a chance. He might have a life left to live. I sobbed again, but this time, they were tears of joy.

Panthea sauntered over to Andrew. Grabbing him by the front of his shirt, she hauled him to his feet. "You do not even realize how lucky you are." She took her hand and trailed it down Andrew's chest, nails digging into the cloth of his shirt. She leaned into him, practically purring. Standing on her toes, she put her face in his. "You've been given the kiss of eternal life."

She pressed her lips forcefully to his. It wasn't the soft, gentle touch of Ariel's. It was as if she was trying to devour him. Her hands traveled up to his hair. She grasped at his short blond spikes. She pulled on them, forcing his mouth to hers.

Watching my brother make out with a centuries old vampire was not one of the things I'd hoped to witness today, but I was just happy he was alive.

Panthea kissed him with enough force to bruise. Her hands moved hungrily over his body, and she pressed her groin seductively against his. Then suddenly, she spun as fast as lightning, moving to stand behind him. Her left arm circled around his waist and her right buried into his hair, yanking his head back. "He's all yours, baby," she said to Ariel.

Ariel grinned at her, his expression full of amusement. "I am quite capable of doing this myself." His grin widened. "And how long has it been since you've called me such names?"

Panthea returned his grin. "I am not doing it to assist you. I am doing it for my own pleasure."

"That used to be my job," Ariel said with a sly smirk.

I stared in surprise at Ariel. This was a side of him I'd never seen. Grumpy Ariel, I was used to. Angry and enraged Ariel, I was familiar with. The reluctantly seductive Ariel I had seen surface, but never this. This version of Ariel was playful and suggestive, his features taking on an arrogant look. I'd seen arrogance before, but not like this.

He strode toward Andrew with a confident gait. "This brings back memories of Rome." He licked his lips, looking at Panthea over Andrew's shoulder. "The high-class noblewoman sneaking into a prisoner's cell for a good fuck."

Panthea closed her eyes and gave a soft sigh. "And it always was."

Ariel pressed his body flat against Andrew's and grabbed Panthea around him, his hand grasping her hair. He yanked her forward and kissed her roughly.

Andrew gave an uncomfortable squeak of protest, obviously not enjoying being trapped between them. I couldn't blame him for his uneasiness at being used as a tool for their foreplay.

When Ariel finally pulled away, Panthea took a deep breath. "There's the man I miss."

"You always did bring out the worst in me," Ariel said, his voice half a growl.

"That's my favorite part."

Ariel shook his head, his expression going momentarily sad. "And that's why we could never be together."

Panthea rolled her eyes with a soft smile. "You and your good heart. Always wanting to do the right thing. Always wanting a commitment."

Ariel laughed under his breath. "Sucks, doesn't it?" With that, he lowered his mouth to Andrew's neck.

Andrew cringed and his hands balled into fists. He didn't look as if he was in pain. He just looked uncomfortable with the situation. Not that I wouldn't be in his position. Who wouldn't be uncomfortable with Panthea holding him or her down while Ariel fed?

After a few minutes, Andrew's eyelids began to droop. He blinked very slowly as if fighting off sleep. When his eyes re-opened, they looked glazed and unfocused.

I almost spoke up, but held my concern in. I trusted Ariel knew what he was doing. He was the vampire, after all.

Suddenly, Ariel stumbled away from Andrew. The first thing I noticed was the paleness that had stripped Andrew's face of color.

My eyes quickly flicked to Ariel as he fell to his knees and clutched at his stomach. He tried to stand, but collapsed back down to one knee. "I have to finish," he said through clenched teeth.

Panthea shook her head. "You are weakened. Let me finish the job." She stroked the side of Andrew's face as she spoke.

I looked down at Ariel, puzzled and a little frightened at his inability to get to his feet. "What's wrong with him?"

Panthea, who had lowered her head to Andrew's neck, lifted only a set of pale blue eyes to look at me. "You just had him pump his body full of poison, of that toxin. He has enough of that shit in him to kill a hundred humans, yet he cannot die. He suffers the most painful part of death without the peaceful release. It is killing him, yet he cannot escape into sweet oblivion. He is trapped, suffering all of the agonies with no relief in sight."

I turned horrified eyes to Ariel. He knelt on hands and knees, his head bent to the floor. His hands were balled into fists and they quivered with his pain.

"He will be like this, tainted, until he gets fresh blood." Panthea bit sharply into her wrist and watched as blood ran down to drip onto the floor. "If he attempted to finish your brother himself, he would be pumping that virus back into his system. Your brother needs pure, clean vampire blood for this to work. It's still no guarantee, but it will help his chances of survival." She offered her wrist to Andrew, who looked at it in fear.

Ariel gave a suffer-filled scream from the ground.

I dropped to my knees next to him, a hand on his back. "Ariel, I'm sorry. I didn't know... I didn't..."

He looked up at me, and there were tears streaming down his face. In that moment, I realized it was more than pain that had put that look in his eyes.

"I pumped poison back into her veins." He gave a miserable sob, his jaw clenching with his anguish. "Banning was there. He was right there, and I insisted on doing it myself."

I wrapped one arm around his shoulders, my other hand brushing hair away from his face. "You didn't know. How could you have known?" I'd never seen Ariel this way. Not only was he in physical pain, he seemed unreservedly defeated. The sorrow he endured knew no boundaries. I looked up to Panthea for help.

Her head was thrown back, eyes closed in ecstasy as Andrew sucked vigorously at her wrist. The expression on her face was one of undulated pleasure. She wasn't going to be much help to me.

I lay my head against Ariel's back, tears coming to my own eyes. "I'm so sorry, Ariel...for everything." I swallowed back a sob as a wave of guilt washed over me. I'd done this to him. "I need you, Ariel."

He put his head back to the floor, sobbing quietly. With each passing moment, his sobs grew more violent, shaking his body.

I gasped in surprise when I realized it wasn't his crying

that was shaking him, but a seizure. "Ariel!" I screamed fearfully, my worry for him rising to new heights. I held him to me, pulling him into my lap. I looked up at Aldrich, tears cascading down my cheeks. "Help him!" I attempted to hold Ariel still to minimize his convulsions. "Do something!"

Aldrich looked at Ariel, his expression unsympathetic. "I think we may have a spare packet of blood in the van."

"Go get it!"

He gave a nod and slowly turned to leave the room without another word.

Once he was gone, I returned my focus to Ariel. "I'm so sorry," I said, my voice catching with a sob. "I didn't know. I didn't know."

He groaned something that I couldn't make out.

I leaned in closer to him, concern filling me. "What?"

"Move!" He lunged out of my lap and back to his knees. I heard the wet splash moments before I realized he was throwing up. If I hadn't been so concerned, I might have been astonished at the sight of a vampire throwing up his lunch. I stared in wide-eyed horror at him, unable to do anything to help. There was a thud to my left, and my eyes moved slowly toward the noise.

My brother's body lay on the ground next to me, blood seeping out of his neck onto the carpet. His eyes were wide and glassy, his body unmoving. I let out a scream of horror at the sight.

A hand clamped over my mouth, and I glanced back to find Panthea crouched beside me. "Shh. He is in enough pain as it is," she said. "Do not shatter his eardrums."

I had thought Andrew dead at first. Now, I could see his shoulders rising and falling raggedly as he struggled for each breath pulled through his lungs. I sat on the floor and watched helplessly as two men I cared about suffered. There was nothing I could do to alleviate the pain for either one of them.

Aldrich reappeared agonizing minutes later with a bag of blood. He stared with disgust at Ariel retching on the floor. "This is not the job," he said darkly. "You disappoint me. How can you do your duty like this?" He suddenly reached out and grabbed me by the throat. "I could kill her right now, and you wouldn't be able to do a damn thing about it."

"That's what he's got me for," Panthea said. "Let it go,

Aldrich."

He stared darkly at her for a moment before releasing me with a push.

I stumbled backwards, but quickly found my footing. I gave him a look to match the one he gave me and snatched the bag of blood out of his hands.

I marched back to Ariel and dropped to my knees in front of him. "Here. You've got to drink this." Me telling a thousand-year-old vampire what he needed to do to survive seemed quite ridiculous, but I said it all the same.

"Thank you for stating the obvious." Even now, in as much pain as he was, Ariel still managed to summon up enough energy to be sarcastic.

I chose to ignore the comment. I carefully tore open the side of the package then slid my body underneath Ariel's to help him sit up. My knees were on either side of him, and he leaned weakly back into my chest. I instructed him to open his mouth as I positioned the bag in front of him. Then I slowly and cautiously poured the amber liquid down his throat.

As soon as the blood hit his tongue, Ariel gave a low growl in the back of his throat. The growl vibrated through his chest to mine, sending a hum down my body.

I expected to be repulsed at the sight of him drinking. Instead, I was intrigued by it. It seemed so right, so natural. I was finally seeing a vampire in his natural element without it being completely terrifying.

I felt each pull of blood through the bag my hands supported. It felt almost as if he were actually drawing the blood from me instead of the plastic pouch. I breathed deeply with each firm suck he took, feeling it down to my core as I silently prayed each drink brought him closer to a healthy state.

His rhythmic drinking lulled me into a serene haze. Through some vampire power, I was beginning to feel sleepy, my eyelids heavy. I knew the effect wasn't natural, but it felt too soothing to fight. I wanted this, wanted the feeling of absolute peace in a world of horror. I let my eyelids flutter closed, giving into the pull of otherworldly power.

"We will take the human to the van," Panthea said, voice full of amusement. "We'll be back in a few minutes. Hopefully, the two of you will be done with your blood play when we return."

I opened my eyes to look at her, the action more of an effort than it should be. I started formulating a comeback to her unwanted suggestiveness, but before I could voice the words, my eyes drifted closed of their own will. By the time I forced them open again, she was gone.

I let out a gasp and quickly forgot about Panthea as I felt the brush of invisible hands against my skin. The sensation left me tingling and shivering with the craving for more. I knew it was a trick, some vampire deception used to get victims to submit, but I couldn't stop myself from responding to the caress. It felt like a lover stroking ever so gently along my flesh, ramping my body up for passion. I gave a ragged pant of desire, and my hands closed tightly around the bag, forcing what was left in it down Ariel's throat.

With the bag depleted, he slapped it to the side. Grabbing me around the waist, he flipped me, pinning my body underneath his.

I could feel his erection hard against my hip and knew from the lustful look in his eyes his intentions went far beyond blood. His domineering expression made it clear he wanted to take me with ferocity like I'd never experienced before. This was the Ariel Panthea had told me about. Here was the passionate, sexual man he'd hidden within himself.

I gave an involuntary shiver that was followed by a whimper at the promise in his deep blue eyes. I wasn't sure if my reaction was from fear or enthusiasm. No doubt it was a bit of both as I was alarmed at my zeal for his touch.

Ariel groaned deep in his throat and ground his hips against mine. He put his mouth next to my ear, his breath hot on my skin. "If only I had the energy..." He suddenly pulled away from me and struggled to his feet. "But this vitality won't last. I'll need more blood soon. If not, I'll be on my hands and knees again in no time."

I let out an exhale of relief. I was glad Ariel climbed off of me because I didn't have the willpower to tell him to do so. I'd been silently telling myself it was wrong to consider sleeping with Ariel, but after having him on top of me with that look in his eyes, I couldn't think of any good reason to label it as such.

When I fed Ariel, it hadn't even been from my own neck.

He hadn't penetrated my skin, yet it felt like he had stroked me in places I didn't care to admit. I couldn't even imagine what it would be like if I opened a vein to him.

Ariel pulled me to my feet, crushing me against his chest. He traced a long, elegant finger over my lips. "Do not think on it so much. Simply enjoy it."

His voice was a velvety purr that caressed along my skin. I closed my eyes, sinking into the lull of his voice.

"I wish I had time to show you," he said regretfully. "You have so much to learn."

I wasn't sure if I was ready to learn the things Ariel wanted to teach me.

Ariel wrapped his hand around my upper arm. "We have to move quickly. We need to get back to the mansion. The sun will be rising in a few short hours. We need to sneak your brother inside and brief Alexandro before daybreak."

"Sneak Drew inside? Why are we sneaking?" I let Ariel pull me down the stairs, barely aware of the fact he was rushing me.

He stopped, turning to look at me. "If Alexandro finds your brother, he will have him killed."

"What?" I shook my head in disbelief. "Only if he turns into a zombie, right?"

"Regardless," Ariel said. "Our ratio to humans is way too high. All of us were instructed no new vampires were to be made. If any were discovered, they were to be put down." Ariel's hand tightened on my arm in anger. "And I agreed with him. Damn it, I agreed."

"I won't let him kill Drew," I said firmly. Fear welled up inside of me to the point it was nearly overwhelming. I wasn't sure how we could ever hope for a positive outcome to this situation. It wasn't as if we could hide Andrew for the next few hundred years. Surely, someone would notice.

"No," Ariel agreed. "I won't either. I'm going to be far too weak to defend him for a while, though. We have to keep him hidden until I'm able to take a stance on his behalf."

I nodded my head vehemently, for once prepared to follow any instructions he gave. I was willing to do anything to keep Andrew alive. Allowing Ariel time to heal was much better than the original thoughts whirring through my brain. This I could happily do.

As we made our way toward the waiting van, Ariel stumbled a little. He used his grip on my arm to steady himself, his fingers digging into my arm.

"You're getting sick again." I shot him a worried look, wondering if he'd even be able to make it back into his apartment without collapsing.

"I'm weak. I just need a few days to regain my strength," he said through clenched teeth.

I glanced at Ariel and silently vowed he would get everything he needed for a speedy recovery. He'd put himself through intense and excruciating pain for me. The least I could do was offer him my assistance while he could use it.

As we made our way slowly along the sidewalk to the street, Panthea returned with Aldrich at her side. "We need to hurry," she said, snapping me out of my stupor of concern for Ariel. "Sunrise is quickly approaching, and we need to sneak the two injured men inside without my brother finding out."

I nodded, ready to follow any commands if it meant protecting Andrew and Ariel.

"I need someone trustworthy to assist us, to drive our van and help us get inside undetected." She paused thoughtfully. "We need to keep all of the others out of our vehicle as well. The less people who know, the better." She made a noise of displeasure. "Too many people know already. I had to leave your brother in the hands of Diego while we came back for Ariel." She let out a sigh that held a hint of nervousness to it.

I think Panthea, the terror of all vampires, was actually worried about Ariel.

"We have myself, Aldrich, and Diego…we will need one more person if we are to do this. Two men to transport Ariel, one for your brother, and a final man to park the van before it is noticed." She turned her eyes to Aldrich. "Go find Banning. Bring him to me." As he turned to walk away, she added, "Tell the second team we must return early. Make something up. Make it believable."

Aldrich's expression never changed. Looking completely disinterested, he headed through the yard toward one of my neighbor's houses.

"I don't like that he knows," I said softly.

Panthea waved it off. "Aldrich will not say anything. For him to say something, he would have to care, and Aldrich cares about nothing."

Her statement reminded me once again how scary some of these men were. Who could have no emotions whatsoever toward their own comrades? How could he not care about anything? It was downright sociopathic.

It didn't take long before Banning came rushing into my yard, his expression concerned. It was touching that he cared. Here he was, an immortal being, a warrior, and he was worried because something had happened in my old house. That emotion written plainly across his face made me like him even more.

Banning's eyes landed on Ariel, and he quickly looked up to Panthea. "What happened?"

Panthea's eyes locked onto his, and she shook her head silently.

"We...we attempted what was done to Angelina." Ariel rasped out his explanation, clutching at his aching stomach.

Banning's eyes widened. "*You what*?"

Panthea grabbed Ariel by one of his arms, trying to keep him on his feet.

Banning quickly moved in next to her, grabbing Ariel under the other arm.

As soon as the weight wasn't solely on her, Panthea answered him. "Your little human's brother was bitten. Ariel had a moment of weakness, and the two of us attempted to turn him. He's in the van. Diego is with him."

Banning stayed silent, but I could see by the look in his eyes this was a major deal. He looked...almost terrified. "What have you done?" he asked in dismay.

Ariel grumbled, but didn't say anything intelligible.

I wasn't sure if he *could* say anything, judging by the way his feet shuffled and his head began lolling to the side as if he was about to lose consciousness.

Panthea and Banning made their way swiftly to the van where Diego slid the door open for them. "You're trying to get us all killed, aren't you?" he accused.

Panthea hopped backwards into the van, pulling Ariel to lie across the middle seat. "Life isn't fun unless a person is having sex or risking death. Anything less isn't worth living for."

Andrew was already in the back, pitiful moans escaping his lips.

As soon as Ariel was securely on the seat, Panthea waved her hands for us to get moving. "Quickly. Quickly. Before the others see."

Diego slid into the driver's seat while Aldrich took the passenger. I was about to climb into the van when a moan behind us caused me to spin around.

Grace Smith was shuffling toward us, arms outstretched. Her skin was starting to decay, falling off of her face in clumps. Underneath the peeling skin oozed some form of liquid. I didn't want to know what it was.

"This is what happens when they don't get to eat," Banning said, nodding toward Grace. "Disgusting, isn't it?" He lifted his sword, preparing to end her undead existence.

I reached out and put a hand on his forearm. "No."

Banning turned to me with confused eyes. "She's far beyond help."

"I know." Taking the gun at the waistband of his jeans, I turned to Grace. I fired three quick shots into her chest, feeling better with each one. I then raised the gun, ice gripping at my heart, and with the fourth bullet, I killed her.

The round entered her rotting forehead and exploded the skull, leaving a gaping hole. It had been like smashing a rotten pumpkin against the sidewalk. I stared down at her, at the wreckage that had once been her face, and didn't feel an ounce of pity. "That's for infecting my mom."

Banning's eyes lit with realization. Gently, he took the gun from my hand. "We'd better get going," he said softly.

I think he was unsure of what else to say to me. I didn't need him to say anything to comfort me, though. Putting a bullet between Grace's eyes had been comfort enough.

I was just about to get into the van when there was another noise behind me, a shuffling in the bushes.

Banning raised the weapon he'd taken from me, ready to fire.

At the last second, I frantically grabbed his forearm. "Banning, no!"

He hesitated, sliding gray eyes to me. "What now?"

I went to rush to the bushes when he put his free arm out across my chest, stopping me. "It's Muffin!" I said, as if that would explain anything to him.

Banning held the gun steady on the bush, not willing to put it down. "There's a breakfast food rattling the bushes? What the hell have you humans done to breakfast?"

"No. Not breakfast muffins. Muffin is...was my neighbor's kitten. We can't just leave him here."

"Are you sure?" He opened his mouth to say something else, but his sentence trailed off. Banning lowered his weapon in acceptance at the soft mewing that came from the bushes. "Okay. You win. It's a cat. What exactly are we going to do with a cat?"

"You don't need to do anything but feed it." I gave him a disbelieving look. "You've been alive how long and you've never owned a cat?"

He shrugged in a noncommittal way. "Never had much use for a cat."

I pushed his arm out of my way and crouched down in front of the bush. "Muffin? Here, kitty kitty." I rubbed my fingers together, trying to convince the kitten I had only good intentions.

A small, gray, fuzzy face peeked out of the brush, and he finally crept toward me. He looked scrawny and malnourished, a side effect of your owner turning into a zombie, but he was alive. That in itself was a miracle, making me wonder if the zombies had attempted to get at him or if their diet was strictly human.

Scooping him up into my arms, I clutched him to me, laughing softly at the immediate purr. When I turned back toward Banning, he ushered me in the direction of the van. "Fine, you can keep him, but if you ask me, a cat is going to be a major pain in the ass."

I hopped into the van, ignoring his comment. I didn't believe him for a minute. Muffin would survive just fine at the mansion, and I had no doubt Banning would be fawning all over him soon enough. Muffin had that effect on people.

Besides, Banning didn't really have an issue with me grabbing Muffin. Banning didn't seem to have issues with much...except Ariel turning Andrew. That seemed to bother him quite a bit. It concerned me that the happy-go-lucky Banning was terrified over Ariel's decision to save my brother.

There wasn't room on the seats, so I found a spot on the

floor between Ariel and Andrew, wanting to keep my eye on them both. Banning sat next to me, trying to keep me from seeing the worried expression on his face. I'd never seen him look so troubled. His eyes stared straight ahead, and I couldn't help but notice that his hands trembled slightly.

I knew what I'd asked of Ariel had been huge. I knew he was suffering. I had put them all in a bad position. I'm sure if Alexandro found out, they would all be punished for having a part in it.

I sat Muffin in my lap, letting him curl up against me. Then I slid my arm through Banning's, clasping his hand with my own. I leaned my head against his shoulder, trying to block out the groans of pain coming from both seats. I pretended I didn't notice the look of fear on Diego's face.

When my head touched his shoulder, Banning glanced down at me. He gave me a sad look before squeezing my hand.

I sat in silence, holding tightly to Banning as Panthea leaned over to speak to us.

"I have to leave," she said quietly.

My eyes widened, and my mouth dropped open.

Banning had said Panthea would never settle down, that she took off whenever she felt like it, but this was bad timing. This was a really, really bad timing. How could she take off now, with the danger we faced?

"I have no choice," she hissed under her breath. "I was to meet Sterling and Sebastian at a rendezvous point on a certain day at a certain time. I cannot simply abandon them. I only came here because I was concerned for my brother. I was to check and make sure things were stable here while Sterling and Sebastian searched for survivors. Then the three of us were to meet back up." Her eyes locked on Banning's. "You need to keep Ariel hidden. Keep both of them hidden until I can return. I should be no longer than three or four days. This needs to stay between this small group until I can return and deflect my brother's wrath."

She bit her lip, running her hands through her thick mane of hair. "I would confront him before I leave, but you know he would detain me. This is an argument that will take at least a month to sort out. He would cruelly make me choose between protecting Ariel or my reunion with Sterling and Sebastian. I can't choose between them. I wouldn't be able to. That's why you need to keep this quiet. Give me four days. I promise I will return."

"When are you leaving?" Banning asked, his tone dull and void of emotion.

"Tomorrow night as soon as the sun sets."

Banning sat back, his whole body screaming with tension. "Okay," he said softly. What more could he say? I knew he wouldn't deny her a reunion with her lovers after all she'd just done for us. It wouldn't be fair.

"We're back," Diego said, ending the conversation as he pulled up alongside the mansion.

Banning jumped into action, taking charge of the group. "Panthea, you take the boy. Diego and I will get Ariel to his room. Aldrich, you can park the van, get the cat inside, and then disappear." He turned to me, giving me a serious look. "Aurora, I need you to watch the front doors while we move. If someone so much as attempts to look outside, I need you to distract them. Panthea, Diego, and I will go in through the small emergency exit to the left. There is an elevator in that hallway. We'll sneak upstairs. Once we get inside, head in. I'll meet you in the front hall once everything is settled." He gripped my shoulders tightly. "Give no signs about what happened tonight or your brother will die." With that, he jumped out of the van and into action.

I didn't have time to think on what we were doing. I just reacted. As soon as my feet hit the pavement, I ran for the front door. I could hear them moving behind me, but I didn't dare look back. I trusted they would do everything they could to keep us safe.

I slipped into the front hall and stood blocking the door, trying to appear casual. If anyone asked, I would tell them I was waiting for Banning. For what, I couldn't be sure, but it was a good start.

I'd barely been keeping watch three minutes before a figure started coming toward me in the hallway. My heart pounded wildly and I licked my lips, preparing myself to do everything I could to distract the person.

As the person drew nearer, my fear escalated when I realized it was Kieran. How was I going to get him to do what I wanted? As for distracting him from my actions, he was much more into causing me physical harm than finding out what I was doing. I guess that was one advantage. He wouldn't be worried about what was happening outside, because he'd be too consumed with thoughts of hurting me.

When his eyes landed on me, his lip curled up in a sneer and he stopped short. "Back already, princess? I was hoping you got eaten."

I glared, hating him with every atom in my body. "Yes, we're back. Not that it's any of your business."

Kieran glanced around, as if looking for someone. "You're back...and you're all alone. How did I get that lucky?"

I tried to block his view of the door. I didn't know what else to do. I was alone. If I ran screaming for help, there was a chance Kieran would find out what we were trying to hide. I had to stand and face him...and hope he would show me some mercy.

"I-I'm not alone," I said, hoping the lie sounding convincing. "I was...I was with..."

"She was with me." Banning's voice came from behind me as he stepped through the front door.

I turned quizzical eyes to him. How had he gotten back so fast? I silently thanked that supernatural speed. It had possibly just saved my life.

Kieran's eyes shifted to Banning, and he scowled. I was getting the impression Kieran really didn't like Banning all that much. Though to be fair, he didn't seem to like anyone all that much.

Banning gave him a bright smile full of sparkling white teeth, pretending to be oblivious to the vile look he was receiving. "Rory and I were just about to take a midnight stroll." His smile widened. "She wanted to check out the horses." He put his hands on my shoulders, rubbing up and down. "She was coming in for a jacket because it's a little chilly out there..."

He looked down at me affectionately. "I say we forget the jacket, though." He wrapped his arms around me, hugging me tightly against his chest. "I can think of a few other ways to keep you warm."

I wrapped my arms around Banning's waist, pressing the front of my body to his as I eyed Kieran nervously. This had to be believable. If he thought for one second we weren't sneaking off for a romantic midnight stroll, he would start investigating. I desperately didn't want him to investigate. With a coy smile, I spoke in my sexiest voice. "That sounds much better than a jacket."

Banning brought his hands to my face and my arms tightened around his waist. Simultaneously, we moved in to kiss each other.

The kiss was slow and full of tongue. It was not the kind of kiss one would want to be doing in public...unless you were Banning. It was the kiss of two people who were about to do things best left behind closed doors. With my little experience where men were involved, it was a type of kiss I'd never experienced before. Despite the entire thing being for show, my entire body lit with desire at the sensual way his mouth moved against mine.

"You are fucking disgusting," Kieran said, his voice dripping with revulsion. "Nothing better than a vampire slut." He thrust passed us, shoving me in the back as he went.

He was just pushing out of the building when Banning broke away from me to ask, "What are you going out for this late? The sun will be up soon."

Kieran spun to face him. "I'm waiting for the second crew to get back. There are a few people on Aldrich's team I trust to fill me in on exactly what happened out there tonight." He turned and stalked off into the darkness.

I tensed in Banning's arms. I didn't think anyone else had seen us, but I hadn't accounted for where each and every person was during the incident with Andrew. Someone could have been watching from the shadows.

Banning looked down into my worried eyes, his hands still cupping my face. "No one saw," he said softly. "Aldrich made sure of that. He sent everyone in the opposite direction. For now, we are safe." He ran his thumb gently across my lips, which were moist from his own. He seemed to realize what he was doing. He dropped his hands, released me, and took a step back. "Go to Damian. Go quickly and make no stops. Ariel and your brother should be safe until at least sundown, but I arranged for Orion to sit with your brother just in case. When I wake, I will make sure we have someone guarding your brother regularly until Panthea returns. It will take some effort, but we might be able to pull this off."

I nodded, relief easing through my body, making me groggy with exhaustion. "Thank you so much."

Banning nodded, his eyes avoiding mine. I knew he wasn't thrilled with the situation, but he was doing everything he could to help. He didn't have to, but he was.

Stepping in, I hugged him tightly around the waist. "I really mean it. Thank you. Without you..." I didn't even want to think on that one. Without Banning, Kieran would have probably killed me already. Without him, my brother might possibly be dead. Without him...things would have been much worse.

Banning held me tightly to him for a moment, running his hand over my hair. "Don't worry about it, sweetheart. I vowed to protect of you, and I never back out of a promise...no matter how much shit you get us into." He said this with a little laugh, letting me know he was only teasing. Kissing the top of my head, he said, "Let's get you to bed."

I nodded tiredly into his shoulder before pulling away. "Bed sounds wonderful."

We made the walk to our hallway in silence, both of us lost in our own thoughts. Outside Damian's door, I paused, turning to look at him. "Well..."

He crossed his arms over his chest, an amused grin on his face. "Well..."

I faltered, unsure of what to do. This hadn't been a date, so I doubt he was expecting me to kiss him, but...what he had done for me was completely selfless. He deserved some sort of acknowledgement. What did I give him, a handshake? That seemed almost insulting. Moving awkwardly, I stepped in and went to press my lips to his cheek.

At the last second, he moved his head, causing my lips to brush against his. He captured my mouth with his own, drawing me unexpectedly into a very slow and sensual kiss.

Pulling back slightly, I stared up at him, knowing my eyes must be wide with shock. "You shouldn't have done that." The words came out breathlessly, letting him know I'd enjoyed it much more than my protesting led on.

"No," he admitted, stepping back with a wicked grin on his lips. "I probably shouldn't have done that, but I needed something to help along the dirty dreams I plan on having about you."

I let out a tinkle of laughter and shook my head as he waggled his eyebrows in playful suggestion. "That little scene in the hallway wasn't enough to fulfill your dirty dream pre-show?"

It was his turn to laugh. "Yeah...yeah...that would have given anyone dirty dreams. Thanks for reminding me." He gave my elbow a quick squeeze before moving down toward his room. "I hope you have sweet dreams yourself."

I knew the next comment was coming, and I was chuckling even before he said it.

"I know I will."

Chapter 16

I entered Damian's room, eager to talk about all that had happened this evening. I knew he wouldn't believe it. Hell, I still had trouble believing it. I had Muffin in my arms, cradled tightly in against my body. Diego had caught up to me, holding the squirming cat in his hands just before I entered Damian's room. Apparently, Muffin was my problem now. Just as well. I thought he was adorable anyway. I was going to have to give him plenty of TLC to get him back in healthy condition.

As I entered, I spotted Damian stretched out along the couch, an arm thrown over his face. I flounced over and dropped to my knees in front of him. I put my hands on the armrest of the couch and placed my chin on top of them, the kitten perched in my lap.

Damian turned his head slowly to look at me, lifting his arm away from his face. He was about to speak when Muffin let out a low growl, his claws digging into my legs.

With a nasty hiss, the kitten scurried out of my lap to hide underneath the bed.

Damian's eyes widened in alarm at the extreme reaction. "What the hell was that thing?"

I stared after Muffin in shock. That...that was a cat and...he never does that. I don't know what got into him."

Damian looked slightly uncomfortable with the conversation. "Maybe I startled him when I moved." He cleared his throat awkwardly. "Cats...they, uh, don't tend to like me very much." He quickly spoke again, changing the topic. "You're awfully chipper for someone that was out looking for death and mayhem."

"I was looking for survivors," I said, correcting him.

"And?"

"We found my brother." I practically squealed.

"No shit?"

"Unfortunately, he was bitten, but Ariel turned him." I began explaining the events of the past couple hours, still having a hard time believing them myself. It was all just so incredible. I left out the part where I almost had sex on the floor with Ariel. I didn't think he would have enjoyed that piece of information very much. I filled him in on the basics—Ariel turning Andrew, sneaking back into the mansion, Kieran's attempted assault.

Damian sat up in interest as I spoke, taking in the story with a look of surprise on his face. After I finished, he let out a low whistle. "Sounds like you had an interesting time."

"I did. It was worth the trip out there if my brother survives." I sprung to my feet in excitement. "I have to tell Ginny."

Damian was on his feet an instant later. "No!"

I jumped, startled by his outburst. "No?"

"It's not a good idea. Why don't you just stay here? Stay with me a little while."

I eyed him as if he were crazy. "Why? Is she sleeping? She won't mind if I wake her up for this. It's important."

I turned on my heels to leave when Damian grabbed me by the wrist. "You can't go up there."

I gave a nervous laugh as I tried to shake his hand from my arm. "What is wrong with you?"

Damian averted his gaze, looking down at the floor before finally looking back up at me.

I could tell by the expression on his face something was wrong. "You're starting to scare me." I yanked my arm out of his grip. "You can't stop me from going to see her, Damian. Just tell me what the hell is going on before I go find out for myself."

Damian reached for me again and thought better of it. He dropped his arms to his sides with a sigh. "Something happened."

My blood ran cold with fear as I envisioned all of the horrible possibilities. Had Kieran done something to her? Had one of the other vampires hurt her? Had she fallen and hurt herself? I turned and took off toward Ginny's room, desperate to know. I was halfway up the stairs by the time Damian caught up to me.

"Aurora, wait!"

He was right on my heels when I swung the door to her room open.

I made a surprised noise in the back of my throat when I found the room empty. "Where is she?" I spun on him, my voice low and angry. "Where is she?" I stormed toward the bed, looking around as if she might suddenly appear.

"She had cancer, Aurora," he said apologetically.

"Where is she?" I screamed.

Damian looked at the ground. "She's dead."

My head swam with confusion. Dead? How could Ginny be dead? I'd just seen her yesterday. "How is that possible?"

"She was sick," he said softly. "You knew that."

I shook my head, anger creeping into me. "Where is she?" I ripped the blanket from the bed, throwing it to the floor as if I expected her to have magically been underneath the whole time.

Damian grabbed me from behind, pulling my arms in against my chest. "Aurora, she's gone," he whispered in my ear.

I spun in his arms to look up at him, tears brimming in my eyes. "But where did she go?" My lips trembled against my will, and my emotions threatened to overwhelm me. There'd been so much loss lately. I just couldn't take any more. Not like this. I felt completely blindsided.

"We buried her out back."

I gave an indignant cry and tried to push away from him. "You buried her in the *backyard*? How could you do that? You just threw her in a ditch like she was some kind of dog!" I fought back a sob and it came out a strangled wail.

Damian tightened his grip on me, not letting me wriggle out of his grasp. "We had to. Don't you understand that? There isn't the neighborhood mortuary to take her to anymore. There was nowhere to take her for the type of care you're asking for. We did what we had to."

"We?"

"Orion and I."

I let out another sob, my hand coming up to cover my mouth. "She was all alone. I was out and she was all by herself. She was probably so afraid."

Damian held me tightly to his chest, trying to offer what little comfort he could. "I was with her," he said softly. "I held her hand and...and I stayed with her." His voice broke and I buried my face into his chest so I wouldn't have to see the look in his eyes.

Heart-wrenching sobs shook my shoulders as I clung to him. I cried until my knees went weak and my head started to throb. When I thought I had no tears left in me, I looked up at him. "We're going to die here, aren't we? We're sitting ducks just waiting for something or someone to kill us."

"No," Damian said emphatically. "We're survivors." He put his hands on either side of my head, brushing my hair back from my face. "We're not going to end up in a ditch somewhere. You're going to make it through this, and I'm going to be beside you the whole way."

Tears started to brim in my eyes again, blurring my vision. I was a little surprised to see a tear well in Damian's eye and spill onto his cheek.

He leaned his head down, his hair framing my face and tickling along my skin. His lips brushed over my cheek, kissing away the tears. He kissed a slow path along my face, taking tears with each soft press of his lips. His mouth then moved to my lips and faintly grazed them. It wasn't a kiss really. It was more of a comforting caress. He rubbed his cheek against mine, nuzzling my skin.

I let the tears fall freely down my face, and I closed my eyes. I let his gentle touch comfort us both. Finally, he rested his forehead against mine and closed his eyes. "We're going to be okay."

"What was the point?" I asked softly.

Damian pulled back to stare at me in confusion. "Point of what?"

"Going to the hospital, suffering through all that horror. For what?" I asked. "She died anyway."

"What was the point?" Damian asked in surprise. "Aurora, you may not realize it, but you did save Ginny. Sure, she died. She knew she was going to. She was terminally ill. But she didn't get eaten alive. She wasn't hunted down and shot. She told me..." He stopped, voice wavering before he could continue. "Right before she died, she told me she was so grateful to you for letting her die in peace, for letting her get to see the sun one last time. She died happy. You made that possible."

I felt a fresh wave of tears brimming. "I can't stay in here."

"I know." Keeping his arm around my shoulders, Damian guided me out of the room.

My legs were unsteady with grief, feeling rubbery and unstable. I teetered on my feet, nearly stumbling into the wall.

Damian swept me off my feet into his arms and I gave a soft gasp of surprise. He lifted me with ease, cradling me to his chest. "Once you get some sleep, you won't feel as bad."

I doubted it. I had witnessed too many terrible things today to just sleep away the memories. It felt nice to pretend I might be able to, though, that I might make it through a few hours of sleep without the faces of people I used to care about haunting my dreams.

I nuzzled into Damian's chest as he carried me down the steps, comforted by the steady thump of his heart. "You're so strong," I said softly.

I meant what I said in more than one way. He was like a rock. Steady. I hadn't seen him lose control yet. Besides the slight tremble in his voice and a few tears, he was in charge of what was going to happen to us. He was so sure of himself. I also said it because of his physical strength. He had scooped me up and carried me like I weighed nothing at all.

A look of anxiety flitted across his face and I wondered why my statement would receive that kind of reaction. He shifted me in his arms as if suddenly registering the weight. "I guess I didn't notice. My mind was so distracted I didn't realize..." He trailed off, discomfort written plainly in his features.

And they say women are hard to understand. I stayed silent for the rest of the walk, afraid to say anything else that would offend his delicate manly ego.

I had thought sleep wouldn't be of any help, but by the time we reached his door, I was dozing off. I was in a fuzzy haze when he kicked the door shut behind him. I came partially back to my senses as he lowered me to his bed. "No." I barely managed to mumble the word out.

He slid his arms out from underneath me. "I know, Aurora. I'm taking the couch."

"No," I said again, more clearly. I balled my fists into his shirt, not letting him go.

He rested his forearms on the bed next to my shoulders, his face close to mine as he strained to hear my whispering. "What do you want?"

"Stay."

His breath caught in his throat and he gazed down at me with an expression of longing. "With you?" he asked.

I gave a sleepy nod. If I weren't half asleep, I would have noted and contemplated the look that crossed his face at my suggestion.

Damian carefully climbed into the bed next to me. He lay on his side, head propped up on his hand. He stared down at me, his face a mask of confusion.

I could see he was debating something internally, pondering over a question I couldn't figure out.

He reached his free hand down and ran it over my hair. "I meant what I said about sticking through this together." His thumb moved to gently stroke my cheek. "I'm going to take care of you. I promise."

My mind came out of the haze enough to realize what he was considering. He wanted to kiss me. My heart gave a thump, warring between panic and anticipation.

This was Damian. We hated each other. Of all the terrible hook-ups I'd had, this would be the worst. The outcome would be bad, very bad.

Yet, I anticipated it, wanted it. I wanted to know what his lips would feel like against mine, what his masculine hands would feel like on my body. With my heart pounding wildly, I scooted closer to him. I took a hold of his free hand and placed it flat against my stomach. I looked up at him and felt fear creep into me.

When I was with Banning, or even Ariel, I was consumed with physical attraction, sexual attraction. This felt different. This thumping in my heart felt heavier, more terrifying. I felt that if I let go, I'd never come back from it.

A slow grin spread across Damian's lips. He let the hand on my stomach curve around my waist, and he pulled me closer. He leaned down, his face inches from mine. "You think too much."

My heart swelled, feeling as if it was going to burst out of my chest. "I've been told—"

I didn't get to finish my sentence because his lips closed over mine. His hand traveled up my waist, up my ribs, and over my neck to cup my face in his palm.

He kissed me gently, his lips a light brush against mine as if he were afraid anything more would freak me out. His lips searched mine slowly, deeply. When he finally pulled away, my eyes were closed and I took in a shuddering breath. "You need some sleep," he whispered in my ear.

I slowly opened my eyes to look into his. "Uh-huh."

He moved away, but remained propped up on his elbow. "Relax and get some shut eye, kitten."

Now that he'd stopped kissing me, I could feel myself slipping back into the clutches of exhaustion. "Kitten," I said tiredly. I blinked and it lasted a good thirty seconds. When I forced my eyes open again, I could see his grin.

"You like that, huh?"

I closed my eyes again. "Mmm-hmm." This time, my eyes never reopened. I felt him lean in and press a kiss to my temple, but I couldn't stir up the energy to look at him.

I drifted off to sleep, the first completely peaceful sleep since we'd gotten here, because I knew Damian was watching over me.

Chapter 17

When I awoke, the sun was still streaming through the window and onto the bed, but it was starting to slip into the horizon. Nightfall wasn't far away. I sat up, stretching my arms over my head, and turned to look next to me.

Damian lay sleeping, his hair falling over his forehead. My heart skipped a beat and my lips involuntarily curled into a smile. I liked waking up to him.

Fear gripped at my chest. This was bad. This was very bad. I could not be falling for the bad boy. I reached my hand to brush his hair back and he sat upright, eyes wide in panic.

He looked out the window, then turned fearful eyes to me. "You have to go."

I was still a little groggy from sleep, so his reaction caught me off guard. I blinked at him with a dumbfounded expression. "Huh?"

He scrambled out of the bed. "You have to go now. You have to leave." He grabbed me by the arm and hoisted me out of bed. "I'm serious, Aurora." He frantically shoved me toward the door.

I turned to face him, walking backwards with his nudges. I experienced the sinking feeling of dread. I couldn't help myself. Damian was having the morning after attitude, and a bad case of it at that. Funny thing was, we hadn't had sex. "I...I don't understand."

"I just need to be alone for a little while, okay? I need some private time." I guess he could see I was hurt by the look in my eyes, because he grabbed my arms and pulled me to him. He kissed me firmly before pulling away. "Please, Aurora. Just give me a little time. Find me when the sun comes up."

He walked me backward into the hallway. A second later, the door slammed in my face. I was completely confused. Not simply about the fact that I was just kicked to the curb. I was leery of the fact that I cared so much that he forced me to the hallway. It could only mean one thing. I really was falling for him.

I couldn't be. This couldn't end well. I'd done the rugged, bad boy thing before. I'd been duped into giving it up in the back seat of a car and was forgotten the next morning. I did not need another incident like that. My heart wouldn't survive it.

Though it was the bad boy who'd saved me from man-eating zombies while the preppy college boy left me for dead. I shook my head, clearing away that thought. I had more to worry about at the moment than Damian and my feelings for him. Like my brother. Just thinking about Andrew had me longing to see him. I needed his familiarity. I needed the comfort only a big brother could offer. Suddenly filled with the need to see Andrew, I made my way to Ariel's room to ask where my brother was being hidden. Outside the door, I faltered.

Ariel wasn't in the best health. If he was asleep, I didn't want to disturb him.

Spinning on my heels, I crossed to Banning's room. I tapped lightly on the door, waiting for a response. When I received nothing, I knocked a little harder. "Banning!"

Still nothing. With a sigh, I cracked the door and peered in. "Banning?" And then I spotted him.

He was asleep on the black leather couch.

I tiptoed over. "Banning?" I leaned over him. "Are you awake?" It was apparent he wasn't, but the sun had gone down. It felt like a rule that he should be up. I knelt on the edge of the couch, putting my face inches from his. "Banning," I said persistently.

His eyelashes fluttered and he opened his eyes, looking groggily up at me.

I was a little surprised at the bleary look in his eyes. I'd assumed vampires jolted awake at sunset, fully aware. Guess that was another thing I could add to the myth column.

"What a nice way to wake up," Banning mumbled, shifting to a sitting position. "Seeing your pretty face makes me almost forgive how absolutely rude it was for you to break into here." His eyes roved over me predatorily and he gave a murmur of appreciation.

"Hey! You're not going to distract me with all your sexual mumbo jumbo."

Banning gave a laugh. "Honey, you haven't seen my sexual mumbo jumbo yet. You've only seen what comes naturally." He reached his hand out and tucked a strand of my hair behind my ear, his fingertips grazing gently across the skin.

When I only gave him a halfhearted smile, he seemed to realize something was wrong. His face suddenly grew serious. "What do you need?"

"I wanted to see Drew," I said softly. "I didn't want to wake Ariel. I didn't know who else to go to."

"And you thought of me. How sweet," Banning said a little sarcastically. He stretched his arms above his head with a yawn. "You're supposed to say, 'Banning I need you. I can't live without you,' not, 'You were my last choice.'"

"I never said you were my last choice."

Banning tapped a finger to my nose. "Not exactly, no. You said you had nowhere else to go. In other words, I was your last resort." He climbed to his feet, his eyes level with mine, hand to his heart. "I have an ego to keep fed, you know?"

"Do I ever." I crossed my arms over my chest and stared stubbornly at him. "Well, are you taking me to see Drew or what?"

"What is it worth to you?" Banning asked, voice low with seduction. He leaned in, his lips inches from mine. "Is it worth a kiss?"

My eyes narrowed and I stared daggers at him. I didn't want to give in to his playful banter and have him dissuade me from my goals.

Banning backed away with a laugh. "Can't blame a guy for trying." When my face didn't soften, he laughed harder. "Okay, maybe you can." He gave a long-suffering sigh. "Are you going to stand there and pout all day or are we going to see that brother of yours?"

"Well, why didn't you say so?" I asked with a grin. On impulse, I pressed my lips to his cheek.

Banning gave a low groan. "You're such a tease."

"You like it." I felt a shiver go through him at the words I whispered against his skin.

"It's been a long time since a woman has thrown me the way you do." His eyes roved over my face for a moment before he pulled away and walked passed me.

I followed him with a smile, shaking my head. I didn't want to admit it to him, but he threw me, too.

As I trailed silently after him, my thoughts slowly returned to my brother. I found myself lost in my concern for Andrew. We stopped at a door that was around the corner from Ariel's room and down the corridor a little.

Banning tested the door and gave an approving nod when he found it locked. He knocked lightly and stood back.

A few minutes later, the door inched open and Orion stuck his head out.

Before I could enter, Banning grabbed my upper arm, halting me. He spun me to face him, pulling me in close. "This is not going to be pretty. The person in there may not be your brother. It could be a monster." His breath was hot on my face, a gentle caress over skin. For someone dead, he was awfully warm and inviting.

"I know that," I whispered back. I didn't know why I was whispering, but it would have felt obscene to speak any louder.

Banning searched my face for any signs of uncertainty. Finally, he sighed and stepped back.

I pushed past him into the room, rushing toward the bed. I sank down into a nearby chair and scooted it to rest by the head of the bed. "Drew," I said softly. "Drew, can you hear me?"

Sweat beaded across his forehead and the hair on his arms prickled up with goose bumps. It took a second glance for me to realize he was strapped down to the bed. His arms were restrained at his sides and his feet roped to the footboard.

I didn't have time to protest this before he opened his eyes and looked at me. His expression was full of pain and regret. "I tried, Rory. I really did." His voice was so full of misery it sent a shiver of alarm down my spine. "I couldn't save them, any of them."

My heart ached for him. He had been forced to kill our parents, to put them down like rabid dogs. That was something nearly impossible to recover from; it was something he'd never forget no matter how hard he tried. I understood that. "I...I think Mom was long gone. Grace bit her a day before things got bad," I said quietly.

"I know that, but...but...Dad." He paused. "And Christine."

"Christine?"

"When things started to get bad, really bad, I left and went in search of Christine."

"Did you find her?" I didn't want to know his answer, yet I had to ask.

"Yeah." Andrew breathed laboriously, his chest rising and falling in an awkward motion. "I found her. A little too late, though." He closed his eyes in pain. I wasn't sure if it was from mental or physical anguish, probably both. "While I sat at home, she was waiting for me to rescue her. She waited for me and I did nothing."

"That's not fair," I protested. "You were with Mom and Dad."

"And Christine died because of it!" A mournful sound escaped him before he continued. "Do you know how she died?"

I shrank back against my chair at his cold tone. I knew he wasn't angry with me. He was just upset, but it was still hard to hear the hatred and bitterness in his voice.

"I'll tell you how she died. She put a bullet in her own fucking brain. She waited until the last possible second. When I never showed, she...she didn't want to be one of those things. She took her own life." He paused and his shoulders shuddered from suppressed sobs. He forced his sorrow into anger, narrowing his eyes. "I let Christine die. I killed our parents. I should be with them. I should be dead right now. Instead, you're going to turn me into a bigger monster than I already am."

"Drew, you're not a monster. You did what you had to do. We all did," I said with pain in my voice.

He wasn't the only one who had killed to survive. I thought back to my trip to the hospital. When Diego and I were overrun, I had killed without a second thought. It didn't make me a monster. It made me a survivor. At least, that's what I hoped.

I went to say something else when Andrew lunged upward at me. The restraints caught him, wrenching him violently back down to the bed.

Banning reached out and yanked me out of the chair. He lifted me to my feet and curved his arms protectively around me.

Andrew's teeth had come very close to closing down on my arm. They might have if Banning hadn't pulled me away.

Banning held me tight against his chest. "Do not get so close to one of the infected," he said in warning.

I watched as my brother started to convulse, horrid moans escaping his throat. "What's happening to him?"

"He's dying."

I pulled away from Banning in a panic. "*What*? I thought he had a chance to survive after what Panthea did." I wanted to run to Andrew, to comfort him, yet I knew what would happen if I did.

"He will die," Banning said softly. "He will suffer and then he will die. It is what he will be raised as that is still a mystery." His arms tightened around my shoulders. "You do not need to witness his suffering. You have done all you can. Leave the rest to us."

I nodded in agreement, feeling like a coward. I did not want to watch my brother suffer. It was too much to ask.

Banning guided me out of the room. Once safely behind the door, he spoke again. "While you tended to your brother last night, I had my team collect some of your personal belongings. Half were sent to Ariel's room, the second half will go to Damian's room later this evening." He crossed his arms almost bashfully. "I kept one outfit in my room because I expected you this evening. I figured you might like to get a shower after you saw your brother."

I stared at him for a moment, completely shocked. He had brought my things. The thought of curling up in a pair of fuzzy pajamas that actually belonged to me was overwhelming. Tears formed in my eyes before I had a chance to fight them. "Th-thank you."

Banning had a look of uncertainty on his face. He knew sex. Beyond physical pleasures, he seemed out of his element. He stood, just staring at me for a moment. Then he gathered me into his arms. "Hey," he said softly. "It's only, uh, clothes."

I held tightly to his waist, sniffling. "That was the nicest thing you could have done for me."

"That's not the nicest thing I could do for you, but I guess it's high on the list," he said huskily in my ear.

An involuntary tremor ran through me and I quickly pushed away from Banning before I did something I might later regret. "You're incorrigible." I laughed, wiping at my tears.

Banning grinned down at me with a look of fondness. "You'll give in to me eventually." He ran his hand over my hair, gently rubbing a few strands between his thumb and middle finger.

I stared silently up at him. The thought of giving in to him crossed my mind...and I wanted to. I couldn't think of a single good reason not to. I'd been through so much pain and suffering; it was time I experienced something good.

Banning stepped back, a grin on his face. "It's at least something to think about." He turned and led the way back to his room.

It was something to think about. And think about it I would. I shuffled along behind him, watching his confident swagger in admiration.

He was so sure of himself, yet he never came off as conceited. He was just good-looking. It was a fact, nothing else. He was comfortable in his skin and he didn't mind letting others know it.

There was something about that I found terribly attractive. He didn't have the uncertainty and insecurities most young men had...not that Banning was young. He merely looked it.

We reached his room and he quickly produced a familiar pair of pink pajamas and a stuffed teddy bear.

A sob escaped my throat before I could stop it at the sight of that stupid bear. I clamped a hand to my mouth, letting my tears fall silently. "I'm sorry," I mumbled. "I...just...my bear..." The bear was the breaking point for me. The violence of this place became too much. Seeing my innocent, non-aggressive bear in this place reduced me to tears.

Banning held it out for me, a look of pity on his face. "I forget sometimes that you are not used to such violence."

I took the bear and hugged it to my chest. "Your world

sucks," I said softly.

Banning nodded. "Sometimes." He gave a shrug. "Though for some of us, it is better than the alternative we were offered."

I let out a sniffle, not commenting.

Banning gave me a soft smile, running a hand comfortingly up my arm. "You should get a shower."

I nodded again, my mind too numb to do much else. I shuffled to the bathroom, moving almost mechanically. After locking the door firmly behind me, I stripped free of my clothing.

I turned the water on as hot as my skin could bear it. I stood underneath the scalding spray for a long time, trying to force my mind to stay blank. It didn't last.

I was consumed with guilt over the decision I'd made with Andrew's life. Was it wrong? Was it a selfish decision? Was I really turning him into a monster? The others didn't seem like monsters to me...well, at least not all of them.

My guilt shifted to Ariel. I'd asked him to put himself into unconditional agony. I had asked him to risk his life, his safety, for a man he had never met. It had been too much to ask of him, yet he had done it.

He had willingly laid his life at my feet...and I had taken it. I was sure if Alexandro found out, it wouldn't only be Andrew that paid for what we had done. It would be Ariel as well.

The fact that my parents were both dead hit me suddenly. Deep down, I'd known it. I had known from the very beginning, but seeing them and hearing about it firsthand still shook me. I would never live to forget my brother's shaking voice as he confessed to bringing our parents' lives to an end.

And Christine. Poor Christine. She had been all alone and terrified. I couldn't imagine having to put a gun to my own head and pull the trigger.

Andrew's luck was amazing. How he managed to make it to Christine's and back without getting overtaken was beyond me. No doubt, he had seen many horrible and terrifying things along the way. And he had seen them alone.

I thanked my lucky stars Damian had been with me. The fact that we hadn't gotten along great in the past didn't matter anymore. He was the one person left I could trust.

I turned the water off and slipped into the clothes Banning had given me. There was no use lingering on the past. What was done couldn't be changed. My parents were dead and I had requested Andrew be turned into a vampire. There was no turning back. The future was rocky enough without obsessing over what couldn't be altered.

I was so caught up in thinking about what was to come I didn't see the person waiting for me outside the bathroom. I gave a yelp of surprise and backed into the door.

Seeing who it was didn't give me reason to relax. Kieran was leaning against the opposite wall, arms crossed over his chest. He gave a snide chuckle at my nervousness. "All alone, are we?" he asked softly.

It was the softness in his voice that sent shivers down my spine. He could speak so calmly, so coolly, yet I could see the barely restrained violence behind his eyes, waiting to escape. "B-Banning is nearby," I stammered nervously.

Kieran's lip curled up in a sneer. "The little princess has a flock of followers, does she?" Before I could answer, he asked, "No Ariel today?"

My body stiffened. I'm sure he could sense it, but I hadn't been able to help myself. Banning said it was very important no one knew what had happened last night. Many lives depended on it and Kieran was the last person we wanted to find out. "I thought he could use a rest."

"A rest, eh?" Kieran practically whispered. "So it's true then, is it? Our princess is a little whore."

I glared at him, refusing to answer.

"Only not to your friend Damian. Word has it, he kicked you out this morning." The uncertainty must have shown on my face, because he laughed. "Did I bring up a sore subject?" Kieran asked. He pushed off the wall, gliding to my side. His right hand entwined itself in my hair. "Mr. Deshea may not find you appealing, but I do. If you are looking to replace him in your little band of fuck buddies, I'd be more than willing to take his place."

"I would never have sex with you," I spat in disgust.

Kieran laughed again, his voice rumbling in his chest. He pressed his body to mine, pinning me against the door. "The choice might not be yours to make."

I put a hand to his chest and pushed. "Get off of me."

Kieran looked down at my hand and grinned. "I'd like to

see you try and make me."

I would like to have been able to. Even if he didn't have superhuman strength, I wouldn't be able to do much. He was much larger than me physically. There was nothing I could do to stop him and he knew it. I realized too late showing my fear at that thought was a bad idea. Kieran was fueled by fear. He fed off of it.

His laughter turned into a growl, chilling me to the bone. "You know there's only one way this can end between us."

"You're right," I said, anger creeping into my voice. "This can only end in death...yours that is."

Kieran scowled. With a snarl, he grabbed me by the wrist. His hand fit easily around it and he squeezed tightly. "You had better think twice about threatening me."

I pulled, trying to free myself from his grip.

He tightened his hold and I felt my bones scream in protest.

I gave a soft yip of discomfort, unable to stop myself.

Kieran's hand clenched down more firmly and my knees buckled from the pain.

"Do not issue a challenge you don't intend to see through. If you wish for things between us to end in death, I will give it to you."

The pain in my arm was nearly unbearable. I knew he would break it without an ounce of remorse. Hell, he would probably get off on it.

He used my arm to yank me to my feet. Black spots swam before my eyes and I had to blink them back as a shudder ran through my body.

"I will make you beg me to kill you," he hissed. "You're not the first spoiled rich girl I've dealt with. I know what makes them tick and I know just which buttons to push." His fingers tightened and I rewarded him with a cry of pain. "In the end, they all beg for death. Just as you will." He released me suddenly, taking off down the hall as if nothing had happened.

I did not doubt him when he said he had tortured many women. I'd heard as much from the others. Kieran was bad news. Kieran was also wrong about Damian. I hadn't been kicked out. There was a completely understandable reason for why Damian asked me to leave. All I had to do was ask him what that reason was.

Determination filled me and I made my way toward Damian's room. I would find out what had been bothering him. I would prove everything was fine between us. In the back of my mind, I was slightly concerned that Kieran knew Damian had shoved me out into the hall. What was Damian doing, telling everyone in the house? Or more worrisome, was Kieran following my every move?

When I came to the door of Damian's room, I skidded to a stop in surprise. It was wide open. So much for needing private time alone. Looked like he just wanted private time from me.

I forced my way into the room. "What was I thinking—" I broke off, my entire body tensing. I expected to find an arrogant, attractive man. Instead, what I saw made my blood run cold.

Lying across the bed was the largest wolf I had ever seen. As soon as it saw me, it let out a ferocious growl, its lip curling up in anger.

I stumbled backward, clutching the doorframe for support.

The wolf sprang to its haunches, twitching as it prepared to launch itself at me.

I backed slowly out of the room, my heart pounding wildly in my chest. How the hell did a wolf get inside Damian's apartment?

As soon as I was out of the animal's view, I took off barreling down the hallway. A moment later, I heard the pounding of huge paws on the floor behind me. "Ariel!" I screamed in a strangled voice as I was thrown to the floor.

My hands hit hard against the ground. I was barely able to keep my face from smashing into the hardwood of the floor. I rolled onto my back in an attempt to fight off my attacker.

I was surprised when the wolf didn't strike. It pinned me to the floor, but it had stopped growling. It lowered its snout to my neck and sniffed, blowing air out of its nose into my hair.

I let out a little yip of fear, squirming underneath it.

I heard footsteps above my head and Banning's voice whisper, "Shit."

I was too terrified to say anything or look to him. I stayed frozen, not wanting to set the wolf off. Out of the corner of my eye, I saw Banning creep closer.

He was holding a hand out cautiously to the wolf. "Don't move, Aurora. I'm going to get you out from under him in a moment."

He took a tentative step forward and the wolf let out a low growl in warning.

I saw a flash of teeth as its lip curled back at Banning. My stomach did a somersault of terror. I was going to die. I was about to have my throat ripped out by this rabid animal.

Banning took a quick step backward. "Calm down, boy," he said soothingly.

I could tell it was the voice he used to calm his horses. This wasn't a horse, though. It was a wolf. The biggest fucking wolf I'd ever seen.

Amazingly enough, when Banning took a step back, the animal relaxed. The growling stopped and the teeth disappeared back into its mouth.

I still didn't dare move. I was still pinned underneath it and I was afraid that any movement would set it off again.

After a tense moment that seemed to stretch forever, the wolf simply sat back on its haunches at my feet. It kept sending wary glances to Banning, but its eyes stayed mostly on me.

"My God," Banning said softly.

I cautiously sat up, my eyes never leaving the animal in front of me. "What?" I whispered.

"He knows you."

My eyebrows narrowed in agitation. "What the—"

"Aurora," Banning said, interrupting me. "Hold your hand out to him."

"Are you out of your fucking mind?" My voice was shrill and panicked. I so did not want to touch the wolf that had moments ago tackled me to the ground with snarls escaping its lips.

Banning shook his head slightly. "No." After a pause, he said, "I have a theory."

"You want me to touch a wild predator on a theory?"

Banning gave a brisk nod.

I had no clue what was running through his mind, but I trusted him. With a shaking hand, I reached out toward the wolf. I felt more than saw it tense.

Banning must have sensed it, too. He began talking to it again in his soft, cooing voice.

The wolf emitted something close to a whine, but it seemed to calm slightly.

I slowly extended my hand and my fingertips brushed across its snout.

The wolf's haunches quivered nervously, but it nudged my hand softly with its nose.

I gave a disbelieving laugh and patted its head. When I looked back at Banning, he had a countenance of astonishment on his face.

"I don't believe it," he breathed.

"Believe what?"

"He recognizes you. He is soothed by your presence."

I gave Banning a look of exasperation. "He recognizes me? How? I've never been this close to a wolf before in my life. I don't even know if I've seen one at a distance. It's impossible for him to recognize me."

Banning went to say something, but stopped, pressing his lips together. That action had my hackles rising with misgiving.

"What?" I asked suspiciously.

"You were not supposed to know."

"Damn it, Banning!" I huffed. "I've got my hands on a wolf, a wild wolf. I feel I'm on a need to know basis at this juncture."

Banning looked as though he was about to argue with me and then changed his mind. "It's Damian," he said cautiously.

"What's Damian?"

He motioned toward the wolf. "The wolf is Damian." He rushed on before I could question him. "You weren't supposed to see this. At sundown, he was supposed to have locked himself in."

"He did," I said numbly, thinking of how he had forced me from his room. I was still having trouble grasping what he was trying to tell me. "He made me leave."

Banning frowned. "How did the door get opened? Did you see anyone else down this hallway?"

"Yeah," I said, anger rising in me at the memory. "Kieran."

Banning hissed in anger and I could feel hatred radiating from him. "He gets more and more careless each passing night. We had no reason to believe Damian would not have attacked you. He took a huge risk with your life for the sake of terrifying you."

Something dawned on me that sent a shiver of fear down my spine. "He wasn't trying to scare me," I said softly. "He was trying to kill me. He was hoping Damian would attack. That way he could join in on the fun and not take the fall for it."

"He is out of control," Banning seethed. "He is out of Alexandro's command."

I absentmindedly patted the wolf's head. "You think?" I asked sarcastically. My mind suddenly caught up to what my hand was doing. I looked at the wolf, then back to Banning in puzzlement. "How can this be Damian? I don't understand what you're saying."

"I'm saying that the animal you've got your hand on is Damian. He's a werewolf and there's a full moon."

I looked at the animal in shocked disbelief as it all started to sink in. "I...I...how...when?" I asked Banning accusingly.

He shrugged. "You would have to ask him. It happened before he was here."

I sat gaping at him in stunned silence. It was impossible. How could he have been a werewolf before this nightmare? That would mean he had probably been that way the whole time I'd known him. Many things started falling into place.

When Damian told me he had to work from home due to his condition, I assumed it was medical, not because he was a werewolf. Now, I understood why he had been so upset when I told him he gave off an aura of trouble. Vampires gave off their own aura and I would bet werewolves did, too. Me saying what I did had probably been a slap in the face to any hope he had of normalcy, and that was what Alexandro had meant by "his kind" dying out.

The fact that he claimed to love the outdoors was ironic. Of course he did. He ran around at night howling at the moon. Muffin, cats in general for that matter, being so frightened of him suddenly made much more sense. To them, he was like a dog. It was like coming face to face with the biggest, scariest, fiercest dog in the world. There was also the fact he had been confident the zombies would go after him before me. And Kieran said something about his blood...

Banning's voice interrupted my thoughts. "Are you alright? Say something."

"Is his blood warmer than normal?"

The question seemed to throw him, but he answered. "Yes. Werewolves tend to have a higher body temperature. In rare cases, some have reached boiling point."

"And zombies like that?"

Banning nodded. "Being what Damian is seems to be the opposite of what we are. Zombies stay away from us. Our blood is too cold, our skin too gummy. Why eat frozen food when humans are walking around with warm, fresh blood pumping through their veins? Even better to eat a werewolf with superheated blood that pumps twice as fast as a mortal. To them, a werewolf is a delicacy. The odds of their race surviving..." He shook his head sadly. "I'm not even sure how Damian survived."

Now that everything was starting to sink in, I felt anger rise in my chest. "And you knew," I accused. "All of you knew. Everyone knew and no one bothered to tell me."

"It was Damian's wish—"

"What about *my* wishes?"

Banning took a step backwards. He seemed shocked at my outburst.

I'm sure he was expecting my reaction to be of fear or horror, not anger. I had felt enough fear lately. I didn't have any left. "I should have known about this. I've been with him the whole time! You act as if you're concerned about my safety, yet I don't even get a warning."

"He was terrified you would be afraid of him. He thought you would hate him."

"Why would I hate him?" I asked, some of my anger dissipating. "That's like hating someone with diabetes. I'm sure he didn't infect himself."

Banning chuckled softly. "Many people would have a problem with him being a werewolf. People fear what is different. They fear change. Think of all the rights movements throughout your species' history. Think of all the violence and resistance. Imagine the fear Damian probably faced in coming out. Then imagine telling your biggest secret to someone you have a thing for. The risk of rejection was too much for him to bear."

I could see his point. I guess if I were in Damian's position, I would have been reluctant to spill the beans on that secret, too.

The end of Banning's speech suddenly sank in. "Wait," I said, unable to hide a goofy grin. "He has a thing?"

Banning rolled his eyes. "Don't play dumb. You know perfectly well there's a thing. The man was a walking zombie target. He should have hightailed it out of that diner as fast as he could, but instead, he was more concerned about saving you."

"That was nice of him."

Banning let out a deep, loud laugh. "That's it? You're hard to impress. Most women would be acting out his craziest sexual fantasy by now. You give a flippant thanks. I'm going to have to step up my game."

I arched an eyebrow at him. "I wasn't aware you had any to begin with."

He put a hand to his heart. "Ouch."

I climbed cautiously to my feet, not wanting to startle the wolf. Just because Damian hadn't attacked me yet didn't mean he wouldn't. When I was sure I was safe, I turned to Banning. Laughing, I shook my head. "You have to be the goofiest vampire I've ever met. I thought you guys were supposed to be scary."

"I'm plenty scary when I need to be. Trust me."

I eyed Banning up and down, taking in his healthy physique. I had no doubt he could be terrifying. I'd seen it firsthand. I was more than a little relieved to know he was on my side, because when he drew his weapon, it would be against my enemies.

The fact that I had enemies caused me to let out a weary sigh. I just wanted to hide somewhere, somewhere I felt safe, and somewhere Kieran wouldn't dare intrude. "Can I see Ariel now?"

Banning gave me a thoughtful look. "He's probably not in the best health and I'm sure his attitude is shit."

"But..." I said hopefully.

"But I'm sure he would appreciate the company. Seeing your face might remind him of why he did what he did last night."

As Banning led me toward Ariel's room, I began having

doubts about going to see him. He was suffering because I had begged him to. If Andrew lived and Ariel recovered, he still might be forced to forfeit his life. Because of me.

As his door loomed into view, I found myself walking slower. I was terrified of how Ariel would react when he saw me. Seeing Andrew hadn't helped. He'd been angry with the way things turned out, regardless of the fact that he had agreed to the terms.

Banning seemed oblivious to my anxiety. So much for super senses. "I'll leave you two alone." His eyes traveled down to Damian, who had been happily trotting along beside me. "That means you too." Banning took a step back and called for Damian to follow.

The wolf watched him with big, wary eyes before looking up at me for confirmation.

"Go on," I encouraged. "Banning won't hurt you."

Damian gave a snort and followed after Banning, staring over his shoulder at me.

As soon as they were out of sight, I let out a nervous sigh. It wasn't much good to put this off. If I stuck around outside, Kieran was likely to show up. Looking at it that way, facing Ariel didn't seem quite so bad.

I knocked lightly on the door before nudging it open. I peered anxiously into the dark, listening to his ragged breathing. "Ariel?" I asked softly.

"Come in." His voice was a hoarse rasp that sent a jolt of guilt through me.

I continued inching forward until I could make him out in the darkness. He looked pale. Well, paler than usual. His forehead was covered in sweat and his face seemed to be stuck in a permanent grimace.

I sat down on the edge of the bed. "How are you feeling?" I mentally kicked myself. He was in unrelenting pain because of me. How did I think he felt?

Ariel opened one beautiful blue eye, staring up at me. "Peachy fucking keen," he said sarcastically. He reclosed the eye and let out a shaky sigh.

Seeing the pain he was in made me realize all over again the sacrifices he'd made for me. I leaned down and brushed my lips across his. "Thank you," I whispered. "Thank you so much."

His mouth curved into a faint smile. "Now you kiss me."

The drawn and tired look on his face made me realize how tired I was as well. I'd spent the day sleeping, but I was so emotionally and physically exhausted. I felt as if I could sleep another twelve hours. With a yawn of my own, I slumped down next to him, laying my head against one of his many pillows.

Ariel tensed slightly. "What are you doing?"

"I wanted to stay with you."

"Does that have to include staying in my bed?"

I hadn't even considered he might be bothered by it. I should have remembered his issues with humans. "No," I said. "I can move if you want me to."

"No," Ariel said quickly. "You can stay."

The desperation in his voice took me by surprise. Did the big, bad Ariel want company?

"So you want me to stay?"

Ariel let out a groan. "Rub it in why don't you? You can't just let things go."

I laughed and moved in closer to him, leaning my head on his arm. "I like to see you squirm."

The last bit of tension drained from his body. "I kind of figured that when you had me pump poison into my veins." Before I could apologize again, he added, "How is your brother doing? I'd hate to have done this for nothing."

I closed my eyes and drew in the scent of him. "He's still hanging on. Banning said he's in the process of dying. They won't know much more until he does."

"What's wrong?"

I didn't realize I'd given an indication that something was wrong. Damn those vampire senses. "Drew wasn't exactly friendly when I went to visit him. He said I should have just killed him."

"He didn't mean it. He's just in pain."

"He said he didn't want to become a monster." As soon as the words left my mouth, I regretted them. I felt Ariel close down emotionally.

"You think I'm a monster," he asked, voice low.

"No!" I leaned up on my elbow and looked down at him. "You're not a monster. Ariel, how could you even think I feel that way? You've saved my life how many times?"

"Look what I did to your arm. I nearly ripped it out of the socket."

"You also kept me alive to this point, even when you didn't want to."

He chuckled softly, closing his eyes again. "I always wanted to keep you alive. I just wanted to strangle you as well."

"Gee thanks." I laughed and collapsed next to him. This close, it was hard to ignore how handsome he was. Even deathly sick, he looked gorgeous.

"Hey, you wanted the truth, didn't y…" He trailed off when he saw me looking at him.

We were both silent, staring at each other. The air between us felt thick and heavy. I was finding it hard to breathe.

In what felt like slow motion, Ariel leaned forward. His lips brushed softly against mine.

I leaned eagerly into him, pressing my body to his.

His hand moved to the back of my head, his fingers sliding through my hair. After a few wonderful moments, he pulled away. "Once again, now you kiss me."

I laughed softly and laid back down, resting my head on his shoulder. "Maybe because I know it's safe."

Ariel let out a weak laugh. "Life with me is never safe." He ran a hand lightly over my hair.

I closed my eyes, relaxing at his touch.

"I'm sorry I'm not better company," Ariel whispered, pain creeping into his voice.

I nuzzled into his shoulder. "I'm not here to have you entertain me. You've done enough for me, more than anyone should. I don't know how I can ever repay you."

"You don't need to repay me. You being here now is enough."

I felt my heart go out to him. All the years he had lived, all the things he had seen, yet he was alone. I couldn't imagine how sad that had to be.

I shifted so I could press my lips softly to his cheek. "Well, then I'll stay." I couldn't pass up the opportunity to catch him off guard. "It's not like I've got much else to do. Especially with Damian being…incapacitated tonight. He's cute when he's furry, by the way."

"I haven't had the opportunity to see him in wolf form yet." His brain caught up with his mouth and his eyes widened. "How did you—"

"How did I find out? When he lunged for my jugular."

Ariel seemed to take this information in stride. "I see that you are unharmed. Is your friend Damian as lucky?"

"He's fine." I waited a beat before saying, "I'm kinda pissed you kept me in the dark."

"It was—"

"I know. I know. It was his wish. Well, what about my wishes?" I didn't keep up the argument, though. Neither of us had the energy for it. "He was stupid to think I would hate him for being a werewolf. I could just…I could just kick him."

Ariel let out an unexpected bark of laughter. It sounded good on him. "You want to kick a poor, defenseless wolf, but you don't hate him?"

I playfully shoved his shoulder. "I don't want to kick the wolf. I want to kick the guy."

Ariel's eyes sparkled in amusement. "You're such a little sweetheart. You wanna kick me too?"

"Maybe."

Ariel reached out and tickled my waist. "You're terrible."

I giggled and squirmed against him. I attempted to roll off of the bed, but he pulled me back.

He rolled on top of me, pinning me beneath him, his fingers tickling me relentlessly.

I gave an indignant cry that was drowned out by laughter and arched up against him. It was that movement that turned the situation from playful to something else. I could see the change in his eyes. They went from sparkling with laughter to smoldering with sexuality.

Before I could process what was happening, his mouth covered mine.

My body responded to him before my brain had the chance to talk me out of it. I arched my lower body up into his again just as he pressed his down against me. I closed my eyes at the sensation, tilting my head back.

Ariel took advantage of this, attaching his lips to my throat. I gasped as he ran his tongue slowly along my neck. He mumbled something in a foreign language, possibly Greek, into my ear, his breath tingling along my skin.

I hadn't the slightest idea what he was saying, but it made my legs feel weak. "Ariel…" For a moment, I felt guilty.

I had kissed Damian merely hours before. How could I be doing this? How was it possible to feel so strongly about two different men? I didn't even want to think about Banning. That just added to the confusion.

Ariel's fingertips ran gently across my inner thigh and I suddenly didn't care. I wanted him so badly. I couldn't worry about my reservations any longer. I let myself go, relaxing into his touch.

It was at that moment, when I was totally relaxed, the moment I fully gave in to him, that I felt a sharp, piercing sensation against my throat. I gasped in shock.

"Fuck!" Ariel pulled away from me, rolling to the other side of the bed.

I bolted upright, my hand flying to my neck. "Did you bite me?"

Ariel's head bobbed and it took him a moment to finally verbalize a response. "Almost." He knelt on the edge of the bed, holding an apologetic hand out to me. "I usually have better control...with me being injured..."

I stared up the length of his body. He was completely aroused. Unfortunately, his teeth were elongated along with other parts of his anatomy.

"I need blood," he said, his words practically a growl. "I should have known better...I could have drained you..."

I was still trying to control my breathing, trying to make sense of what had happened. "Do you want me to get you some blood?"

He nodded his head. "That would be a good idea." He groaned in aggravation. "I am so sorry."

I crawled across the bed to him and pressed my lips firmly to his, carefully avoiding fangs. "Don't you dare apologize."

He stayed silent for a moment, as if not knowing what to say to me. Finally, he just gave me instructions on where to find him blood and suggested I find Orion for assistance.

I rushed out of the room, my heart pounding in my throat, wondering what I had gotten myself into.

Chapter 18

It took me nearly forty minutes to track down Orion and have him assist me in getting Ariel blood. It took a few minutes after that to heat it to body temperature. As we walked back to Ariel's room, Orion gave me a puzzled glance. "I don't get it," he said with a shake of his head. "I've been helping flush out Ariel's system. I had his blood to a schedule. He was in a minimal amount of pain. I don't understand what would set him off early."

There was no accusation in his tone, only bafflement. It still made me blush and stare at my toes. "I'm not sure." *Liar*, I mentally hissed. *You know exactly what set him off.*

"Oh well," he said with a shrug. "We'll just have to give him a little extra." He paused and glanced sideways at me. "I'll warn you, though. He's probably going to get sick. He still does about three-fourths of the time. Without fresh blood, it's taking him longer to heal."

Seeing as it was completely my fault he would be getting sick, I felt it was my duty to deal with it. "I think I'll be able to handle—" I broke off in mid-sentence as I entered Ariel's room. Instead of finding the disgruntled blond beauty, I found Kieran.

He was stretched across Ariel's bed, feet crossed at his ankles, arms behind his head. "Well, well, well," he drawled, "look at what we have here."

"Where's Ariel?" I attempted to keep the fear out of my voice, but failed.

Kieran sprang to a sitting position, his feet hitting the floor with a thud that made me jump. "Oh, I believe he's off in a dungeon somewhere being tortured unmercifully."

I wanted to accuse him of lying, but the evil gleam in his

eyes told me he wasn't. He was far too happy. I started inching backwards out the door before I realized he would catch
me easily. Being in shape was no competition for superhuman speed. Instead, I opened my mouth and screamed.
"Banning!"

"Banning!" Kieran threw back his head and laughed.
"Sorry, baby doll, but your little fuck buddy is a little busy at
the moment. I would guess they've got him chained to a wall
and are tearing chunks of his flesh out about now."

I felt my knees go weak and my head swim. Beside me,
Orion shrank back in fear.

"I know for a fact Ariel has," Kieran said, "because I took
the first piece." He held his hand up and I noticed for the first
time it was covered in blood.

He raised a hand to his mouth and sucked on his index
finger. "Nothing more invigorating than vampire
blood...especially one so old." He held his hand out toward
me, examining a drop of blood that clung to his fingertip.
"Would you like some?"

I would have fallen over had Orion not pressed a firm
hand to my back, keeping me upright.

"Have I finally shocked you speechless?" Kieran's lip
curled up into a sneer. "Have you finally decided to shut your
fucking mouth? It's not so easy to talk shit without your fuck
buddies around, is it?"

I could tell he was getting angrier with each word, and
this time, I didn't have a warrior to protect me from him.

Kieran crossed the room in two strides of his long legs.
He reached for me, but Orion cut him off, blocking me from
his reach.

"You can't hurt her. Alexandro wouldn't—"

"Alexandro doesn't give a fuck what I do to her. She
broke his laws!" Kieran's hands balled into fists. "No new
vampires were to be sired during this crisis. None! That's
why Ariel and Banning are being tortured. That's why they've
probably already driven an axe through the newbie's skull."

I gave a strangled sob at that mental image, clutching
the back of Orion's shirt. Had they killed my brother? Was he
already dead?

"Alexandro won't punish me if I torture, rape, and kill
you. He'll be a little pissed at first, but he'll come to realize

what a pain in the ass you were." He sneered at me around Orion, his lip curling back to expose fangs. "It's been a good day. Ariel dies, your brother dies, I get to kill you, and hopefully they'll execute Banning as well. He's only supposed to get tortured for a few weeks, but sometimes our enforcers get a little carried away." His eyes slid back to Orion. "Move out of my way."

Orion took a deep breath and squared his shoulders. "No."

Kieran bristled, a low growl escaping his throat. He took a few intimidating steps in Orion's direction. "You don't have to die today. Get out of my way."

"No."

At the other man's refusal, Kieran lunged, taking Orion to the ground. He straddled the smaller man and began driving his fists into Orion's face. He hit him with inhuman force, causing blood to splatter into the air.

"Stop it!" Racing over, I jumped onto Kieran's back, trying to pull him off of Orion.

Kieran reached back and grabbed a handful of my hair. He yanked me forward over his shoulder and to the floor. I hit roughly, my hip taking the brunt of the fall. While I was still stunned, Kieran jumped to his feet and drove his booted foot into my stomach.

My breath left me in a whoosh of air. The pain was immediate and intense. I clutched at my stomach, curling in a ball as I attempted not to vomit.

Kieran turned his attention back to Orion, kicking him in the jaw.

I heard the sound of bones crunching and let out a strangled sob. "Stop."

Orion fell to his back on the carpet. His nose was crooked and bleeding, one of his eyes was swollen shut, yet Kieran never relented. His booted foot came crashing down onto Orion's throat, rewarding him with a wheezing croak.

"Stop," I begged. "Don't kill him! Please, please, don't kill him."

Kieran halted, his eyes sliding slowly to me.

I was cowering on the ground, one arm wrapped around my aching ribs. A shiver of terror raced through me at the grin that crept across his lips.

"I told you you would beg." He lifted his foot and shoved my shoulder with it, forcing me to my back. "This is only the beginning. I will have you pleading with me. You will cry and scream...and in the end, you will beg me to take your life."

He sat down on my stomach and stared at me with the look of a predator. His tongue flicked across his fangs, saliva causing them to glisten in the light.

I wanted to scream. I already wanted to cry and beg him not to hurt me, but Banning had already warned me. The more I begged, the more violent it would be. If I had no choice on whether I would have sex with him or not, at least I could make it on my own terms.

The thing I did next shocked even me. Kieran wanted to bring fear out in me. I wouldn't give him the satisfaction. I was going to have sex with him whether I wanted to or not, but I wouldn't let him rape me. If he wanted to hear me scream, he wasn't going to get it. I was going to take all the fun of torturing me out of his little plan.

Sitting up, I touched my lips to his, kissing him slowly, passionately.

Kieran pulled back as if burnt. "What the fuck are you doing?"

"If it means Orion's life," I said, my voice wavering, "I'll have sex with you."

A spark of interest lit Kieran's eyes. He loved pain and torture, but I could see in his expression that this proposition intrigued him. My willingness to cooperate was ammunition to use against the men I truly cared for. He would torture them with it.

"This won't save Ariel," he said, voice low. "They're still going to kill him."

Tears welled in my eyes and I tried to force them back. I had to do what I could for the people I still had the ability to save. "I know."

His hand grabbed my throat, squeezing, forcing me to look him in the eyes. I held his gaze, letting him see I was serious. His hand was still caked in Ariel's blood. I could feel it sticky against my throat. My stomach turned and I closed my eyes to fight back nausea.

Kieran took this as an invitation. He slid his hand down my neck, leaving a trail of blood as he went.

I shivered, fighting back a sob. This was Ariel's blood. Ariel was suffering somewhere and I was trapped here, unable to help him. He would probably die while I was having sex with the monster in front of me.

Hatred took root in my heart and I opened my eyes to stare steadily into his, mine full of steel. I hated him. With everything in me, I hated him. Reaching up, I grabbed his hair roughly in my fisted hand. I yanked his head toward me, placing his face inches from mine. "I hate you."

A grin curved over his lips and, for the first time, he was actually attractive. I could do this. For the sake of my life and Orion's life, I could survive this.

"I know." Then his lips crushed to mine. The fact that I despised him seemed to fuel him on. It was as if he was trying to devour me, his mouth so forceful against mine I got jagged with a fang.

Kieran groaned in delight. He drew my lower lip into his mouth, sucking roughly to draw more blood. Both of his hands grabbed the front of my shirt, balling into fists.

I gave a startled gasp when he tore it completely from my body.

Kieran was still resting on my legs with me sitting up to reach his lips. He seemed to realize this because he forced me to lie back and got to his knees in front of me.

Grabbing me by the ankles, he forced my knees to bend. He then drew my legs apart and crawled up my body. He kissed me again, slowly and softly. He kissed me with a gentleness I didn't know he possessed.

I tried to force myself to relax. Maybe this wouldn't be so bad. Maybe I could close my eyes and pretend he wasn't the terrible monster I knew him to be.

"I'm going to fuck you so hard your legs go numb," he whispered against my mouth. "I'm going to fuck you until you cry...and there will be blood."

I was unable to fight back the small sob of terror. How could I have thought this could be anything less than horrifying?

He rolled his hips forward, grinding himself against me to show how much the idea excited him. "All of it yours." He got back to his knees, his hands moving to the button of his jeans.

I tried to hide my look of surprise as Orion rose up behind him. *Kill him*, I silently pleaded. *Please, kill him.*

Orion had a large knife in his hand. Before Kieran could even realize anyone was behind him, Orion drew the blade across his throat.

Kieran's eyes widened in shock as blood gushed from the injury. It spurted out of the wound onto my bare stomach, splattering across my breasts. He collapsed to his hands and knees, his body still over mine. Blood continued to pour from his throat, splashing down onto me.

I scrambled backwards, frantically trying to get away from him. As soon as I cleared him, he fell to his face, blood pooling around him.

Orion grabbed my arm and pulled me to my feet. "Oh, God...are you okay? Are you okay?" His hands touched my face, gently feeling for injuries. "He didn't hurt you, did he?" He glanced down my body and gave a cry of protest. "That bastard." He pulled his shirt over his head and pressed it into my hands.

I gratefully took the shirt and shrugged into it, my hands shaking so badly I could barely manage the simple task. Just as I finished pulling it down, I saw Kieran rise up behind Orion. My eyes widened in horror.

Orion's eyes shone with knowing fear a second before a sword was shoved into him from behind. It went clean through, the tip coming out the front of his chest.

I let out a scream of absolute terror. "Orion!"

He clutched the point of the sword, his eyes traveling down to look at it. Blood began escaping from the corners of his mouth and he collapsed to his knees.

"Oh, God," I breathed, backing slowly away from him. "Orion."

The next instant, Kieran was on me. He grabbed me by the shoulders and threw me against the wall.

"I'm going to make you suffer!" He started marching toward me, murder in his eyes, but before he reached me, he was thrown backwards by a furry shape.

It took my mind a minute to realize it was Damian in wolf form.

Kieran went down with a horrible shriek that was nearly drowned out by the sound of the wolf's snarl as it tore into him.

I didn't wait another second. I took off running down the hallway, heading for Alexandro's office. If I had any chance of getting out of this alive, I would need his protection. That thought terrified me. Everyone I relied on had been taken from me. Ariel and Banning were being tortured. Orion lay bleeding on the ground, and I didn't know how long Damian would be able to hold Kieran off.

I didn't want to think about what Kieran would do if he got the upper hand on Damian. Damian couldn't heal wounds like the rest of them.

I reached Alexandro's door and threw myself into the room.

He glanced up from a stack of papers in front of him. When he saw me, he couldn't hide the look of disgust on his face.

"Help me," I begged. "Please, please." Sobs tore from my throat as I stood before him, covered in blood and desperate. He was my last hope.

He remained silent, staring at me. He didn't move. He didn't breathe or blink. He just watched me. "You didn't knock."

I nearly collapsed from the fear overwhelming me, and I felt tears trail down my cheeks. "Don't kill Ariel. I need him."

This set Alexandro off. He jumped to his feet, fists slamming down to his desk. "Ariel broke my rules. In my own home!" He grabbed a vase from his desk and threw it at the wall where it shattered into a thousand pieces. "And he did it for a mortal. A mortal!"

I cringed at his anger, shrinking back. "He doesn't deserve to die."

"How would you know? You've known him a week. I've known him centuries. I think I know what he deserves better than you do."

"He doesn't—"

"Even if he didn't deserve it, it's too late. He knew the consequences! If your brother lives, Ariel dies."

I felt as if I'd just been slapped. Ariel had known. He knew that if he successfully saved my brother, he would be forfeiting his own life in return. In essence, he had given his life to make me happy.

"Our numbers are too high. We can't afford to have any more of us. We all agreed to that."

"So that's it?" I cried tearfully. "It's all a numbers game? Ariel's life is a fucking statistic?"

There was a broom leaning against the wall near his elbow. He grabbed it and threw it in my vicinity. It hit the wall behind my head and broke into three pieces. "Don't blame me for your actions! This is *your* fault! He was never meant to have feelings for you! He was supposed to scare the shit out of you, maybe beat you around a bit."

"So you're punishing him because he has a heart?"

Alexandro turned his back on me as if he couldn't bear to look at me. He stayed silent, his body tense.

I knew I didn't have much time. Kieran was coming for me, of that I was certain. Bending down, I picked up a piece of the broken broom, clutching it in my hand. "Is it really just numbers to you?" I asked Alexandro softly. "Or are you still punishing him for Angelina?"

Alexandro spun on me and, for a moment, I thought he would strike me. He held back at the last second. He was so close that his breath was hot on my face.

That was good though. If he was breathing, that meant I was getting to him.

"It is about the numbers, but I won't lie that I am happy to see Ariel finally get what he deserves. He deserves to suffer. He deserves to rot in hell...and now, thanks to you, he will."

I had never seen anyone so consumed with hatred. He was blinded by it. A few hundred years of holding it in had made him bitter beyond sanity. Trying to keep my makeshift weapon hidden against my leg, I asked, "If this is about numbers, does that mean you would let Ariel live if someone else were to die?"

Alexandro gave a shrug, his face contorted with a sneer. "It probably doesn't make a difference anymore, but I suppose." He gave a cruel laugh. "Do you plan on finding someone willing to lay down their life for your precious boyfriend?"

I was so tired of defending my single status I didn't even bother to object to his choice of words. "No," I said darkly. "I plan on someone breaking a rule that's punishable by death."

"And what would that be?" he asked with a cocky smirk.

"Trying to kill me."

It was at that moment the door was thrown open. I heard it bust off its hinges, heard it splinter.

"You bitch!" Kieran's voice rang through the room.

I had my back to him and was very grateful for that. The look on Alexandro's face told me enough. Orion had sliced Kieran's throat and then a werewolf had savagely mauled him. I could only imagine how mangled he must be.

His words had come out as a burble and I could hear the sound of blood splashing to the floor every couple of seconds.

"You fucking bitch. I'll kill you!"

My eyes caught Alexandro's and, in that instant, realization hit his eyes. "Kieran, no!"

Kieran was too consumed with rage and bloodlust to listen. He came at me with the intent to kill. His fist curled into my hair, yanking my head back to expose my throat.

I had a fleeting thought where I prayed I had at least one vampire legend right before I drove the busted piece of wood backwards.

Kieran's fangs, that had just grazed my neck, suddenly pulled back. He gave an inhuman shriek and made a frantic attempt to get away from me. The first blow hadn't found the heart, hadn't gone all the way through.

I pulled back and shoved again, putting my body behind the thrust.

He gave a shriek as the wood forced its way into him.

I felt it jar all the way up my arm, sending tingling pain down through my fingers. The broom handle hit bone, grinding against it, before sliding off and hitting heart.

Kieran gave another howl that was cut short as his body disintegrated into dust.

I released the handle and it clattered to the floor. Then I collapsed to my knees next to it, my fingers moving to my throat.

I could feel blood seeping from the slice Kieran's fangs had created. I pulled my hand back and stared at the red liquid. I made sure Alexandro saw it as well, forcing him to come to terms with what I had been forced to do. "Let Ariel go."

Alexandro was staring at me with a confused expression on his face. He looked as if he were torn between disbelief, anger, shock, and horror. There was respect in his gaze as well. Finally, he said, "He had lived more years than you could possibly hope for."

"Well, he outstayed his welcome."

"Such boldness for such a young creature."

"That's because I just realized how much you need me. You're not going to have me killed for someone that had it coming. And you won't kill Ariel either, because you know if you do, I'll never have sex with Damian. Ever. We need things from each other, and unless we're both willing to co-operate, everyone dies."

I fell silent, letting him take that in. I was using sex with Damian as collateral for Ariel's life. At this point, I didn't even know if Damian was still alive. I tried to keep that uncertainty from my face as I stared into Alexandro's unforgiving eyes.

The silence seemed to stretch on forever before he finally said, "I like a woman who can play hardball." He studied my face, eyes narrowed in concentration. "You have the look of someone who has the weight of the world on their shoulders."

"That's because I do," I said softly.

Alexandro let out a soft sigh of resignation. "If he truly means that much to you, I will spare him."

Relief flooded through me and I couldn't help the tears that cascaded down my cheeks.

"Only know that I am not doing this as a favor and I have no love for Ariel. This is a pact that you will try to mate with the wolf. If you break this promise, I will have someone you care about killed."

I nodded numbly, willing to give him anything if it meant saving Ariel.

"Good. Then we have an understanding." He walked over to me and pulled me to my feet. "Let's go."

I followed after him, anxiety tearing at my chest. For all I knew, Ariel could be dead already. Banning could be dead. Hell, so could Damian and Orion. If everyone got out of this alive, it would be a miracle.

We walked for what felt like forever, going down long corridors and twisting staircases. We finally reached a large, heavy door. From the other side came the sound of a suffer-filled holler. Ariel. I was torn between relief that he was alive and horror at what was being done to him.

Alexandro threw open the door. He didn't seem disturbed by the room, but I was.

The walls were covered in chains and manacles. At least a dozen tables pressed against the right wall, covered in instruments of torture. The floor held drains. Easier to get rid of the blood that way. One of those drains held a pool of amber liquid.

I followed the trail to a familiar pair of booted feet. My eyes made their way up the body attached to those boots and I shrank back in horror.

Ariel was a bloody mess. He sagged against the chains that held him. They were the only thing keeping him upright. He was so bloody I couldn't see where one wound ended and the next began.

He glanced up at the sound of the door and I got a glimpse of his face. It was barely recognizable. His left eye was swollen shut, so puffy I wondered if he still had an eye at all. A large chunk of his right cheek was missing altogether, exposing a set of bloody teeth. Most of his visible skin was bloody, boiling up.

My hand went to my mouth to cover the sound of a strangled sob.

Alexandro's voice broke through the silence. "You can let them go," he said dully, as if it didn't matter to him either way. He then turned and left.

One of the men who had been torturing Ariel only moments before began unchaining him, his expression as dead and uncaring as Alexandro's.

I rushed to Ariel's side. As soon as the chains were released, he toppled to the floor. I held him by the waist, trying to make the fall less painful. We both collapsed to our knees, facing each other. "Ariel..." I went to touch his face but stopped. It would probably cause him pain. "Oh, Ariel." I cried into my hands, the sobs wracking my body. Since he had agreed to protect me, he had been through so much, all of it because of me.

"Don't cry," Ariel said weakly. "If you're this upset, it means my face is mangled beyond recognition." He spat a stream of blood out onto the floor.

I was unable to stop the tears that flowed down my cheeks. "Kieran said...Kieran...he said..."

"That he helped?" Ariel offered. "He did. He got the sadistic ball rolling." He looked at me with his one good eye. "Hey, don't worry about me. I did my job. You're still alive. That's all that matters."

"That isn't all that matters," I said tearfully. "You matter...and Banning...and..." I broke off when the next name popped into my head. "And Damian...oh, God, Damian." I broke into a fresh round of tears. "And poor Orion."

"What happened?" Ariel asked, concern thick in his voice.

"Kieran happened. He attacked us...Orion and me." I quickly told him of the ensuing scuffle. He seemed quite impressed Orion had fought back and stood his ground against Kieran. I finished with Damian getting in between Kieran and me, giving me time to run. I looked into Ariel's eyes, tears brimming in my own. I brought my hands up and ran them gently over his hair. "Kieran will never hurt you again. He'll never hurt any of you again."

He closed his eyes, leaning into my touch. "You can't know that for certain," he said softly, "but thank you anyway."

I leaned forward and kissed a clean spot on his cheek. "I do know. He won't touch you ever again, because I killed him."

Ariel jerked back, his good eye widening in disbelief. "You *what*?"

"I killed him." I could see the question in his eyes before he asked it, so I explained. "I killed him right in front of Alexandro. He left me no choice."

"I'd say he fucking deserved it."

I spun to the owner of the voice just in time to see Banning popping his shoulder back into place by pressing his palm flat against the wall and jerking his body to the side.

I cringed slightly. After everything I'd seen in the past few weeks, a dislocated shoulder was nothing.

Banning didn't look nearly as bad as Ariel. He had a black eye and his jaw was bruised, but that was it. It looked mostly like he had fought back while they chained him. It appeared as if they had chosen to torture one guy at a time.

Banning didn't seem too concerned with his injuries either. Walking over, he put a hand under Ariel's arm. "Help me get him upstairs."

I did as instructed, wondering what was going to happen next. I wanted to find out if Damian and Orion were alive. I wanted to spit on the dust that used to be Kieran. I wanted to find my brother.

As we deposited Ariel in his bed, I felt adrenaline leave and exhaustion take over.

Banning seemed to notice this as well. "You need rest." He came to my side and lifted me up into his arms.

"No. Orion...Damian...Drew..." My eyes felt so heavy. I could barely keep them open.

"I'll take care of them."

That was the last thing I remembered before my head hit his shoulder and I passed out.

Chapter 19

I awoke at sunset. The light fading from the room caused shadows to hide in the corners. It drew an instinctive shiver of fear from me.

Orion was sitting in a chair beside the bed, his face a mask of concern.

Seeing him sparked my memory. "Orion!" I quickly sat up. "You're alive!"

He gave a bashful smile before staring intently at his hands. "Yeah..."

"I don't think I can ever repay you for what you did for me."

His head shot up and his dazzling eyes were full of surprise. "Me?" He shook his head. "No, I should be thanking you. You killed Kieran when I couldn't."

"*Me*? Orion, do you realize Kieran would have raped and murdered me if it hadn't been for you and Damian?" I grew suddenly tense at the thought of Damian. He still hadn't been accounted for. "Orion...where's Damian?"

His eyes avoided mine. "I was instructed to get Banning the moment you awoke. He wishes to discuss all of the past events with you."

Before I could say another word, Orion was out the door.

I stared after him, my concern deepening. He had run out of the room at the mention of Damian. The horrible thought that he was dead filled my mind. My breath caught in my throat and I fought back tears.

Banning made his way into the room a moment later. He must have seen the tears glistening in my eyes, because he rushed over to me. Sitting on the edge of the bed, he pulled me in tight against his chest. "Don't cry."

I don't know why, but this made the tears spill harder.

He brought his hand up and ran his thumb lightly over my cheek, brushing away the tear.

"Damian's dead, isn't he?" I whispered.

"Oh, baby," he said with a laugh, running a hand through my hair. "That's why you're crying?" Grabbing my face in his hands, he pressed a kiss to my forehead. "Damian's alive."

Relief rushed through me in a wave. Damian was alive.

"He's not looking too hot. He had the shit beat out of him, but he's still breathing."

I put my head in my hands, giving myself a moment to let the terror leak away. "Good." I looked up and gave a genuine smile. "That's great."

Banning nodded, an amused smile on his face.

"So what was Orion's deal?" I asked. "Why did you need to tell me everything?"

"You've been asleep for nearly two days. Many things have happened in the past forty-eight hours. I wanted to make sure nothing was left out when you were brought up to date."

I couldn't believe I'd slept for two days straight. I guess my body had finally given out under exhaustion.

He took one of my hands in his, gripping it, as if trying to prepare me for a blow. "Your brother died this afternoon."

I gave a gasp of terror and tried to yank my hand from his.

He tightened his grip. There was no beating vampire strength. "He died in a good way. He wasn't beheaded or tortured. He died in his bed this afternoon." He shrugged. "We won't know what he will rise as for at least a few more hours. What was done to him was very complex."

I sighed in relief. Andrew was dead, but he wasn't dead dead. He was the kind of dead we'd expected. "Okay."

Banning smirked, seemingly pleased with how well I took that. "As you can see," he said. "Orion is completely healed. He healed at a rate that was almost alarming. I've never seen a wound like his heal in an hour." He shook his head. "He has almost always been bruised and bloodied. With a healing rate as fast as his..." He let out a soft whistle. "No one was aware of how badly Alexandro was beating him."

I clenched my jaw, anger creeping up my spine. "He's not staying with Alexandro anymore. Alexandro said I could keep Orion and I intend to. Tell everyone he's mine."

Banning's eyebrows shot up in surprise. "You're claiming Orion?"

I nodded. "Yes, and if anyone so much as looks at him funny, I want you to hurt them."

"You're fierce," Banning said with a chuckle. He leaned back on the bed, propping himself up on his elbows. "Speaking of how fierce you are..." He shook his head in disbelief. "You really killed Kieran?"

He made it a question, but I think he already knew the answer.

"Yeah," I said, a little shocked myself. "I did what I had to."

"Alexandro collected his ashes for Panthea. He thought she might like them."

I was a little confused by this statement, but Panthea's name sidetracked me. "Where *is* Panthea?"

"She has not yet returned. She has no clue what has transpired since the night we found your brother."

"I figured not."

Banning watched me, his eyes roaming lazily over my face. "Ariel's in bad shape, you know?"

I stared silently at my hands, not wanting to know the extent of Ariel's injuries, yet needing to. If Ariel were human, he'd be dead. Even with vampire healing, he was in bad shape. "I know."

"Without fresh blood, his wounds will heal slower. There's nothing that can be done for him. He'll just have to wait it out. He and Damian both."

"Can I see them?" I asked softly.

"Sure." Banning climbed to his feet, holding a hand down for me. "Keep in mind they are very battered. I don't want you getting upset."

"I'm just glad they're alive." I took his hand and let him help me to my feet.

He pulled me flatly against his chest, his lips twitching in amusement. "I was thrown in a dungeon and chained to a wall for protecting you. Did I earn myself a real kiss yet?"

I tilted my head to the side, staring into his gray eyes. "I suppose." Wrapping my arms around his neck, I gave him a small smile. I was feeling generous. My entire group had lived and Kieran was no longer around to torment me. I was in too good of a mood to torment Banning. "Anything for my knight in shining armor." Leaning in, I brushed my lips against his. "Or is it my cowboy in shining stirrups?" I kissed him again, my lips a gentle caress against his. I felt his fingers curl into the fabric of my shirt. I pulled back to look at him.

His eyes were tightly closed and he looked as if he were fighting for control. "You can't do this..." He opened his eyes to look into mine. "You will drive me out of my mind. It has been...too long since a mortal woman has kissed me like that."

My heart went out to him. He had suffered so terribly under Alexandro. Being banned from the one thing he craved for nearly four hundred years to then have it flaunted cruelly in his face without being allowed to have it was torture.

"If I don't drive you crazy, we just might have some good times together."

Banning laughed and grabbed hold of my wrist. "Then take me to the brink, sweetheart." He touched his lips to my wrist and I knew he was feeling for the pulse. Pulling back, he squeezed my fingers. "Let's go see your guys. We have them both in the main area of Ariel's room for safety reasons. Kieran had some allies who may wish to retaliate. Safety in numbers is probably a smart plan to follow."

I shadowed him to Ariel's room, my light mood evaporating. I couldn't imagine the amount of suffering the two of them had gone through...were going through. I didn't want to witness either of them suffer, yet I didn't want them to go through it alone. Steeling myself for the worst, I pushed into the room. I saw Damian first.

He was lying on the bed closest to the door. Banning was right. It looked like someone had beaten him within an inch of his life. His face was a mask of bruises, his lip busted. One of his arms was in a sling and two of the fingers on his left hand were taped.

"Oh, Damian." I sank down to the mattress of his bed. My fingertips brushed along the back of his hand, needing to touch him.

His eyes fluttered open. "Aurora?" His hand suddenly clutched at mine and he squeezed my fingers tightly. "Rory, you're alive. Banning said, but...I needed to see with my own eyes." He slowly, painfully sat up, gently stroking my cheek.

I nodded, tears springing back to my eyes. I was an emotional roller coaster. "Me too...I thought you were dead." The hand that wasn't in his moved to his face. I couldn't help myself. I desperately needed to touch him. I wanted to make sure he was real.

"I would have died if I weren't—" He broke off suddenly, cutting his sentence short.

"Damian," I said softly, realizing what the end of that sentence would have been, realizing what he was concerned about telling me. "I don't care if you're a werewolf. That doesn't matter to me."

Damian's face filled with emotions as he pulled me toward him with his one good arm. He hugged me tightly to his chest. Burying his face in my shoulder, he mumbled, "I was so afraid to tell you."

I held tightly to him, rubbing my cheek against his. I took comfort in the feel of the couple days worth of stubble, letting it prickle along my skin.

"I thought you would never speak to me again if you knew."

I pulled back, looking into his warm, chocolate-colored eyes. "I will never turn my back on you. You're all I've got left."

Damian let out a giant sigh of relief. "You're everything to me, Rory." His free hand moved to the back of my head, fingers entwining in my hair. He leaned forward and brushed his lips against mine.

My eyes fluttered closed and I relaxed into him. The kiss was slow and tender, making my heart pound forcefully in my chest. I was once again reminded that kissing Damian was so much different than kissing Banning or Ariel. In my mind, I told myself it was the difference between werewolves and vampires.

One had cold blood, while, apparently, the other's was hot. One was dead while the other vibrated with life. They were opposites in every way. Why should this be any different?

Damian pulled back a moment before gently pressing his lips to my forehead. "Thank you for being so understanding." He nodded to the second bed. "You can go check him out. I think he's a little worse off than I am."

I looked over at the bed that Ariel occupied. He looked slightly better than two nights ago. His skin had begun to heal and wasn't nearly as charred. Healing or not, he still looked like shit. "Ariel?" I asked tentatively. I ran my hand along his golden blond hair, angered at the patches where it was shorter and shorn.

"I hear you," he said through cracked lips.

"I'm so sorry. Look what they did to you..."

"It's all part of the job," he said with a slight shrug. "Give me a week tops and I'll be back in working condition."

"Part of the job?" I didn't know what job included torture and murder as an everyday occurrence. He looked horrible. He looked as if he would never be alright again. Yet if things were different and he had someone to feed from, he might be healed instantly. Vampire genetics were amazing. "If you had fresh blood to feed from..." I trailed off, leaving the end of my sentence open for him to finish.

"I would heal much quicker, practically overnight. Unfortunately, that is not going to happen."

I couldn't believe what I was about to suggest. I had to be out of my mind. I felt I owed him, though. He was injured because of me. "Drink from me," I said before I could lose my nerve.

Ariel's eyebrows shot to his hairline. "Excuse me?"

"Drink from me. Take the little that you need to heal. Why suffer for weeks when you could be as good as new by tomorrow?"

Ariel stayed silent, staring at me uncertainly. I could tell he wanted to accept my offer, but he looked like he was waiting for me to change my mind.

"Ariel, drink from me. I want you to. It's the least I can do."

He slowly sat up, wincing in pain. "This isn't something to be taken lightly. Are you sure about this, Aurora?"

"Completely."

After a moment's hesitation, he leaned forward, leaving a soft kiss against my neck.

Out of the corner of my eye, I saw a wounded look cross Damian's face before he rolled over, putting his back to us.

I put my palm flat to Ariel's chest and pushed him away. "What's wrong with Damian?" I asked, my voice barely audible.

Ariel leaned in, putting his lips next to my ear. "Vampires are not the only creatures who can heal through blood."

It took me a moment to realize what he meant. "You're saying..."

"You could heal him, yet you extended the offer to me. It is a close bond, an intimate exchange. He is bothered by this because he loves you."

My breath caught in my throat and my heart began pounding wildly. Here it was again, this reaction to Damian. I had a hard time blaming it all on his werewolf powers. I had such a strong reaction because I knew what Ariel said was true. Damian loved me.

The thought brought a goofy smile to my lips and made my heart swell. It made me think there was something in this world still worth living for. "Can I feed you both?"

Ariel's eyes darkened in arousal. Apparently, my suggested ménage à trois of terror thrilled him. Keeping his voice carefully neutral, he said, "You could. Only keep in mind that feeding a werewolf is not as gentle as a vampire. Their teeth are rougher, larger. They don't slide as easily into the skin and Damian is a baby. He does not have the control, experience, or knowledge to make it an easy feeding." His shoulders arched slightly into a shrug. "Doing it would create a bond between the two of you that would be nearly unbreakable. I don't know if you are prepared for that or not, but he is. He would follow you to hell and back...he has."

"Would you and I have a bond?" I asked, trying to figure out just exactly what I was getting myself into.

Ariel shook his head. "Not like you would with him. With us, it would be like a fun secret, like good sex with a friend. With Damian..." He shrugged again. "It would be like sex with your soul mate."

What Ariel was getting at was that it would mean quite a lot more to Damian than it would mean to him. "His teeth would leave a scar," Ariel continued. "In essence, he will be marking you as his mate."

I gave a frustrated little groan. "Why does everything have to be about sex with you guys?"

"It is what we know." Ariel paused, as if trying to think on his next statement. "Vampires communicate through sex. It is our primal instinct." He gave me a pitying look. "I'm sure things have probably been hard for you the past few weeks. When we, vampires I mean, communicate through sex...it can be a bit much to handle. We cannot help what we are, though. To have a deep connection with one of us, you would need to have a sexual attraction." He paused thoughtfully. "Of course, some of us are different. Others sometimes have a different way of communicating. Orion has known only fear, so he uses that. You were terrified in his presence many times while you were here and it made it possible for him to form a bond with you. Now that the bond is in place, the two of you don't have to share only fear with one another. Fear only made it possible for you to understand each other. Alexandro uses power to communicate with others. You do not hold the power you have over the heads of others, so it makes it hard for him to see you as anything besides a meal."

I felt a sudden rush of understanding. The only time Alexandro had looked at me like I was anything but a nuisance was when I had told him he needed me and unless he was willing to work with me, then we would all die. I flaunted the fact that he needed me, that I had power over him. I hadn't known it at the time, but I had probably used the only weapon Alexandro could understand—power.

"Kieran used terror," Ariel said. "Obviously, the two of you didn't click with each other. You don't take pride in hurting others. Kieran is one of the few of us who has never been able to communicate through sex. I think someone in his human life wounded him psychologically in regard to sex and he was never able to recover. That is why he had such an adverse reaction to the bond you formed with the rest of us. Sex was an abomination to him. Sex was a snide insult to the victims he chose to torture. He used the one thing he didn't understand to torment those who knew the social rules of the act." Ariel paused, running his hand over my cheek. "You, Banning, and I share sex as a primal instinct and that is how we chose to bond. I'm sorry if this has caused any inner turmoil to you." He dropped his hand and let out a sigh, as if things were terribly complicated.

"As I said," he continued. "Vampires communicate through sex. It is our primal instinct to do so. Human instincts are much easier and more definable—food, shelter, and sex. Ours are intertwined. There is shelter. You know Alexandro came to power because of this. Without shelter, the sun kills us. But food and sex..." He shook his head. "To us, they are the same. We get food and sex from the same place. We get food from a human body. We get sex from a human body, sometimes the same one. It can be confusing to some. Think of it this way, you would not eat only pasta for the rest of your life, would you?"

I shook my head, wondering where he was going with this.

"Of course not. Well, human blood has variation. Everyone has his or her own distinct taste. You would not only eat pastas and in the same respect, we would not eat from only one human. Seeing as sex and food are interchangeable, we would not have sex with only one person either. A mortal might frown upon this, but to us it is merely fulfilling our basic instincts. There are some of us who could survive on...pasta," he said for lack of a better word. "I guess you would consider them vegetarians." He chuckled at this. "Kenya and Diego are in this group. They manage, but most cannot." He shook his head sadly. "When Angelina was alive, I fed off of her alone. I hate to admit that Panthea was right, but it made me weak. I cannot survive on one person alone. I'm sorry."

I suddenly got what he was saying. He liked me, but he would never be with just me. He was old enough where he didn't necessarily need to feed, but he needed sex from other women. It wasn't in his nature to be faithful to just one.

"Banning is the same way, maybe more so because his power deals with sex. If he does not keep his powers healthy...then he will become a target for anyone who wishes to hurt him."

I knew Banning had super hearing and that he was probably hanging on to Ariel's every word. I glanced across the room at him and caught him guiltily staring down at his shoes. So Ariel was right. Without sex, they became weak. If sex was interchangeable with food, it was like starving themselves.

"But Damian..." Ariel brought my eyes back to him. "Damian needs only you to thrive. Nothing more. A wolf will pick one mate and stay with them until the bitter end."

He squeezed my hand almost sadly. "Know that Banning and I care for you, but you belong to Damian."

"I belong to no one."

"You are Damian's," Ariel repeated. "He will be dedicated to you alone, give you children, his protection, anything you need." Ariel smiled softly. "Being what he is, Damian understands our instincts and knows that Banning and I care greatly for you. He will not forbid Banning and I from those instincts. He will share because he knows we do not pose a permanent threat to what is his and, trust me, werewolves are not kind to anyone they consider a threat to their mate." Ariel looked me dead in the eyes, his full of intensity. "If you feed him, you are letting him mark you as his mate. You need to think about that before you go through with this."

With a small sigh, I thought over my options. It was terrifying to me to let Damian mark me as his property. I was only trying to heal him, not pick out curtains. It was also a little odd that Damian was giving his permission for me to feed and have sex with Ariel and Banning. When did the three of them have time to sit down and discuss that? How did a person broach such a subject? Was it merely animal instinct alone that had created their agreement?

Another thing, who said I even wanted to have sex with Ariel or Banning? True, they were both terrific kissers, but...there was a lot more to sex than that. The fact that I was attracted to them wasn't even my choice. The way Ariel explained it, it was some primal survival instinct that had me weak in the knees anytime they were in the room.

Though I suppose just because Damian was giving his permission didn't mean I was forced into anything. It just meant the option was open if I chose to take it.

I was confused about many things. The only thing I was certain of was that I wanted Damian to keep looking at me the way he had tonight. If that meant spilling a pint of blood, so be it. I knew if I chose to feed Ariel and left Damian out, it would put a rift between us.

My mind made up, I climbed to my feet and made my way back to Damian's bed, placing my hand gently on his shoulder.

He jerked in surprise before climbing to a sitting position. He faced me with questioning eyes. "Rory?" His voice was cautious and fearful, trembling slightly when he spoke.

Him calling me by my nickname was proof enough that I had made the right decision. The tremor in his voice made me want to make sure I never hurt him again. How could I have gone from practically hating him to needing him so desperately? Sometimes life didn't make any sense.

I took his hand gently in mine and lowered my lips to his, kissing him tenderly. "I want you to join us. You need to be healed as well."

The look in his eyes nearly brought tears to my own. I'd never had anyone look at me with such love before. It shook me to the core.

I took his hand and silently guided him to his feet. I pulled him over to Ariel's bed, walking backwards, my eyes never leaving his. I hadn't realized Ariel stood until I bumped into him.

His arm snaked around my waist while the other gently brushed my hair back from my neck.

Damian gave Ariel a mischievous grin before wrapping an arm around the opposite side of my waist and stepping in against me. He didn't seem to mind sharing with Ariel. He seemed to find it amusing actually.

One pale arm appeared on one side of me while a darkly tanned one disappeared around the other. So different, yet both so lovely. One fair-haired and pale, the other dark in hair and complexion. One hot, one cold. One dead, one alive. Both of them beautiful in every way.

Ariel's fangs sliding gently into my neck interrupted my thoughts. I froze up for a moment until I realized it didn't hurt. In fact, it felt good. Very good.

Damian brushed his lips against mine. "Is it alright?"

"Yes," I whispered shakily.

"Are you ready?"

Ariel sucked gently at the wound he had made and it caused my knees to go weak. Pleasure swept through me. Sex and food... My eyes fluttered closed and I couldn't think around my desire. I barely managed to get out my consent to Damian.

I forced my eyes open to look at him. What I saw sent a shiver of terror down my spine, momentarily eradicating my arousal.

His incisor teeth were elongating. They grew to massive size, much larger than Ariel's fangs. They grew to the size of a wild cat. More accurately, they grew to the size of a wolf's fangs.

I would have screamed, but his teeth sank savagely into my throat, silencing me. I nearly collapsed, but Ariel held me firmly against him, keeping me upright. The moment of fear passed as Damian lapped sensually at my throat with his tongue. Pleasure returned, mingling with the pain.

Desire pooled between my legs. I could feel their erections pressed firmly against me. Ariel ground against my backside while Damian rocked his hips against the front of my slacks. Sex and food. Sex and food...

Ariel's hand lifted to my breast and he squeezed. In the next instant, I felt his power wash over me in a suffocating wave. He forced pleasure into my body, bringing me to new heights I'd never experienced.

I only had a moment's notice before an orgasm tore its way thought my body with an intensity that robbed me of speech, robbed me of sanity. My muscles spasmed, seeking pleasure from men who'd never even taken their pants off.

Ariel groaned low in his throat, and Damian inhaled in sharp surprise. I had a suspicion they'd both experienced their own form of climax from our little tryst.

I was panting and trying to get my raging lust under control as a second orgasm threatened. It was only when I forced myself to pay better attention that I realized both Damian and Ariel were still drawing blood from me at a rapid rate. I was starting to feel dizzy.

"S—" I tried to tell them to stop, but I couldn't finish the word, couldn't do anything to protect myself. I was too far under their spell and I'd already lost too much blood. The fear that they might kill me flitted through my mind moments before I lost consciousness.

Epilogue

I awoke with Damian and Ariel at my bedside. Both were apologizing profusely about nearly draining me. Ariel promised if I gave him another chance, he would make feeding him much more pleasurable. I didn't hold anything against either one of them, but I didn't think I'd be letting them feed off me again anytime soon.

After the apologies were out of the way, they filled me in on everything that had happened while I was recovering from loss of blood. Both of them had healed completely, not a blemish to their skin. After they nearly drained me, Banning had gone for help.

They kept Orion by my side with his newfound healing powers for the first few hours. After that, he was rushed away when Banning's rescue team brought in another survivor. They had found the battered and bruised body of Geneva Scott, but she was still living and that was all that mattered.

I also found out Geneva had the same...nocturnal issues as Damian. That's what her whole self-defense class had really been about—teaching new werewolves control over their second forms. Turned out the self-defense was a farce just like I'd claimed it to be those long weeks ago. Geneva wasn't just a survivor in my eyes. She signified hope. Maybe the fate of humanity wasn't a loss.

Another bright spot was that Andrew was going to live. Well...not exactly live. He was going to be a vampire, which was fine by me. He wasn't going to be a flesh-eating zombie, and that's what mattered.

As I lay in Damian's bed, taking in this information, I felt optimistic. I thought there just might be a future for all of us after all. The one thing I knew for certain was that the two men with me would be at my side for whatever was to happen next.

The End

About the Author

    Melissa lives near Pittsburgh, Pennsylvania with her husband, Jeremy, and her son, Marshall Frost. Her favorite genre to write is Paranormal Romance.

    Melissa attended London School of Journalism where she received her certificate in Novel Writing in 2011. She writes a monthly short story column titled *Frequent Flyer* for a government newsletter.

www.ingramcontent.com/pod-product-compliance
Lightning Source LLC
Chambersburg PA
CBHW021536250626
47154CB00006BA/2139